DEATH IN DU

CAROLE COPLEA

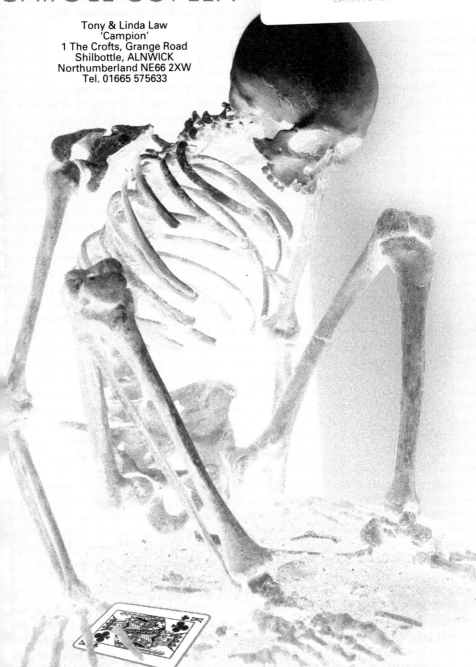

Master Point Press • Toronto, Canada

Master Point Press
331 Douglas Ave.
Toronto, Ontario, Canada
M5M 1H2   (416)781-0351
Email: info@masterpointpress.com
Websites: www.masterpointpress.com
              www.teachbridge.com
              www.bridgeblogging.com
              www.ebooksbridge.com

Library and Archives Canada Cataloguing in Publication
Coplea, Carole, author
      Death in duplicate / Carole Coplea.

Issued in print and electronic formats.
ISBN 978-1-897106-98-3 (pbk.).-- ISBN 978-1-55494-244-2 (pdf).--
ISBN 978-1-55494-476-7 (html).--ISBN 978-1-55494-727-0 (mobi)

      I. Title.

PS8605.O684D42 2013   C813'.6   C2013-902150-7
                                                 C2013-902151-5

We acknowledge the financial support of the Government of Canada
through the Canada Book Fund for our publishing activities.

Editor   Suzanne Hocking
Copyeditor/Interior format   Sally Sparrow
Cover and interior design   Olena S. Sullivan/New Mediatrix

1 2 3 4 5 6 7   17 16 15 14 13
PRINTED IN CANADA

IN MEMORIAM

I dedicate this, my first novel, to my sister Lois Maxwell (1927-2007),
the original actress who played Miss Moneypenny.

ACKNOWLEDGEMENTS

First and foremost, I wish to thank Camille, my daughter, for providing the inspiration for this novel right from the beginning. Her insightful comments and suggestions were instrumental in formulating the plot and characters.

There are a few trusted friends who helped: Lesley and Peter, for giving me my first audience; Nita and Ken, for their sincere comments and honesty; David and Katie, for their help and support; my bridge buddies in Oakville who believe in me; Wayne in Ottawa who helped with some details and the ending; and my brother, Victor.

I can't thank George Holland enough for his unwavering support. He donated countless hours to mentor me on the bridge content and provided detailed comments on every chapter. He graciously agreed to appear as a real character in the story.

Finally, and not the least, I wish to thank my publisher, Ray Lee, for having the courage to take on this project, and my brilliant editor, Suzanne Hocking, whose helpful comments in the final stages made my heart sing.

AUTHOR'S NOTE

I wrote this novel to entertain my fellow bridge players, and also to reach a wider audience of people who are not currently involved in bridge but who may want to learn more about it.

All the characters are fictional, except for George Holland, who appears as himself.

People of all ages play bridge, either at home, in clubs or online. Bridge Base Online (BBO), attracts thousands of players across the planet every day. BBO also broadcasts tournaments where you can watch world class players in real time.

Bridge is an instant friend-maker — no matter where you go in the world, you can always find a bridge game or attend a bridge club and make new friends. If you want to enjoy bridge on your vacation, you can go on any number of cruises in exotic locations, sponsored by professional bridge players.

Bridge often becomes a life-long passion. There is no limit to improving your understanding of the game and your skill in playing it.

School students are discovering bridge. A growing number of teachers are promoting the game and setting up bridge clubs in their schools in recognition that bridge helps to develop communication and social skills as well as mental acuity.

To learn more about the fascinating world of bridge, contact your local bridge club, national association, or the World Bridge Federation.

And happy bridging!

Carole Coplea, 2013

Mary, Mary, quite contrary, how does your garden grow?
With silver bells and cockleshells, and pretty maids all in a row!

PROLOGUE

📅 PRESENT DAY, THURSDAY — 11:45 P.M.

Brian Jackson strolled into my office. He settled his tall, lanky body into the chair opposite my desk and chewed on an apple. He looked bored. It was a slow evening in the Beaumont P.D. It had been a slow week, too.

Our noon-to-midnight shift was almost over. It was Thursday, the last day of our four-day rotation, and I was feeling tired. We did four twelve-hour shifts a week, with three days off to rejuvenate. It worked out well for my husband Paul and me, as we took turns looking after our two school-aged children during the week. I got them off to school in the morning, and he took care of them after school.

Brian shifted in his chair as he flicked the apple core into the garbage can beside my desk. I looked up from my paperwork.

"What's on your mind, pard?" I asked.

"Just wondering how you do it, day in, day out... same old stuff all the time. Don't you get tired of it?"

"You lookin' for some major crime action? Can't blame you. Keeping the peace in a place like this won't get the adrenalin pumping," I said. "But we have had our share of interesting cases over the years, you know."

Brian perked up. As a new recruit, Brian loved cop talk. He was always keen to hear about cases that involved more than routine police work.

"So, tell me, Dee-Dee, what's the most intriguing case you ever worked on?" He was a fresh-faced twenty-two-year-old who had recently graduated from the police academy. He was assigned to me to "learn the ropes", so to speak. I have a new recruit every couple of years and I help them through their probation period to get on permanent status. From there, they usually move on to bigger and nastier places for crime control, like Buffalo, Pittsburgh or New York City. Here in the back hills of the Adirondack Mountains, our crimes are garden variety: drugs, theft, domestic violence, drunk and disorderly and illegal gambling with the occasional knifing or shooting thrown in. You might call it Dullsville, if you were a cop.

I like it fine here. It suits me because I have two young kids, a boy and a girl, and I don't want to raise them in a big city where they are exposed to serious social and criminal problems. A child's time for pure innocence and joy of life is limited... why rob them of something so precious? For the sake of ambition? Sure, I'm ambitious, but I'm also Italian by heritage, and family comes first, so I'm biding my time. When the kids are grown and off to college, then I'll be ready to make a move. In the meantime, I take university extension courses to improve my credentials, and one day, I hope to make Inspector or something even higher. For now, I have settled for a low-profile career as a cop in the Adirondacks.

After more than ten years in Beaumont, I've come to enjoy having a low-stress job that also allows me to have a decent family life. But when the occasional challenging criminal case comes my way... well, that's when my heart rate speeds up and I feel the primitive excitement of the hunt coursing through my veins. I think this passion comes from reading too many mysteries as a child. Nancy Drew and the Hardy Boys were my favorites. As a teenager, I moved on to Agatha Christie's Hercule Poirot and Arthur Conan Doyle's Sherlock Holmes, and challenged myself to try and solve the crime before they did. Now, as an adult, I'm constantly searching for new murder mysteries to devour by authors like Harlan Coben and Linwood Barclay. Lately, I have been reading Scandinavian crime mysteries (in English, of course) for something a little different. I would certainly enjoy the intellectual challenge of solving difficult crimes in my jurisdiction, but unfortunately they are few and far between.

To break the monotony of life in Beaumont, we often get together at the local pub after our late shift... Brian, Captain Juno, myself and others. The stories we've told! Cap has the best stories from when he was a detective with the Chicago P.D.

"The most intriguing case," I mused, in response to Brian's question. "Let me see." I paused in my paperwork. I knew which case I wanted to talk about, but I needed to organize my thoughts first. How to tell young Brian about this one?

"The Digman/Boland file is probably the most intriguing case I worked on. Happened a few years ago, shortly after I made detective." I paused again, wondering if I should go down this road. It would take a few hours in the telling.

"So... what was so special about it?" he prodded.

I checked my watch. It was almost quitting time. I closed the binder I was working on and let my mind go back to December 2008, when the case fell into my lap.

"Well, let me start at the beginning. My partner and I were on our usual patrol one night in Mount Salem. It was a couple weeks before Christmas. We got a 911 call about two suspicious deaths at Kensington College."

I got up and went to a filing cabinet in the corner of my office. I opened the second drawer.

"I made photocopies of some of the media coverage. Was gonna make a scrapbook for my kids one day," I said, chuckling. "Look at this... I have a drawer full of news reports." I took out a folder and opened it.

"Sharon Sharpe, reporter at the *Beaumont Record* locked onto this case right from the start. She's a thorn in Cap's side, that one! Always calling him about something or other. I think she's got a thing for him, you know. But he's having none of it." I read the clipping out loud.

THURSDAY, DECEMBER 11, 2008
POLICE INVESTIGATE SUSPICIOUS DEATHS AT LOCAL COLLEGE

Late Wednesday night, police were called to Kensington College after two people collapsed and died while playing cards in the faculty dining room.

Details are sketchy, as the news came in just before our midnight press time.

Dr. Gayle Primrose, President of Kensington College, was present at the scene, along with 17 other people.

Captain Juno of the Beaumont Police Department had no comment, except to say the police were conducting preliminary interviews of eyewitnesses.

Detective Christina diLongo is in charge of the investigation. Our sources speculate that the deaths were not from natural causes.

"If you want me to tell you the whole story, let's go for a beer after we sign out tonight," I suggested. "We've got the next three days off, so we can afford a late night. I'll text Paul and let him know."

"Sounds great," Brian said eagerly.

Half an hour later, with beers in hand, we settled into a booth at our local pub. I opened the folder of clippings.

"It was my first big case as a detective," I began. "My partner at the time, Skip Crane, did some awesome background checking and helped me with some of the critical thinking that we needed to do. I conducted most of the interviews, and eventually we pieced together the whole sordid story. And it was quite a story! We made the national media by the time we were through." I chuckled at the recollection. "But it wasn't very funny at the time. We were all stressed out to the max. Cap was breathing down my neck to wrap it up. He was getting heat from the media and higher-ups. And the parents of the college students were on his case. And, of course, he was worried about overtime."

"Some things never change!" Brian commented, smiling wryly. Brian had been with us for only a week, but he's a smart kid, and he had already picked up that Cap's primary focus these days was working on the budget and keeping costs, especially overtime, at a minimum. Can't blame him, really. With the local economy still in the soup, the tax base was eroding while crimes were on the upswing. Cap was in the pivot point between the two, and he found that position to be increasingly uncomfortable. However, in my opinion, it was more important than ever to keep law and order strong and viable in our communities, and that means more police vigilance, not less. It was an argument that Cap and I got into almost every week, as these budget restrictions made our jobs as enforcers difficult.

"There were twenty players in the bridge club, and two of the players died, which left me with eighteen witnesses. I didn't know what I was investigating at first. Was it an accident, like food poisoning? Was it a deadly virus? Was it something more sinister? If it was homicide, then all my witnesses were suspects. We had to assume the worst and hope for the best. So we treated it like a crime scene, and waited for the M.E.'s report."

"And what did the M.E.'s report tell you?" asked Brian. He leaned forward in his seat. I could tell he was eager to get this important detail, but it was way too soon to reveal that. To be fully appreciated, the story needed to be told from the beginning, and that would take some time.

"I'll get to that! But first, I need to give you some background."

I settled back on my bench. The news reports had refreshed my memory, and that energized me. I knew that once I got started with the details, it would be a long night.

"It all started with a Halloween party on October 31, 2007. The bridge players got dressed up like famous characters in the movies. It ended thirteen months later, with two people dead. And as I learned through the investigation, bridge players are not just a bunch of old timers sitting around in their retirement homes. Our investigation exposed hidden agendas, secret lives... all kinds of things you might find surprising!

"But I'm getting ahead of myself. To really understand this case, you have to know some things about the bridge club and how the players related to each other."

"Okay," said Brian. "I'm listening."

CHAPTER 1

📅 WEDNESDAY, SEPTEMBER 10, 2008 — 5:00 P.M.

The Kensington Faculty Bridge Club got its start in the 1930s, when playing bridge was a popular and inexpensive pastime. In those days, there wasn't much else to do during the long winter months on Mount Salem, high in the Adirondacks where the college was located. There was no TV or Internet, of course. The nearest movie theater was thirty miles away in Beaumont. The bridge club offered players some comfort and companionship along with friendly competition to keep their spirits up.

In recent years, the club membership was limited to twenty players, which made it rather exclusive. Dr. Gayle Primrose, the director of the club, was also the college president. Other members included her bridge partner, David Bartholomew, who was head of campus security, Jill Wilmington, director of human resources, and several professors, including the head of the English Department, Daniel Post.

With membership in the bridge club, players enjoyed access to the corridors of power at the college, which was a big draw for some people. In addition, Gayle was renowned for her magnificent soirees and over-the-top dinner parties. It was a holdover from her upbringing in the South. She always invited special guests of high repute, of both local and international fame, and went to great lengths to ensure an enjoyable time for everyone.

Gayle reserved four seats in the club for students in each of the participating faculties: History, English, Business and Psychology. These seats were highly coveted. Students were known to switch majors in an effort to earn a seat in the bridge club.

Competition to gain a seat was also fierce amongst the staff. Six years earlier, when Daniel Post joined the English department, he wanted to get into the bridge club so badly that he concocted a rumor that one of the players, another professor in the English department, was in possession of child pornography. Even though the rumor was never substantiated, the besmirched professor left the college under a cloud, thus opening up his seat in the bridge club.

Since not all club members could attend every Wednesday night, Gayle insisted that they confirm their attendance by noon on Monday. If they didn't confirm in time, she would invite people, usually her friends, to fill the table. She would boot players out of the club if they persistently failed to show up.

Gayle ran the club in her own inimitable way, and no one dared to complain.

Playing bridge helped Gayle to de-stress from her exhaustive administrative duties. Sometimes, when she was having a particularly tough day, she would open her laptop and log on to a website where she could play bridge with Internet friends. However, she preferred playing bridge in person at the club, as it could be very entertaining when strong personalities and towering egos clashed over the bidding or the play of a hand.

In September 2008, a new school year was beginning, with a crop of young students arriving on campus for the first time. Gayle was tired from all the work involved registering and orienting the new students and dealing with anxious parents. On the afternoon of Wednesday, September 10, Gayle finished writing a report for her staff. She picked up the phone to call David Bartholomew, her bridge partner, who was head of security for the college. He helped her with the bridge club preparations each week.

"Hi, David," she said wearily. "Are we all set for bridge tonight?"

"So far, so good," he said. "Everyone has confirmed, so we have a full house."

"Good! I'll see you there at seven o'clock."

The school year had begun much the same as any other. However, within three months, Gayle would be faced with the biggest challenge of her career when two bridge players suddenly and gruesomely died at the bridge table. The resulting media attention threatened her college's image and put her own personal reputation at risk.

CHAPTER 2

📅 PRESENT DAY — 12:30 A.M.

Our beers were half-finished when I pulled out another press clipping.

"You have to understand," I said to Brian, "the bridge club at Kensington College was full of super-smart, competitive people, some of whom were also very devious. On the surface, however, they all seemed like regular folks — perhaps a little more high-strung than most. Know what I mean? Here's a transcript of a news report the local radio station put out that set the tone for the whole investigation. Did I mention that Sharon Sharpe from the *Beaumont Record* also doubles as the radio station's crime reporter?"

Brian shook his head.

I showed the radio report transcript to Brian. "From the moment it happened, students at the college started messaging their parents and friends with exaggerated details. Almost immediately, parents were calling the police station wondering if students were safe on campus."

I sipped my beer while Brian read the news clipping.

THURSDAY, DECEMBER 11, 2008

ANNOUNCER: News Radio 1015 has learned of two suspicious deaths at Kensington College last night. Our reporter, Sharon Sharpe, has just filed this report. Sharon?

SHARON: My sources at the college said that a man and a woman died suddenly in the faculty dining room around ten o'clock last night. The police investigating have not released the identities of the victims at this point, pending notification of their next of kin. The victims were playing bridge.

The bodies were taken to the county morgue to be autopsied as the cause of death is unknown at this time.

The police will make an announcement once they have the medical examiner's report.

ANNOUNCER: When do you expect his report?

SHARON: It typically takes six to eight hours for an autopsy for each body. The medical examiner is not making any promises, but he thinks he'll have something by six o'clock this evening.

ANNOUNCER: Is there any speculation on the cause of death?

SHARON: Well, nothing solid, but the rumor mill is working overtime. Some people are saying it's food poisoning or an allergic reaction to the meal that they ate before they started playing cards, and some people think it's a targeted attack on the two victims, or possibly a random act of violence, or even terrorism. Nothing has been confirmed at this point. I spoke to Dr. Gayle Primrose, the president of the college. She was present at the scene. She said she has called in off-duty security guards as a precaution, and she urges calm.

ANNOUNCER: Thank you, Sharon.

When Brian looked up I took another sip of my beer and then resumed the story. "Shortly after the case was solved, a history professor by the name of Professor Schultz explained to me that playing bridge is much like solving a mystery you read in a book. Each hand contains clues in the bidding and the play of the cards. A good bridge player is able to correctly decipher the clues to uncover the best line of play."

"I don't read mysteries," said Brian. "I go for true crime."

"Bridge players can also be very devious," I continued. "Professor Schultz told me you can make incorrect bids, called psyches, to throw opponents off track... and you can misdirect your opponents with the card you choose to play — that's called falsecarding. So some of the clues are false, and you have to take that into consideration when you are playing the hand."

"I get it," Brian responded. "I have friends from high school who got into playing bridge when their math teacher started up a bridge club. He got them interested in the mathematics of the game, calculating percentages and all that. They talked about it all the time, especially bidding systems. They were big into that. They said it's like fighting in a war... you try to deceive your enemies at the same time as you are planning to outflank them or pull them into an ambush."

"Yeah, sounds like a good analogy. My parents play bridge with their friends, just for fun, not the competitive bridge that the Kensington crowd plays. My parents really enjoy the game. But I digress. I'll get back to the story. As I recall, it was a cold, rainy night, just before Christmas. Skip and I were dealing with a minor incident in Mount Salem when we got the 911 call."

📅 WEDNESDAY, DECEMBER 10, 2008 — 9:30 P.M.

Two police officers drove slowly down a rain-soaked street in the quaint village of Mount Salem, where trendy cafes, upscale boutiques and several art galleries attracted visitors to enjoy the village's charm.

At the village center sat the magnificent Lakeside Inn. The Inn became famous in the 1920s as a fishing lodge for wealthy businessmen and their families. Over the intervening years, the owners improved the Inn's accommodations to include modern amenities like Wi-Fi and Jacuzzis.

On this dark December night, the almost-freezing rain was driven by strong winds coming in off the lake, making it difficult to see clearly. The cruiser slowed to a crawl.

Detective diLongo was driving. She motioned to her partner, a young sandy-haired recruit named Skip Crane.

"You see that guy over there in the red hoodie? I bet he's going to boost something in a minute."

Skip was originally from the Midwest. After graduating from the Buffalo Police Academy, he joined the Beaumont Police Department, where he hoped to earn his stripes as a law enforcement officer before moving to the big city for some major crime action.

His father, now retired, had spent his entire career in law enforcement. He even became a local hero after breaking up a massive organized crime ring in Indiana. Skip had always wanted to follow in his father's footsteps and make his mother as proud of him as she was of her husband.

Since joining the department in June, Skip's job functions had been routine deskwork, mostly processing criminals and writing reports. No serious crimes, just drunk driving, petty thefts, domestic disputes and small-time drug trafficking. He thought he had a murder on his hands back in the summer, but the knifing victim didn't die, and it turned out that the victim was the aggressor!

Skip was disappointed that the whole incident had petered out into nothing much. No murder, no headlines, no big trial and no big investigation on that one. As a young man looking for action, Skip had not exactly fulfilled his crime-fighting dreams with the Beaumont P.D. He wondered when he would see some hardcore police work.

When diLongo stopped the cruiser, Skip got out and positioned himself next to the front door of the mini-grocery store. The Quick Mart was open 24-7. As they waited, Skip could feel his heart rate increase with anticipation of the confrontation. He unfastened his gun holster. He knew from his training that as a police officer with a visible weapon, he would intimidate most common offenders, who were often impaired with drugs or alcohol, and they would be slow to react. But if this guy was a hardened criminal, he could be dangerous, so Skip wanted to be fully prepared, just in case.

Skip looked over to his partner; she was leaning against the cruiser, arms folded, raincoat glistening in the lights. They nodded to each other, and Skip gave her a thumbs-up.

It wouldn't be long now. Skip tried to keep his focus as he waited. The seconds seemed like minutes, and the minutes seemed like hours. Skip could feel the cold dampness seeping through to his skin. He shifted from one foot to the other, and rubbed his hands to keep them warm… waiting… waiting. He let his mind wander back home, and he smiled to think that his mother would be so proud of him now, as he was about to make his first real arrest.

Suddenly, the glass door swung open and a red blur came bursting out. Before Skip could react, Hoodie was already disappearing into the wet, dark night.

"Stop! Police!" diLongo shouted the words, and Hoodie stopped. Skip drew his gun and strode purposefully over to the middle of the street where diLongo was talking to Hoodie.

"Let's see what you've got there!"

Hoodie, as it turned out, was a teenager. His white-rimmed eyes darted back and forth looking for an escape route, but there was none.

"Come on," diLongo said impatiently.

The young man slowly raised the bottom of his hoodie, revealing three packages of meat and a whole chicken hidden in his clothes.

"Go back in there and replace those items right now," she ordered.

The young man turned and slowly sulked back into the store. A minute later he came back out.

"Show me," said diLongo. Hoodie raised his clothes again. This time he was not wearing any food.

"Go home," she said, hands on hips, trying to impress him with her words. "This is your last warning. Next time I find you boosting food or anything else, I book you. Understand?"

He nodded, and looked down at his feet.

"Now git."

Hoodie turned and quickly disappeared into the night.

Once Hoodie was out of earshot, Skip turned to diLongo in amazement.

"Shee-it! Why did you let him go? We had him dead to rights!"

"Skip, I know that boy. He's only fifteen. His father took off. His mother worked at the local recycling plant, but she got sick with cancer and now she can't work. He steals food because he and his mother are hungry. If he's not stealing food, he's rooting through garbage bins. If I arrest him, his mother has no one to help her, and he could go to juvie for Lord knows how long. That's not a good result."

"Oh."

"Come on," she said, returning to the cruiser. "I'll contact the HOPE organization. Helping Other People Everywhere. They can get some food for his family. And maybe we should see about enrolling the boy in a Teens-4-Teens group. It's our answer to teen gangs, which is where our young friend is heading if we don't do something to help him."

Skip shuffled his feet nervously, trying to process all this information and calm his nerves at the same time.

"You can holster your weapon now," said diLongo, smiling.

Skip immediately did so, patting the holster to make sure it was secure. They got back into the cruiser.

"It's our job to arrest criminals, but there's often a gray area where you have to use your own judgment on how to handle a situation in the best interests of the community. Do you agree?" asked diLongo.

"I... dunno."

"Don't worry, Skip, there's bound to be some bad-ass criminals to deal with, sooner or later," she said.

"That guy's already a criminal," Skip said. "He stole stuff from the grocery store. That's theft. That's a crime. We should have arrested him."

"Whatever. Let's get back on patrol, and maybe we'll stop by Donut Heaven for our break. Sound good?"

"Yeah, I guess." Skip pulled out his notebook and searched his front pocket for a pen.

"You're not going to write this up in your notebook, Skipper. Let it go. Trust me, it's not worth it."

Skip replaced his notebook and stared straight ahead. He was starting to think that his decision to join the Beaumont P.D. was not the smartest move he'd ever made. It served a collection of rural towns that were just too peaceful for him, and it was getting on his nerves. He felt like a Ferrari forced to drive in second gear at 25 mph, when he had the horses under the hood to do 200 mph or more.

He wanted to sink his teeth into something that challenged his training and intellect, something that would make his family proud, something that would give him the heart-pounding satisfaction of good sex, something that would inspire him to greater heights of accomplishment and ingenuity, something that would confirm for him, once and for all, that he was meant to be a cop.

He knew he wasn't ready to take on crime-fighting in New York or even Buffalo, but he was concerned that he would never earn his stripes if he stayed in this backwater of tranquility.

As he pondered these and other matters, he realized the cruiser was slowing down. Donut Heaven's neon sign glowed faintly through the cold rain.

Skip checked his watch. 10:10 p.m. He could use an energy drink. DiLongo parked the cruiser and they hurried into the warmth of the coffee shop.

"How can I help you?" the girl behind the counter asked.

"I'll have a Red Bull and something to eat," he said. The donuts didn't look very fresh, but he wanted something sweet. "I guess a couple of those chocolate chip cookies, the ones with oatmeal. You know, the healthy ones." DiLongo chuckled.

After the officers picked up their orders, they found a table next to the window. Skip watched the raindrops trickle down the window as he munched on a cookie. "This is really great," he thought. "If my mom could only see me now, watching raindrops instead of fighting crime. She'd be so impressed!" He sighed heavily.

Then diLongo's cell phone rang. "Yeah, diLongo." There was a long pause. "Okay, we're on it." Then to Skip she said, "Let's go, Skipper."

From the look on his partner's face, Skip realized something was up. He nearly tipped over the table in his haste to get out of Donut Heaven.

"What's going on?" he asked, slamming the car door shut.

"Emergency at Kensington College," she said in a grim voice. "Two dead."

As they exited the parking lot with lights flashing and siren blaring, Skip grinned in anticipation of some real police work ahead.

CHAPTER 3

📅 WEDNESDAY, DECEMBER 10, 2008 — 10:45 P.M.

Detective diLongo and her partner, Officer Skip Crane, turned their cruiser around and drove through town towards Kensington College.

"We have to get to the college as fast as possible," diLongo said.

"Fill me in?" Skip asked.

"Don't know much yet. A 911 call. Two people dead. We have to go check it out and see if there's anything suspicious."

Mount Salem had not changed much over the last century. It had one main street that was loosely strung out along the shoreline of Lake Salem. There was one set of traffic lights at the T-intersection where Highway 11 met the main street. Situated at this intersection was Lakeshore Inn, a rambling six-storey structure made of thick, sawn logs. The Inn sat between the main street and the edge of the lake. Next to the Inn was the Delish Deli. It had an outside patio that faced the lake. The front of the deli was all glass, and fresh baked goods were displayed enticingly in the window every morning. The deli was famous for its sandwiches.

On the next block were small stores and fancy boutiques selling local crafts and designer fashions. Further down the street was a hardware store that also doubled as the Post Office. Next to the hardware store there was a gasoline station and a small office building. The Quick Mart was on the corner. Across the street was Poppa John's, a hamburger and pizza joint that also offered cheap draft beer, a favorite hangout for students. Next to Poppa John's was an old villa that had been converted to a four-star restaurant called Dolce Vita. Further along the main street were more cafes and restaurants interspersed with small boutiques, hair salons and spas, a laundry and dry cleaning service and a store that sold computers and other electronics. One of the side streets offered a supplies store for fishing and hunting, a sports store for sales and rentals of skis, skates and snowshoes, and a marine store for sales and rentals of boats and boating supplies. The main street carried on around the end of the lake, as the commercial buildings petered out, to be replaced with houses and small apartment buildings. The street then veered away from the lake to climb Mount Salem, twisting and turning up the steep slope, through clusters of large homes and expensive townhomes towards Kensington College near the top of the mountain.

Kensington College had a mesmerizing effect on students, administrators and teachers alike. In its spectacular mountain setting, it looked more like a Victorian country estate than an institution of higher learning. Tall spires on the main buildings mimicked the towering trees that surrounded the campus. Stone and brick exteriors blended into the natural landscape of rough granite boulders and exposed rock. Mossy growths added splashes of green along the stone foundations, while ivy spread its spindly arms up the stone walls, almost obliterating the wrought iron-framed windows that dotted the façade of each main building.

It would be hard to be depressed in such a setting. The spires, the trees and the mountain itself, high above the commotion of normal life and everyday concerns, had an uplifting effect on the human spirit.

Of course, appearances can be deceiving, and usually are.

Skip could hardly contain his excitement. Two D.B.s! He started chattering nervously. "Okay, so this could be a murder or it could be an accident. Or maybe someone collapsed. They had a heart attack and the other person tried to help them and they slipped and fell down or something and hit their head. Or maybe there was a fight, yeah, students fight sometimes. They get drunk and get into a fistfight. Or maybe it's... I don't know... a drug deal gone bad? Or a jealous husband? Or..."

"Skip! Shut the fuck up, will ya? Call the station back and find out where we're supposed to go when we reach the campus."

Skip was startled to hear diLongo use the f-word. She was a mild-tempered woman in her late thirties, married with two school-aged children. To his knowledge, his partner was very careful about using swear words. He figured it was because of her kids. In any case, he shut up and did as he was told.

"Okay, I got it," Skip said, after calling the station. "We're going to the administration building where they have some kind of faculty lounge or dining room. It's at 10 Winding Road Crescent."

"No problem, I know the building," said diLongo. "I took a course there last year."

The driving rain forced diLongo to reduce her speed. It took longer than she would have liked before they pulled up at their destination.

They drove in silence up the narrow, twisting highway towards the campus.

The drive was very pretty in daylight, but on this dark December night, the dense forest on either side of the highway obliterated any signs of life. Skip felt his heart rate increase.

"There it is," diLongo said, as they rounded a corner and saw an opening in the forest. She drove through the entrance to the campus and pointed to a tall building with turrets and a high, peaked roof.

"Third floor," she said. "That's where the faculty dining room is located."

A tall, well-dressed woman was waiting for them inside the front doors. "Officers, I am so glad you're here. There's been a terrible accident. Two people died here tonight while we were playing bridge. Upstairs. Please follow me."

"And who are you?" asked diLongo.

"I'm Dr. Gayle Primrose, the president of this college." She spoke over her shoulder as they climbed the wide stone stairs that led to the second floor. "And who are you?"

"I'm Detective diLongo, and this is my partner, Officer Skip Crane, from the Beaumont Police Department. We're here to assess the situation."

At the top of the stairs, Gayle turned right and led them up a narrower set of stairs. "I'd call for the elevator, but it's faster to take the stairs," she said.

"No problem," diLongo said, as she and Skip followed Gayle up to the third floor. At the top, they turned right down a short hallway, opened a set of heavily carved oak doors and entered a large room with a vaulted ceiling.

DiLongo took stock of the people in the room. She could see shock and confusion in their faces.

"Our doctor checked the bodies," Gayle said. "He confirmed they are dead."

DiLongo nodded, then took Skip aside and said quietly, "Who knows what happened here tonight. If the deaths are suspicious, everything we do from this point on is critical. So just do as I say and don't ask any questions."

Skip nodded. DiLongo wasn't sure what to do next. This was her first death scene investigation since she had become a detective. In the past, there had always been a senior officer who took charge of the situation. Now it was her turn to be in charge. She recalled what her captain had told her to do.

"It's all in the details," he said. "Get every detail you can, as fast as you can, and go from there."

"Did you call 911?" diLongo asked Gayle.

"Yes. I asked them to send an ambulance, but it will take an hour to get here at least. You know what it's like to get medical attention way up here on the mountain. We have our own clinic for most medical emergencies. Our doctors and nurses are on staff 24/7."

"I'd like to look at the bodies, Dr. Primrose." Gayle showed diLongo where two people were lying on the floor. DiLongo took a close look at the first body, a man lying on his back. His face was distorted in a horrible grimace. DiLongo thought he looked vaguely familiar, but it was hard to tell with all the blood and vomit smeared over his face. "Who is he?" she asked.

"Professor Terry Digman. He teaches in our psychology department," Gayle said. Then diLongo realized why he looked familiar. She had taken a course with him the year before. Criminal behavior.

"Has anyone touched him? Or removed anything from the body?"

"Well, uh…" Gayle hesitated as she groped for the right words. "It happened so fast. I think someone tried to revive him, but he was convulsing and spitting up blood and I don't know who exactly might have touched him."

Then she pointed to the other body lying a few feet away. "Anne-Marie Boland over there, she collapsed on the floor and her husband, Chris, went to her immediately. And then Dr. Morrison came in, and he probably touched the bodies… but they were already dead by then."

"Okay, we'll sort this out later," diLongo said. Then she turned to the room where people were standing in small huddles, and in a forceful voice said, "I am Detective diLongo of the Beaumont P.D. I want you all to go back to where you were sitting when the trouble began. Do not touch anything, do not drink anything and do not eat anything. We'll be with you shortly."

DiLongo turned to Skip. "Call the station and get them to send the M.E. here immediately. And call 911 to tell them we're handling this. They don't need to send paramedics or the fire department. It's a crime scene now. Dr. Primrose called it in a while back."

DiLongo then turned to Gayle.

"Who is the doctor who responded to your call?"

"Dr. Morrison," Gayle said, pointing to the man in the gray jacket standing at the bar. "He's one of our campus doctors."

"I'll speak with him in a minute." DiLongo took out her notebook and started writing.

"Okay," Skip said a few minutes later as he got off the phone. "The M.E. is on his way."

"Good." DiLongo spoke to Skip in a low voice. "We don't know what we're dealing with yet. Maybe accidental food poisoning, maybe a deadly virus, maybe something else. For now, we'll assume it's an accident, but we'll handle this like a crime scene, just in case. You see all these tables where people are sitting down? I want you to identify who's who at each table and get their contact information. They were playing bridge, so there should be four people at each table. I want you to make a diagram of exactly where everybody was sitting when the victims collapsed."

Skip nodded. Then diLongo addressed the people in the room. "I want to ask you for your cooperation tonight, folks. It's unfortunate that two of your colleagues have died so suddenly, and we don't know what caused their deaths at this time. The medical examiner will be here shortly. As you are all witnesses, I need to interview all of you before you go home tonight. It might take a few hours, and I apologize in advance for the inconvenience."

The bridge players looked at each other and murmured their concerns, but no one spoke up to object to diLongo's instructions.

Skip went around to each table and wrote down the names of all the players, while diLongo walked over to speak with Dr. Morrison. "Good evening, doctor," she said, extending her hand. "I need some information from you."

"I understand."

"Please tell me, in your own words, what happened here tonight."

"I got a call just after ten o'clock from Dr. Primrose. Actually, my assistant, Jennifer Schnell, took the call. She said there was an emergency. I grabbed my bag and ran over from the clinic. It's in the Lowe Building, just across the way." He pointed with his finger.

"Okay, so Jennifer said it was an emergency. Did she say anything else?"

"Just that Dr. Primrose said someone had collapsed," he said.

"How many minutes had elapsed by the time you arrived on the scene?"

"Oh, I'd say not more than five minutes. It's just a quick sprint across the quad."

DiLongo recorded this information in her notebook.

"So, what did you see when you got here?" she asked.

"People looking sad and confused, and scared. They were huddled in groups, crying and comforting each other. I had to move some people out of the way to get to the bodies. Well, I didn't know they were dead until I got up close to them. Anyway, they were not breathing by the time I saw them. I checked for a pulse, and tried to resuscitate them, but it was too late."

He took another gulp of scotch, draining his glass. "One thing I noticed, the hemorrhaging of the eyes. Haven't seen that before," he said, studying the bottom of his glass.

DiLongo raised an eyebrow. "That's unusual?"

Dr. Morrison shrugged and said, "It just seems a little suspicious to me."

"Okay. Did you notice any bruising, wounds or other signs of violence?"

"No, not really, just some vomit and blood." He shuddered. *Strange,* thought DiLongo, *a doctor should be used to dealing with blood and other bodily fluids.* But he looked so young, and his face was pale.

"So, what do you think, doc? What's your professional opinion of what happened to these people?"

"I honestly have no idea. I don't usually deal with dead bodies." He smiled weakly. He was obviously uncomfortable with the whole situation.

"What do you typically deal with here on campus, doctor?" she asked, to put him at ease.

"Oh, you know, sprains, broken bones, unexpected pregnancies, colds and the flu, alcohol and drug abuse, STDs, those kinds of things. Typical sickness and injuries you see in a college full of young people." Then he lowered his voice. "This is my first posting as a doctor. I don't like working in hospitals…"

"I don't blame you," diLongo said. "I avoid hospitals. I find them depressing. Okay. I may need more information from you later. Please give me your direct lines at home and at work so I can contact you if necessary." She wrote the numbers into her notebook. "I'd like you to stay here until the M.E. arrives. He may have some questions for you. After that, you're free to go."

"All right," he said, and turned back to the bar for another drink, but diLongo stopped him. "Don't touch anything," she said. "This is a crime scene, until we know it isn't." Dr. Morrison looked at her glumly, and nodded with a sigh.

DiLongo returned to where Gayle was now sitting at her table. "So, Dr. Primrose, you were sitting here when the commotion began?"

"Yes, I had just called the next round of play after the break."

"What was happening before the incident? Anything unusual or re-markable?"

"Not that I noticed. Tonight was a special Christmas dinner, so everyone turned up early."

"Anything else? Maybe something out of place? Or someone saying they were not feeling well, anything like that?"

"No, I have to say, nothing comes to mind," Gayle said.

"Okay, thanks," diLongo said, and she walked away. "Are you finished, Skip?"

"Yeah, I got them all." He showed diLongo his diagram of the room with all the players indicated at each table.

"Good work." She motioned to Gayle to join them.

"Dr. Primrose, we need to set up a place to interview people privately. Are there any rooms available besides the dining room here?"

"Yes. If you go down the corridor that way," she pointed towards the double oak doors, "there are several offices that you can use."

"Perfect."

Gayle spoke to David Bartholomew. He fished a key ring out of his right pocket and went to unlock some office doors, then returned to his seat.

Meanwhile, in a loud voice so everyone in the room could hear, diLongo said, "Okay, folks, can I have your attention for a minute?" When the room was quiet, she continued. "I realize this has been a shocking night for you, so we are going to try and get through this as quickly as possible. Do any of you have young children at home?"

Four hands shot up.

"Okay, we will talk to you folks first, and hopefully it won't take too long," she said.

One of the hands that went up was Christopher Boland, husband of Anne-Marie Boland, the first victim.

"Excuse me, officer, I must speak with you," he said, rising from his chair and walking over to diLongo. He was a tall, good-looking man in his forties, with a close-cropped beard and short hair.

"That's my wife lying there," he said, his voice shaking. "We have five kids at home. I don't know what to do! Should I stay with my wife, or should I go home and take care of my kids? If I stay here, I need someone to help with the kids and let my babysitter go home. She's just a teenager…" He looked genuinely distraught.

Gayle put a hand on his arm. "We'll call around and find someone to help out. Come and sit with me for a minute." She guided Chris over to the bar where they contacted some people on his cell phone. A few minutes later, Gayle told diLongo that one of Chris's neighbors had agreed to relieve the babysitter and stay with the children until Chris got home.

In the meantime, diLongo directed Skip to take the other parents to separate rooms. DiLongo showed Skip's diagram of the room to Gayle.

"This diagram shows where everyone was sitting when the trouble began. Is it accurate?"

"Yes, this looks right," Gayle replied. "He even indicated the movement of the boards and the players with the arrows. Nice."

"What do you mean?"

"Well, we play duplicate bridge," Gayle explained. "There are four hands per round. At the end of each round, the boards are moved to the next table and the East/West players move in the opposite direction."

"What do you mean, 'the boards'?"

"Oh, right, well, the board is a holder with slots in it for each hand. We keep the hands separate when we play, and then when we finish each hand, we put the cards into a slot on the board. Then the boards go to the next table, where the same hands are played and scored. So the players at each table not only play against each other, they also play against all the other pairs who played the same hands."

"I see," diLongo said, not really seeing at all, but not wanting to dwell on that. "Please tell me what happened after you started playing bridge tonight."

"Well, we played three rounds, which is twelve boards. Then, at 9:30 we broke for coffee and dessert."

"Do you recall when you noticed the first sign of trouble?"

"Yes, I was on my second hand after the break, so it must have been ten o'clock or shortly thereafter. I didn't look at my watch. Sorry."

"I understand," diLongo said. "Okay, I need you to stay here until we have finished interviewing everyone. I may have some more questions for you later."

"Yes, officer. I'll be available for as long as you need me."

Skip walked back into the dining room and reported to diLongo. "Mr. Black is in room 301. Mrs. Black is in room 303. And Melissa Fielding is in 305. Mr. and Mrs. Black are very anxious to get home. Their baby was being fussy and they don't want to be out too late. Melissa Fielding says her husband is out tonight with his buddies at a bachelor party, and she needs to let her babysitter go home."

"Of course. I'll talk to Mrs. Black first." To Gayle, she said, "Dr. Primrose, I need to start the interviews now. Would you mind keeping an eye on the others in the dining room? Don't let anyone leave. And let me know when the medical examiner arrives."

"Of course," Gayle said. She watched as Daniel Post, the head of the English department, got out of his seat and walked over to her. "I heard what that officer said to you," he said. "I want to help. What can I do?"

"Oh, thank you, Daniel. I appreciate that. We have to keep everyone calm. Why don't you offer them tea or drinks… Oh wait, I forgot. The officer said not to touch anything. I guess we just have to sit tight. But if some people have to go to the washroom, perhaps you can escort them? We can't let anyone leave the building."

Daniel returned to his table where Emily Warren, his bridge partner, and David Bartholomew were sitting. He sat down with his hands folded in front of him, looking slightly aggravated.

"What's going on, Daniel?" Emily asked.

"Nothing. I offered to help, and Gayle said if you have to go potty, I should walk you there and back. They're waiting for the medical examiner to turn up, and the detective will interview all of us before we can go home. Looks like we're going to be here for a while."

"Oh dear," Emily said. "I have to get home to feed my cat."

Daniel snorted. Emily looked down at her hands. Then she said, "What do you think happened to Terry and Anne-Marie? They both got so sick, so suddenly. I've never seen anything like it."

"I'm not a doctor. How should I know?" Daniel snapped.

"Even Dr. Morrison over there doesn't know what happened," David said.

"It could be a virus," Emily mused. "You know, something like the Avian flu virus that kills people."

"Don't be ridiculous," Daniel said. "Avian flu!"

"My bet is it's something they ate. Maybe some bad meat in the sandwiches," David suggested.

"But Anne-Marie's a vegetarian," Emily pointed out. "She doesn't eat meat."

"Well, there's got to be a simple explanation," David said. "People don't just drop down dead for nothing, you know."

Daniel nodded in agreement. "I'm sure there's a simple explanation," he said. "Let the police do their work. The medical examiner will be here soon. Maybe he'll shed some light on the subject. All this idle speculation will get us nowhere."

Emily looked around the room. Players were sitting at their tables, chatting in low voices or staring into space. The four students were huddled together at a table with their cell phones, sending text messages to friends and family members.

"The news is getting out," she said to Daniel, indicating the students.

"Well, I'm not surprised," Daniel said. "It's not every day something like this happens. The police will have to investigate it."

David looked concerned. "You think there's foul play?"

"How should I know? I'm not an expert in these matters! What are you worried about?"

"Not a thing!" David said, eyeing Daniel.

"Okay, then, shut up!" Daniel said. "You keep speculating and you'll have everybody in a panic!"

CHAPTER 4

 PRESENT DAY — 12:45 A.M.

We finished our beers and I noticed the bartender was wiping down the tables, indicating the bar would soon be closing.

"We have to leave here," I said. "Let's go to Donut Heaven for coffee after this, and I'll finish the story."

"Yeah, sure. We're both off tomorrow, and I can sleep in as long as I want."

"Well, I have to get the kids ready for school, but I can always catch a nap in the afternoon."

"So, you and Skip were at the scene. Then what happened?" Brian asked, as he got some money out of his wallet.

"Well, we started interviewing the witnesses, one by one. You know, these bridge players took the game very seriously! We wondered if they took it seriously enough to kill over it. Everyone seemed nice enough on the surface. It was only after we did some intense interviews that some surprising information started coming out. For example, we learned about this funky Halloween party where players got dressed up and acted like their characters, you know, role-playing. We also learned some things that did not reflect well on the college administrator, Dr. Primrose."

"So she's not so squeaky clean?"

The waiter came to our table. We gave him money for our drinks and I picked up the folder of clippings. "We'll look at these over coffee. Let's go. We'll take my car."

Brian nodded in agreement. Donut Heaven was a popular 24-hour coffee shop on the highway halfway into Mount Salem. The donuts weren't great, but the coffee was always hot and fresh. It took about fifteen minutes to drive there.

"Tell me about the Halloween party," Brian said as I pulled out of the parking lot.

"It was thirteen months prior to the event. All the players were there," I began.

🗓 THE HALLOWEEN PARTY, WEDNESDAY, OCTOBER 31, 2007 — 6:45 P.M.

Children screamed in wild excitement as they careened around the neighborhood in their colorful costumes, collecting candies and other goodies at each other's homes. It was Halloween night, that time of year when children of all ages indulge in their super-hero fantasies or explore their dark side — all in good fun, of course.

But there was another kind of dark side brewing on the mountain that night, a darkness of the soul that would result in mayhem and death a year down the road.

At 6:45 p.m., the sky was darkening with black clouds and the wind was rustling the dying leaves as Gayle Primrose stepped out of her townhouse and doused the candles in the jack-o-lanterns outside her door. She filled a big bowl with candy bars and left it on the front step, since she would not be around to shell out. It was bridge night at Kensington College.

As she drove to the campus, Gayle's mind drifted back to her childhood in the deep south. She recalled how excited she had been as a young child to experience Halloween. She especially enjoyed dressing up in outrageous costumes, mostly characters she knew from nursery rhymes, fairy tales and Disney movies. It was a fun way to escape from the rigid rules and restrictions of her family life, and it was the highlight of the year, even outshining Christmas.

She was the eldest of four children in a large, extended family near Savannah, Georgia. Her parents believed in the literal truth of the Bible and the whole family attended church every Sunday. Her parents didn't drink, didn't smoke, didn't swear and didn't allow their kids to play with friends on Sunday. They were dyed-in-the-wool southerners and they religiously maintained their traditions. While they schooled their children in fundamentalist Christian values and southern hospitality, they also exhibited a common feature of life in the south, a fear of interaction with African-Americans. This fear permeated traditional white society with their need to 'keep negroes in their place'. The antagonism between the races finally boiled over in the 1960s when Martin Luther King began his campaign against poverty and the segregation of schools. 'Busing' became the nation's hot potato as protests and riots broke out against the forced busing of children to integrate the schools.

Gayle felt uncomfortable living in a society that discriminated against people on the basis of race. It seemed un-Christian to her. The busing issue motivated Gayle to pursue a career in education and escape the intellectual prison of the small town where she grew up. She studied hard and graduated high school with very high marks. Then she applied for, and received, a scholarship to attend Columbia University in New York City. As choked as it was with smog, cars and people, the big city was a breath of fresh air for Gayle's inquisitive mind. She could never go back and live with her family after that. She met a young man, Garry Primrose, on campus, and after graduation, they married and moved further north to Syracuse, where she could focus on her intellectual pursuits. She studied for her Ph.D. at Syracuse University, and started writing books about improving education and learning. She was truly happy for the first time in her life.

The young married couple visited Gayle's hometown at Christmas each year, to see her folks and keep tabs on the siblings. They also attended family weddings and funerals, when their schedules permitted.

They moved to Mount Salem when Gayle was hired to teach in the education department at Kensington College. She had already published five books and was working on her sixth, her last as it turned out. It was the biggest tragedy of her life when Garry got caught in a sudden storm while he was sailing by himself on Lake Salem. His small boat capsized and he drowned.

The memory of that day still haunted her. "He should have bought the Marshall sailboat," she told her parents. "It's the most stable in choppy water. Instead, he bought that other boat to save a few thousand, and that's what killed him." She had the boat destroyed.

Within a year of Garry's drowning, the president of the college became too ill to continue, and he passed away. Gayle applied to the Board of Governors for the job, and presented an ambitious plan to modernize the curriculum and promote the image of the college. She was just thirty-two, far too young to take on the responsibilities of running the college, but she got a break when the candidate they selected, a man in his fifties, suddenly dropped dead of a heart attack. The Board of Governors turned to Gayle, and she never looked back.

Gayle bought the townhouse where the previous college president had lived, lock, stock and barrel. She got a great deal because it had to be sold as part of the estate. She removed the stuffy old furniture, except for some fine antique pieces from the Pennsylvania Shakers, and brought in sleek modern furniture imported from Italy. She also invested in paintings and sculptures from artist friends she had met as a student in New York City. They often invited her to exhibitions in various places around the country, and she always bought one or two pieces to show her support. Over the years, her townhouse filled up with modern art that she treasured, not because they were expensive pieces, but because her friends had made them.

With no husband and no children, and her family far away, she devoted the next twenty-five years to the college, and to her favorite pastime, bridge. Playing bridge was a hold-over from her childhood. Gayle's mother belonged to a ladies bridge club that met every Tuesday afternoon in Savannah. She taught Gayle to play bridge at the age of twelve, saying that bridge was a necessary social skill for a young woman, along with cooking and domestic management. Even at that age, Gayle was more interested in reading, writing and politics, but she found bridge to be mentally challenging, and she enjoyed the competitive aspect. At university, she joined the student's duplicate bridge club, and later took lessons to improve her game. It was under Gayle's leadership that the bridge club became such an important part of campus life at Kensington.

As director of the bridge club, Gayle was the one who organized regular events, including the annual competition. In advance of Halloween night in 2007, Gayle sent out this memo to bridge club members.

FROM: GAYLE PRIMROSE
TO: FACULTY BRIDGE CLUB MEMBERS

Halloween falls on Wednesday this year! I have decided we'll get in the spirit of Halloween for our regular bridge night. And you, dear friends, will be the entertainment.

We can't let children have all the fun on Halloween night, now can we?

I am mandating that everyone turn up in costume for bridge on October 31st. Not just any costume. I want you to choose one from the attached list of movie characters. And I will be handing out prizes.

For the top prize of $500, you must stay in character for the entire night! So don't be shy and don't be late! The food will be potluck and the cocktails are on me!

And wear your dancing shoes. We're going to have a bloody good time!

Gayle had attached a list of characters to the memo. She knew the $500 prize would entice some of the players to make an effort to win it.

When Barb Baker, the manager of mail and printing services at the college, saw the memo, she dialed the extension for Jill Wilmington. Barb and Jill were bridge partners, and over the last three years, they had also become quite friendly. Jill was the human resources manager for the college.

"Hey, Jill," Barb said in greeting. "Did you get Gayle's memo?"

"About the Halloween party? Yeah."

"She's offering a pretty big prize for the best character portrayal," Barb pointed out. "So, what do you think? Do you have a costume in mind?"

"Yes, I'm going to be Hot Lips Houlihan."

"Cool!" Barb said. "I remember her from that TV show, *M*A*S*H*."

"And the movie, too. She made quite a splash!" Jill said, laughing. "What about you?"

"I haven't had time to think about it."

"Well, if you need help, let me know. I'm good at putting costumes together."

"Okay, thanks," Barb said. "I'll probably take you up on that offer." She hesitated for a moment, and then she said, "Tell me something, Jill. I never asked you this before, but I've always been curious. How did you first get into playing bridge?"

"Well, it was a long time ago," Jill said. "I was a high school student. It was on a dare, actually. A cute guy in my class dared me to play 'strip bridge'. I didn't know what that was, but I figured it was probably like strip poker. I liked the guy, so I agreed to do it. Sounded like fun," she said, and paused.

"So, what happened?"

"Well, when my parents were away one Saturday afternoon, the cute guy came over to my place with another guy and a girl, and we went into the rec room downstairs. He told me how the game is played. He said that aces are worth 4 points, kings are worth 3, queens are worth 2 and jacks are worth 1, and if I add up the points in my hand and I have 13 or more, I can bid my longest suit. Well, to make a long story short," Jill said, laughing, "the guys kept changing the rules and we kept losing, of course, and stripping off our clothes, until we were down to just our panties.

"I forget the girl's name, but I'll never forget her tits. They were small and firm, with big brown nipples that got really hard and stood straight out. Don't know if she was just cold or getting turned on! My nipples were also sticking out, and I was definitely getting turned on. Anyway, the boys kept staring at us until they started losing games and stripping off their clothes. Just as they were about to lose their shorts, my big brother walked

34 | *Death in Duplicate*

in on us! You can imagine the uproar that caused! So anyway, that was my initiation!"

"Were you embarrassed?" Barb asked.

"Me? No, I didn't do anything wrong. But the guys got red-faced when my brother saw the bulges in their shorts and started bellowing at them, so they got their clothes back on and left in a hurry."

"I bet they did." Barb laughed. "Well, I better go. Tons of work piling up here."

"Okay, see you later," Jill said, and rang off.

Over the next two weeks leading up to the Halloween party, the bridge club buzzed with anticipation as players made their plans and got their costumes organized.

For the event, Gayle wore a snug-fitting English schoolteacher's outfit similar to Maggie Smith's costume in *The Prime of Miss Jean Brodie*. Her pumps added another three inches to her already tall, curvaceous figure.

"I look like a force to be reckoned with," she thought. She parked in her reserved spot next to the Baxter building, the administrative building that contained her office and the faculty dining room. She was pleased to see some grinning jack-o-lanterns greeting her on the front steps.

She had hired a local events company to transform the dining room into a dungeon, with black curtains and cobwebs hanging overhead. There were skulls glowing in the dark corners and creepy creatures of the night clinging to the walls.

Gayle checked the preparations and was satisfied to find everything in order. There was a table for food and candies against one wall, with another table for refreshments.

David Bartholomew was already there. A barrel-chested black man in his early fifties, David was in charge of security for the campus. For this event, he was dressed up as Captain Hook, with a big floppy pirate's hat and a fake hook in one hand.

"Why, Captain, you look devastatingly dangerous tonight," Gayle said flirtatiously in greeting.

"Watch yer tongue, me beauty, or I'll throw ye over me shoulder an' take ye down below. ARRRRR," he growled. Then he grinned and she giggled.

"Later," she said, and winked at him. "I do hope we see some exciting costumes tonight!"

Chris and Anne-Marie Boland, a husband and wife team, arrived next. They came dressed as the young innocents, Brad and Janet from the *Rocky Horror Picture Show*. Anne-Marie worked in the accounting department, and Chris was an engineer who worked off campus. They were born-again Baptists, and Gayle suspected their bedtime reading every night was the New Testament. That's what her parents used to do. She was surprised they even knew about the *Rocky Horror Picture Show*.

"Is there a party going on here?" 'Brad' asked as he and 'Janet' walked timidly into the room. "We just want to use the phone."

"Yes, we're having a party! But the phone is out of order! So help yourself to drinks and something to munch on. You're going to stay a while," Gayle responded, as more players entered the room.

Daniel Post, the head of the English department, came in next, as Klinger, the cross-dresser from *M*A*S*H*. His printed frock came just below his knees, exposing the bottom half of his hairy legs. He also wore elbow-length gloves and a floral hat. Over his shoulder he carried a fake rifle.

"Klinger, come over here," Gayle ordered. He hurried over to talk to her. "I just want to say I love your style," she said approvingly.

"Well, I love your style too," he replied smoothly. "Where did you get that smashing outfit? I got mine from the Sears catalogue."

"Well, I got mine at the Sally Ann!" she replied, laughing.

The next players to arrive were Terry Digman and Sally Brighton, two professors in the psychology department. Terry wore a top hat and tails and held a lethal-looking plastic handgun. Sally came dressed for a garden party, with a wide-brimmed hat and a string of pearls. When Terry saw Gayle, he suddenly crouched, raised his gun as if to shoot and moved stealthily towards her. Sally trotted behind him, fluttering and twittering. When Terry reached Gayle, he bowed and said, "Let me introduce myself. I'm Bond, James Bond. And this is my loyal assistant, Miss Moneypenny. At your service, madam."

"Well, Mr. Bond," Gayle said, "I'm pleased to make your acquaintance."

"Just call me 007," he said, tipping his hat to her.

"Oh, James," cooed 'Moneypenny,' fluttering her eyelashes at him.

"Children!" 'Miss Brodie' said in her best fake English accent. "I want you to be on your best behavior tonight. So help yourself to drinks and find your seats," she ordered, and pointed to the refreshments table.

'Bond' nodded and said to 'Moneypenny,' "Make mine a vodka martini. Shaken, not stirred."

She fluttered again and said, "Anything else I can get for you, James?"

Gayle noticed a few more players arriving and she went over to them, raising her glass of wine in greeting. "Please help yourself to refreshments and get settled at your desks, I mean, tables. We'll start the lessons soon, I mean, the bridge games. Oh, dearie me, I think I need another drink…" She carried on for a while like this, chatting with each player as they came through the door.

Emily Warren, Daniel Post's office assistant and bridge partner, came dressed as the evil Nurse Ratched. She had borrowed a nurse's uniform from a friend who worked at a local psychiatric hospital. Emily had a pleasant, round face with big, blue eyes, and wore her chin-length brown hair swept up in the style of Louise Fletcher. She carried a very large syringe in one hand. A black dildo dangled from her waistband like a nightstick.

When she saw Gayle, Emily said, "I expect everyone will be on good behavior tonight, or else I'll keep them in line with this!" She brandished her syringe, squirting some clear liquid in the air. "It's just vodka," she whispered to Gayle, "but don't tell anyone!"

Then a whole group of players showed up at once. Two students came dressed as the dynamic duo, Batman and Robin, and two others came as Princess Leia and Han Solo. Karl Schultz, a portly history prof, turned up as Friar Tuck with his young bridge partner as Robin Hood.

Then Jill Wilmington made her entrance, wearing only a white towel and a pair of bright red wax lips in her mouth. Jill, a tall, slender blonde, seemed perfectly at ease in her character as Margaret 'Hot Lips' Houlihan.

Gayle called her over and said, "I say, Hot Lips, you look ravishing as always. Your comrade Klinger is here already. And who's this fine-looking gentleman with you?"

Barb Baker was dressed as the Godfather. She took the cigar from her mouth and growled, "I'm gonna ask you once, or I'll make you an offer you can't refuse. Where's the booze?"

Gayle laughed and pointed to the tables set up for food and drinks as the remaining players arrived. They crowded around the refreshments tables, trying to stay in character as they chose their drinks and picked up some homemade goodies. The most popular items were sugar cookies shaped like ghosts, a pumpkin pie made to look like a jack-o-lantern and cupcakes decorated with orange icing and black jellybeans.

Eventually the players settled down at the bridge tables, and Gayle made some brief announcements before starting the first round. On this night, Gayle kept the play moving along quickly so they could finish early and have time for dancing.

As usual, the players took the bridge game very seriously, since the results would be counted towards the annual prize. After consuming many scotches, bottles of beer and glasses of wine, the players became quite vocal, with the occasional "Whoopee!" or "Oh, no!" or "Partner, why did you do that?" breaking through the chatter.

At ten o'clock, Gayle asked the players to move the tables to the side. Then she turned on the sound system and told everyone to get up for some dancing to "Monster Mash," "Purple People Eater," "Time Warp," "Twist and Shout" and other funky dance tunes from the 1960s and 1970s. Players stayed in character as much as possible throughout the evening, and between the drinking, the dancing and the role-playing, they all had a very good time.

At midnight, Gayle turned up the lights to make her announcement. "There are three prizes tonight," she said. "One is for the most amusing couple, one is for the most outrageous character, and one is for the best character overall — that's the big one," she said with a grin, waving an envelope.

"For the most amusing couple, it was a close race between Brad and Janet and James Bond and Miss Moneypenny, but I had to go with Bond and Moneypenny. Well done!" And she offered them a bottle of Mumm's champagne. "I'm sure you'll know what to do with this, James."

"I do, indeed," he purred, and winked at 'Miss Moneypenny.'

"For the most outrageous character," Gayle said, "no one is more outrageous than Klinger, a woman after my own heart." She handed Daniel Post a bottle of Scotch.

"Much appreciated," he said. Scotch was his favorite drink.

"For the top prize tonight, for the best character, I must admit I had a hard time choosing. There were several strong contenders. I want to give a gold star to my bridge partner, David Bartholomew, for being such a splendid Captain Hook." She nodded in David's direction. "I also want to give a gold star to Jill Wilmington as Hot Lips, for taking time out from her shower to join us this evening, in her very simple and, shall I say, flesh-baring costume," she said, to hoots and howls of approval. "However, I was most impressed with Nurse Ratched. She stayed in character the whole night, and put the fear in me, I must admit. Well done, Emily!" She handed the envelope with a check for $500 to Emily Warren.

"Thank you so much, Gayle," Emily said. "This means more to me than you can possibly imagine."

CHAPTER 5

📅 PRESENT DAY — 1:00 A.M.

I finished my account of the Halloween party as we drove into the Donut Heaven parking lot. We went in, got coffee and sat at a table next to the window.

"This is the same table Skip and I were sitting at when we got the 911 call that night," I said, smiling at the coincidence.

I took a clipping out of the folder. "Anyway, here's another radio report. Sharon Sharpe broadcast the names of all the people who were playing bridge that night. It turns out she had a contact at the college who was feeding her information. That made it difficult for us to keep a lid on things."

"She's a good reporter."

"Yeah, I guess so. She was just doing her job." Then I read the transcript to him.

> THURSDAY, DECEMBER 11, 2008
> POLICE QUIZ WITNESSES IN THE BRIDGE CLUB DEATHS
>
> News Radio 1015 has learned the identities of the persons who were present last night at the Kensington College Bridge Club.
>
> Sharon Sharpe has been on the story since it broke late last night. Sharon, what do you have on this now?
>
> SHARON: The two victims are Terry Digman, 40, a psychology professor, and Anne-Marie Boland, 45, an accountant on staff at the college, and the mother of five children.
>
> Detective Christina diLongo has confirmed that all the witnesses were detained for several hours while the police conducted interviews.
>
> The deaths were particularly gruesome, according to our sources. The victims fell to the floor, convulsing,

vomiting and bleeding from their eyes. The medical examiner is now conducting autopsies to determine the cause of death.

Those present at the scene were:

Gayle Primrose – the high-profile president of Kensington College. She is also the director of the Faculty Bridge Club and the host of a private New Year's Eve event that attracts international celebrities every year.

David Bartholomew – Chief of Security for Kensington College.

Christopher Boland – husband of victim Anne-Marie Boland and a computer engineer with a local firm.

Sally Brighton – a psychology professor at Kensington College and bridge partner of victim Terry Digman.

Daniel Post – acclaimed international author of crime fiction and a professor of Creative Writing at Kensington College.

Emily Warren – a secretary in the English department at Kensington College.

Jill Wilmington – Human Resources Manager at Kensington College.

Barb Baker – Manager of Mail Services at Kensington College.

Samantha Black – a programmer in the IT department at Kensington College.

Phillip Black – also a programmer in the IT department at Kensington College and Samantha Black's husband.

Melissa Fielding – an administrator at Kensington College.

Karl Schultz — a history professor at Kensington College.

Tracey Kingston — a nurse at Beaumont County Hospital.

And five students, whose names are not released at this time.

ANNOUNCER: So, Sharon, what are the police saying about it?

SHARON: They are waiting for the M.E.'s report, and then they will make an announcement.

ANNOUNCER: Is there any indication as to whether this is an accident or a homicide investigation?

SHARON: The police aren't saying, but speculation is that it could be anything from a terrorist plot or a random act of violence to an accidental case of food poisoning. The police have not ruled anything out at this point.

ANNOUNCER: Thank you, Sharon.

"So, I guess you interviewed the witnesses. What did you find out, if anything?" Brian asked.

"That first night, it was late and we didn't know the cause of death. So it was difficult to question people under the circumstances. After the initial interviews to get their details on what happened, I tried to get the witnesses to talk about each other. I wanted the inside scoop on what was going on at the college. I figured that the witnesses must know something that would help us understand what happened, and why, even if we could not connect the dots immediately. It often goes like that in an investigation. You collect masses of information, and at some point, you have enough to solve the case. That's when your critical thinking skills really take over. Of course, you have to know when you reach that point. That's the key."

Detective diLongo walked down the hall to conduct interviews with the parents who needed to go home to look after their children. First up was Mrs. Black, a plump blonde in her thirties.

"Hello," diLongo said, smiling to put her at ease. "I know you are anxious to get home to your baby, so I'll keep this brief. How well do you know the victims, Anne-Marie Boland and Terry Digman?"

"I play bridge with them," Mrs. Black said. "Other than that, we don't run in the same circles. I work with the computer system, and I rarely see either of them. Do you think there's been some foul play?"

"If you don't mind, at this point I'll ask the questions, okay?" diLongo said.

"Sorry. I'm just a little jittery after all that's happened tonight."

"I understand. So, tell me what happened, in your own words."

"Everything was fine," Mrs. Black said. "We were bidding the hand and suddenly Anne-Marie started coughing and choking and she fell on the floor gasping and making gurgling sounds, and then she seemed to go unconscious. And, of course, we all stopped playing at that point. I got up to see what happened. Next thing I knew, Terry was having a problem and he fell on the floor too. It was really creepy you know. First Anne-Marie collapsed, and then Terry, and blood was coming out everywhere. It was awful. People were shouting and crying all at once. Everyone is so confused. What caused this? It's not contagious, is it? I have a baby at home."

DiLongo wrote some things down in her notebook. "Did you feel okay? You know, after the meal. Any upset, nausea, increase in heart rate or other unusual symptoms?"

"No, nothing like that. I just felt full. I over-ate a bit," she said, patting her tummy.

"Okay, that's all for now. Please wait here for a few minutes while I talk to your husband."

DiLongo walked to the next office to speak with Mr. Black. His story was the same as his wife's. DiLongo debated whether or not to let them both go home to their baby, and she felt she had little concrete reason to keep them any longer.

What would Cap do? she wondered. She decided to let them go home. "Until we know the cause of death, don't contact anyone and don't go anywhere," she warned. "I want you to stay at home for at least twenty-four hours. Understand?"

"Like a quarantine? In case it's contagious?" Mr. Black asked anxiously.

"Look, I'm asking for your cooperation here, since we don't know what we're dealing with yet. Do I have your promise to stay home for the next twenty-four hours?"

After they agreed to the self-imposed quarantine, she told them there might be more questions once the cause of death was known, so they should not plan to go out of town. Both Blacks expressed their gratitude, and then they left.

"Two down, sixteen to go," diLongo said to Skip. "I wonder when the M.E. is going to get here. I need to know what we're dealing with! Is it an accident or something else?" Skip just shook his head. "I want to talk to Terry Digman's bridge partner and Christopher Boland next," she said. "Bring them to the rooms the Blacks were in, please. And, we shouldn't leave Mr. Boland alone. He looks pretty wrecked. Ask Gayle to stay with him, okay?" DiLongo had another reason to ensure Chris was not alone. It was his wife who had died. In cases of murder, nine times out of ten, the husband or lover was responsible. She was well aware that Chris's grief could be less than genuine, and she thought that if his guard were down, Gayle might notice something about him that would give a clue to his guilt, if indeed he were guilty.

While Skip went back to the dining room, diLongo went into Room 305 to interview Melissa Fielding.

"So, Mrs. Fielding, how are you doing?" diLongo asked, as she entered the room.

Melissa was an attractive Latina in her late 20s, with impossibly long eyelashes. She was wearing a short leather skirt and a low-cut, sequined top that showed off her large, round breasts. "I'm all right," Melissa said, and waited.

"No tummy aches or anything?"

"Nope."

"So, how do you know Anne-Marie Boland and Terry Digman?"

"Bridge." And she licked her lips that appeared very dry.

"Feeling alright?" diLongo asked.

"Whadyamean?"

"You seem very tense. Does it make you nervous to talk to the police?"

Melissa suddenly launched herself off her chair. "Christ! What do you think? Two people died tonight, right in front of my eyes! One minute they're doing fine, next minute they're dead. And it wasn't a pretty sight." She started pacing up and down. "You think I'm nervous? I'm fucking out of my mind! What the hell happened to them? What if it's a killer virus? What if I catch it? Will I infect my baby? I'm freaking out here!"

"Okay, okay, Mrs. Fielding, please take a seat," diLongo said, trying to calm her down. "This won't take long. I just need to know what you witnessed tonight, during dinner and afterwards. Did you notice anything unusual?"

"Unusual!" Melissa responded, clearly in an agitated state of mind. "You don't get it. Two people died in front of me. I'd say that's unusual."

"Take it easy, Mrs. Fielding," diLongo said in a softer voice.

Melissa gave diLongo a pained look. "I want to go home to my baby," she said.

"Is there anything else unusual you can tell me about — other than the two people who died?"

"No, nothing. We were just playing fucking bridge!" Melissa said, and pressed her lips together.

DiLongo sighed, and decided to let her go home. She gave Melissa the same instructions as the Blacks, to stay at home for 24 hours, or until notified. "That's all for now, Mrs. Fielding. I may have more questions for you later, so don't go on any sudden vacations or anything."

She then walked back into Room 301 where Sally Brighton, Terry Digman's bridge partner, was waiting, drumming her fingers nervously.

"Hello, Professor Brighton," said diLongo. "First, let me say I am very sorry for the loss of your bridge partner. But I have to ask some questions to fill in my report. Can you tell me about your personal relationship with the victim, Professor Digman?"

"What makes you think we have a personal relationship?" she asked, sounding agitated.

"Just routine questions," diLongo said, giving her a long look.

Sally took a deep breath. "Well, we both work in the psych department as assistant professors. I teach child psych and Terry teaches — I mean, he taught — criminal behavior and related material. A while back, when Terry came on staff, we became bridge partners. That's about it."

"Notice anything about him recently that might explain his collapse tonight?"

Sally hesitated before answering, "Well, I probably shouldn't say anything about it, in case it's not true, you know. But I got the feeling he might be using drugs. You know, not prescription drugs. He just seemed a little hyper and obnoxious at times. He's not your typical, dry academic type, if you know what I mean."

DiLongo wrote in her notebook: *Terry Digman — drugs?*

"Okay," diLongo said, "back to this evening. Anything unusual tonight? People, things, smells, anything?"

"No. Terry and I were getting some top boards and I think we would have been first again. But that's not unusual," she said, rather smugly.

"Professor Brighton, did your bridge partner have any enemies that you know of, anyone who might want to do him harm?"

"You mean, kill him?" Sally paused. "Oh my God, he was murdered? Oh my God… oh my God…" She starting wringing her hands.

"So you think he was murdered?" asked diLongo.

"I don't. At least, I don't know if he was. You said… Why are you asking me these things? You think I did something to Terry? Am I a suspect? Do I need a lawyer?" With that, Sally stood up to face diLongo straight on.

"Calm down, Professor. I'm not accusing you of anything. Look at it this way," diLongo continued in an effort to get Sally on her side. "If it turns out to be foul play, don't you want me to do everything I can to find out who did it?"

"Well, of course."

"All right, then. Answer my questions. Can you think of any reason why someone would want him out of the way?"

"Not exactly," Sally said. "I don't go around wondering why people might be murdered, you know!"

"Let's get back to this evening, then. What were you doing when Mrs. Boland collapsed?"

"Terry was declarer in four spades, and I was the dummy," Sally said. "He was having some trouble making the contract."

"What kind of trouble?"

"Do you know anything about bridge?" asked Sally.

"A little," diLongo said. "My parents play with their friends sometimes."

"Well, he had four losers, but to make the contract he could afford to lose only three tricks. So he set up an endplay to eliminate one of his losers. When Anne-Marie collapsed, Terry ignored her and kept on playing the hand. I got up to take a look at Anne-Marie and see if I could do anything to help, but she was having convulsions and I didn't know what to do. And then Terry started screaming and clutching his throat and the next thing I knew, he was on the floor, convulsing and vomiting and bleeding. It was very upsetting!"

"At the break, what did you do?" diLongo asked, to change the subject.

"Nothing. I… I just got some coffee and dessert and waited for Gayle to call the next round."

"Did you have a tummy ache, headache, cramps, anything?"

"No. I felt fine."

"And what did Mr. Digman do at the break?"

"Well, he went up to the dessert table and got some tea and a cupcake, and came back to our table. I was eating a cookie and then I ate a cupcake. He made some crack about how my blood sugar levels would go through the roof." DiLongo noticed Sally was wringing a tissue in her two hands as she talked.

"Was there anything unusual prior to the incident?"

"Terry was sweating and frowning as he was playing the hand, but I thought it was just because it was a difficult hand. And I know he badly wanted to win. That's what he talks about all the time: beating everyone at bridge and winning the year-end prize. It's like he has to prove something to everybody, how smart he is or something."

"What's the annual prize?"

"It's a competition we have every year. Each time we play, the top pairs for North-South and East-West win some money. The pair that are in the money the most throughout the year gets to attend Gayle's New Year's Eve dinner party. It's a big status thing for the bridge players to win this prize."

"I see. Are you in the running for it?"

"Yes, we're tied for first," she said. "But some other pairs are close behind. Anyone can win at this point."

"Now, let's go back to what happened this evening. I want you to tell me again about the last few minutes before your friend collapsed. Go back to the break. Close your eyes and review it in your mind, like you're watching a movie."

DiLongo figured that something must have happened before, during or after the break to affect the two victims. Sally closed her eyes and concentrated. DiLongo could see her eyeballs moving under her lids.

"Okay, I go up to the dessert table. There's a bunch of people milling around, chatting about stuff, catching up on news and plans for Christmas. Emily comes along to get some tea, and I tell her how much I enjoy her cupcakes. She seems very pleased. I go back to my seat. I review my scoresheet. Terry is still at the dessert table, chatting to some people. After a while, he turns around to come back. He bumps into Emily and almost drops his cupcake and she nearly splashes hot tea all over him." Sally paused.

"Good, Professor Brighton. Please go on," diLongo said, making notes.

"Okay, he comes back and sits down. He starts talking about the hands and how well we're doing. He peels the paper off the cupcake. He sips his tea. He takes the jellybeans off the top of his cupcake and pops them in his mouth and says, 'I like them black' and winks at me. He's always making little comments like that, just a little off color."

"Right. Go on."

"So he's chewing the jellybeans and shows me his tongue which is turning black from the jellybeans, and he says, 'How would you like some black magic up your…' you know what."

Then Sally opened her eyes. "I have to tell you, he's a big flirt, but I don't take him seriously."

"I can imagine he was popular with the ladies. He was a good-looking guy. Was he married, single or what?"

"Single — at least, that's what he told me. I didn't know much about his personal life, though."

"Okay, go on."

Sally closed her eyes again. "He's still munching on the cupcake when Gayle calls the round, so he puts it back on his plate. Our new opponents, Karl and Ben, come to the table. Terry made a snide remark to Ben, something like, "Where's your chopsticks?" We start bidding the hand. Karl wins the auction and plays the hand in 3NT, but we manage to put him down one, which is a good board for us. Then we start the next hand. Terry ends up in four spades. Then he starts playing the hand as I watch, because I'm dummy. Terry is frowning as he plays the cards. Then Anne-Marie collapses, and I get up to take a look. Then Terry keels over."

Sally opened her eyes at this point, and looked straight at diLongo.

"I can't do this anymore. I'm feeling really drained."

"All right. Take a break," diLongo said, sensing that Sally had more to say but she didn't want to push too hard at this point. "Go back to the dining room and try to relax. I may have more questions for you later, so don't go home just yet."

Sally walked back to the dining room, and diLongo went to the next room where Christopher Boland was waiting for her. Gayle was also in the room sitting next to Chris. She was doing her best to comfort the grieving husband.

DiLongo indicated that Gayle could stay with Chris for the duration of the interview.

"Mr. Boland, I'm Detective diLongo. Let me say how very sorry I am about your wife. I will do everything I can to find out what happened to her. The medical examiner should be here soon, and he will hopefully have some news for us tonight or perhaps tomorrow. We'll find out why this happened. I promise."

"Thanks," he said, looking down at his hands.

"How are you holding up?"

"My... my wife just died," he stammered. "I... I can't believe she's gone." He stared back at diLongo with the look of a deer caught in the glare of oncoming headlights.

He looked so shocked and confused that she was afraid any attempt at expressing her sympathy would result in his grief spilling over, preventing her from being able to elicit vital information.

Unless he's guilty, she thought. *He's a pretty good actor, if that's the case.*

So she kept her questions to the point.

"How was your wife feeling tonight?"

"I don't know what I can tell you. Annie was in good health. She was feeling fine. She was in a good mood. And then, boom, she's gone. It's like God just decided to turn the lights out. I don't understand. Why? Why?" He face crumbled as he blinked back some tears.

"I cannot answer that right now, but I promise I will keep working until we know exactly what happened to her." He let out a sob and looked down at his hands. DiLongo stifled a sigh. Dealing with grieving witnesses was not her strong suit.

"Just for the record, Mr. Boland, do you know if your wife had any food allergies? You know, to seafood or peanuts, that kind of thing?"

"No, she didn't. She was perfectly healthy!"

DiLongo made a note and continued her questioning.

"I'm sorry to have to ask you this, but just in case there might be some foul play involved, can you think of any reason why anyone would to hurt your wife?"

Chris brought his head back up to look at diLongo, his eyes brimming with more tears.

"No. She was a wonderful person and everyone loved her!"

"Okay, but just so you know, we may have to look closely into her life, and once we start looking into a victim's life, we usually uncover some things that are hidden from view, even from those closest to them, and it could get ugly. So, if you know anything, no matter how insignificant you think it might be, now is the time to tell us."

"I know my wife, and there's nothing," he said mournfully. "We're God-fearing, church-going Baptists."

"So, what is your wife's connection with Mr. Digman? Could they be more than friends, do you think?"

"No! Impossible. My wife and I have a good marriage. We're happy together, or we were."

"How's your financial situation? With five kids to support, things could be tight."

"We do okay. We're careful with our money. It's not a problem."

"Tell me please, what investments or other assets are in your wife's name, including any life insurance?"

Chris stared at diLongo, and then jumped up. "I don't believe this! You think I did something to my wife to collect her life insurance? Good grief! This is too much!" He marched out the door. "I'm leaving. I'm going home to my family, and you can go to hell," he shouted as he strode down the corridor, down the stairs and into the night, without even collecting his coat.

"Hmmm, that went well," diLongo commented dryly to Gayle who pursed her lips.

DiLongo wrote into her notebook: *C.B. — refuses to answer questions about insurance — leaves in a huff — need to re-interview.*

Skip came into the room and said, "The medical examiner has arrived. He's on his way up now."

Thank God, diLongo thought, as they walked back towards the dining room. *Maybe now we'll find out if we're investigating an accident or a crime.*

Sam Baldwin was a short, bearded man in his mid-fifties. He had been the county's M.E. for at least twenty years. He was a man of few words, and preferred to spend his free time at the end of a fishing pole.

Sam arrived with three assistants who wheeled in stretchers for the bodies and equipment to collect evidence. Gayle led Sam over to the bodies in the dining room.

"They haven't been moved?" he asked, as he knelt down beside Terry.

"No sir," said diLongo.

Sam took a close look at Terry's face. He looked into his bloody eyes, opened his mouth, felt around his head, poked and prodded his abdomen, and then stood up.

"He's pretty fresh. No obvious signs of physical trauma," he said. "I need to get him back to the morgue. Let's see the other one."

He went over to Anne-Marie and went through the same cursory exam.

"Okay, boys, you know what you have to do now," he said to his two assistants. "When you're finished collecting evidence from the bodies and getting all the shots I need, you can wrap them up and take them back to the morgue."

Then he took diLongo and Skip aside and said, "I'll do autopsies and run some tests. I have to say, I'm intrigued by the bloody eyes."

"Maybe they caught a virus like Ebola," Skip suggested helpfully.

Sam looked at diLongo as if to say, "Where did you get this clown?" and ignored Skip. He spoke to his assistants. "I want you to collect all the food, drinks, containers, garbage bags, liquor containers, used napkins, playing cards, dishes, etc. and bring them back to the lab. I don't know what we're dealing with yet, but I think we'll find out when we examine this stuff." Then, in a lower voice so only diLongo could hear, he said, "I'm almost convinced it's a deadly toxin they consumed, but I can't be sure until I run some tests."

"Okay," diLongo said, "I'll check in tomorrow, and you can bring me up to speed. That's Dr. Morrison over there. He first examined the bodies to confirm they were dead. Want to talk to him?"

Sam nodded, and went over to speak with Dr. Morrison.

"I'm Sam Baldwin, M.E.," he said by way of introduction. "Do you know what happened to these two?"

"Not a clue."

"Do you know anything of their medical history?"

"I'm not their family doctor, but as far as I know, they seemed to be in good health."

"Were they dead when you got here?"

"Yes, about ten minutes or so."

Sam turned around and trotted back to Gayle Primrose. He pointed to the bodies. "How did they seem before they collapsed — any signs of distress?"

"No," Gayle said. "They seemed perfectly normal to me. We had a meal, then we played bridge for a couple of hours, then we had a break for dessert. There was no indication of anything amiss."

"I see. Well, that's all for tonight," he said, and just waved as he trotted out the door. His appearance at the scene had lasted no more than eight minutes.

diLongo told Dr. Morrison he could go, turning her attention back to the dining room where the remaining bridge players still congregated. She told them to stay clear of the bodies and let the M.E.'s staff do their work.

"I want to interview each one of you before you go home," she said. "Emily Warren, please go to Room 301. Professor Post, Room 303. Ben Chong, Room 305. Professor Schultz, Room 302. Barb Baker, Room 304. Jill Wilmington, 306. Professor Brighton, 307. David Bartholomew, 308. Dr. Primrose, and the rest of you, sit at those tables in the corner, out of the way."

"But she already interviewed me," Sally grumbled as she walked out to the corridor with the others.

"Everyone in a room?" diLongo asked Skip a few minutes later. He nodded. "Then, let's get started," she said. She headed for 301, where Emily was seated at the desk, doodling on a piece of paper. Emily was in her late twenties, quite slender with her brown hair pulled back into a ponytail. Although looking a little pale, she was pleasantly attractive with deep-set blue eyes.

"Hello, Miss Warren," diLongo said, glancing down at her notebook. "How are you holding up tonight?"

"I'm okay. I think it would be hard to sleep after what's happened tonight. Poor Terry... poor Anne-Marie... poor Chris! He has all those kids to look after now!"

"Yes, he'll have to come up with a plan for that," said diLongo.

"Yeah, he's the planning type. You should see him play bridge. He always takes his time to plan out the play before he begins, like a real expert."

"We have to consider the possibility that this was not an accident. There could be foul play. So, I ask you, for the record, is there any reason that you can think of why anyone would want to kill Mrs. Boland?"

Emily shrugged. "I can't think of any reason off the top of my head. Everyone liked her, or had very little to say about her. She keeps to herself, anyway. She's an accountant, you know. What's to dislike about someone who crunches numbers for a living? I'll need some time to think about it. If anything comes to mind, I'll let you know."

DiLongo made a note.

"Fine, then let's move on. How well do you know Professor Digman?"

"Not well. I just see him in the bridge club, and sometimes around campus. He has a bit of a reputation, you know, as a womanizer. He says he's looking for a wife, but I think his mission is to get into the pants of every woman on campus while he's searching. Or at least, that's the impression he gives."

"Has he ever tried to get into your pants?"

"Well, he teases me sometimes," Emily admitted. "I mean, he teased me," she said, and frowned.

DiLongo sighed. "Okay, so he was a flirt. I understand. Do you know of anyone who's had a sexual encounter with him? Any office gossip going around about that?"

"No."

"Because if it turns out to be foul play, we have to look into the lives of both Mrs. Boland and Professor Digman, and that means overturning every rock and every pebble of their lives. We will find out what they are hiding, and why someone would want to do them harm."

Emily looked concerned. "I don't think there's foul play here. I think it must be some kind of accident. But I'm not a doctor yet, so I don't want to speculate what it might be."

"Okay then, let's talk about what happened tonight. Where were you when the trouble started?"

"Well, we were on the third hand after the break. I was playing the contract in four spades. I was studying the dummy when I heard something. I looked up to see Chris jumping up from his seat and screaming his wife's name. The others who were sitting close by went over to see if they could help. Gayle got on her cell phone and called the medical center to get a doctor to come over and check on Anne-Marie. Daniel and I stayed in our seats. He said not to go over there, that we'd just get in the way with so many people crowding about.

"We stopped playing and waited. The next thing I knew, Terry fell over on the floor, screaming and rolling around on the floor. I got up and saw blood. Daniel said, 'Maybe he cut himself. See the blood?' Anyway, Terry just kept convulsing and spitting up vomit and blood. It was pretty awful to see." Emily paused.

"Go on."

"Daniel and I went over to him and we were trying to help him when he suddenly went quiet and stopped breathing. I tried CPR, but it didn't work. Anyway, the doctor showed up a few minutes later and said they were both dead."

DiLongo made some notes as Emily paused in her recounting of the events.

"So, Miss Warren, what did you do during the break?" diLongo asked.

"Nothing."

"You didn't visit the dessert table?"

"No. Daniel offered to get my dessert for me."

"And what did he bring you?"

"A date square and a brownie, as I requested."

"I've been hearing about your cupcakes, Emily. People seem to really love them. But you chose a date square and a brownie. Why?"

"I have plenty of cupcakes at home. I made four dozen and brought two dozen tonight and I froze the rest. So I just thought I'd have something different. Does it matter what I ate for dessert?"

"Not sure. We'll ask everyone what they consumed, in any case. What else did you do?"

"I told you, I sat down at the table. I didn't talk to anyone. I looked at my score sheet to see how we were doing and where we might have some good boards. Daniel brought our tea and coffee and then he went back to get our desserts." Emily paused to take a breath. "He got himself a cupcake. He said he loves my cupcakes, but he doesn't like the jellybeans because they stick to his dental work, so he gave them to me and I ate them. That's about it."

"Nothing unusual there."

"No, nothing unusual. Well," Emily paused, "I didn't like my coffee. It was too strong, so I took my coffee cup back and got some tea. And then I returned to my table and waited for the next round to begin. Daniel and I discussed our score sheet. We always do that at the break."

"So you did go to the dessert table. Did you see Professor Digman when you got your tea?"

"No."

"Really? You didn't bump into him?"

"Oh, yeah. We kinda collided."

"What did he say to you?"

"Nothing."

"Nothing? Not even sorry, or oops?"

"I don't remember," Emily said, frowning.

DiLongo sighed. She felt she was not getting anywhere with the questioning. She didn't have enough information about the cause of death, so these interviews were like shooting at ducks in the dark. Even if she hit one, how would she know?

"All right, Emily. That's enough for now. But don't leave yet. I may have some more questions for you."

DiLongo left the room, leaving Emily staring into space.

Next, DiLongo went into Room 303 to speak with Daniel.

"So, Professor Post, we meet again," diLongo said, greeting Daniel with a smile. "You were in our office a month ago, was it?"

"Yes, I was looking to do some research for my new book. Some of my books are bestsellers, you know."

"Right. I'll check the library next time I go," she said. "Maybe you can tell me what happened tonight?"

"What do you want to know? I'll help any way I can."

"These are preliminary interviews, so we're just gathering information. We'll sort through it later. So, you and Emily were sitting at Table 5, at the end of the line, so to speak."

"Right. We like the end spot. Less of a chance someone can cheat by looking at your cards," he said.

"Let's cut to the chase, Professor Post. Did you notice anything unusual tonight? Any sounds, smells, comments from people… anything weird happening around you?"

"Other than two people dropping down dead? No. Only weird thing is Emily making four spades twice in a row. She got top boards both times, too. She's been playing most of the hands tonight, and I've been the dummy. Now, that's weird, if you ask me," he said, and he laughed dryly.

Bridge players are strange, diLongo thought. "So, what's your theory on the cause of death?" she asked aloud.

"Hmmm, good question. I can't imagine. Maybe they were allergic to something, like peanuts, and someone unwittingly put peanut oil in the salad dressing. That might cause sudden death, since we all ate the same food…" he said, as his voice trailed off.

"So you think there's a simple explanation for it, like a nut allergy?"

"Who knows? I'm not a doctor. Wait for the M.E.'s report. That's what I would do if I were investigating this…" He paused for a moment. DiLongo frowned. Daniel realized his remark could be interpreted as being presumptuous. "I've… I've done a lot of research into police matters, you see, for my books. I don't mean to tell you how to do your job. I know you have procedures you must follow, and I want to help any way I can. It's important for my new book, too."

DiLongo regarded Daniel skeptically, but decided to play along with him for the moment. "Well, I don't know yet if we're investigating a crime or not. It could just be an accident, as you suggest. We didn't have any cases going on before that would be suitable for your book, but maybe this is an opportunity for you, if it turns out to be homicide. I have to eliminate you as a suspect first. Then, if my Captain says it's okay for you to observe our investigation, I won't object. It's for a good cause, right?"

"I will write another bestseller, if you call that a good cause."

"Okay, Professor Post, stick around. I may have more questions for you later."

DiLongo strolled down the hall toward the dining room. She thought she was missing something. Everyone she'd talked to so far seemed unlikely to be involved in anything criminal, but the M.E. said it looked like the victims had consumed some kind of toxin. She was starting to think that maybe someone from outside the college had introduced a deadly substance into the food or drinks. If so, why was it that two people died and the rest were unaffected?

So maybe, just maybe, only some of the food was contaminated, she thought, *and the two victims were just unlucky to have chosen the wrong things to eat or drink. But that would mean it was a random act of violence — like a terrorist attack — and how likely is that?* She stopped in her tracks for a moment to ponder this. No, it was more likely the two victims were selected for some reason. *Look for a motive,* she instructed herself.

DiLongo stopped outside the dining room door to write in her notebook: *motive?*

"Skip!" she called to her partner, who was leaning against the wall on the other side of the staircase.

"Yo," he answered.

"Come here a minute," she said, and ripped a page out of her notebook. "I want you to talk to all the players who are still here and record everything they ate and drank tonight. Get it all, even if it's water from a bottle. And tomorrow, I want you to follow up with the people who have left already, and find out what they ate, too. And tell everyone not to go anywhere for twenty-four hours, like a quarantine. If they ask, just say it's a precaution."

Then she entered the dining room and found Gayle sitting at the bar, fiddling with her cell phone.

"So, Dr. Primrose, what do you think happened tonight?"

"I don't know, Detective, but I have a bad feeling in my stomach."

"Really?" diLongo said, sounding concerned.

"No, it's not something I ate. I'm just mystified and worried. What if it's foul play and not an accident? I have to think about the reputation of my college!"

"We'll know more when we get the M.E.'s report," diLongo said. "For now, I can't rule anything out, so I have to treat this as a crime scene. We'll put up some tape when we leave here."

"That's fine," Gayle responded.

"I'm just wondering, Dr. Primrose, when you were waiting with Chris Boland, did he say anything that seemed odd to you?"

"No, nothing odd. He is very distraught. He talked about his kids, and how upset they will be when he has to tell them their mom is dead. That was his biggest concern. I must say, you could have been a little gentler with him. Now he thinks he's a suspect."

"Until we know what happened to the two victims tonight, everyone in the room is a suspect," diLongo replied. "If it turns out to be foul play, the crime must be investigated and every detail is critical. I'd really appreciate your cooperation."

Gayle looked at diLongo for a long moment, then nodded. "Of course."

"So, what do you know about the victims? They both worked here at the college, right?"

"Yes. Anne-Marie works with me in the Baxter Building. Terry works in the Macintosh Building on the other side of the quad. Rather, I should say worked," Gayle said, frowning.

"I know that building. I actually took a night class with him last year. Criminal behavior."

"Oh, really?" Gayle said, surprised and a little amused. "Yes, he is an expert on the psychology of crime. He's worked with law enforcement agencies here in the States and Canada, to help them solve difficult cases."

"I see," diLongo said. "What do you know of his personal life?"

"Well, he's not married. I think he may have one or two girlfriends. He's a very good-looking man, and he can be very charming. I don't know much else about him." DiLongo noted that Gayle continued to speak in the present tense about Digman, as did most of the other witnesses.

"Do you know his next of kin?"

"Ah, no, but we can look it up in his personnel file."

"Where was he working before he came here?"

"He was in Ottawa consulting with the R.C.M.P., I believe. It was a big fraud case that went on for several years."

"And before that?"

"I think he was a consultant while he was working on his Masters in criminal psychology at the University of Toronto. Then he came here."

"So he's Canadian?"

"No, he's an American, but he went to Canada to study and that's when he got involved with the R.C.M.P. in Ottawa."

"Okay, let's talk about Mrs. Boland. What do you know about her?"

"She's been with us for about ten years. Nice woman. Steady, dependable. Comes from a good local family, the Simpsons. She has a nanny who comes in days to help with the kids. She has five kids, two boys and three girls."

"What about her personal life? Any problems in the marriage?"

"Not that I know of. She and Chris seemed quite happy, if a little stressed out at times. Can you blame them, with five kids underfoot?"

"That sure is a challenge these days."

DiLongo next went to speak with Karl Schultz, in Room 302. He was a portly man with a white beard. He stood up when diLongo entered, and extended his hand.

"Good evening, detective. Professor Karl Schultz."

"Good evening, Professor. How are you doing?"

"I am a little tired, I'm afraid."

"I understand. Past your bedtime," she said, smiling to put him at ease. "So, you were sitting at Professor Digman's table when he collapsed. Did you notice anything amiss with him before he became sick?"

"Well," he said, looked at her over his glasses, "I can't say that I did. He was his usual obnoxious self — arrogant, I mean. I put it down to poor breeding."

"Professor Schultz, do I detect a slight accent? Where are you from originally?"

"I'm from the old country," he said. "I came here as a young man forty years ago, and I'm a bona fide American citizen for the last thirty years. And I'm proud to be an American. America is my home now," he said.

"You know, my folks came here about the same time, from the old country. Italy," she said, smiling. "They still speak Italian at home. Italian is my first language, but now I only speak it when I visit the folks."

He nodded.

"So, you were playing bridge. Then what happened?"

"We heard the commotion with Anne-Marie. Terry was playing the hand when Anne-Marie got sick. Terry insisted on finishing the hand, because he had endplayed my partner and he wanted to get the score recorded — probably a top board for him."

"What's an endplay?"

"Oh… it's when you manipulate the play of the cards to put an opponent on lead to eliminate a loser in your hand. In the right circumstances, he has to lead something that gives you an extra trick."

DiLongo shook her head, not comprehending this piece of information. "I guess I'll have to take some lessons," she said dryly. "So you didn't get up to help Anne-Marie?"

"No, the others were doing that. We didn't think it was serious at first, I mean, not life-threatening."

"So, what happened next?"

"We kept playing. Sally got up to take a look at Anne-Marie — Sally was the dummy — and she said something like 'Anne-Marie looks bad'. Terry was still focused on playing the cards, but then he started clutching at his body, like this," Karl hugged his chest, "and the next thing we knew, he was writhing on the floor, bleeding and groaning."

"What do you think caused their deaths?"

"I don't know." He shrugged. "I wish I could tell you, but I just don't know."

"Your bridge partner, Mr. Chong... what's he like?"

"Oh, he's a good kid. A real keener. Very smart. Very motivated. And a very good student."

"If you don't mind my saying, you're a rather odd couple."

Karl laughed. "Oh, not so odd. He's one of my students, and each year I teach one student to play bridge. I've been mentoring Ben since September. He's coming along quite nicely. He already knows Jacoby transfers and Blackwood."

DiLongo really didn't want to talk about bridge. She was more interested in what the players were doing and saying that evening.

"Would you say Mr. Chong and Professor Digman got along?" she asked.

"I don't think there was a problem. Except that Terry was always trying to intimidate Ben. You know, he made stupid comments to undermine Ben's confidence. But that's bridge!"

"Indeed," diLongo said, unimpressed. "So, there was no bad blood — no reason for Mr. Chong to do something to get back at Professor Digman for bullying him?"

"Well, I wouldn't call it bullying. It's just a little psychological intimidation to gain advantage. And I'm sure Ben wouldn't do anything to harm Terry," Karl said. "He's a good kid."

"Okay, Professor, thanks," diLongo said, as she got up to leave. "Please stay here a while longer, as I may have more questions for you."

DiLongo next went to Room 305, where Ben Chong was waiting. He was a slight young man of average height, with thick, black hair. He wore dark-rimmed glasses that were slightly tinted. Something about him looked odd. Then she realized that while his features where Asian, his eyes were blue. He started to stand up when she entered the room.

"Hi, Mr. Chong," diLongo. "Don't stand. This won't take too long."

"Okay," he said, and sat back down.

"Where are you from?"

"Hong Kong."

"You're a long way from home. What brings you here?"

"My parents are friends with Gayle Primrose. And this is a good school to learn business."

"So your parents expect you to do well?"

Ben nodded.

"They paid a lot of money for you to go to this college?"

Ben didn't answer.

"Okay, then, what can you tell me about this evening? What happened here tonight?"

"I don't know anything," he said.

"What is your relationship with Professor Digman?"

"I don't have one."

"What about Mrs. Boland?"

"I don't know her, either. We just play cards. That's all."

"You speak English very well, Mr. Chong. Why don't you have a Chinese accent?" diLongo said, changing the subject.

"My mom is English and we speak English at home. I went to English schools in Hong Kong."

"I see," diLongo said, and paused. Ben fidgeted in his seat, unwilling to meet diLongo's gaze. "So if we find out there was some foul play that caused the two victims to die tonight, we're going to look into the lives of everyone who played bridge here tonight. Is there anything that you can tell me about your relationship with either of the victims?"

Ben just shook his head.

"Okay, then," she said. "Stay here for a while. I may have more questions for you."

She made a note: *B.C. — very quiet, what's he hiding?*

Next, diLongo went to Room 304 where Barb Baker, a heavy-set girl with plain looks and short, dark hair, was waiting.

"Hi there," diLongo said. "You are Barb Baker? You work at the college in the mail room."

"I'm the manager of mail and printing services here at the college," she said, lifting her chip up slightly.

"Right. How did you get into this snooty bridge crowd, anyway?"

"I play bridge — very well, I might add. Bridge is not just for high-minded academics, you know. Some of the best bridge players I've known worked in the post office. Just because you work with your hands for a living doesn't mean you're stupid."

"Hey, I hear you," diLongo said. "Some of the best cops I know are still walking the beat." Barb smiled and nodded.

"So, what can you tell me about Professor Terry Digman and Mrs. Boland? You know them well?"

"Terry is an asshole, and Anne-Marie is a goodie-goodie," Barb said emphatically.

"So you don't like them much?"

"Nothin' in common with them," Barb said, and shrugged.

DiLongo knitted her brow, wondering what to ask next. Barb did not have much to offer, it seemed.

"Is there anything else? I'd like to go home and try to chill out after what happened tonight," Barb said.

"Hang on, I'm not finished," diLongo responded. "I may have more questions after I speak with the others. I'm sorry if it's late, but it is essential to get information as quickly as possible, before you forget."

"I don't forget things. I have a memory like an elephant," Barb said proudly.

"Wait here. I'll be back," diLongo said, and went outside to the corridor. Next on her list was Jill Wilmington, Barb's bridge partner, in Room 306.

"Hi, Miss Wilmington," said diLongo. Jill, in her early thirties, was an attractive blonde with a slim, athletic build. She was pacing back and forth.

"Hello," Jill replied.

"How are you doing?"

"I'm starting to get a little antsy, to be honest. When can we leave?"

"I just have a few questions for you," diLongo said, "so it shouldn't take long. Tell me about you and Professor Digman."

"What do you mean?"

"Your relationship. How was that going?"

"I don't like him," Jill said flatly. "I'm not having a relationship with him. What are you trying to suggest?"

"I'm sorry, Miss Wilmington. Sometimes I have to ask personal questions in an investigation like this. And I just thought… a beautiful woman like yourself, single, smart, and he's available. I might go for him myself, if I were single."

"I don't have any problems attracting male attention and I don't need someone like Terry in my life. He's trouble, with a capital T."

"What makes you say that?" diLongo asked.

"Terry is a dangerous, disgusting man and I wouldn't let him near me with a ten-foot pole. But I didn't do anything to put him out of his misery," Jill said.

"Why do call him dangerous?"

"I'm a good judge of character, and he's someone to avoid. In my opinion," she added.

"I hear he has a reputation as a womanizer on campus."

"Could be."

"Did he come on to you?"

"Ha! He wouldn't dare. I'd smack him down! Not literally, but I would slap him with a sexual harassment suit if he tried anything like that with me."

"What about bridge?"

"He's a good bridge player, I'll give him that. I get great satisfaction when I beat him at bridge."

"Okay, thanks. Stay here. I'll be back soon." DiLongo left the room. Her next stop was Room 308, where David Bartholomew was waiting.

"Hey there, how you doin'?" diLongo greeted him.

"Could be better, could be worse," he said in a deep, gravelly voice. He was a middle-aged black man, going gray at the temples. He chuckled, "You know how it is."

"Yes. I understand you're head of security for the college, and you play bridge with Dr. Primrose. You're her partner?"

"Correct."

"Have you had any run-ins with either of the victims?"

"No, they keep themselves out of trouble, you know," he said, smiling.

"Any bad stuff going on here at the college?"

"Well, you know, we have the normal pranks that you get at any college. Some kids let their drinking get out of control. But nothing we can't handle."

"What about drugs?" diLongo asked. "Do you ever see students getting high?"

"Well, yeah, there may be some of that. It's hard to stop. You can't strip search the student body." He chuckled. "Drinking is rampant. We get the occasional complaint from the residences, people throwing up on the quad or in the hallways, drinking and driving around, making noise. Shit happens, you know. My job is to make sure people are safe and secure on campus. I have staff doing regular patrols day and night. If I see someone acting out, or I get a complaint, I take care of it. If something serious happens, I call in the police. Like the time someone stole a car out of the parking lot. I called the cops to look into it that time."

"So, what do you know about Professor Digman's activities? And I'm not talking about his teaching job."

David looked surprised at the question. "Nothing."

"Ever had a complaint about his behavior towards women — maybe being a little too forward? I don't mean an official complaint. Maybe someone just said to watch him or something."

"No, nothing like that. He seemed okay to me, you know. He was a good guy."

"What about Mrs. Boland? What do you know about her?"

"Nice lady. Don't see much of her, except at bridge," he said.

"What do you think we'll find out when we start tearing her life apart, that is, if we discover there was some foul play tonight?"

David raised his eyebrows. "Foul play?" Then he chuckled and said, "Go for it. As far as I know, she's an accountant, a wife, a mother and a regular at church every Sunday. Apart from that, she could be a madam with a whorehouse in town, but I wouldn't know."

"All right, thanks. Stay here. I'll be back." DiLongo left the room, looking for Skip. She found him waiting by the stairs.

"Anybody leave?"

"Nope. All's quiet on the Western Front."

"They're being accommodating, aren't they?"

"Yep."

"Who's left to interview?"

"We have four students — John Murphy and Bess Thompson, who play as partners, and Heather Bean and Mike Stokes, also partners — and Tracey Kingston, who works off campus as a nursing assistant. She's Melissa Fielding's guest tonight."

"Okay, I'll go to see them now." DiLongo turned to walk towards the dining room.

Inside, the four students were sitting at a table.

"Hi guys," diLongo said, approaching the group. "Sorry to keep you waiting so long."

"No problem," John said. "We're night owls anyway."

"Understand that you are witnesses and we may have questions for you as we investigate what happened."

"We want to know if it's some kind of deadly virus or something," Bess said. "Can you tell us?"

"I won't know that until we have the medical examiner's report. We'll inform everyone at the appropriate time. But, to put your mind at ease, we don't think it's contagious. That's not official," she said.

They didn't look very reassured, but diLongo couldn't tell them anything more.

"Just wondering," diLongo continued, "did any of you have a relationship with either of the victims? I mean, outside of regular college activities and classroom interactions?"

They all shook their heads.

"All right. You can go back to your rooms or your apartments or wherever you live. My partner has recorded your names and other information, so we'll get in touch with you later."

DiLongo then spoke to Tracey Kingston, a dark-haired lady who looked more like a Sunday school teacher than a potential murderer.

"What is your relationship with the two victims?" she asked Tracey.

"I have no relationship with them," Tracey said. "I met them for the first time tonight playing bridge. I have never played here before, but my friend, Melissa, asked me to sub in since her husband had to do something tonight."

DiLongo wiped her brow with the back of her hand. "Okay, we have your contact information. We'll be in touch if we need anything else from you. You're free to go home now."

"Detective, I'm a nurse. What is it? Are we at risk too?" she asked.

DiLongo took a deep breath. "What do you think?"

"I think it's something serious. I've never seen anyone expire like that before. It's like something out of a horror movie. I'm scared out of my wits. So tell me, are we all at risk?"

"Between you and me," diLongo said slowly, "it's probably something they ate. However, we won't know for sure until we get the M.E.'s report, so don't go to work until we give the all clear."

Tracey looked worried, but she nodded as she walked away. DiLongo went over to Skip.

"That wasn't very fruitful," she said, frowning. "It's hard to know what questions to ask when we don't know the cause of death. Oh well, round two. I'm going to talk to Emily Warren again. Something bad went down here tonight and people are not telling me everything they know. I'm gonna get to the bottom of this, if it's the last thing I do."

CHAPTER 6

📅 THURSDAY, DECEMBER 11, 2008 — 1:30 A.M.

"Miss Warren," diLongo said, settling down in a chair opposite Emily. "Tell me about Professor Post. Don't people think it a little strange that you play bridge with your boss? What else do you do together?"

"I don't think it's strange that we work together and play as bridge partners," Emily said. "It just happened that he needed a bridge partner and I wanted to get into the bridge club, so we talked about it, and I guess he figured out that I am a pretty good player. Anyway, not too many other players want to be his partner. He's a little eccentric, and he sometimes gives people a hard time. I've had to modify my bidding to adjust to his game, and that took some time, but now we're on a good track."

"So you like him?" asked diLongo.

Emily blushed a little. "He's my boss, so I try and get along with him. He's a famous writer, and writers tend to be somewhat unconventional, you know. I feel sorry for him, actually."

"And why is that?"

"He was married for a long time to Marion. She basically kept him on track. Then she died quite suddenly. Since then, he's been like a rudderless ship, spinning around and not getting anywhere. I know he's having a hard time with his new book. Gayle… I mean Dr. Primrose, the president of the college, gave him a year off to work on his book so he hasn't been teaching this year, just writing and mentoring some students. He's also responsible for running the English department and conducting staff meetings. I provide all the coordination for that."

"And what about his bridge game?"

"He's been really keen on bridge this year. He wants to win the annual prize. That's something we all want to win."

"Why is that so important?"

"Apart from the pride and satisfaction we get for coming first? The winners get an invitation to Gayle's New Year's Eve party! It's a big event every year, at least in this neck of the woods. She has so many famous friends from all over the world. Celebrities like writers, artists, politicians and actors. She always gets a good crowd, and puts them up at the Lakeside Inn. Daniel is — or was — a famous writer. Winning the prize would make him feel better about himself, I think."

"Why do you say that?"

"Well, he hasn't published a new book in several years. He's been quite down about it. Depressed, even. He's been working on the same book since he came to Kensington. He keeps starting over. I think he misses the limelight. He used to be on Letterman and Jay Leno a lot. He used to be a big celebrity."

"I see. And what about you? Do you want to win the prize too?"

"Of course! It would be fun to meet famous people, don't you think? And the connections might help my career."

"You seem like a bright young woman. What are you doing working in a secretarial job?"

"Pays the bills," Emily said.

"Are you involved with anyone? Thinking of getting married at some point?"

"Of course, I'd like to get married one day and have a family, but there's nobody around here who I'm interested in," she sighed. "I was going to college for a medical degree. I wanted to be a doctor and join Doctors Without Borders and go to third-world countries where they desperately need doctors. But my dad died, and my mom got sick, and there was no money left for my education. So instead, I applied to work here. I'm saving up and one day I hope to get that medical degree. But it's going to take a long time to get the money together," she said. "My Plan B is to join a publishing house as an editor and researcher. Maybe work in New York."

"Well, Miss Warren," diLongo said, "good luck to you. Tell me more about your boss. He's writing a new book. What is it about?"

"I don't know too much about it. He's had writer's block. He's under pressure from Gayle to finish it by next April, so I've been helping him with the research. He's going to give me a credit in the acknowledgements. That could help my career too."

"What kind of research are you doing for him?"

"Whatever he wants. Lately I've been mapping out locations using the Internet."

"Can you be more specific?" diLongo asked.

"No. I'm under an NDA. You'll have to ask him."

"Okay, I will," diLongo said. "So, let's see. You've been working here how long?"

"Six and a half years."

"So, what is he like to work with?"

"He's up and down a lot," Emily said. "Some days I think he's depressed, but then he'll snap out of it and be happy for a while, and then things will get on his nerves and he'll be difficult again. He's unpredictable that way. I think he goes on and off his meds. When he walks in the door you never know if he'll be Happy Daniel or Cranky Daniel."

"That could make it hard for you, working for someone like that."

"Yeah, but I don't take it personally. I just do my job."

"Okay, Miss Warren, that's all for tonight," said diLongo.

"May I go home now? I need to feed my cat," she said.

"Yes, you can go home, but we'll likely have more questions later. So don't go on any sudden vacations!"

DiLongo next went into Room 303 to talk to Daniel Post.

"How's it going?" he asked diLongo as she entered the room.

"Going," she said. "Just a few more questions and then you can go home. I want to learn more about the people in the bridge club. Perhaps you can help me, starting with your assistant, Miss Warren. What can you tell me about her performance?"

"She tries hard. I've been coaching her, and she's getting better, slowly."

"You mean at work?"

"No! I mean bridge. I'm trying to get her up to speed so we can win the prize this year."

"What about work? That's what I was asking about. How is she doing at work?"

"Oh, I see. She makes a lot of mistakes and I have to constantly correct her work. But that's my job as her boss, of course."

"Right," diLongo said, making a note. "Would you say her performance is adequate?"

Daniel nodded.

"So tell me about your book."

"Can't talk about it. It's not finished," he said.

"I offered to let you look at some old case files when you came to the station. You still want to do that?"

"Yes," he said. "As part of my research."

"Okay, contact me later and I'll arrange it," said diLongo.

"Thank you. Much appreciated," Daniel responded. DiLongo took a long look at Daniel. He was in his sixties, tall and slim with a close-cropped moustache. He seemed alert, if a little stressed, and his eyes were puffy with dark circles.

"Dr. Primrose gave you the year off to finish the book, isn't that right?"

"Yes. What about it?" he asked.

"So can you tell me how it's going? How much of it do you have done?"

"That, my dear officer, is confidential!"

"Don't you have a deadline to complete it?"

"Yes, I do. April 1st."

"All right," she said. "So what can you tell me about the victim, Professor Digman?"

"He's just another psych prof," Daniel said. "Other than that, I know nothing about him. I keep to myself."

"What about the other victim, Mrs. Boland?"

"Like I said, I keep to myself. I don't know these people, and I don't care to know them, either. We just play bridge. I don't have much in common with any of them."

"I see. Do you have any idea why anyone might want to kill them? I'm looking for any connections that would explain why they died, in case it's not accidental," she said.

"Honestly, Detective, I have no clue about their lives. If there is a connection between them, I would be the last one to know about it, I can assure you," he said.

"What do you know about Dr. Primrose, then?"

"She runs the college. She has a Ph.D. in education and has written several books. Her husband died many years ago. She's the director for the bridge club. Other than that, I don't know much about her, except she likes to do gardening. We talk about gardening sometimes, since my wife died. My wife was a great gardener."

"What about her personal life?"

"Well, Gayle knows a lot of high-placed people in business, media, academia, show business, etc. I don't know who she's dating, if anyone, if that's what you are asking."

"And her partner, David Bartholomew?"

"He's okay. Not a bad bridge player — a little unorthodox. He seems to be doing a good job of keeping the campus clean and orderly."

"And Professor Brighton?"

"She's not a great bridge player. She makes a lot of defensive errors — no wonder Terry always tried to play the hands. I don't pay any attention to her, and I don't know much about her personal life, either. I have too much work to do to bother with the riff-raff around here!"

"Okay, well, that about wraps it up for tonight," diLongo said. "You're free to go home. We may have more questions later, after the M.E.'s report comes out with the cause of death. And I want to thank you for your assistance tonight."

"Absolutely! Anything I can do, just ask. If there is a crime to investigate, I'd like to be let in on your theories, how you analyze the evidence and come to your conclusions. And I'm sorry I cannot tell you about my book, Detective. It's just that it's a work in progress. Things are in flux. I might change my mind several times before it's finished, and I don't want to talk about it at this stage. It's my creative process, you see."

When she nodded, Daniel said goodbye and left the room.

DiLongo returned to the dining room where Gayle was sitting in her chair. Her hands were clasped so tight the knuckles were white. DiLongo noted that the M.E.'s assistants were wrapping up after taking photos and collecting the evidence they needed. The bodies of the two victims were placed on stretchers and wheeled out of the room.

"Dr. Primrose, I just have a couple of questions for you, and then we can all go home," diLongo said.

"That would be really great, Detective. I'm sure everyone is tired. Even you look tired."

"And you look like you could use a drink, Dr. Primrose," diLongo said, smiling.

Gayle nodded. "I'll do that when I get home."

"Okay. Well, I have a few more questions. We're just gathering as much information as we can tonight, while it's fresh in people's minds. What can you tell me about Professor Post?"

"Daniel? He's a celebrated author. I had to give him a very good contract to get him to agree to come here."

"What kind of contract?"

"Well, the details are confidential. But he teaches and writes, and I pay him six figures a year to do that."

"Are you happy with this arrangement?" diLongo asked.

"Yes, of course. You see, when you have someone of Daniel's stature on staff, you can attract a better caliber of students and charge higher fees. So his reputation helps to build my college's image and marketability."

"What about his new book?" diLongo asked.

"That's a problem," Gayle admitted. "He was supposed to have it ready years ago, but when his wife Marion died, that seemed to derail him for a while. I think he's getting on with it now."

"How do you know? Have you seen a draft?" asked diLongo.

"No, I haven't, but he told me it's coming along." Then she paused for a moment. "This is confidential, Detective. I've put him on notice that he must finish it by the spring, or I'm canceling his contract with the college."

"So you're tired of waiting?" diLongo suggested.

"Exactly. With no new books coming out, I can't get the publicity I want for the college. It's harder for me to attract the best students and justify the fees, which means I can't afford his salary much longer."

"So, there's a money motive," diLongo mused, making a note.

"Yeah, to get that book done. For him and for me. No book, no job. It's as simple as that."

"So, tell me about the other players. David Bartholomew, for starters."

"David is my head of security, and he's fantastic," Gayle said. "He's really cleaned up the problems we had on campus a few years ago with some bad bikers and drug dealers causing trouble. I strive to provide a clean, safe and secure environment for my students. That's what their parents are paying for."

"What can you tell me about Professor Brighton?"

"Sally is very dependable and hard working," Gayle said. "She's been on staff here for about four years, and she's doing a tremendous job with the students. I don't know much about her personal life, but she is a real pro when it comes to her work."

"And Jill Wilmington?"

"I like Jill very much. We're not exactly friends, but we work closely together. I rely on her for advice on staffing issues and any problems that arise. She manages our hiring process, as well as staff performance and discipline. I have the highest regard for Jill as a professional," Gayle said, "and as a bridge player."

"Okay," diLongo said. "What about her bridge partner, Barb Baker. What can you tell me about her?"

"Barb is a dedicated worker, and very competent in her field of responsibility. She's also a very smart bridge player. All I know about her is that she used to work for the post office before she came here. The job she has here, as manager of our mailroom and printing services, is a big step up from what she was doing before, so I think she is very happy to have it. I've had no issues or problems with Barb."

"And Professor Schultz?"

"Karl is a dear," Gayle said. "He's been with the college as long as I have. He has devoted himself to teaching and he's always done a great job with the students. He's a bit old-fashioned, I know, and a little eccentric. I put that down to his European roots."

"And what do you know about his partner, Ben Chong?"

"Just that he's Karl's student. Ben is very polite and quiet, so I really haven't had much interaction with him. I do know his parents, and they are very nice people."

"Okay. And Mr. Boland, the victim's husband, what's he like?"

"Chris is as solid as a rock. He works as a computer engineer at a local firm. He's a great guy, a little quiet and shy, and a good husband, as far as I know," Gayle said. "Chris and Anne-Marie are very religious. They attend church every Sunday, and all their kids go to Sunday school, except the toddler, of course."

"And the Blacks?"

"They work together in our IT department. I don't know much about them, other than that they are good bridge players and seem to get along with everyone in their department. I've had no bad reports about them."

"Okay, I'm going to talk to the others now, just to wrap up for the night, and then we'll head out. Officer Crane will put some tape over the dining room doors until we can determine if this is a crime scene or not. Please instruct your staff to stay out of there in the meantime."

"Done," Gayle said, reaching for her cell phone and typing out a text message.

DiLongo returned to the corridor and entered Room 307, where Sally Brighton was waiting.

"Professor Brighton," diLongo said, "have you had a chance to relax a bit and get some energy back?"

"To be honest, I'm feeling a little shaky. I really want to go home," she said.

"Soon, I promise. I just need to know more about your partner, Professor Digman. What do you know of his personal life — any enemies?"

"Well, he might have enemies, but I don't know that for sure. He likes flirting with women. Maybe he flirted with some woman who took him seriously and she got jealous. I really don't know. He had an odd teaching style, so not everyone appreciated that. You know, I think his death could be an accident, if he was taking some bad drugs that interacted with his beer. Can I go home now?" she asked.

"All right, Professor Brighton, you may leave. But we may have more questions for you later, once we have the M.E.'s report. Don't leave town."

"Good night, then. Good luck with the investigation," Sally said, as she strode quickly out of the room.

DiLongo then went to see Karl Schultz, who was dozing in a chair when she entered the room.

"Professor Schultz," she said, "I know it's getting late. I don't have much more to ask you at this time, unless you can tell me about Professor Digman. Do you know if he had any enemies on campus?"

Karl roused himself and rubbed his eyes before replying.

"Terry? No enemies that I know of. He was popular with the ladies," he said, yawning, "and he seemed to be in with David Bartholomew, the security chief."

"Really?"

"Yeah, they seemed like good buddies, except at the bridge table. They could really go at it sometimes. David said Terry was a cheater, but I think he was just trying to throw Terry off his game."

For Pete's sake, thought diLongo, *these bridge players are worse than children in a schoolyard.*

She opened her notebook. "Have you ever noticed Professor Digman behaving strangely, like he might be on drugs?"

"No, not really. He always seems sharp, at least at bridge. I don't socialize with him, so I don't know what he does for recreation."

"Right. Okay, I think that's enough for tonight. You may go home now and get some sleep."

"Thank you, Officer. I wish I could do something to help you. Let me know."

"I will," she said.

Next, diLongo talked to Ben Chong.

"Hi there," she said. "We're wrapping up for the night but I have a couple more questions for you."

"Okay."

"Any idea why anyone would want to hurt either of the two victims?"

"No."

"So tell me about your partner, Dr. Schultz. How did you wind up playing bridge with him?"

"He's my history prof. At the beginning of the semester he asked if anyone wanted to learn to play bridge. No one else wanted to, so I put up my hand."

"Why did you do that?"

"He said that bridge players are successful in life, and I thought it might help my grades in history if I spent more time with Dr. Schultz. My parents introduced me to bridge when I was a teenager, so I already knew the basics."

"So you get in good with your prof and with your parents, kill two birds with one stone?" diLongo suggested.

"Something like that," he replied.

"Okay, Mr. Chong. It's late. Go back to your room. Here's my card. If you think of anything else, call me. I'll be in touch with you if we need anything further."

Next, diLongo talked to Barb Baker.

"Miss Baker, it's already been a long night. You've had some time to think about things. Anything else come to mind since we last talked?"

"Well, I was thinking." Barb said. "Thing is, if these two were victims of foul play, why Anne-Marie? She's harmless. She does accounting for a living. How boring is that? I can't see why she would be targeted by anyone. I can understand Terry, he's the type of guy who could piss you off. I never liked him. But what's the connection between the two of them? They don't exactly hang out together. You ask me, I don't think anyone killed Terry and Anne-Marie. Doesn't make sense. It must be some kind of weird accidental thing, like they handled something that was poisonous and got it on their fingers and put their fingers into their mouth. Can't be the food! We all ate the food and no one else got sick. So it must be some kind of accident."

"That's good reasoning, Miss Baker. I'll make a note of that," diLongo said, and she did. "So, let's focus on Terry for a minute. I'm curious why you don't like him. Did he do anything to you, say anything to you, that made you dislike him?"

"No, but he makes stupid remarks at the bridge table, just to rattle you, you know. He's a real player, in more ways than one. I just think he's creepy."

"He has a reputation on campus as a womanizer. Did he ever come on to you in that way?" diLongo asked.

"Oh, give me a break. He's not my type, and I am certainly not his."

"So, what is his type?"

"You know, cute, slim, young, anything with a wiggle. See, I jiggle, I don't wiggle," Barb said.

"So, you are telling me you've never had any kind of encounter with him outside the bridge club?"

"Well, I see him sometimes when I'm doing my rounds. I have a golf cart to drive around the campus to deliver the mail."

"So you handle his mail?"

"I handle everyone's mail. It comes in from the post office in big bags. I sort it for the buildings and deliver it to the offices. The secretaries handle it from there." Then Barb paused for a second, before continuing. "I just remembered something. A week ago, I was on my usual mail run and I saw Terry and David get into a fight outside the Arts Building."

"Really? What were they fighting about?"

"I don't know. When I asked Terry about it later, he was very evasive, which is strange for him. He usually just makes a joke or says something obnoxious to you. It made me think there might be something going on between Terry and David. But I don't know what it could be."

DiLongo made a note: *Check into Terry and David's relationship.*

"Okay, thanks. Could be nothing. That's all for tonight, Miss Baker. You may leave."

"What about Jill?"

"I'm talking to Miss Wilmington next," diLongo said.

"I have to wait for her. She's giving me a lift home."

"Okay, then wait here. I won't be too long."

DiLongo went nextdoor to talk to Jill Wilmington.

"Miss Wilmington, you work in H.R. What can you tell me about Professor Digman and Mrs. Boland? You must have access to their files."

"I can't tell you that, it's confidential."

"Right. Okay, we'll get permission from Dr. Primrose or we'll get a warrant. So, we'll leave that for now. Tell me how you and Miss Baker wound up as bridge partners. What's the connection?"

"Well, when I hired her, I found out that she plays bridge, and I needed a partner to get into the bridge club. Bridge players don't care what a person looks like, or where they're from, or whatever. We don't discriminate on age, sex, race or anything else. If they play good bridge, that's all that counts."

"So, the only thing that these bridge players have in common is they like to play bridge, is that it?" diLongo asked.

"The way I see it is, we're all smart and we like to challenge our abilities to think, remember, plan and execute. And, above all, we like to win," Jill said. "There's a lot of ego on the line at the bridge table. We like to think we can outsmart our opponents."

"I see. Well, that's all for tonight. I believe Miss Baker is waiting for you in the next room. You're giving her a ride home?"

"Yeah, so I'd better get going. Good night. Keep me informed, please. Like everyone here, I want to know what happened. And, let me know when you get permission to look at Terry and Anne-Marie's personnel files. I'll be happy to get them out for you."

DiLongo followed Jill into the corridor and paused before going into the next room where David Bartholomew, the security chief, was waiting. *There's something going on here, but I can't put my finger on it,* she thought. Then she opened the door to see David Bartholomew sitting on a swivel chair, feet up on the desk, looking relaxed..

"Hello, Mr. Bartholomew," she said. "Long night, huh?"

"Yes, ma'am," he said.

"I'm nearly done. What's your take on what happened tonight? Why are two people dead, when everyone else seems quite healthy?"

"Yeah, I've been wondering about that," David said in his deep-voiced drawl. "I just can't figure it. Some kind of nasty bug got into their system, I guess."

"Okay, what do you know about the victims. Digman first."

"Like I said before, a good guy. Seems to work hard. Always on the go, doing something or other, you know."

"He hasn't been here very long," diLongo prodded.

"No, he came on staff about fifteen months ago."

"Do you know anything about him, I mean about his past?"

"Well, not really. Gayle asked me to check him out when he applied for the job here. So I checked references, criminal record, landlords, credit, that kind of thing, you know. Everything was in order."

"Okay. I might need to look at that report later on, depending on the results of the autopsy. If there's foul play, I mean," she said.

"Of course."

"So you didn't suspect him of being a drug abuser or anything like that?" she asked.

"Nope. If he did use drugs, he kept it hidden from me," David said.

"Any other deviant behavior?"

"Ha-ha, unless you call skirt-chasing deviant, I'd have to say no."

"And what about Mrs. Boland. What can you tell me about her?"

"Nothing much. She's worked here for quite a few years. Never heard anything bad about her. She plays a good game of bridge, being an accountant and all, you know."

DiLongo made a quick note.

"Well then, that's all for tonight," diLongo said. "You can go home now."

"Alright. Keep me posted on any developments, okay? I need to know what's going on, for security reasons," he said.

"I will be sure to keep you in the loop," she said, "as soon as we clear you as a suspect. Oh, one more thing," she said, as David rose to leave.

"Yes?" he asked.

"What about your personal relationship with Professor Digman? Tell me about it."

"Well, we play bridge. That's about it," he said.

"Ever had any problems with him, on a personal or professional level?"

"Nope," he said.

"Okay, then we'll catch you later," diLongo said, eyeing David closely. *He's hiding something,* she thought.

DiLongo went back to the dining room to see Gayle. The M.E.'s staff had already left with the bodies and the evidence.

"We're wrapping up for the night, Dr. Primrose," she said. "I've talked to everyone and sent them all home. So, you can go now, too. We'll walk out with you."

Gayle got her coat and locked the door to the dining room while Skip taped up the dining room doors. Then the three of them walked down the stairs, and Gayle entered the alarm code to lock the building.

They said good night, and diLongo and Skip got back into their cruiser.

"We need to organize our notes before calling it a night," diLongo said, with a sigh. "You drive, Skip, I'm too tired."

It was turning out to be a very long night.

As David walked to his car, he remembered the comment diLongo had made about clearing him as a suspect.

I'll have to talk to my buddy Earl at the police station about this, he thought, *especially if it gets serious.*

CHAPTER 7

 PRESENT DAY — 2:00 A.M.

I went up to the counter and ordered another coffee. Brian switched to a Red Bull. "That's what Skip always drank," I commented, "whenever we came here at night."

Brian grinned. "Well, I get tired of drinking coffee."

We settled back into our seats and I resumed my story. "The bridge club consisted of faculty members, students, administrative staff and some others. I had to treat them all as suspects initially, until we knew what we were dealing with."

Brian nodded.

"Remember, I was still pretty green. This was my first big case, and I didn't want to make any mistakes, but at the same time, I didn't have any real experience to draw from either. Cap wasn't much help. He just said 'Do your best, and wrap it up asap!' He had the mayor on his case, the D.A.'s office and the media, and also the parents and the public who kept calling the station."

"Sounds like a zoo," Brian commented. "What about the suspects?"

"They all seemed innocent enough, and no one had an obvious motive. The only thing they had in common was bridge. They were very competitive at the card table. I didn't think a card game could be as important to people's lives as it was to these people," diLongo commented. "But there's more to this game than you might think, as I learned during the course of the investigation."

FIRST DAY OF CLASS
MONDAY, SEPTEMBER 8, 2008 — 10:30 A.M.

The rotund professor with a shaggy white beard surveyed the students in his lecture room as they settled in their seats. They gazed back at him with a range of expressions on their faces, from 'eager keener' to 'bored with life and wanting out of here'. He turned his back on the class and wrote two words on the whiteboard: Karl Schultz. Then he turned and smiled at the students before beginning his speech.

"Good morning, and welcome to Modern History. I am Professor Karl Schultz. I don't know who you are, so I'd like you to write your names on these labels, and place them on your desk where I can see them, please. Then we'll be on a level playing field, don't you agree? You will know my name, and I will know yours, at least for the duration of this class." And with that, he distributed the labels to the students.

As the students complied with his request, Karl stood behind his lectern and reviewed his notes. Then he turned to the whiteboard and wrote one word below his name: Bridge.

"Before we begin our investigation of modern history this semester, I have a little project for which I'd like a volunteer. And it concerns the word 'bridge'." He indicated the word on the whiteboard. "What does this word mean to you?" he asked. "You there, John," he said, pointing to a burly young man sitting near the back. "When I say bridge, what do you think?"

"I dunno," John replied, pausing, "'Bridge Over Troubled Waters'? You know, the song."

"That's good. Anyone else?" Karl asked.

"Bridge the gaps," said Brian, sitting next to John. "In business, you need to bridge the gaps in your marketing and finances."

"Also good," Karl said. "Anyone else?"

"Suicide," Valerie said, a dark-haired girl sitting up front. "As in, jumping off a bridge." Several students giggled.

"Well, that's a new one for me. Good, Valerie. Anyone else?"

"San Francisco," Peter piped up, a short fellow with glasses sitting next to Valerie. "Golden Gate Bridge."

"Those are all good answers. There is one other meaning that you missed, but that's not surprising."

The students looked at him expectantly.

"Are you familiar with the card game called bridge?" Karl asked.

"Oh, sure. That's for old farts," John called from the back, and laughed. Other students glanced around at each other, murmuring. "Bridge? What has bridge got to do with history?"

When Karl heard the comment about history, he said, "In fact, there's history in every card game. Back in the middle ages, card playing was banned in France and other countries because the authorities thought cards were evil and encouraged anti-social activities, like gambling.

"The royal characters on the cards also depict figures in history. It is said that the king of spades is David, King of Israel, the king of clubs is Alexander the Great, the king of hearts is the French King Charlemagne, and the king of diamonds is Caesar, although not everyone agrees with these designations. There is a great deal of speculation about the queens. Perhaps someone in the class can do some research on this subject for an essay topic and provide us with insight on the origins of the kings and queens," he suggested.

"Card games have historically been a way for people to occupy their leisure time and provide a distraction from the hardship of their lives. Prisoners play cards. Soldiers and sailors play cards. Older retired people play cards. A deck of cards is small and easily transportable and cards don't require modern technology like the Internet to make them work." Some of the students snickered at this comment.

"Speaking of the Internet, it has had a tremendous impact on the popularity of card games in recent years. Look at the way the Internet has transported poker out of the smoky backrooms of low-class bars and gambling dens into the global spotlight. Being a poker player these days is a respectable and rewarding occupation attracting millions of players around the world. In the same way, the Internet has created a new age for bridge."

Here, Professor Schultz paused as he gazed across the room of upturned faces.

"Many bridge players in America today are over the age of fifty. Why? They probably learned when they were college students, like you, or they learned from their parents. Bridge was an important and well-respected activity in the 1920s and 1930s, like team sports are today. In fact, the results of bridge tournaments were publicized on the front page of many newspapers back then, and even today, newspapers publish a daily bridge column and some still print the results of local bridge clubs. But bridge lost popularity when less mentally challenging forms of entertainment like movies and video games came along. However, there's a new age of bridge developing today, and it's being promoted on the Internet all over the world. If you go on a bridge website, like Bridge Base Online, you can watch live bridge games. Young people from every country you can think of are discovering this game, and playing it at all hours of the day and night. Only in North America do people still view it as a pastime for old folks." He paused.

"I am sure you've heard of Warren Buffett and Bill Gates, two of the richest men in the world. Did you know that they play bridge? They have donated a lot of money to finance bridge programs in schools so young people can develop the valuable skills required to play bridge, such as decision-making, critical thinking and teamwork. These are the same skills you need in real life, in business and other pursuits.

"If you do some research, you will discover that when these two gentlemen are not working, they are playing bridge at tournaments or online. In fact, Warren Buffett was quoted in the media as saying he is so obsessed with bridge he does not notice if a naked woman walks by his table while he is playing!"

The students reacted with laughter and guffaws.

"I see bridge as a metaphor for life," he continued. "As in life, a bridge player sets his goals and prepares a plan. The partner he chooses can help, or hinder, his progress. Bridge, you see, is not just a card game. It is a constant learning process, sometimes frustrating, but ultimately very satisfying. It's just like your academic career. If you apply yourself and allow yourself to be challenged, you can become very successful. Now I have an announcement," Karl said, pausing again.

"Every year, I accept one student from this history class as my bridge protégé. You must have the interest and ability to excel in life and want to learn how to play this fascinating game. So, who will it be this year? Anyone?" he asked, surveying the room.

One hand shot up near the front of the room, and a young man spoke up.

"Sir, my parents play at their local bridge club. They taught me the basics, but I'd like to learn more," he said

"Excellent. So, Ben," Karl said, noting his name on the label, "if you accept, you can be my bridge protégé this year. We have lots of work to do, and you will need to study some bridge books and practice your game online to develop your card-playing skills. Are you prepared to do that?"

"Yes, sir."

"Then stay for a few minutes after class and I will give you your first assignment."

And with that, Karl opened his binder of lecture notes. He already knew them by heart, but felt the thick binder would impress his students.

"Now we begin. Who can tell me what is meant by the term Modern History? Anyone?"

While Karl was introducing his class to the two passions of his life, history and bridge, the college president, Gayle Primrose, had an appointment with a prospective new student and his parents.

"Good afternoon, Mr. and Mrs. Seymour. This must be Julian?" Gayle asked, extending her hand. She indicated the comfortable couches and chairs that encircled an oval coffee table in her office. "Please have a seat. May I offer you some water or juice?" she asked.

"Water would be very nice. Thank you so much," Mrs. Seymour said.

"For me as well," Mr. Seymour said.

"Please, may I have some juice?" Julian asked.

Gayle fetched cold drinks from the small bar she kept in her office. She smiled and said, "I am very pleased to meet you and introduce you to our campus. As you know, Kensington is one of the nation's leading schools for arts, humanities and social sciences."

Mr. Seymour nodded and said, "Julian will be graduating high school this year and this is one of the colleges we wanted to look at to see if it is suitable for him."

"Kensington," Gayle stated firmly, "is a school for serious students who want to achieve at a high level, and I'm not talking about the altitude up here in the mountains." She chuckled at her own joke while the Seymours glanced at each other, smiling weakly. "I am pleased to say that, upon review of Julian's high school transcripts, he's in the top five percent, and that qualifies him for a spot here at Kensington."

The Seymours looked fondly at their son. Julian smiled and studied his hands in embarrassed silence.

"Let me tell you a bit about our college," Gayle said enthusiastically. "Over the last hundred and fifty years, we have grown from a single building with sheds out back for the horses and carriages, to a modern campus with twelve academic halls, separate residences for young men and women, some co-ed residences for the senior students and, of course, several fraternity and sorority houses. We have a world-class sports facility including gyms, swimming pools, tennis and squash courts and outdoor playing fields. In addition, we have a theater and music center and an entertainment and games center for students to relax and enjoy some downtime. And we have several clubs that students can join, for example, hiking, skiing, tennis, theater and bridge. At Kensington, we believe in exercising the mind, body and spirit!

"Our teaching staff is second to none," she continued. "I personally recruit and hire the brightest minds available from around the world. Our international staff includes a former prime minister of Sweden, a leading economist from France, an award-winning physicist from Germany, a brilliant mathematician from India and a bestselling author from the U.K., in addition to several academics who have earned excellent reputations right here in America.

"At Kensington, your son will be able to pursue his dreams in a challenging and supportive academic environment. We may be small compared to Harvard or MIT, but what we lack in size we make up for in quality," she said with conviction. "We provide a safe campus with our own security service that is on the job 24/7, patrolling the campus and keeping it free of undesirables, so to speak. We also have medical and counseling services on site with doctors and nurses available at all times."

"We understand," Mr. Seymour said. "Your college was highly recommended to us."

Gayle smiled. "I am pleased to hear that," she said. "We are fortunate in being able to attract the very best students from all walks of life, including many very prominent families. We also provide scholarships for students who demonstrate that their superior academic and athletic skills would be an asset to the college. At least ten percent of the student body is on a scholarship. I personally am very proud of this achievement, because I firmly believe that the best and brightest among us are not only from the elite of society. And I want to provide the opportunity for students from all walks of life to shine and reach their full potential. You might say that my mission is to promote 'la crème de la crème', no matter from where they get their start in life."

The Seymours nodded. "I'm very happy that you would consider our son for acceptance at the college," said Mr. Seymour.

"The scholarship program," Gayle continued, "is a particularly important program that sets Kensington apart from many other similar campuses. I am extremely grateful to have generous support in the way of annual gifts and other donations to our scholarship fund from the more fortunate families whose children have attended Kensington. These generous gifts make it possible for us to provide the needed opportunities for our less fortunate students to make their way in the world." At this point, Gayle paused and looked expectantly at the Seymours.

Mr. and Mrs. Seymour looked at each other, and then Mr. Seymour spoke up. "Of course, Dr. Primrose, if Kensington is our choice, we would be honored to participate in your scholarship fund," he said. "I'll write a check as soon as Julian is enrolled."

"Very well," Gayle said, and smiled broadly. "Now, Julian, how do you feel about joining a college that is known for producing students who go on to brilliant careers in science, politics, business and the arts?"

"I'm very excited, ma'am," he said. "I want to be a writer one day, and I understand there's a very good creative writing department here."

"Yes, there is," she said. "As a matter of fact, the head of our English department is a world-famous author, Daniel Post. He's written several bestselling novels, and I'm sure you will learn a lot from him about the craft of novel writing. You may also be interested to know that the motto of our college is *in studio nostrud intelligere*. Do you know what that means?"

"No, ma'am," he said.

"Well, roughly translated, it means 'in the pursuit of creative intelligence'. I firmly believe that it is our duty, as educators, to help you learn about a wide range of subjects and to help you become a well-rounded, intelligent human being. But knowledge is only part of the equation. As a society, we need to graduate creative thinkers, people who can assess and interpret our society and lead us to a better place in the future. I believe, located as we are up here in the mountains, far away from the distractions of the big city, that Kensington College provides the ideal environment for the pursuit of higher learning and creative thinking. As a student here, you will acquire the skills and knowledge that will help you to be successful in your life, no matter what path you choose to take," she said.

The Seymours nodded, and Julian smiled.

"So," Gayle said, turning to the parents, "let me show you around the campus, and then, if you think this is the right college for Julian, I'll give you the application form before you leave." She smiled brightly.

Gayle relied on her college's stellar reputation to attract students from the best families, and to obtain the generous donations that helped her pay the salaries of her high-priced teaching staff. She guarded this reputation like a mother bear guards her cubs, that is to say, fiercely. In the months to come, she would face the biggest challenge of her career: to keep her college's reputation intact.

Ben waited after class to talk to Karl about the next steps for his bridge instruction.

"So," Ben said, "what do I have to do first?"

"Come back to my office after your last class today. We will deal out some hands and review basic bidding. Then, you will go online and watch some live bridge tables. You will read some books on bridge theory and play, and you will memorize the Standard American bidding system. And you will do all that in the next week, because we start playing at the Faculty Bridge Club next Wednesday."

"So soon?" Ben asked anxiously.

"You bet. That's why we start today."

A FEW WEEKS LATER
WEDNESDAY, OCTOBER 1, 2008 — 4:00 P.M.

It was a crisp, sunny day on Mount Salem. Barb Baker slouched in her wooden swivel chair behind a desk piled high with printing dockets and other paperwork. She was taking a break, drinking a Diet Coke and smoking a cigarette, when her cell phone buzzed.

She recognized the number on the display. "Hi, Jill. Wassup?"

"Oh, not much. Just taking a break before I fire a guy for coming to work drunk for the umpteenth time. He refuses to get help. What can you do?"

"Yeah. Tough."

"Hey, did you hear that we may have a special guest at the bridge club tonight?"

"No, do tell."

"Well, you know Belinda in the English department? She heard Daniel Post giving Emily grief because Emily forgot to send in an email to confirm their attendance at bridge tonight. I guess when Daniel called Gayle about it, Gayle told him there were no seats available because she had invited some guy called George Holland to play with his partner, to replace Daniel and Emily."

"George Holland? Haven't I seen him in expert games on BBO?" Barb asked. "Daniel will be so pissed if he doesn't get to play! He thinks he has a chance to win the New Year's Eve prize this year! Wouldn't that just fix his britches if he loses the prize because Emily forgot to confirm!" Barb took a long drag on her cigarette.

"You'd think with a boss like him, she wouldn't forget something like that!" Jill said. "She's usually very competent, but I think he intimidates her so much that she loses her focus."

"Yeah, I feel sorry for Emily. I don't know how she can put up with him all day long in the department, and then play bridge with him at night. She's a glutton for punishment, that one!"

"Well, I sent in our confirmation days ago, so I'll see you tonight, sweetie."

"Thanks, Jill. See you later."

Barb stubbed out her cigarette and placed the ashtray in her bottom drawer. Smoking at work was forbidden, but she snuck the occasional cigarette when things were slow and she was bored. She didn't like doing all this paperwork, but she loved her job. At 37, she was only halfway through her working life. As a single female, with a stocky build, short black hair and average looks, she wasn't expecting to find a husband and become Mrs. Susie Homemaker. Anyway, she liked having a job and the feeling of responsibility and control that she got from managing the college's internal mail and printing service. She made sure that her dockets were always up to date and the mail was delivered on time.

Her interest in bridge had started years ago, when she was a mail handler in a local post office. During the many slow periods, some of the fellows who worked on the dock played cards to amuse themselves. One of the mail handlers was from India. He had a Ph.D. in engineering, but could not find a job in his field, so he wound up working for the post office. He was also a very good bridge player, and he got some of the mail handlers interested in the game. From the first hand she played, Barb was hooked. She signed up with the American Contract Bridge League, joined a local club and read every book and magazine she could find about bridge. She soon learned basic bidding and the usual conventions, but she couldn't find a regular partner with whom to practice. That's when she discovered Bridge Base Online. She didn't need a regular partner to play online, so she played on her computer at home after work every night, to improve her game.

When the post office downsized and she was laid off, Barb applied for a job with Kensington College. Jill Wilmington handled her job application. She noted that Barb's hobby was playing bridge. The two hit it off immediately, and after the job interview they talked about bidding systems for an hour. Barb was thrilled to learn, a week later, that her job application had been approved. She immediately started looking for an apartment in Mount Salem and gave her notice to her landlady in Beaumont. That was three years ago, and she could not have been be happier about the move.

Once ensconced in her job, Barb asked Jill to play with her online, and when two seats became available in the Faculty Bridge Club, Gayle offered the seats to Jill and Barb.

On the surface, Jill and Barb were quite different. Barb's father worked in a factory and her mother was a retail clerk in a local clothing store. Barb was proud of her working class origins and had no ambition to climb the social ladder. Jill, on the other hand, was a polished professional, and she dressed the part. She used her engaging smile and personal charm to put everyone at ease, from the janitors to the professional teaching staff.

Jill's persona changed when she played bridge. She always bid her hand to the max, and thrilled in opportunities to disrupt her opponents' bidding and steal the contract. Barb admired her for her bridge skills and for her ability to slough off the antagonism from other players.

"Who cares?" Jill would say. "It's just a game." But Barb knew that bridge was much more than a card game for Jill. It was her consuming passion.

At 4:30 p.m., Barb's phone rang, interrupting her paperwork.

"Are you and Jill playing tonight?" It was Sally Brighton, an assistant professor in the psychology department. She lectured in child psychology.

"Yep. We're playing tonight, as usual. Are you?" Barb asked.

"Oh yes. I wouldn't miss it. I hear we may have a special guest: George Holland."

"I heard. He has a little star by his name on BBO!" Barb said.

"I know," Sally said. "I often kibitz his table. What's he doing here?"

"I have no idea," Barb said.

"Oh well, you never know anything." Sally hung up.

"Bitch!" Barb said to the dial tone.

Sally got on Barb's nerves. She had tried to explain it to Jill one evening over several glasses of wine.

"Sally aggravates me so much, Jill. She thinks she's so smart. She's not even that good of a bridge player, in my opinion. Terry plays most of the hands. And then she takes so long to bid. It drives me nuts. I just want to throttle her. And that so-called boyfriend of hers, Terry, he's some piece of work, I tell you. I hear all kinds of stories about him from the girls in the psych department. If he doesn't get fired for sexual harassment one of these days, I'll eat my jeans."

The call from Sally made Barb so aggravated that she lit another cigarette and puffed away on it for a few minutes before returning to her paperwork.

Barb's cell phone rang again. This time it was Jill.

"Barb, I just finished firing that guy. Did not go so well," she said, groaning. "I'm ready to knock off early and go for a beer and a burger at Poppa John's. Want to join me? My treat."

Barb glanced at her watch. It was 4:45 p.m. She could easily escape now, without anyone making a fuss.

"You're on!" she said. "We can go over Bergen raises again. Burgers with Bergen!"

"You are obsessed!" Jill said, laughing.

"You know, that bitch Sally Brighton just called me to ask what I knew about George Holland coming tonight. I'm surprised she hasn't called you already. She must have been talking to Gayle."

"I wonder why he's playing with us. He's never been here before."

"You know Gayle, she collects celebrities. He's probably a friend of hers."

"Well, you know, Gayle is a celebrity in her own right. She wrote some important textbooks years ago, before she became president of the college. How do you think she got the job?" Jill pointed out.

"Yeah, I know, I'm just saying," Barb replied, letting her sentence hang in the air.

"Okay. We'll go over Bergen tonight," Jill said, changing the subject. "I'll pick you up in five."

Poppa John's was a local beer and burger place in the heart of Mount Salem, popular with both college staff and students. The burgers were flame-broiled and made to order. The draft beer was cheap, too, attracting people on a limited budget.

Two other bridge players, Karl Schultz and Ben Chong, were sitting in a corner booth at the other end of the room, enjoying a meal and talking bridge. Karl was pleased to have such a bright young man as his bridge partner, and he was sure Ben would turn into an outstanding player.

In the three weeks since Karl had first started tutoring Ben on the game, Ben had read some bridge books and memorized the Standard American bidding system. He was a quick study and was already using some basic conventions, like Jacoby transfers after his partner's notrump opening.

Over dinner at Poppa John's, Karl was talking bidding theory.

"It's like having a conversation, but in a different language, the language of bridge," Karl said. "Everything you say at the bridge table has multiple possible meanings, and the context tells which one applies in a given auction."

Ben nodded again.

"Look, there are Jill and Barb, both very good bridge players," Karl said. "Looks like they had the same idea to eat here tonight before bridge."

"Yeah, I like the burgers here," Ben said, licking his lips to remove some crumbs. Then he noticed someone in the far corner.

"Excuse me a minute, Karl," Ben said. "I have to go to the washroom."

He got up and walked to the other side of the room, stopping briefly to chat with a friend who was sitting alone at a small table eating a burger.

"Hey, Mike," Ben said.

"Hey," Mike replied, through a mouthful of food.

"Call me tomorrow and we'll hook up," Ben said.

Mike nodded. "'Kay," he said. Ben continued to the washroom; a few minutes later, he returned to the table as Karl was signing the credit card slip to pay for their meal.

Jill and Barb got up to leave, and noticed Karl and Ben. Jill gave a cheery wave to them. As they were leaving Poppa John's, Jill commented to Barb, "I wonder how Emily is doing. Will they turn up tonight? Will Daniel make a stink?"

Barb shrugged and pulled a face as if to say, "Who cares?" They got into Jill's car and drove back to the campus.

While David was setting up the tables for bridge, Gayle was entertaining George Holland and his lady friend over dinner. George, a good-looking middle-aged man, was a long-time friend of Gayle's. He just happened to be attending a bridge tournament in Marble Island, Vermont. His partner, Mary Givens, was a striking blond and an expert player in her own right, although not as accomplished as George. She liked to play tournaments with George so they could practice their new bidding system.

Gayle knew that the bridge club members would be thrilled to have George and Mary join them for the evening, but she was a bit nervous about Daniel Post, who had contacted her in a huff when he learned he wasn't allowed to play. When she told him about the special guests, he insisted on attending anyway as a kibitzer. It was obvious that Daniel did not want to lose the opportunity to meet a big-name player like George Holland.

When Gayle and her guests arrived at the bridge club, the North players had already prepared the scoresheets that traveled with each board, and the South players had filled in the slips that indicated which players were seated at each table. They had also set up their own personal scoresheets to record their contracts and scores. Gayle showed her guests to Table 1.

George sat in the North seat, and Mary sat in the South seat. Then Gayle stood by the fireplace to make some announcements.

"Good evening, folks," Gayle began, when she had everyone's attention. "I trust everyone has picked up the results from last week? Yes? This is the most important time of year for the bridge club because this is the final stretch towards the annual prize. I don't need to remind you that my New Year's Eve party is not to be missed! This year I have already confirmed two couples who are household names in America for their contributions to political life and their philanthropy. We'll also have a leading movie star. Is it a male or a female? I cannot reveal at this time," she said teasingly, "and there are several others of international fame and distinction." She paused for effect. There was a round of enthusiastic applause.

"Next, I would like to introduce to you our special guests tonight. I am very pleased and honored to have my good friend George Holland join us this evening, with his delightful companion, Mary Givens. I first met George back in 2005 playing online. My nickname on BBO is 'DaWoman,' and one day, I saw someone playing whose nickname was 'DaMan.' I figured we might have something in common! Later, we spent some time together at a national tournament in Orlando, and we've been great friends ever since," Gayle said, smiling in George's direction.

"George hails from Halifax, Nova Scotia, and he's a former president of the Canadian Bridge Federation. On BBO, his table attracts lots of kibitzers when he teaches Mike Rippey, also known as 'radiators'. The commentary between George and Mike is so hilarious that people watch for the entertainment as much as the bridge lessons.

"Those of you who play frequently online will know that George is one of the colorful characters who make this game so interesting and exciting. I am thrilled that he has agreed to join us this evening. George, would you care to say a few words?"

Enthusiastic clapping brought George to his feet.

"Why, thank you kindly, Gayle. It's a real pleasure to join you all for an evening of bridge. You know bridge has always been my favorite pastime, even more so now that I'm semi-retired, because I can travel and play more tournaments. I often play online with some of my old buddies who I've known since my student days in the 1970s, many of whom used to play for money in the Student Union Building at Carleton U. in Ottawa. How do you think I paid my way through university?" he said, patting his wallet as he waited for the laughter to die down.

"Some of you may know that bridge has attracted many rich and famous people all around the world. Omar Sharif, for one, who is famous for movies like *Doctor Zhivago* and *Lawrence of Arabia*. You probably know that Bill Gates and Warren Buffett are bridge addicts. They have also invested in Bridge Base Online. There are many others, like Isadore and Rosalie Sharpe, a husband and wife team who live in Toronto. Izzy is the chairman of the board for the Four Seasons hotel chain. Then there's Vijay Singh, the golfer, Jimmy Cayne, former Chairman of Bears Stearns, Charles Lazarus, founder of Toys-R-Us, and George Rosenkranz, CEO of Syntex Corp and inventor of the birth control pill — I've been to his hacienda in Mexico by the way, which is surrounded by high walls with barbed wire. He even has a Picasso in his home. His wife was kidnapped at a national bridge tournament and held for ransom, but that's another story," George said, chuckling. "With people of this caliber so intensely involved in a card game, you know there must be something to it!

"I am often asked why I became a lifelong student of the game of bridge. Even though I now teach bridge, I still call myself a student of the game because I don't think you ever stop learning and improving your bridge skills and knowledge."

George paused to take a drink of water.

"No matter what level you play at, I think what attracts people to this game is the thrill of the hunt, seeking out the clues and using logic to unravel the mysteries of each hand. Bridge challenges your capacity for deductive reasoning, inspiration and daring, while your opponents try to distract you with blatant bluffs, outright lies and miscommunication," he said. "And for that reason alone, it's a lot of fun!

"Bridge helps you develop skills in other ways, too. That's why I think it's important for young people to take up the game. I was pleased to hear that Gayle has set up this bridge club to encourage students to play bridge, and I notice there are a few young faces in the room here. I also understand that Karl Schultz... where are you Karl?" he asked, as Karl held up his hand. "Karl has also done his part to encourage students to take up the game. I understand he takes a different student under his wing each year," George said, and he clapped his hands to show his approval.

"I'd like to see more young people involved in playing bridge. The game helps to develop important mental skills, and it can also help your career. I know of some bridge players who got a job or a promotion because they played bridge with the boss and impressed him with their ability to think, plan and execute!

"The links between the world of bridge and the world of business are numerous. Something for young folks to think about!"

George ended his speech and sat down to enthusiastic applause.

Gayle rose from her seat. "George, thank you for your comments. I am sure I speak for all here tonight when I say we appreciate hearing your thoughts about this game we all love. Now, I have a practical problem that I'd like you to help me solve. Daniel Post and Emily Warren wanted to play with us tonight, but as it turned out, we already have a full house. Daniel asked to join us as a kibitzer, but that is not ideal. What I'd like to do is set up a half-table with an East-West sit-out. Daniel and Emily will sit East-West tonight and have the first sit-out, and David and I will sit East-West and have the last sit-out. That way, I can enter the scores into the computer and have the results before you leave this evening. Is that acceptable? Please raise your hand if you agree with this arrangement." A show of hands indicated that Gayle's solution was acceptable.

Gayle took David aside and said, "Would you please call Daniel on his cell and tell him to get over here lickety-split, so we don't have a delay?"

David didn't have to make the phone call, because Daniel and Emily were just outside the dining room and had heard the entire discussion. They casually walked in as David was dialing Daniel's cell phone number.

"Daniel! I'm glad you are here," David said. "We have a half-table tonight and you're sitting East-West in the first sit-out. Too bad you missed George Holland's talk. It was most inspirational."

"Well, as a matter of fact, I did hear his little speech, and I didn't think it was inspirational at all," Daniel said caustically, and steered Emily over to the sit-out table.

The evening progressed in a normal fashion. Twice, Gayle, as director, was called away from her table to settle a dispute when a player bid out of turn, and another player reneged during the play of the hand, but there was nothing unusual in that.

At the break, Ben Chong jumped up, and walked over to the coffee table where George was pouring two cups of coffee.

"Mr. Holland," Ben said, just as Daniel Post was extending his hand to George. "May I have a word?"

George swiveled his head around, and smiled at Ben. "Certainly," he said. "But please call me George."

"I'm a novice player," Ben said shyly, "but I'm really keen to learn and improve. What would you suggest?"

George gave Ben his business card. "Look, as I said, I think bridge is a great pursuit for young people, and I'm always happy to help them. If you seriously want to get into this, contact me and I'll give you some introductory lessons on BBO. But only if you are serious, okay?"

"Thanks!" Ben said, and he stuffed the business card into the pocket of his jeans.

Daniel Post waited impatiently for George to wind up his conversation with Ben, and then he stuck out his hand again.

"Hello," he boomed, "I'm Daniel Post. Pleased to meet you, George!"

George shook his hand and said, "And likewise."

"Are you playing in the Fall Nationals this year?" Daniel asked.

"Thinking about it. If Mary wants to play with me, of course," George said. "Excuse me. I'm supposed to be getting this coffee for her."

George walked back to his table with two cups of coffee. Daniel poured himself some tea and returned to his table where Emily was sitting.

"Not the friendliest bloke," Daniel mumbled to Emily, who smiled back at him.

Gayle called out, "Okay, folks, time is marching! Please return to your seats and we'll get started on the next round."

The players settled in for the remaining rounds of play. The last table finished at 10:30 p.m. Gayle entered the scores into her computer to generate the results. She announced the winners and dispensed the prize money. She also announced that the evening's scores would not count towards the race for the annual prize. She said she wanted to keep the playing field equal for all, in consideration that not everyone had to play against George and Mary.

Daniel objected loudly. He and Emily had got two good boards when they played at George's table. On one hand, George and Mary bid a 50% slam that went down one, and on another, Emily was in four spades doubled, which she made on an endplay that even George couldn't avoid. Daniel and Emily were the top East-West pair, and this result would have secured their place as the front-runners for the annual prize, had it counted.

"Never mind, Daniel," Emily soothed. "We'll still get there."

Daniel ignored her and walked over to the bar to get a Scotch before heading back home. Gayle rounded up George and Mary and ushered them out the door, leaving David to clean up the room and put all the bridge equipment away.

"How do you put up with that dreadful man?" Sally asked Emily as they put on their coats. Daniel was leaning on the bar with a sour look on his face.

"Daniel? He's not so bad, once you get to know him," Emily said. "Anyway, it makes things a lot easier in the office if he's in a good mood, and having a good result at bridge improves his mood."

"Is that why you partner with him? I always wondered about that, since you're a much better bridge player than he is. You could win more often with a nicer partner, I think."

"We do all right," Emily replied, defensively.

"Emily, you know what I mean. He behaves as though you make all the mistakes, but it's him making the mistakes! We all see it," Sally said.

"I'm not sure I know what you mean," Emily responded, as she turned to walk away. Sally placed her hand on Emily's arm to stop her retreat.

"He's just like the Hideous Hog, Emily! He's a bridge bully, always trying to maneuver the bidding so he can play the hand. How many times does he bid 3NT when you should be in hearts or spades? It's a classic sign of hand-hogging, my dear."

"Sally, I don't appreciate your comment, and furthermore I don't think it's true," Emily said, removing Sally's hand from her arm. "Daniel is a fine bridge player and we do well together. And if you're just trying to rattle me, it's not going to work!"

Sally raised her hand in mock capitulation. "Whatever you say, Emily. You want to live in a fool's paradise, that's your problem." And with that, she swiveled on her heel and walked out of the room.

As she walked back to her car to drive home, Emily thought about her exchange with Sally, and she wondered if she should raise the issue of hand-hogging with Daniel. It was true that he preferred to play 3NT contracts whenever possible, even if 3NT wasn't the right spot. It is hard for the opponents to double a 3NT, so he often got away with a top score by going down one or two when the opponents could have made a partscore contract. However, it was also true that he tended to manipulate the bidding to be the declarer, bidding notrump when he should have supported her suit.

There was not much she could do about it, though. They were one of the top pairs in the club, so it was hard to argue with success. However, she also knew that as the end of the year drew nearer, the competition would heat up and Daniel's unconventional bidding tactics could backfire on them, especially as his play of the hand was often more pedantic than inspired.

She also feared that he could make her work life miserable if she raised the issue with him. His tendency towards unpredictable arrogance had worsened since his wife died, and the pressure he was getting from Gayle to finish his book was making him crankier than usual. He became very obnoxious at any mention of the book.

Emily pondered these issues as she drove home. She lived in a cozy walk-up apartment a few blocks from the center of town. There was a parking area at the rear of the building. She unlocked the back door, went up the stairs to the second level, then unlocked the back door to her apartment. Her calico cat, Patches, greeted her with a yawn and a long stretch, and followed her into the small galley kitchen. Emily poured herself a glass of water and checked the cat's food dish. It was empty. Patches sat next to her dish, looking up at Emily with an expression that said, "So feed me already." Emily dutifully opened a tin of Deelish, a gourmet mixture of meat and vegetable matter that smelled to high heaven. Patches took a whiff and immediately set upon the contents with delicate gusto. Within a minute or two, the dish was empty and Patches stretched out beside Emily on the couch, purring in contentment.

As Emily sipped her water and watched the news on TV, her mind wandered back to the exchange with Sally. *I'm not going to let that woman get to me,* she thought, pushing away any thoughts that Sally might continue to try to undermine her bridge partnership with Daniel.

Emily smiled as she reflected on the hand where she made four spades doubled at George's table. She had bid spades twice but Daniel had still bid 3NT. *If I hadn't pulled the contract to four spades, we'd have gone down for sure,* she thought. *I had only one club stopper.* It was a typical example of Daniel making poor decisions because he insisted on playing the hand himself.

I will just have to take control more often, Emily thought, *if we're going to have any chance to win the annual prize.*

Emily was starting to realize that Daniel was not the superior intellect that he portrayed himself to be. She often noticed mistakes in his presentations and accounts, small things that she corrected for him, but mistakes nonetheless. And this last episode, forgetting the confirmation for the bridge game, was a case in point.

Every week, on Friday, Gayle (via David) sent out an email to all the club members to remind them to confirm their attendance at the Wednesday night bridge session. The deadline was Monday at noon. If a pair did not confirm by then, Gayle would invite someone else to sit in for the evening.

On the previous Friday when the email came through to the office, Emily asked Daniel if she should confirm. He said to wait, because he might have something to do on Wednesday evening. He said he would let her know Monday morning if he was available.

Daniel didn't let Emily know on Monday morning, so she didn't confirm with Gayle, and therefore their seats became open. So Gayle had invited George and Mary to come as her guests.

When Daniel found out, he was livid.

"You stupid girl!" he said, angrily confronting Emily at her desk. "I am getting really fed up with your incompetence, Emily! You failed to confirm us for bridge, and now we'll miss it, and George Holland is going to be there. Do you know who he is? Of course you don't. Do you know that he is a commentator on BBO's vugraph broadcasts from the biggest tournaments around the world? And he's going to play and we won't be there because you forgot to confirm! This is unacceptable and unforgivable!" And with that, he strode back to his office and slammed the door.

The other secretaries pretended not to hear this exchange, but of course, they did, and before long, the news got out. Daniel already had quite a reputation for angry outbursts, so no one was surprised that he'd had a go at Emily. But Emily just took it in stride. She knew it was not her fault.

Emily wasn't sure if it was from grief over his wife's passing that he acted strangely at times. She often wondered if his mood swings were a sign of something more serious, or if he was just being eccentric, but in any case, she had developed quite a thick skin.

While Daniel was obnoxious when things did not go his way, he could be very considerate at other times. When Emily's mother was ill, he let Emily take a week off so she could travel to D.C. to help her mother after an operation. Another time, he surprised Emily by arranging a celebration for her birthday in the office, with cake and flowers.

Emily figured that, underneath all the bluff and bluster, Daniel was just a scared little boy who had never really grown up, and she sometimes felt quite protective towards him, as a mother to her child.

But in the last few months his behavior had gone downhill, to the point where she sometimes wondered if he was 'all there'. She kept watching for indications of a medical problem. She knew he took pills for depression and other issues. On the other hand, it was possible he was just an arrogant SOB, as Sally suggested, and needed to be put in his place.

Emily sighed, tickled her cat and decided to call it a night.

CHAPTER 8

 PRESENT DAY — 2:30 A.M.

My coffee cup was empty again, so I went back to the counter to get a refill. Brian took the opportunity to visit the men's room.

When we got settled back into our seats by the window, I resumed my tale.

"We learned through our interviews that the writer, Daniel Post, was having major problems writing his new book. Then he came up with this crazy idea that he could write a real crime into his book. That's when he starting calling the station, asking to be included in our investigations so he could get some material for his book. He was under extreme pressure to finish it. Made him real cranky."

"Yeah, well he sounds desperate. It's like a Hail Mary play in football… just throw the ball as high and far as you can, and hope that it lands in the right hands," Brian mused. "You talked about the annual bridge prize. Why was it such a big deal? It's just a party, after all."

"Right, but when you look at these bridge players, they are all super-competitive with each other, so winning the prize was a huge ego boost. Digman, in particular, really wanted to win it. He was planning to leave at the end of his contract, so he had one last chance to show off his bridge smarts. Barb Baker wanted to win it to gain the respect she thought she deserved. Emily Warren wanted to win it so she could rub shoulders with celebrities and further her career. Daniel Post wanted to win it because he thought he belonged there as a celebrity himself. Jill Wilmington, Sally Brighton and the others were in it to win for their own personal gain. Wouldn't you like to spend New Year's Eve at a fancy party with world-famous people? Think of the bragging rights!"

Brian nodded. "There must have been a lot of tension between the players on the back stretch."

"You got it," I said.

"But how does all this figure into the murder of those two players?"

It was a dreary Monday in early October, with steel-gray skies, gusty winds and a light drizzle. Emily yearned for the glorious days of early fall when the sun shone brightly in brilliant blue skies, and the trees turned the hillsides into a raging fire of orange, yellow and red.

She shrugged off her gloomy mood as she entered the English department office. Her cubicle was just outside Daniel's private office door. She settled into her chair and turned on her computer. While she waited for the machine to boot up, she glanced outside, noting again that she was lucky to have a window next to her desk. But the drizzle and low-hanging clouds seemed to drain the campus of life. She looked away.

The light was blinking on her phone. She dialed in to pick up the message.

"Emily, this is Gayle Primrose. Please tell Daniel to come to my house today for lunch and an important meeting. Twelve-fifteen. On the dot."

By 10:00 a.m., Daniel still had not arrived in the office. Emily was starting to get worried about him, but a few minutes later he strode in, raindrops dripping from his hat as he bustled past her.

"Good morning," he boomed, and immediately disappeared into his office. Emily gave him a few minutes to get settled and then tapped on his door.

"Come in, Emily," Daniel said. "I always know it's you by the timid way you knock. I can hardly hear you. Can't you put some muscle power into it?"

Emily ignored his comment. "How was your weekend?"

"Oh, same as ever. I puttered around in the garden. You know, my wife was quite the gardener in her day. She did all the planting and upkeep. I've been trying to figure out what's growing in there. Tedious work, I tell you."

"You could hire someone," Emily suggested, but he just dismissed that idea with a wave of his hand.

"Okay," she said, "today, you have two students coming in for consultations — one at 10:30 and one at 11:30. And we have a staff meeting at 4:00 p.m. And Gayle wants to see you for an important lunch meeting at 12:15 today, at her place."

"She does?" Daniel seemed a little surprised. "Okay, we'll leave here at noon."

"She didn't include me in the invitation, Daniel."

"Well, you're coming anyway. I want you there to take notes of official department business, so I don't have to," he said.

Emily went back to her desk and reviewed her emails and to-do list. The grad students arrived one at a time for their appointments with Daniel, who was advising them on their courses and thesis work. He ushered the second student out of his office at 11:45 a.m., and told Emily to 'go potty' if she needed to, before leaving for their lunch with Gayle.

Emily visited the washroom down the hall to check her make-up and hair and then went back to the office to get her coat. Daniel was waiting on the curb when Emily pulled up in her Mazda to pick him up. By now the rain had stopped and the sun was starting to break through the clouds.

Emily knew the route to Gayle's house, having been there several times before when Gayle held staff meetings (called 'think sessions') at her home. "I want those creative juices flowing," she would explain. "You need to get out of the office and away from the phone and email so you can open your mind and come up with new ideas." Gayle wasn't just wagging her tongue. She had done a lot of research on the workings of the human mind while writing her books on improving education through creative thinking and learning.

It was unusual, however, for Gayle to summon professors to her home. She would usually use her office for one-on-one meetings. Emily was very curious to see what this meeting was all about.

Gayle lived in an exclusive neighborhood located halfway between the campus and Mount Salem village. Her three-story townhouse was an end unit on a hillside overlooking the lake and valley below. This time of year, the sky was full of V-shaped formations as flocks of magnificent Canada geese made their way south to avoid winter's wrath.

Emily pulled into Gayle's driveway and parked behind her sleek, blue Jaguar. Gayle was standing in her front yard when they arrived, trowel in hand, surveying a group of shrubs near her front door.

"There you are," she called, as Emily and Daniel emerged from the Mazda. "Want to check out my garden?" she asked Daniel. She knew that he was learning how to take care of his own gardens since his wife died.

"Why not?" Daniel said, and Emily murmured the same.

"I'm experimenting," she said. "I've moved some plants from the back to the front."

"What's that vine over there?" Daniel asked. "I think I've seen it in my garden."

"I'm not sure. A friend gave it to me two years ago. He said it's a very popular decorative garden plant," Gayle said.

"It's called Rosary Pea, I think," Emily said. "My mother has them in her garden. I recognize the little red berries."

"Well, isn't that interesting. And what's that one over there?" Daniel asked, pointing to another plant.

"Oh, that's a barberry bush. Every garden should have one. They grow very well in this climate," Gayle said. She then led them around her front garden, pointing out the specific features of each plant. Next to playing bridge, gardening was Gayle's favorite pastime.

A few minutes later, another car drove up and parked beside Emily's Mazda. Jill Wilmington got out.

"My goodness," Gayle said, glancing at her watch. "It's time to have lunch." She turned and greeted Jill and then ushered her guests into her elegant home. She had a table set up on the back deck so they could take in the view of the valley below while they ate.

"Thankfully, it has stopped raining so we can sit outside," Gayle said. "If you find it cool, keep your jackets on."

The sun was breaking up the overcast sky, but there were still large patches of dark clouds that threatened rain.

Gayle provided an extra place setting for Emily and poured home-made lemonade into their glasses. She placed soup bowls in front of them, with slices of goat's cheese and nuts in the bottom. She then brought out a soup terrine and ladled steaming broccoli soup into the bowls, covering the cheese and nuts. She sprinkled chopped coriander on the top and said with a flourish, "Voila!"

Daniel fished a small pill container out of his pocket. He took a pill with some water and said, "I keep forgetting to take this in the morning with my breakfast."

Gayle said, "What is that for? Blood pressure?"

"No," he said, "it's some new-fangled drug the doctor prescribed for my anxiety issues. My happy pills, but I'm not so sure they're working, eh, Emily?"

Emily was embarrassed. She didn't know what to say, so she just sipped her soup. As the cheese melted, it became a little creamy. Daniel grumbled. He wasn't a big fan of broccoli, but he ate the soup anyway. Jill remained quiet and crumbled some crackers into her soup before eating it.

Gayle then brought out a tray of ham and cheese sandwiches on rye. The group chatted about the weather and national politics while they ate, and Emily began to wonder about the purpose of the lunch meeting. It wasn't like Gayle to have a private lunch with college staff just for the heck of it.

When the teapot came out, so did the purpose of the meeting.

"So, Daniel," Gayle spoke as she poured the tea. "How's your book coming along?"

"Oh, you know," he said, avoiding eye contact. "So-so."

"I see. So not much progress in the last six months?"

Daniel nodded.

"You know, I gave you this sabbatical so you could finish the book," she reminded him. "You don't need to do any teaching, just act as an advisor to the grad students and provide direction to the department. That's not too much to ask, is it?" Her tone belied her frustration.

"No. Yes," he said.

"So, when can I see the first draft?"

"You'll see it when it's ready," he said testily.

"But why do you not have a draft ready yet?"

"Because I haven't finished it," he retorted.

Gayle straightened up. "Daniel, need I remind you that you are skating on thin ice?"

"Oh, really? Need I remind you that I am a bestselling author whose reputation as an internationally acclaimed writer attracts students to your college?"

Emily shrank down in her chair as this storm of clashing egos gained momentum. Gayle turned to her, "Perhaps you could give us a minute or two here, Emily?"

"Oh, no," said Daniel sharply, "I want her to stay. You've got Jill here as a witness, I want Emily to hear whatever you have to say."

Gayle folded her napkin and looked straight at Daniel. "All right, then. Need I remind you, Daniel, that you are well past the original deadline that we agreed upon when I first hired you?"

"No, you need not remind me for the umpteenth time that I am past the deadline," he responded. "But you of all people should realize that genius does not bend to artificial deadlines. World-class creativity doesn't happen overnight. You have to give it time to develop," he argued. "You think Rome was built in a day?"

"This is serious, Daniel!" Gayle exclaimed. "I did not invite you here to lecture you and give you another extension."

"So, why did you invite me here, then?" he demanded.

"I invited you here to make it clear, one last time, that I need you to finish that book. I need it to be available for next year's Creative Writing curriculum. And I need to start promoting that curriculum in the spring. I have commitments! You must have the completed manuscript to your publisher by April 1st. It's do-or-die time, Daniel. Get it done, or I will be forced to cancel your employment contract. I will be sending you a written memo confirming this, for the record," she said, her eyes blazing.

"You wouldn't dare!" Daniel snapped.

"Try me," she snapped back. Gayle glared at Daniel, not giving an inch. Daniel glared back. Jill looked calm, a veteran of many such scenes. Emily waited, breathless, looking down at her folded hands. She suddenly felt quite small. If Daniel lost his job at the college, what would happen to her job as his secretary?

Suddenly, Daniel pushed his chair back. Emily gulped. Daniel half rose, then settled back down in his seat, shifting his weight to one side, leaning forward.

"Oh, come on, Gayle," Daniel said, changing his tone. "It's not like I haven't tried, but you know my dear wife Marion was my muse. It's much harder for me to write inspired fiction without her. It takes so much longer to get going. I am making an effort every day, believe me." Gayle did not look convinced. "I'll put more effort into it, I promise," he said. "I will have the first draft by Christmas."

Emily stole a glance at both her boss and her boss's boss to see if the confrontation was over.

Gayle waited a moment, and then matched his conciliatory tone. "I know, Daniel, I know. Losing Marion was a terrible blow. I realize how much she meant to you. But you have to know your reputation has diminished somewhat since your last book was published — how many years ago now? Six? I'm having a harder time attracting top students because you haven't published anything in years. I've given you more than enough time to finish this project. Get Emily here to help you. I need you to finish that book, and fast!"

As the tensions eased at the table, Emily started breathing again. Jill poured herself more tea. Daniel reached for one of Gayle's Peek Freans. Gayle took one too. They sat in silence for a few moments, gazing out towards Lake Salem.

"Nice view you have here, Gayle," Daniel said.

"Yes, it is. I enjoy it every day," she responded.

Jill smiled and Emily sipped her tea silently. She wished she hadn't been dragged along to this lunch meeting to witness the confrontation, but at the same time, she recognized the importance of Gayle's message.

Do-or-die is what Gayle had said. *She's not going to back down this time,* Emily thought.

With the lunch meeting over, Gayle ushered Daniel and Emily out the front door, and said to Jill, "Wait a minute, please."

After Daniel and Emily drove off, Gayle turned to Jill and said, "So, you heard everything. If Daniel doesn't produce a manuscript soon, I'll have to start the process to end his contract. I've given him ample warning and too many extensions already," she said. "Thing is, I hate to let him go. I like him and I think he's had a rough time. But I can't keep paying his huge salary if he doesn't produce. It's as simple as that!"

Jill nodded. "I understand. I'll draft a memo for your signature confirming what you told him, and we'll put a copy in the file. Then if you decide to fire him, it's all documented properly."

"Thank you, Jill," she said. "I know I can always count on you."

As Emily drove with Daniel back to the campus, she pondered this new situation, and it gave her much cause for concern.

She finally said to Daniel, "If you don't get the book done, Gayle will fire you and I will be out of a job!"

She glanced at Daniel, who showed no signs of having heard her. Emily continued, saying, "The job market for secretaries is not that robust anymore, and I need a job to pay my bills."

Daniel continued to ignore her.

"I still want to finish my medical degree and become a doctor," she said. "But since my dad died, my family has had no money to support my studies. You know I've been taking some odd jobs on my own time to save up money to finish my medical degree."

Daniel finally looked at her and said, "I understand, Emily. I'm doing the best I can."

"After six years here, I only have $25,000 saved up," she said. "I can't afford to lose my job!"

"I said, I am doing the best I can," he said irritably. "You think I'm happy about this? I'm not at all happy. What I need is inspiration. That's where Marion was such a great help!" He sighed. "She could always figure out the critical issues and help me plot them out. In fact, without her, I probably would not have written so many books. That, by the way, is not for public consumption," he said pointedly.

"What are you going to do about it?" Emily asked.

"Well, my dear child, I'm going to get inspired," he said. "After all, I have my reputation as a brilliant novelist to uphold!"

"How can I help you?" Emily asked.

Daniel was silent for a minute. "Well, maybe you could do some research," he said. "I hate doing research."

"Sure, I'd love to," she said. "Will you give me a credit in your acknowledgements?"

"Well, why not?" he said.

They arrived at the college and Emily parked the car in the staff parking lot. They walked back to the office together.

"So, what can I research for you?" she asked.

Daniel thought for a moment while he unbuttoned his coat and hung it up in the closet. "Research why college presidents think they are so damn perfect that they can boss people around willy-nilly!" he growled.

"Daniel! I mean real research that can help you get over your writer's block."

"I don't have writer's block," he snapped. "What I have is lack of inspiration. There's no such thing as writer's block. Anyone can write. Just throw some words on paper. That's what many so-called writers do, anyway. It's just words and words and more words on paper. Any idiot can write!" he said, and threw himself down on the couch in his office with a big sigh. "Go on, get out of here. I'll figure this out myself."

Emily retreated to her cubicle. *I can't help him if he won't let me,* she thought. *It's obvious he needs help. There's got to be something I can do.*

Later, she went back into Daniel's office to bring him some tea. "Daniel, if you tell me what your book is about, I can at least help you identify the areas where you need some research to be done." She watched carefully for his reaction.

"You are a determined little thing, aren't you?" he said with a sigh.

"Give me a chance," she said. "I have time available, and I can get a lot of information on the Internet and at the college library."

"You have to keep it confidential," he said. "You will need to sign an NDA — a non-disclosure agreement."

"So long as you give me a credit for the work I'm going to do," she countered.

"Okay, it's a deal." Daniel opened a file in his computer. He opened a document, made some changes and printed it. Emily read it and they both signed it.

"I guess this means we're in business together," he said with a wry smile.

"I want that credit," she said firmly. "One day it might come in handy if I need to get a new job."

"Right. It's in the agreement," he assured her. "You'll get the credit."

"So, tell me about your book," she said, gently but firmly.

Daniel hesitated as he mentally tried to force back the dreadful anxiety that always accompanied discussions about the book. "I'm having some trouble with the writing," he said. "I have the story in my head, but when

I try to write my thoughts down, they somehow get scrambled up. You could help me by reading some of my notes and seeing if they make sense to you."

"Okay, we can start with that," she said.

Daniel started to warm up to the idea.

"Did you read my last book, about the philandering Cambridge professor Cal Swanson who got mixed up in a plot to steal data from the British defense department?"

"Yes, I read it. You signed my copy, remember?" she asked.

"Oh, right you are. Well, this new book takes off from the first one. Cal is on a sabbatical and travels to the USA, where he winds up at a small college as a visiting professor… like me. There are a series of local murders and the police think that he is the culprit, but it's a case of mistaken identity. Cal has to figure out who the real killer is or go down for the crime."

"Sounds like a good storyline. So, what's the problem?"

"I'm still on page one."

"You can't get going?" she asked.

"Right. I'm stuck in first gear. I need to figure out how the murders were done, and why the cops mistake Cal for someone else. The plot has to have a lot of unexpected twists and turns. I've trained my fans to expect that from me. They expect the unexpected, and they expect the story to be plausible in reality, but also fresh and interesting. You know," he said, frowning, "many writers become stale after the first few books, and they start writing the same crap. It's formulaic writing. They become a commodity for the publishers. Their books are predictable, Emily, and eventually the public becomes bored and turned off. I can't let that happen to me," he said with grave concern. "If I don't give my readers what they really want, my book won't sell, and I'll be known as a washed-up old has-been! I won't be invited as a guest on David Letterman or Jay Leno or even Ellen DeGeneres. They'll just ignore me. That's why I need inspiration! I need Marion! She always gives me good ideas!"

And with that, he propped his feet up on the end of the brown leather sofa, closed his eyes and dismissed Emily with a wave of his hand. Emily retreated from Daniel's office and returned to her cubicle.

Daniel closed his eyes, thinking about Gayle's ultimatum. A plan was beginning to form in his mind of how to develop the characters for his story. He wanted to model one of the characters on Gayle, and then murder her. He loved that idea; it gave him extreme satisfaction, in his imagined world at least.

In the meantime, he had no idea how to get started. He knew from past experience that once he had the inspiration, he could sit at his desk and write for hours on end, day after day, working through all the plotting and sub-plotting, character development and dialogue sequences, until the first draft was ready for editing and subsequent revisions. He didn't mind working with an editor on the revisions. The post-writing work was mostly technical, with some fact-checking and minor refinements, and it didn't require a lot of hardcore mental work. The hard part for him was finding the inspiration.

He decided to take a little nap. He went to his desk and dialed Emily's extension.

"Emily," he said, "I'm going to have a snooze. Wake me up at 3:45, in time for the staff meeting."

"Okay," she replied, and busied herself with some reports that had to be prepared for the meeting.

Daniel went back to the sofa and tried to sleep, but he couldn't clear his mind. He found himself thinking about his dead wife Marion. If he closed his eyes and focused on her, he could actually conjure her up before him, as if she were sitting right there with him in the room, talking to him like in the old days when she was alive. If he concentrated, he could even smell her perfume...

Daniel, Marion said, *you need to get up off your butt and figure this out. What's wrong with you?*

"I'm stuck without you," he muttered.

Well, she replied, *I can't have you lolling about like this. Get on with it! What's your problem?*

"I need a crime, maybe a murder. Something unconventional."

You want a biological weapon, like a virus?

"No, too hard to control."

How about an allergy to nuts or shellfish? she suggested.

"Murder by food allergy?" he mused. "No, that's too complicated. Has to be something based in reality, something my readers will actually believe."

You want a prescription drug that seems harmless but combined with something else, like a common cold remedy or alcohol, it becomes lethal? she asked.

"No, that's been done before," he said with a sigh. "I need something fresh."

I know, she said, *what about murder by mind control! I think I'm dead, therefore I am!*

"Now you are being silly, my dear." Then he sighed.

Don't worry. The right idea will come to you, she said. *Now rest.*

And he finally slept.

Emily woke Daniel from his nap in time for the staff meeting. During the meeting, Daniel's mind kept drifting away. Something about his conversation with Marion had twigged an idea in his brain. It had to do with reality. The public was obsessed with reality — reality survival shows and singing contests, real police chases and bounty hunters, the list went on and on. The public's consumption for reality seemed to hold no bounds.

"What about reality crime?" he thought. The idea appealed to him. He could offer himself as a crime consultant to the local police force, and get involved with one of their actual investigations and model his story (with some invented twists and turns) on a real crime. It could be a quasi-docu-crime-mystery. That would be unique and different!

Of course, the characters would have to be developed, but the real crime story could be woven into the fictional story. He decided to contact the Beaumont Police Department and see if he could get insight into one of their ongoing investigations.

The staff meeting ended and Emily gathered up her notes. "That went well," she said after the rest of the staff left the boardroom.

Daniel had no idea what she was talking about. He said to her, "I know how you can help me with my book! Call the police captain over at Beaumont and set up an appointment for me. I want to talk to him about one of their cases."

Emily said, "Right away," as she walked back to her cubicle and Daniel went into his office.

A few minutes later, Emily opened the door to Daniel's office and said, "Okay, you can see Captain Juno tomorrow at 12:30 p.m. Do you need directions?"

Daniel said, "Great! Yes, get the directions from MapQuest, and the phone number too. In case I need it."

For the first time in weeks, Daniel felt the heaviness in his chest ease a little. He got his coat and left the office to go home. He had a slight spring in his step and started whistling a tune as he walked.

That night, he slept well and woke up feeling refreshed and energized. When he arrived in the office around ten o'clock, he greeted Emily with a smile and said cheerfully, "Good morning."

Emily returned his greeting and walked over to the staff kitchen to make him some tea. When it was ready, she brought the tea to his office, and gave him a folder with the notes from the staff meeting.

"You want to go over these notes and see if they are accurate?" she asked, handing him the cup of steaming hot tea.

"Oh, Emily, I'm sure they are fine. Don't bother me with that right now. I have to prepare for my meeting with Captain Juno," he said.

"Anything I can do?" she asked.

"Not now," he replied. "Wait until I have the meeting, then we'll see. You can go now," he said, dismissing her.

When 11:30 a.m. rolled around, Daniel shut down his computer and opened his briefcase. He pulled three books from his bookshelf. These were the last three novels he had published. He opened each one and wrote a brief message and signed each book. Then he put them in his briefcase, put on his coat and walked out of his office.

"I'm off to see the captain now," he said to Emily. "Wish me luck."

"Luck," she said, smiling.

Daniel walked to his parking spot and got into the Volvo station wagon that he and Marion had purchased ten years earlier. It was still in very good condition. When Marion was alive, they used to go for long country drives through the New England states. They liked to stay in B&Bs and dine in small restaurants that featured the local cuisine. Since her death, Daniel had stuck close to home, just driving to and from work and the grocery store. He had not left Mount Salem in four years.

It took him about forty minutes to drive to Beaumont and find the police station. He was a bit early for the appointment, but he walked into the station anyway to get a feel for the place.

He presented himself to the uniformed officer at the main desk, who told him to take a seat. A few minutes later, the officer led him to an inner office and said to the man sitting behind a big desk, "Cap, Mr. Post is here to see you."

Daniel walked into the office and extended his hand. "It's Professor Post. Pleased to meet you, Captain," Daniel said.

"Have a seat," Captain Juno responded. He was having his lunch, and his mouth was half-full of a tuna sandwich. He swallowed, wiped his lips with his hand and said, "What can I do you for?"

"Well, Captain, first of all, I want to thank you for taking the time to meet with me," Daniel began.

"No problem," Juno said, "But I am very busy, so I don't have a lot of time."

"I understand," Daniel said. "Let me explain my mission. As you may know, I am a writer with several bestselling novels to my credit." Daniel looked at Juno for some acknowledgement, but Juno just smiled back at him. Then Daniel took the books out of his briefcase and handed them to Juno.

"Go on," Juno said, as he glanced at the book covers.

"I am writing a new novel, and I'd like the assistance of the local police department," he said. "It could turn out to be another bestseller."

"I'm listening," Juno said.

"Here's the thing," Daniel said. "I'd like to introduce an element of reality into the novel, and that's where the Beaumont Police Department can come into the picture. If you have a case that I can monitor, you know, as part of my research, I will write the case into my novel and you will get the credit!"

"I see," Juno said. "You want to be embedded in one of our cases?"

"Yes," Daniel said, "If that is not too much to ask."

"Let me think about it," Juno said. "What kind of case are you looking for?"

At that point, another officer walked into the room.

"Oh, diLongo, I'd like you to meet Mr. Post. He wants to write a novel about us," Juno said. "Detective diLongo is one of our top investigators."

Daniel extended his hand to the detective, an attractive brunette in her mid-thirties. "Pleased to meet you," Daniel said.

"Same here," she said.

"We're just talking about cases that might be of interest to Mr. Post," Juno said. "Perhaps you could brief him on the options?"

"Sure," she said. "We don't have much going on, really. Petty theft. Drunk driving. The occasional knifing incident outside the bars. What kind of case are you interested in, Mr. Post?"

"It's Professor Post," he said with what he thought was a disarming smile. "Well, something more serious. I'd like a murder investigation, or perhaps a major fraud case, with corporate corruption and government scandals. Maybe even terrorism. What have you got along these lines?" he asked.

"Hmmm," she said. "In this neck of the woods we don't get much in that regard. But you know something? I took a course last year at Kensington College and we learned about cross-border criminal activities. We're close to the Canadian border so we have to be more diligent about controlling who comes and goes. In fact, there could be terrorists who have infiltrated from Canada lurking here in the mountains, just biding their time until they get the call. So we are on the alert for any signs of unusual activities that could be a terrorist cell.

"The other big issue causing problems for law enforcement these days is identity theft," she continued. "The professor explained how easy it is to steal someone's identity and create a fake one. Combine that with the porous nature of our border with Canada and the threat of external and internal terrorist activity, you have the ingredients for some nasty stuff brewing under the radar," she said. "We already know about the gangs that bring illegal drugs into our area through their connections on the Native American reserves that straddle the border. There are several rival gangs and we get the occasional gunfight with dead bodies turning up. Is that something you might be interested in?" she asked.

"Well, I'm interested in anything that prompts a serious police investigation," he said. "I'd like to write the investigation into my book."

"Well, Mr. Post," Juno said, rising from his seat. "We'll keep you in mind if something turns up, okay?"

"If you'd like to look through some of our older cases, I can have some case files brought out for you," offered diLongo.

"Well, I would prefer a live case," Daniel said. "But I may want to do some research on your old cases at some point. Thanks for the offer." Then Daniel got up and extended his hand to Juno. "Much appreciated," he said. "Good day." He shook hands with diLongo, and then left the building.

On his way back to the college, Daniel reviewed the conversation with the two police officers. He felt encouraged by their apparent willingness to accommodate him. He began formulating a possible plot line for his book, using the cross-border angles the detective had talked about.

"If the police play ball, this could be the breakthrough I need," he thought.

CHAPTER 9

📅 PRESENT DAY — 2:45 A.M.

I took a sip of my coffee, which was no longer hot. Brian was gazing out the window, trying to put all the pieces together.

"So, back to the investigation. You interviewed all the bridge players at the scene and let everyone go home. What did you do next?" he asked.

I cradled the now-empty coffee cup in my hands. "It was already late… about this time of night, actually. We had to go back to the station and organize our information into something that was manageable. I wanted to get a clear picture of what happened and the people who were involved. And I still didn't know if we were investigating a homicide or some kind of freak accident.

"The next day, we had a brainstorming session about the case, and started following up some leads while we waited for the M.E.'s report to clarify the situation."

📅 THURSDAY, DECEMBER 11, 2008 — 2:30 A.M.

DiLongo and Skip headed back to the station after finishing the interviews with the bridge players. Their regular shift had ended at midnight, and they were already two and a half hours into overtime.

When they got back to the station, word had already spread there was a fresh case with D.B.s up at the college. When asked, diLongo just said, "We don't know anything yet… waiting for the M.E. I'll do a briefing at noon." They were on twelve-hour shifts, so their next shift would start at noon.

When she was working a case, diLongo sometimes had to put in a few extra hours, like tonight. She sighed. The sooner she got home to hit the sack, the better. "I'll be running on empty tomorrow," she thought.

"Come into my office," she said to Skip as they entered the station.

"Let's clean off that board," she said, indicating a huge whiteboard on the wall. "We're going to create a big chart."

Skip nodded.

"We're going to write on the chart the names of all the bridge club members and what they ate and drank tonight," she said.

Skip got a marker and said, "Ready."

"Okay. At the top left, write: *Kensington College. December 10, 2008, Faculty Dining Room, 3rd floor, Admin Building. Bridge Club. Two bodies. Cause TBD. Time of death: approx. 10:10 p.m.* Below that, write: *Persons present at the scene.*"

Then they filled in the chart using their notes. When they were finished, they had the names of the bridge club members listed, starting with Gayle Primrose and ending with the two who died, Terry Digman and Anne-Marie Boland. Underneath each name, Skip wrote down the food and drink that each player consumed, and questions that needed more time to investigate. At the far right, they wrote *Others,* for any other potential suspects who might emerge.

It was 3:30 a.m. by the time they finished.

"You think it was homicide, don't you?" Skip asked.

"I would not be surprised, but the M.E.'s report will shed some light on the situation. It's all up to Sam now. Let's go home and get some sleep. Tomorrow will be a long day," diLongo said.

They signed out for the night, and went their separate ways.

DiLongo hoped the M.E.'s report would not be inconclusive. That would be the worst-case scenario, because then they wouldn't know what they were dealing with, and that would make it hard to develop a plan. She did not want her first big case to turn into a cold case. She decided to go back to work early and talk to Sam Baldwin, the M.E., and see if he had any news.

Sam loved to fish, and he owned a place on a small lake close to Beaumont, where he could be found most days fishing off his dock or out on the lake in his little putt-putt motorboat. The only thing he loved more than fishing was cutting up dead bodies, probing them for telltale signs to indicated how they died. Once he got into a case, he could be counted on to work around the clock to uncover all the body's secrets.

One more thing about Sam — he didn't like to be disturbed when he was working. DiLongo had learned that the hard way a few years back when some tourists found a body near their campsite. DiLongo walked into the morgue to get an update while Sam was performing the autopsy, and he roared at her to stay out until he was "damn good and ready to give a report!"

When diLongo arrived in the station later that morning, she was careful to phone Sam's extension at the morgue before going to see him.

"Hey, Sam, how's it going with my two D.B.s?" she asked. She knew he had been working all night. "Anything you can tell me? I have a shift change meeting at noon, so I have to give a briefing."

"I'm still working on it," he said. "I can tell you this much. Both were in reasonably good health. No visible signs of trauma. I've sent their stomach contents and blood and brain samples to the lab for tests. Now I'm going home to catch some zees. Call me later. I may have something for you by six o'clock."

"Okay, thanks, Sam," she said.

She hung up the phone, and started preparing a report for the shift change meeting. The phone rang. It was Sharon Sharpe, a reporter.

"I have no comments for you at this time," diLongo said. "We're still waiting for the M.E.'s report." Then she returned to her briefing note.

"Two bodies, Terry Digman and Anne-Marie Boland," diLongo reported at the meeting. "No known cause of death. Investigation continues. Waiting for M.E.'s report. Have to treat it as suspicious at this point. If it's homicide, there are eighteen possible suspects who were in the room at the time. Here's the list of names, including the two D.B.s. If you know something about any of these individuals, contact me or my partner, Skip Crane."

She gave the officers a copy of the list of suspects. They knew better than to ask a lot of questions at this point.

"Skip, come into my office and let's review what we know," diLongo said, when the meeting was over.

They sat down facing the chart on the whiteboard.

"We're going to treat this as a homicide, until we know it's not," diLongo said. "If it is homicide, we can't waste any time. We don't want to give our perp time to fly the coop if we're behind the eight ball!" she said, smiling at her own mixed metaphors. Skip nodded.

"So, let's work on the chart," she said. "On the left side, I want you to write down: *Means*. Underneath, write *Opportunity*, and underneath that, write *Motive*. When we can fill in all three, we'll have a plausible suspect," she said.

Skip got busy with the marker while diLongo reviewed her notes.

"Put a checkmark beside *Opportunity* for each of the names," she said. "They were all there so they all had the opportunity."

Skip did as instructed.

"So, based on the information we've filled in," she said, "it looks like everyone ate sandwiches and salads from the buffet table and most of them ate dessert. They drank the same coffee and made tea from the same hot water jugs. Some of them had wine, but not the victims. Some had beer from a can, including Mr. Digman. Mrs. Boland did not drink any alcohol, but she did have a bottle of water and some tea."

She looked at Skip. "So, you're a smart young man. What do you make of this?"

Skip squared his shoulders a little and cleared his throat. "Well, I'd say, if it's a homicide, there's some kind of toxic substance that was introduced to the victims at some point during the evening. Maybe it happened before they came to play bridge, and it took a few hours for the toxin to work through their systems. Since everyone there consumed the food, but only two got sick, I don't think the food itself was contaminated. Otherwise we'd have more victims, wouldn't we?"

DiLongo nodded. "So what if it turns out to be poison in the food or drink that only Mr. Digman and Mrs. Boland consumed? How do you account for that?"

"Well," he paused to consider this scenario, "I guess, in that case, someone would've added the poison to their food or drink once they were in the dining room," he said.

"So, in that case, the killer would also have been in the room at some point during the evening," she said.

"And the victims were selected for a particular reason," Skip said, thinking out loud.

"Yes, which gets back to motive," she said. "So, in this case, the timeline for contaminating the food or drink is what, exactly?"

"I'd say between 6:30 p.m., when the bridge players started arriving, and 10:10, when the first victim became ill," he said.

"Well let's consider another scenario. What if the toxin was already in the sandwiches they ate? It's possible to add the poison after the sandwiches were made and before they were delivered to the college. You could poison a couple of them, without contaminating all of them," diLongo said.

"That would indicate the murderer is someone connected to the college, but not one of the bridge players," Skip said, "unless, of course, there is a conspiracy."

DiLongo gave this some thought. "Do you think someone from the college hired an outsider to tamper with the food?"

"Well, Dr. Primrose said the sandwiches were catered by the Delish Deli, so it's possible someone could have tampered with them," he said.

"But that would mean Mr. Digman and Mrs. Boland were not targeted and this is a random act of violence, and that is, well, some kind of terrorism," Skip said. He looked skeptical at his own conclusion.

"How likely do you think that is?" diLongo asked.

"These days? In this area?" He weighed the odds. "I dunno. If it is a random act, it's more likely to be some psychopath or nutcase who has a grudge against the college and decided to do something about it. Wouldn't be the first time someone went off the deep end and committed mass murder at a college," he said.

"What do you suggest we do about that possibility?"

"I think we should investigate the deli and see if anyone there has a history with the college that might turn up a motive," he said.

"Good thinking," diLongo said, pleased that Skip was demonstrating he had a good head on his shoulders. "We'll do that this afternoon, while we wait for the M.E.'s prelim," she said. "Now, let's consider the other scenario, that it's not a random act of violence, but a targeted attack on two people. Any ideas?"

Skip studied the names on the wall. "Nothing really jumps out at me. It looks like Terry Digman was popular with some people, and not so popular with others, but there's no indication of a motive. As far as Mrs. Boland is concerned, people seemed to like her. It may turn out her husband has reason to kill her, maybe for insurance money, or out of jealousy. It's possible she had some kind of secret life going on that she didn't want anyone to find out about, and her husband got wind of it and freaked out," Skip suggested.

"Yes, Chris Boland is a suspect until we rule him out," diLongo said.

"Or maybe someone she was involved with outside of her marriage decided to do her in."

"What about Digman?"

"We'll have to dig into him," Skip said, grinning at his pun. "Find out about his personal life, if he has a girlfriend or two. Poison is the murder weapon of choice for female killers. So it would make sense that if he has a jealous girlfriend, she might want to get back at him."

"Revenge is a possible motive. Yes, and the girlfriend could be one of the women in the bridge club," diLongo suggested.

"Yeah, she would have had the opportunity," he said.

"Right. So what's the connection between Boland and Digman?" diLongo asked.

"I dunno. He's a good-looking dude. Maybe he's doing her on the side," he said.

"Okay, write this down at the top there: *Connection between the victims, question mark*," she instructed. "Can you think of any other explanation why these two might have been targeted?"

"No, I cannot. If they were targeted, the poison had to be introduced after 6:30. But how would the killer know which items to poison?" Skip paused for a moment to think this through. "Okay, so maybe the killer saw Digman go up to the table, and then introduced the toxin to the food on his plate. Same thing with Boland."

"Good thinking, Skip. So we have to presume there is a connection between Digman and Boland, and that's why the killer has targeted both of them. We need to figure out the connection between these two. Are they in cahoots with a third partner in some kind of illegal scheme that goes bad? Or do they have information about a third party that could harm that person, and that person decides to get rid of them? Boland is an accountant, so maybe she had damaging financial information about one of the bridge players. We have to investigate the lives of both victims and look into their backgrounds. Their connection may go way back, before either one of them came to work at the college," she said.

"Okay, I'm on it. Where do we start?" he asked.

"We start with the deli owner this afternoon. I've known him for years. His name is Mason Schwartz. Poison could either have been added to the sandwiches at the deli, or en route to the college. Let's go."

DiLongo and Skip went out to their unmarked cruiser and drove in silence along the winding two-lane highway towards Mount Salem.

They parked in the street in front of the Delish Deli, and walked in. The noon-hour rush was over, but a half a dozen patrons were still seated at small tables set up along one wall, finishing their lunch.

DiLongo identified herself and Skip to the server behind the counter, and asked for the owner.

A minute later, Mason Schwartz appeared. He was a balding, middle-aged man, heavy-set and jovial. He wore a white apron covered with stains from wiping his hands on it in the kitchen. He approached the officers with a big smile and said, "Good afternoon, officers. What can I do for you today? I have a smoked meat special, if you are interested."

"No thanks," diLongo said, "but we'll stop in another time for lunch. I know you make the best sandwiches this side of the Big Apple."

He beamed.

"We're here to ask you a few questions about last night," she said.

"Yes, I heard," he said. He looked around at the diners still in the cafe. "Hey, let's step outside. We can sit at the picnic table."

Mason removed his apron and shrugged into his overcoat. They went out and seated themselves at a picnic table underneath the spreading branches of a huge maple tree. Ice crystals in the grass crunched underfoot, left over from the rain the night before. The sky was a clear, brilliant blue, and the sun shone brightly, warming their faces, even though the early winter air pricked at their exposed skin. There was no wind to chill them, however.

"I heard about the two deaths at the college," Mason said. "Terrible thing. How can I help?"

"We're just looking into a few details," diLongo said. "I understand that Dr. Primrose ordered sandwiches from your deli to be delivered to the college last night."

"Yes. She ordered a few dozen sandwiches with a variety of fillings, some meat, some vegetarian, cut into quarters."

"Right. Who prepared these sandwiches?"

"I did, myself."

"Okay, and who delivered them?"

"My son delivered them. Michael. He's sixteen and I hire him to do deliveries and such. He has his driver's license. That's not a problem, is it?" he asked anxiously.

"Talk to your insurance company about that. Now, let's see. How long have you been in business here?" diLongo asked.

"Forty-five years. I inherited this place from my dad, who started it when he immigrated here after the war."

"Okay. And how well do you know Dr. Primrose?"

"I know her from years of catering her lunches and other events at the college. We just know each other for business purposes. I don't know her socially," he said, smiling.

"Have you ever met Mrs. Boland or Professor Digman?"

"Sure. They come in here for lunch sometimes — not together, as a couple, I mean. I've known Anne-Marie since she was a teenager. She's in here about once a month with some of her coworkers. I've seen Professor Digman here a few times with that guy who runs security for the college. He likes my smoked meat. I get a lot of business from the college crowd, you know." Mason kept smiling, looking at diLongo, then at Skip, then back at diLongo. "What—" he said, suddenly realizing where these questions might be headed. "You think I might have something to do with them dying? You think it was my sandwiches? You think my roast beef was bad or something?" He suddenly looked very worried.

"Thanks, Mr. Schwartz. That's all for now," diLongo said, choosing not to answer Mason's question. "We'll get back to you if we have any further questions." And with that, she and Skip got up and walked back to their cruiser.

As Skip buckled up, he said, "What do you think? He seems pretty straight to me."

"Yeah," she said. "I can't imagine he had anything to do with it, unless he has a private connection with either victim that we don't know about. We need to speak to his son. Michael's a teenager, so he'll be in class today. Let's head over to the high school and track him down."

It took only fifteen minutes to drive to the school, located in the neighboring town, Hillsville. A fleet of yellow school buses collected students from nearby towns and brought them in and out every day.

DiLongo parked the cruiser in the visitor's parking lot, and they went to the main office on the first floor. They identified themselves and asked to speak to the principal. Mr. Wallace, the school principal, came out a few minutes later and invited them into his office. It was a typical administrator's office, lined with bookshelves crammed with manuals and textbooks. There were two computers on his oversized desk.

"How can I help you today?" he asked, settling into his black leather chair.

"We're conducting an investigation into the deaths of two people at Kensington College," diLongo said. "We'd like to speak to one of the students here, Michael Schwartz. We have some questions for him, just to fill in some blanks. And for the record, have you ever had any problems with Michael — you know, with drugs or violence, that kind of thing?"

"Sorry, officer, I can't really discuss Michael's file with you without his parents' permission. But I can get him for you. Just one minute." He summoned his secretary and he looked up something on his computer.

"Michael Schwartz is in 203," he said to his secretary. "Would you please get him out of class and bring him here?"

She left, and while they waited, Mr. Wallace asked, "So, what can you tell me? What happened? Was there an accident?"

"Well, as you can see, we're just investigating right now. When we have something to report, we'll call a news conference in Beaumont, and it will be on the radio and in the next day's newspaper. I'm afraid you'll have to wait for that," diLongo said.

"I know people at the college," he said. The way he looked at diLongo over his reading glasses seemed to imply he had ways of getting information through his own sources.

"Really? Who do you know at the college?" diLongo asked.

"Many people," he said coyly. "Some of my former students work there."

"I see," diLongo said. "I hear there's a lot of misinformation going around on campus."

Mr. Wallace just shrugged, and gazed out the window. Then they chatted about the weather as they waited for Michael Schwartz to arrive.

A few minutes later, Mr. Wallace's secretary opened the door and Michael walked in. She closed the office door behind her and Michael settled into a vacant chair. He was stocky with black hair and a few acne spots on his face.

Mr. Wallace said, "Michael, this is Detective diLongo and Officer Crane. They have some questions for you."

Michael nodded and looked down at his hands.

"Hi, Michael," diLongo said. "How are you doing?"

"Okay," he said.

"Do you know why we're here to speak with you?"

"No."

"No problem. We'll explain. Last night, around 6:00 p.m., you delivered sandwiches to Dr. Primrose at the Administration Building at Kensington College, correct?"

"Yeah," he replied, looking up at diLongo with a puzzled expression on his face.

"We just want to know if you happened to leave the sandwiches unattended, even for a minute or two. Did you stop anywhere en route? Go for a coffee and donut or something? Stop to talk to some friends?" diLongo asked.

"No. I drove to the college, delivered the sandwiches, and then I drove back to the deli," Michael said.

"And what time did you arrive back there?"

"I don't know. I didn't look at my watch," he said, shrugging.

"But you didn't stop anywhere in between?"

"No."

"So, is it fair to say you are the only person who handled the sandwiches after your dad gave them to you to deliver to the college?" diLongo asked.

"I didn't handle the sandwiches!" he said. "That would be gross. I just picked up the platter and carried it into the building and gave it to Dr. Primrose. The sandwiches were covered in tin foil to keep them fresh."

"Do you know anyone at the college, Michael? Students, professors, staff?"

Michael shifted in his seat. "No," he said, but diLongo detected a slight reddening of his cheeks. *He's hiding something,* she thought.

"Okay, Michael. You've been very helpful. Thanks for your cooperation. You may go now," diLongo said.

Michael jumped up and left the office without closing the door behind him.

DiLongo turned to the principal, and said, "Thank you for your time, Mr. Wallace. We may want to re-interview Michael with his parents later, if anything further comes up."

"Okay, but give me a day's notice next time," he said. "Good day, officers."

Arrogant S.O.B., aren't you? diLongo thought as they left, and returned to the cruiser. She had never liked her school principals.

"Wanna get something to eat?" diLongo asked Skip, and he nodded. It was well past lunchtime.

"Okay, we'll pick up a pizza on the way back to the station," she said, and they headed back down the highway towards Beaumont. They stopped at the Slice of Italy on the way.

With pizza and Cokes in hand, diLongo and Skip returned to the station. DiLongo opened the pizza box and handed Skip one of the paper napkins that came with the pizza.

"So," diLongo said between mouthfuls, "what do you think that kid, Michael, is hiding?"

Skip shook his head, indicating that he either didn't know or couldn't say with his mouth full of pizza.

"We need to add his name under *Others* up there," she said, pointing to the wall. "I doubt he had anything to do with the deaths, but I think he knows something that might be helpful."

"Could be a connection," Skip finally said, "with the college crowd. Maybe he knows some of the students. The deli is close to Poppa John's where the college kids hang out."

"Yeah, that's possible. We should check out the scene at Poppa John's."

Skip agreed. He liked the burgers there, and it would give them an excuse to have a burger and fries for dinner.

"Write this on the chart," she said, "*M.S.'s connection to the college, question mark.* Why do you think a college kid would hang out with a high school kid?" diLongo asked.

"I dunno," Skip said, through a mouthful of pizza.

"Well, I can think of a few reasons. One, a college kid is tutoring a high school kid, or writing essays for a fee. Or…" and diLongo tapped her finger on the pizza box before lifting the lid for another slice, "Or the college kid is supplying the high school kid with drugs, or vice versa — pot, coke, maybe even crack. Three years ago, we collared a student at the college for selling pot to one of the high school kids. He was kicked out of the college and wound up in jail."

She removed another slice from the pizza box and took a big bite.

"If there's a connection, it's more likely to be about drugs. You know, you find young people on every campus every day getting high. Dr. Morrison told me he sees cases of drug use. We'll talk to Michael again and see if we can shake some information out of him. But even if there is a drug connection, it may have nothing at all to do with the deaths of these two bridge players. We have to be careful not to get sidetracked."

The office door opened and Captain Juno strode in. "DiLongo, Skip. How's the pizza? Got an extra slice?" he boomed.

DiLongo opened the lid, took out a slice and handed it to Juno.

"So," Juno said, "where do we stand with your investigation on the college case?" he asked before taking a big bite.

DiLongo pointed to the chart on the white board. "Take a look, Cap," she said. "We have eighteen potential suspects in a possible double homicide or some kind of accidental poisoning. Looks like the victims ate or drank something that did not agree with them in a big way. They were all playing bridge, like usual, on a Wednesday evening. There are fifteen adults and five students. All the adults work on campus, except for Chris Boland, who works at a local company as a computer engineer. It's his wife who died, Anne-Marie Boland. Oh, yeah, and this other woman, Tracey Kingston, who works at the hospital in Beaumont."

"Cause of death?" Juno asked through his pizza.

"Waiting for Sam's report. Should have something by six o'clock today. We haven't ruled anything out at this stage, except that there were no obvious signs of trauma. Sam says the victims were otherwise in good health."

"Okay, so what are your leads?" Juno asked.

"We think it's a toxin that was introduced to the food or drinks, so we checked out the sandwich angle today. We interviewed the owner of the deli that catered the sandwiches, and also his son. So far, nothing. Once we have Sam's report, we'll know the actual cause of death and then we can develop some better avenues to investigate," diLongo said. "If the poison turns out to be in the sandwiches, we'll have to investigate Mason

Schwartz, but if it's in something else, we'll look at all the bridge players who provided food or drinks that night."

"Keep me posted," Juno said as he left the room. "I want answers fast. I've already had half a dozen calls from Sharp Sharon," he said. Sharon Sharpe was a local reporter, but Cap called her 'Sharp Sharon' for the way she asked pointed questions. "And I'm getting calls from worried parents looking for answers," Juno said. "I don't have time to answer all these calls."

"Right," diLongo said. "We're on it."

CHAPTER 10

 PRESENT DAY — 3:00 A.M.

I looked at my watch and discovered it was already three in the morning. Strangely, I did not feel at all tired. After checking with Brian, who was cheerfully happy to stay, I continued with my tale.

"Our investigation showed just how weird and eccentric some of the bridge players were, starting with Daniel Post," I said. "He became a big pain in the butt before and during our investigation. He couldn't help it, I guess, as he was under a lot of pressure from Dr. Primrose to finish his book. Anyway, he kept emailing and calling Cap to get embedded in one of our cases. He thought we would appreciate being featured in his book, and he also thought he could help us solve our case, too. The man was pure ego!"

 TUESDAY, DECEMBER 2, 2008 — 10:00 A.M.

"What's going on with Grumpypants, Emily?" Belinda Leone was a tall, curvaceous black woman who had the cubicle next to Emily. She rolled her chair over to the end of the partition that separated the two cubicles so she could talk to Emily without raising her voice. Belinda had given Daniel the nickname 'Grumpypants' four years ago, when his mood and disposition changed after Marion died. "He's looking very strange, like he hasn't slept in days," Belinda said.

"I don't know, Bel," Emily replied. "It's probably just stress."

"What does he have to be stressed about? It's not like he has a big family to deal with. He just has himself! He doesn't even have to work. All he has to do is write his book and conduct a few meetings every week. He should try living my life for a few days if he wants some stress!" Belinda had the sole responsibility for four young sons and her elderly father who lived with her.

"What can I tell you?" Emily said. "One day he's up, the next he's down, like a yo-yo. I offered to help him research his book, but all I'm doing is tracking down basic information that I can't talk about because I'm under an NDA."

"What's that?"

"Non-disclosure agreement. It's a legal document. It means I can't talk about the work I'm doing for him on the book," she said.

"Okay, well, good luck with all that," Belinda said, and rolled her chair back to her desk.

Everyone in the department thought Daniel was busy writing every day. Emily and Gayle were the only people who knew that Daniel had not yet produced one page, let alone a first draft, of his new book.

Emily knew that most of the time he was in his office Daniel was either sleeping on the sofa or surfing the Internet for "inspiration" in between appointments with grad students and meetings with staff.

She thought he was making a little progress when he asked her to do some research on police procedures for certain things, finding out what brand of vehicles they drive (mostly Fords), downloading maps of various cities and towns in New England and researching other seemingly unrelated topics. "Genius at work," she mused. "He'll bring it all together somehow."

From the looks of him lately, unshaven, dark circles under his eyes, clothes more wrinkled than usual, she thought he might be working at night on his novel. He seemed to be completely unaware of his unkempt appearance.

She was surprised when, the next morning, Daniel arrived at the office all spruced up, wearing a clean shirt and tie and pressed pants. He was freshly shaven and had his hair trimmed. His mood was elevated as well.

"I've had a breakthrough," he announced to Emily.

"On the book?" she asked.

"Of course on the book!" he said. "I have the inspiration I've been looking for. I know what's going to happen now. It's clear to me. As Jack Nicholson would say, *Crystal*. Thanks for your help." He disappeared into his office, and then opened the door again to say to Emily, "We on for bridge tonight?"

"Yes, we're confirmed."

"Okay, then," and he closed the door. Then he opened the door again, "By the way, next Wednesday night is the Christmas bridge dinner." The Christmas potluck dinner was a longstanding tradition of the bridge club, having started in the Depression era of the 1930s. "Gayle wants you to bring in some cupcakes — you know the kind I mean, with your special icing and jellybeans. She says they are everybody's favorite."

"Yes, I know," Emily responded. "I got an email from her about it. She's providing sandwiches and some people are bringing a salad or dessert. What are you bringing?"

"I'm on snacks… potato chips, I think. Perhaps you could pick them up for me? I really don't know what to get."

"Sure, I'd be glad to," Emily said. "The dinner will be a nice warm-up to the Christmas season."

"Yes, it will be," he said, and disappeared into his office. Then he popped his head out again. "We're going to win the prize this year, Emily. I can feel it!"

Belinda heard this exchange, and she rolled her chair around the end of the divider between their cubicles.

"What's gotten into old Grumpypants? He's sounding downright cheerful!"

"Beats me," Emily said. "Maybe he's coming out of his funk. About time!"

For the past week, Daniel had been in a very sour mood indeed.

A WEEK EARLIER…

Daniel got up from the sofa in his office and sat down at his desk. He opened his laptop and when it had booted up, he went on the Internet to get the telephone number for the Police Department in Beaumont. He dialed the number and spoke to an officer, who directed him to the Captain.

"Juno!" barked the voice on the other end of the line.

"Captain Juno, Daniel Post here."

"Yes. What can I do you for?" Juno responded in his usual gruff voice.

"You know, I was in to see you a while back about my book," Daniel said.

"Yes, I remember," Juno replied.

"Well, I haven't heard anything since," Daniel said, "so I'm wondering what's happening. Is there a case I can sink my teeth into?"

"Well…" Juno said, trying to recall the details of their previous conversation. "Let me get back to you."

"So, Captain, here's what I've been thinking," Daniel said, ignoring Juno's comment. "Let me come on board as a consultant so I can be on the inside of the investigation. I can write the real story, not just what the news media want to spew out. You know what I mean? Reporters just sensationalize crime and make the police force look foolish just to sell ad space. They don't care about the police officers, how hard they work to solve crimes and keep people safe. I think there's a real story to tell, and I want to get it across to the tax-paying public what a terrific job the police do on their behalf. But I have to be on the inside to do it," Daniel said.

"I'll think about it. We don't have any big cases on the go right now. In fact, we don't get many at all. Mostly drunk driving or petty theft. Pretty quiet in these hills…"

Daniel interrupted him. "Imagine, Captain, if your investigation is the focus of my novel! Millions of people will read about it. You will be famous! And not only that, local people will read the book too, including the politicians who control your budget. When the public understands what bloody good work you do, you'll have more ammunition when budget time rolls around!"

Daniel had done some research and he knew that the Beaumont Police Department was always looking for more money to serve and protect. They'd had to lay off some staff a year ago, due to budget cuts. The only people who rejoiced were the criminals.

"Well, I guess it could be good PR for us," Juno said. "Let me think about it."

"Don't think too long, Captain," Daniel said. "I have a deadline, and I need to work the police angle into my story!"

"Well, I can't guarantee I'll have a case for you," Juno said. "And, I can't give you an answer right now. If something does come up, I'd have to look at the situation to see if it is suitable."

"What do you mean," Daniel asked, "by suitable?"

"Oh, I dunno. We have to be careful not to contaminate evidence and subvert normal police procedures," Juno said, "and, of course, you could not be a suspect in the crime, either. That would definitely put things off-limits," he said, laughing.

Daniel laughed along with him. "As if I would be a suspect in any crime." Then he started coughing.

"Anyway, we don't have a budget for outside consultants," Juno continued.

"No worries," Daniel said. "I won't charge a fee. I'll work alongside your officers as an observer, and maybe help them connect the dots, that kind of thing."

Juno sighed. He didn't want to alienate Daniel, a famous author and respected member of the community, but he found the author's persistence to be irritating and somewhat irrational. *What's his problem?* Juno thought.

"I'm just not sure about this. I have to consider all the possible issues. For example, what if there's a sharp defense attorney who makes an issue of you being involved in a case? If you need real police investigation material, perhaps you'd like to look at some of our old case files. We had an interesting one last year..."

Daniel said goodbye and hung up the phone before Juno could finish his sentence, annoyed with Juno's lack of cooperation.

I'm a celebrated author, he thought. *You'd think he'd die to have me come on as a member of his team. I just want to observe, for Christ's sake. What's the harm in that?*

You are right, dear, Marion butted into his thoughts. *He should never have shut you down like that. It's disrespectful!*

"Marion, I don't know what to do. I feel like I'm running out of time!"

Well, you've taken some action in the right direction, dear. Keep at it. I believe the solution is closer than you might think.

"I'm tired," he complained, "tired of all this pressure I'm feeling. I've got a pain in my gut and it won't go away, even with my new medication. It makes me wooly-headed. I won't take it anymore."

Dr. Primrose needs to be more understanding. Does she even know the effort you've made with the police? How uncooperative they are being? It's time to take the bull by the horns!

"You're right, my dear Marion, as always. I will talk to her right away!"

Then he picked up the phone and dialed an extension.

"President's office," her secretary answered.

"It's Daniel Post. I want to speak with Gayle."

"Hello, Professor Post. Please hold. I'll get her on the line."

A few seconds later, Gayle answered. "Hello, Daniel."

"Gayle. I just want to let you know I've been talking to the police in Beaumont about my book. I've asked them to let me observe an investigation so I can write about it in my book. I've been waiting for weeks to get in, and but they are giving me the run-around. I don't know what their problem is! You'd think they'd jump at the chance to have a respected author like myself involved in one of their criminal investigations so I can write it up in my book! I've even explained to them how it will help them out at budget time, but they are such narrow-minded fools, they don't get it."

"I see," Gayle said.

"I'm not getting what I need to finish my book, so I won't have the draft ready for Christmas like I promised, and it's all the fault of the idiot police captain!"

"Daniel! That's no excuse. You can't blame the police for not completing your book. That's just not acceptable."

There was a long pause.

"Balderdash!" Daniel said, and hung up the phone.

Daniel stewed in his office for a while, pacing back and forth, extremely irritated with Gayle for her negative attitude. Then he sprawled on the brown leather sofa and glared at the ceiling.

"Well, if the police angle is not going to work out, I'll have to find something else. Gayle's not letting me off the hook, so I better come up with something soon."

Yes, you'd better. Now think, dear. Think!

"Stop pestering me! When I want your help I'll ask for it!"

Is that any way to speak to me? Your problem is you've never had a good idea of your own. You always relied on me to give you solutions. Now you're stuck because I am dead. So, what's it going to be? Are you going to just loll about like a pathetic good-for-nothing, or are you going to show me that, for once in your life, you have the stuff great people are made of? What's it going to be?

"Balderdash!"

Daniel got up from the sofa and plunked himself down in his chair. He swiveled around to stare out the window. Dark storm clouds were gathering overhead, a sure sign of bad weather approaching the mountains. The clouds mirrored his mood, but somewhere in those clouds he saw a glimmer of light.

Murder by mind control. Wasn't that what Marion had said to him? He closed his eyes and half-dozed for a while, as images flew into his head and inspiration began to take shape in his mind. He began to write.

A few days later, Gayle sat in her office and pondered the situation with Daniel's book. She was concerned about his ability to finish the book on time. She really didn't want to fire such a valuable member of her staff. No, the biggest issue was the reputation of her college and her ability to attract high-profile students.

She decided to do what she could to help Daniel. She called Captain Juno at the Beaumont P.D.

"Juno," he barked in his usual fashion.

"This is Dr. Primrose at Kensington College," she said.

"Yes, I know who you are. Hello, Dr. Primrose. What can I do you for?"

"It's about Daniel Post's request to be involved in one of your investigations. Daniel Post is an internationally renowned novelist, and he's working on a new book. It's very important, both for him and for my college's reputation, that his book be completed on time. He has confided in me that he wants to use a real police investigation as part of his novel. I would consider it a personal favor if you would kindly allow him to shadow your detectives on a case. Daniel is a brilliant novelist and I'm sure the book will be another bestseller. If this happens, it could reflect very well on your department, and maybe even on your career and the careers of your police officers."

"How very interesting," he responded with little enthusiasm.

"What I'd like to ask is this: would you take him on as a consultant, even if it's a small, insignificant case? I'll pick up the tab for any fees. Let him in on your evidence process, your strategy sessions, interrogations, etc., to give him a close-up view of a real investigation. It's not like he's a news reporter looking to criticize your department. Quite the opposite. He wants to use the experience to reflect positively on the police."

"Hmmm," Juno said.

Gayle chose her next words very carefully. "In recognition of your cooperation in this matter, I'll arrange with the Kensington College Board of Governors to make a rather large donation to the Police Department's Children Christmas Fund."

"I see…" he said.

"Captain Juno, do you think it will be possible to let Daniel in on an investigation?"

"Dr. Primrose, I appreciate your proposal, and I will give it some thought. There is the question of liability if he should get hurt while participating in police business…"

"I'll take care of that," she said, "with insurance."

"And some things may still be confidential or off the record…"

"I understand."

"I'll talk to my people and get back to you or Mr. Post at the appropriate time. Your number?"

She gave him her direct phone number and cell number, and then she said, "Thank you. I do so appreciate your help in this matter."

She decided not to tell Daniel about the effort she had made on his behalf, as he was likely to ask her every day for an update. She would give him the good news, if and when it came through.

CHAPTER II

 PRESENT DAY — 3:15 A.M.

"Daniel Post was not the only unconventional character on campus," I explained to Brian. "The victim, Terry Digman, was also very interesting, as it turned out. He had his fingers in a lot of pies, and he tended to rub people the wrong way. Barb Baker, the mail services manager, for one, did not like him at all. During our investigation, she told us something that helped us unravel his activities on campus and expose the truth about his relationship with David Bartholomew."

"David Bartholomew? The head of security?"

"Yeah. They had a relationship, but it's not what you think."

 WEDNESDAY, DECEMBER 3, 2008 — 3:30 P.M.

Barb Baker loaded up her golf cart with bags of mail, and prepared to zip around the campus to deliver the mail to all the buildings on her route.

This was her favorite time of day, especially in the summer when the sun shone brightly and the air was soft and warm on her bare arms. Winter was not so great, but she bundled up in a warm coat and boots to keep from getting too cold. Luckily for her, the maintenance staff always cleared the snow before her mail rounds so she could easily drive the golf cart around. This day was overcast, but not too cold and there was still no snow on the ground.

Snow's late this year, she thought. *They should have tunnels here to use in inclement weather.*

It was getting close to Christmas, and the mail volumes were increasing. The student residences were first up. This time of year, there were a lot more parcels and letters coming through, some stuffed with cash for the students.

Barb made sure her bags were secure, and then she turned the key to start the electric motor on the golf cart. With the whirr of the motor, she began her rounds.

She was half finished when she noticed an altercation happening behind some recycle bins at the back of the Arts Building. She stopped the cart to take a closer look.

My God, she thought to herself, *it's David and Terry!*

It looked like they were having an argument. David pushed Terry and Terry pushed him back. David took a swing at Terry, but Terry ducked and laughed. David said something and rushed his whole body at Terry, crushing him against the side of the building, where they struggled in a clinch.

Geez, Barb though, *I can't call security! David is the security!*

She waited to see what would happen next. After a few moments of struggle, she saw them separate and glare at each other. Then Terry said something and David nodded. Then David straightened his overcoat and walked away. Terry turned and walked in the opposite direction towards Barb, who quickly started her golf cart, pretending not to have seen anything.

I wonder what that was all about, she thought, and continued on her way with the mail. *I'll have to ask Terry about it at bridge tonight.*

Later that evening during the break at the bridge club, Barb sidled up to Terry at the coffee table. "Hey, Terry, how's it going?"

"Well, if it isn't little Miss Twinkle Toes," he said sarcastically. "Fine with me. How are things with you?"

"Not so bad. Lots of mail these days. Matter of fact, I was doing my rounds this afternoon when I saw two guys going at it around the side of the Arts Building," she said, smirking.

"Oh yeah, how exciting for you," he replied evenly. "Did you get your rocks off?"

"That's not what I mean, creep," she said. "I think you know what I'm talking about."

"Hey, I'm a professor here. Don't call me 'creep'. And no, I don't know what you're talking about," he said. "Why don't you explain it to me?"

"I saw you and David, and it didn't look too friendly," she said. "I almost called the cops."

"You don't say," Terry said, "Well, I don't know what you *think* you saw, but I can assure you it was nothing serious and certainly none of your business. So keep your little pug nose out of it!" With that, he walked off.

Well, Barb thought, *I touched a nerve there! I wonder what they were arguing about?*

CHAPTER 12

PRESENT DAY — 3:20 A.M.

I smiled at Brian, who was now leaning back in his chair, a fresh Red Bull in hand. I commented, "One of the big surprises for me was finding out about Ben Chong, the Chinese kid. He was a smart dude, prepared to take some risks to get what he wanted."

Then I chuckled. "You had to admire the guy. A newcomer to America, and he managed to get into a frat house... but not by the usual route."

TUESDAY, SEPTEMBER 23, 2008
AROUND NOON

It was the second week of class as Ben Chong left his history class and walked over to the Student Union Building to have some lunch. He was feeling down.

Things had not progressed quite the way he wanted since arriving in America a few months earlier. He knew his academic career would take off with no problem, but one of his goals was to make friends and get established in his new college community. This was not happening.

Back in Hong Kong, he had discussed his future with his parents, and they agreed that he should attend college in the United States after graduating from the business college in Hong Kong. His parents chose Kensington College for him, partly because it was in the top ten academic colleges in the country, and partly because Ben's father, Ben Chong, Sr., already knew Dr. Primrose. Ben Sr. had met Gayle at a bridge tournament in England a few years back, and they had stayed in touch. Gayle had told Ben Sr. that if Ben Jr. ever wanted to study in America, she would be happy to help.

Ben was determined to gain acceptance and succeed socially in America where he hoped there would be no stigma attached to him for being of mixed race.

He was very sensitive about his mixed heritage, with a Chinese father and English mother. In Hong Kong, the Chinese students taunted him because of his blue eyes, and the white students shunned him because of his Asian looks. His mother always said he would have the best of both worlds, being half Chinese and half English, but it turned out that neither world accepted him in Hong Kong. That's why he had focused his mind on academics, and it paid off for him now that he was at Kensington.

When he arrived on campus, Ben was assigned to one of the campus residences. It was known as the foreign students' residence. The languages spoken in the rooms ranged from Urdu and Cantonese to Spanish and Russian… of course everyone also spoke English, a pre-requisite for Kensington.

Ben found it easy to get along with his peers in residence. They congregated in the lounges and joked around with each other. They played card games like poker and euchre, and some played backgammon and chess. They even cooked meals together in the small kitchens when they didn't want to eat the cafeteria food. There was only one problem: they were all foreign students. Ben was desperate to be accepted into American society, and hang out with other American kids his age. He wanted to plant his feet firmly in America where he could live and work for the rest of his life, marry an American girl and become a successful business professional. When his parents retired, he planned to bring them to America to live close to him.

That was his American dream. He never wanted to go back to Hong Kong.

Now, at Kensington, he was again stigmatized, this time as a foreign student, living in the foreign students' residence and hanging out with other foreign students. The Americans showed little interest in fraternizing with him or his peers.

He jealously watched the students who lived in the Sigma Chi fraternity house further down Residence Row. Known as the frat brats, they had the best parties and got the prettiest girls.

Ben figured that it would behoove his future plans to become one of these frat brats. He wanted to be invited into Sigma Chi, but he didn't know how to go about it. His natural shyness prevented him from directly approaching anyone in the fraternity.

On this sunny September day, Ben walked into the cafeteria as usual for lunch. He loaded his tray with soup and sandwiches, and looked around for a place to sit. Then he noticed one of the frat brats sitting alone at a table.

"Here's my chance," Ben thought. Screwing up his courage, he plunked himself down beside the other young man and said, "Hullo."

The young man stared at his soup dish. "Yeah, what's up?"

"Not much," Ben said. "I'm Ben."

"Lincoln," the boy replied. "Linc for short." And then he groaned and made a face.

"You okay?" Ben asked.

"Feel terrible... party last night. Went very late," Linc said. His unshaven face was pale.

"That's too bad," Ben said.

"Yeah," Linc said, "and I have an essay due this week, on Kierkegaard... such crap," he moaned. "I hate that guy."

"Really? I studied him in high school. He's cool," Ben said. Then he had a thought. "Maybe I can help you with your essay."

Linc looked up with interest. "That'd be awesome," he said. "You really know this stuff?"

"Oh yeah. My private school was big into this shit," he said. "European philosophers coming out our ears."

"Sick!" Linc said.

"You're sick?" Ben asked, puzzled.

"No sick as in good," Linc replied. "You know... sick."

Ben shook his head, and then said, "Oh, I get it. I thought you meant you were feeling sick... cuz you look kinda sick, ha-ha."

"I'm not sick, just hung over. Got into some bad shit last night," and he shoved his food plate away.

"You a member of the Sigma Chi?" Ben asked.

"Yeah, I am," Linc said. "Got in last year."

"I want to get in, but I don't know anyone," Ben said.

Link took a good look at him.

"Someone like you... don't think it's gonna happen," Linc said. "They don't let in just anyone, you know."

"Well, what would it take for me to get in?" Ben asked.

Linc considered this for a moment. Then he said, "You need to bring something very special to the table — cash, connections, that kind of thing — or you need to offer something special in a different way."

"Like what?"

"You know, score something special for the bigwigs in the frat." He raised his eyebrow.

"You mean girls?" Ben asked.

"No, man. The stuff that gets the girls," Linc said, with another raised eyebrow.

"Oh, you mean booze."

"That's not so cool. I mean stuff that enhances the party experience. Some good shit, man. Do I have to spell it out?"

Ben sat back in his chair. *He means drugs*, he thought. *If I can score some drugs, maybe I can get into the frat house.*

"I'm interested," Ben said. "Can you help me get in?"

"Well, this could be your lucky day," Linc said. "We lost our connection when the last dude graduated, and the shit we've been getting lately from the locals is really bad stuff. And guess what, there's a guy in the frat house whose roommate left after one week. Homesick or some shit. So there's a space available."

"Let's make a deal then. I'll help you with your essay this week, if you help me get into the frat house."

Linc considered the deal, and agreed. It would enhance his reputation with the Sigma Chi bigwigs if he brought Ben, as their new drug supplier, into the frat house.

"You gotta play this real cool," he said to Ben, who nodded in agreement. "Our previous connection got hooked up at this bar in Beaumont." Linc scribbled the name of the bar on a napkin. "You go there, hang out for a while. Tell the big bald guy behind the bar you're looking to score. He'll know what you mean. He'll set you up. Then I'll meet you at Poppa John's in town and we'll make the exchange."

"Okay. But if it's that easy, why don't you do it?" Ben asked.

"Hey, man, I'm already Sigma Chi. Consider this to be your initiation. Don't worry, I'll get the frat boys on board with this. You just do your thing and I'll do mine. It's the only way, man. You'll need about $1,500 in cash to get started. After that, just use the profits to buy the stuff each time." Then he wrote his email address on the napkin.

Ben was intrigued, and also little scared. He could come up with the $1,500, but he knew what he was about to get into was illegal. His student status in America would be terminated if he got caught; he'd be deported back to Hong Kong, or worse, sent to jail. But it was a risk he was prepared to take if it meant he could get a green light into the frat house, where he would have a much better social life: girls, parties and the connections he wanted for his future in business.

"And don't go talking to anybody about this," Linc warned. "If you tell anyone, I'll deny this conversation ever took place."

"Understood," Ben said. "I won't tell. Promise."

"Okay, let's talk about my essay. We can make arrangements for the other stuff later," Linc said. He pulled out a folder from his backpack, and laid it on the table. "I gotta pick one of these," he said, showing Ben the list of topics.

"No problem," Ben said. "I already wrote an essay on this topic here," pointing to the first topic on the list.

"Awesome," Linc said, smiling to himself. *Something tells me I'm into something good,* he thought, as the melody of an old pop tune that his parents used to play filtered through his mind.

LATER THAT EVENING…

Ben borrowed a car from his roommate, Rudi, an engineering student from the Ukraine. The car was an old Pontiac clunker, but it drove well enough on the hilly roads to Beaumont.

Once in the downtown core of Beaumont, Ben cruised around until he found the bar he was looking for. The entrance door was on the side of an old brick building. There were a few steps down to a grungy, dimly lit barroom.

Ben took a deep breath, opened the door and walked in. He could hear music playing in the background from a tape or a jukebox, since there was no live band in sight. Mixed in with the music was the drone of conversation and laughter, which would get louder as the night wore on and the beer kept flowing.

The room was long and narrow, with booths along one wall and small tables scattered about in the middle. There was a bar with barstools on the other wall where the regulars tended to hang out. At one end were two pool tables. At the other end was a raised platform for dancing.

The place smelled of beer and greasy food, like the million other barrooms across the country that catered to the down-and-outs of society.

Ben felt a little out of place, since his jeans were clean and his hoodie was bright white. He pushed the hoodie off his head, walked over to the bar and slid onto one of the empty stools. The bartender came over and Ben ordered a draft beer.

He decided to stay seated for a while to acquaint himself with the layout and the general atmosphere of the room. It seemed like a place where friends would meet for a few brews after their working day, and the regulars would hang out at their favorite tables.

Halfway through his beer, Ben found enough courage to raise his hand and attract the bartender's attention. "Hey, man," Ben said in a low voice. "I'm from the college. My friend said you can help me score some stuff."

"That a fact?" the bartender responded. With his shaved head and muscular arms, he looked more like a bouncer than a bartender.

"Look, I just want a connection. I'll make it worth your while," Ben said, and he patted his jeans pocket where he kept his wallet.

"You a cop? You look like one," the bartender said warily.

"I'm no cop, man," Ben said. "I'm a student at the Kensington College in Mount Salem. Here's my ID," and he showed the bartender his student card.

"Lookit," the bartender said, "I dunno nothin' about nothin', you understand? But sometimes there's a guy in here who… let's say he knows more than me." He winked, knowingly. "Where's my twenty?"

Ben pulled out his wallet and took out a $20 bill and slid it over to the bartender.

"Which one is he?" Ben asked.

"You see those guys in the back booth?" The bartender nodded towards the back of the room. "Talk to the guy in the red shirt over there. He can get what you want. But wait until the other dudes leave. I don't want no trouble."

"Okay, thanks," Ben said, and he slid off his stool to take a closer look. The back booth was on the way to the men's room. He pulled up his hoodie and walked in that direction. As he got nearer to the back of the room, he turned his head slightly and got a good look at the men sitting in the booth.

Holy shit, he muttered under his breath, and he scurried into the men's room before the men could notice him.

Ben leaned against the wall of the men's room. He could not believe his eyes. The man in the red shirt was Terry Digman, the psychology professor at Kensington, and sitting next to Terry was David Bartholomew, head of security for the college. Ben had met both of them at the bridge club a week before. The two men with them were dressed like bikers: leather jackets, big black boots, blue jeans and ponytails.

Ben clamped his hands together, squeezing hard. His heart was racing. *I'm screwed!* he thought. *How can I ask Professor Digman, of all people, to help me get these drugs? I gotta think… I gotta think.*

Then he realized that he would have the upper hand on them because they had not seen him in the bar.

Okay, calm down and think logically, he told himself. *Why would two members of the college staff be meeting with two bikers? The bartender told me to talk to Digman, so he must be the drug connection. Bartholomew is also in on the deal, and he's head of security at the college. So he must be getting a cut of the action. That's why there's no problem getting drugs onto campus — security looks the other way!*

Then he let out a low whistle. *I could go to Dr. Primrose with this,* he thought, *or, for the right incentive, maybe I don't go to her. If I tell Digman and Bartholomew that I know what they're up to, they'll have to strike a deal with me, and I can still get drugs for the guys in Sigma Chi.*

The more Ben thought about this strategy, the more he liked it. After a while, he washed his hands and pulled his hoodie up to keep his face partially covered. When he opened the door and walked back into the barroom, the back booth was empty. He waited a few more minutes, paid the bartender for his beer and walked up the stairs. He looked both ways as he exited to see if the way was clear. He didn't want to accidently bump into Digman and Bartholomew or the bikers.

Satisfied that it was safe to walk out, he returned to the Pontiac and drove back to the campus. It was Tuesday night, and he would be seeing them the next night at bridge. He figured that would give him enough time to clarify his strategy on how to approach them with his deal.

Back on campus, Ben sent an email to Linc, and told him he could meet him in the cafeteria for lunch on Thursday. He had access to his electronic files through an online server account where he backed up all his work. He just needed to download the essay, change a few things and transfer the file to his flash drive. With that little job completed, he decided to relax and listen to music on his iPod before turning in for the night.

In less than twenty-four hours, he would have his plan in place and with luck, he'd receive the invitation to join the Sigma Chi fraternity before the month was up.

CHAPTER 13

 WEDNESDAY, SEPTEMBER 24, 2008 — 7:30 P.M.

The next night, Wednesday, was bridge night. Ben arrived at the bridge club feeling excited and nervous. He planned to talk to Terry at some point during the evening.

Gayle surveyed the dining room as the players arrived. Daniel was already sitting at Table 5, in his usual spot in the North seat. Terry and Sally arrived together, and sat down at Table 2, Sally sitting East and Terry sitting West. Karl and Ben sat North-South at Table 3. A whole crowd of players arrived all at once. Gayle was pleased to see that everyone who confirmed had showed up, and they would have a full house.

When everyone was settled, Gayle made a brief speech. "Good evening, folks. The results from last week are now available on the bar. As you know, we are now in the final stretch for the annual prize! There are five pairs near the top, but even those of you who are lagging have time to pull up your socks and zoom ahead of the pack. Good luck to all."

And she sat down at Table 1 opposite her partner, David, who sat North for the evening. The buzz in the room quieted down as the players started on the first hand of the evening.

After about twenty-five minutes, Gayle called the round, and the East-West players got up and moved to the next table. The boards with the hands that were just played moved in the opposite direction. Terry and Sally moved to Table 3, where Karl and Ben were sitting North-South.

Ben pulled the cards from the board. His hands were shaking slightly as he sorted his cards, and his mouth was dry. He wasn't sure how to engage Terry in a private conversation. He certainly couldn't do it at the bridge table, so he'd have to get Terry alone at some point.

This was the deal, with neither vulnerable:

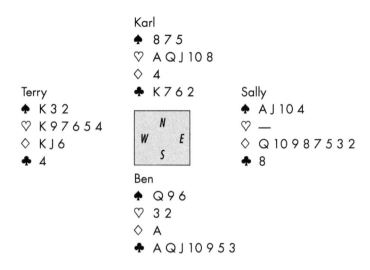

Karl
♠ 8 7 5
♡ A Q J 10 8
◇ 4
♣ K 7 6 2

Terry
♠ K 3 2
♡ K 9 7 6 5 4
◇ K J 6
♣ 4

Sally
♠ A J 10 4
♡ —
◇ Q 10 9 8 7 5 3 2
♣ 8

Ben
♠ Q 9 6
♡ 3 2
◇ A
♣ A Q J 10 9 5 3

Karl passed as dealer, figuring to bid his five-card heart suit on the second round. Sally elected to pass in second seat, even though she had an eight-card diamond suit. She decided to sit in the bushes on the first round, and come into the bidding later in the auction.

After two passes, it was Ben's turn to bid. Terry tapped the table impatiently. "So what's it going to be, Mao? Three notrump with two singletons?" he asked sarcastically.

Ben ignored him and stared at his cards, but he was so nervous he could not see them well enough to get a correct count. He blinked several times to make the cards come into focus. Then he realized he had missorted the suits. He had a club mixed in with his spades.

"Oh, come on, Terry," Karl said. "Ben's new to the game, but he's not stupid! Give him time to think."

When he had re-sorted his hand, Ben wondered whether he should try a preemptive bid of 3♣, since he had seven of them, but then he remembered Karl's instructions and opened with a bid of 1♣, to indicate his point count. He figured he could always repeat the clubs later to show his length in the suit. Terry confidently bid 1♡. Karl elected to pass, hoping for a chance to double Terry in a heart contract later. Sally had no interest in hearts, and bid the obvious 2◇.

Ben was tempted to pass, with Karl not having bid anything, but he didn't want to sell out cheaply, so he decided to rebid 3♣. He didn't really have a good enough hand for that, but at least he had seven clubs!

With good diamond support, a singleton club and a less than stellar heart suit, Terry raised Sally to 3◇.

Now Karl, with hearts over the heart bidder, a singleton diamond and great club support, decided that the hand lay well for their side, and jumped to 5♣. Sally thought about bidding 5◇, but she needed an awful lot from Terry to make eleven tricks, and partner's hearts would be wasted opposite her void. Instead, she decided to chance a double, hoping Terry would lead a heart, which she could ruff — if she could get back to his hand again for a second ruff, they might get a nice score. Everyone passed, and the final contract became 5♣ doubled.

Ben was dismayed to realize that he had to play the hand as declarer, since he was the one who bid clubs first. His heart rate suddenly jumped and his hands got clammy.

Terry indeed led the ♡6. The dummy came down, and Ben saw that he might have three losers in spades. Down one, doubled and not vulnerable, would earn 100 points for the opponents, not a bad result if the opponents could make 4◇. If the contract went down two or three, however, that would be a terrible result for Ben and Karl.

Since Terry had bid hearts, Ben assumed that he must hold the king, but did Sally have any? Ben called for the ♡10 from the board at Trick 1. Instead of a heart, Sally pulled out the ♣8 and trumped! Terry grinned at Ben and said, "Didn't expect that, did you?"

Ben's heart sank. He felt certain he would go down more than one trick now.

Sally considered her next move. She had the ♠A, but she didn't know if Ben had the ♠K or if Terry had it. She decided to play the ♠A next, and see if her partner gave a 'keep coming' signal, or a 'switch suit' signal. Ben played the ♠6, and Terry played the ♠3 as the board contributed the ♠5.

Having won the trick with her ace, Sally now considered her next move. Terry's play of the three did not make her enthusiastic about continuing with another spade. Being void in hearts and clubs, her only other option was to play a diamond, and hope that Terry had the ace.

Following Sally's diamond switch, Ben was now in control, winning with the ◇A in his hand. One of the first lessons Karl had taught him in the play of the hand was to pull trumps early so the opponents could not trump his good tricks.

He played the ♣A, extracting Terry's single trump, while Sally sluffed a diamond, not having any more clubs in her hand.

Ben wasn't sure what to do next, so he stopped to think.

Terry tapped his fingers on the table. "Got a problem, kid?" he asked, grinning.

Ben chewed on his lower lip, trying to decide his next move.

"Come on, we don't have all night," Terry said.

Ben sighed, and decided to play a small club, winning with his king on the board. He knew it was safe to play clubs, since Terry and Sally were now both void in that suit. He watched as they both sluffed diamonds. To give himself more time to think, Ben played another club, winning the trick with the ♣Q in hand. He had four more clubs in hand, with two more potential losers in the spade suit. He knew if he played a heart to the dummy and finessed, he could get one spade pitch on the ♡A, but he would still have another spade loser, for down one.

Ben decided to take all his club tricks first, and then see if something good happened when he finessed in hearts again. As he played out the clubs, postponing the inevitable, Terry became very quiet. He pitched all his diamonds, until the last four tricks. On the next trick, he had to choose between his winners in hearts and spades. If he threw his ♠K, it would make the queen good, but Terry didn't know if Ben or Sally held the queen. If instead he threw a heart, that would make all the hearts on the board good after the proven finesse.

After giving it some thought, Terry realized that he had to sluff the ♠K and hope that Sally held the queen. When Ben saw the ♠K on his last club, he could hardly believe it! Now his ♠Q was good, so he played it next. It was at that point that Ben suddenly realized he would make his contract by finessing against Terry's ♡K.

With a big smile, Ben played the small heart from his hand towards dummy.

Terry threw down his cards in disgust. "Partner! Why didn't you play another spade earlier? We had them down two!"

"You played the three of spades, discouraging," Sally shot back. "I figured you for the ace of diamonds!"

"It was the highest spot I had!"

They continued to argue about the hand as Karl scored up 550 points for their side.

Karl looked approvingly at his protégé. "Good job, Ben. That was a brilliant squeeze play you pulled off."

"Thanks," Ben said, quietly enjoying his moment of victory over Terry. He didn't want to admit that he had no idea he was executing a squeeze when he played out all his clubs. It was purely accidental.

Terry recomposed himself and started the bidding on the next hand. He reached 3NT, and played the hand quickly. They ended the round with five minutes to go.

"I'm going for a whiz," Terry said, as he collected his cards and placed them back into the board. Then he looked at Sally, "Care to join me?" he said with a wink.

She shook her head and made a face at him. He got up, laughing, and walked out the double doors to the men's room in the corridor.

Ben was still feeling pumped after his triumph on the previous hand. He decided he would take this opportunity to speak to Terry.

"I have to go, too," he said, and followed Terry into the men's room.

Ben didn't use the urinal. He just waited until Terry was finished, and then he said, "I know what you are doing, and I want in on it."

Terry looked startled, but then composed himself. "I have no idea what you're talking about," he said, as he zipped up his pants.

Ben looked around the washroom to make sure no one was listening. "I know about your drug deals, and I know how you're getting the stuff."

"And how do you know this?" Terry asked suspiciously.

"That's not important," Ben said. "I want to make a deal."

"Oh, I see," Terry said. "Okay, we can't talk about this here. We'll go for a walk on the quad after bridge tonight."

"I know David is in on it, too," Ben said.

"You're a smart little Chinaman, aren't you?" Terry said. "Never mind. I'll still whip your ass at bridge."

It was just after 11:00 p.m. when the bridge session ended. Ben waited outside for Terry to emerge from the building. Terry and David came out together. They spotted Ben, and motioned for him to join them. They all walked together across the street to the quad. It was a popular place for students to congregate between classes and over lunch hour in good weather, but at night it was usually deserted, except for young couples making out.

This night was no different. A slight wind scattered the leaves on the ground. The clear sky above was dotted with thousands of twinkling stars. The air had that crisp, autumn feeling.

Terry started the conversation. "So, David, I asked you to join us because Ben came to me with a proposition tonight in the men's room," he looked at David, "and it's not what you think," he said smirking.

"So, what's up?" David asked.

"Ben here wants to buy some stuff."

David looked alarmed. "What?"

"It's cool," Terry said. "He knows."

"What the fuck?" David did not sound happy.

Ben piped up, "It's no big deal. I just need some party enhancements for friends. Good quality stuff," he said.

"What makes you think we can help you," David asked, looking worried.

"Don't bullshit me!" Ben said, suddenly feeling agitated. "I saw both of you at the bar with the bikers. I figured it out. Just get me the stuff. I'll pay you."

"And what happens if we don't?" David asked.

"Oh, that's simple," Ben said. "I'll go straight to Dr. Primrose with my information!"

"You have no proof of anything," Terry said. "She won't believe you."

Ben was startled. He realized that Terry was right; he had no proof. He looked down at his feet, thinking fast. Then he remembered something Professor Schultz told him about winning at bridge. "To throw the opponents off their game, instead of following suit with your lowest card, play a high card. Falsecarding might make your opponents think you have a singleton and will trump in on the next round, so they may switch to another suit. It's like bluffing in poker."

He decided to use a bluff. "That's where you're wrong," Ben said. "I took pictures." He pulled his iPhone out of his jacket. "With this."

"God almighty," David said under his breath.

"So I know who your suppliers are, but I don't want to deal with them. I'll buy the stuff from you, and no one needs to know about our arrangement," Ben said.

"Why do you want to get involved, anyway?" David asked. "You hardly, uhhh, you know, seem the type."

"Why does that matter?" Ben countered. "Let's just say the drugs will help me attain another goal."

"Ah-ha, there's a girl in the picture somewhere," Terry said, winking. "Give us a minute." He pulled David aside to speak to him privately.

"Lookit, the kid wants our stuff. So we sell it to him. I don't see a problem, do you?"

"If he tells Gayle, you know I'm toast! And what if he goes to the cops?"

"He won't. If he buys drugs from us, even once, and the cops find out, he'll be on the next plane to Hong Kong, or worse," Terry said. "Don't you see? He's not going to spill the beans on us! If he does, he spills the beans on himself, too."

"Okay, so you think it's just a straight-up deal?"

"Yep. He's a college kid. They want to party. They want what we got, and we want their dough. It's a win-win situation."

"I get my usual cut!" David said.

"Well, of course, pal. We're partners. So, we make the deal with Ben?"

"Okay, you deal with the kid. Just give me my twenty percent," David said.

"Hey, I just had a thought," Terry said. "We need a new pipeline to the high school since the last dude left. So, here's the deal we make with Ben. We supply him with the stuff if he also handles our business at the high school."

"Not bad, Terry. Good thinking," David said approvingly. "Do you think he'll go for it?"

"Let's find out," he responded.

They went back to where Ben was standing. Terry said, "Okay, Ben, we'll make a deal with you. But you have to do something for us."

"What?" Ben asked.

"We have a little business going on with the high school in Hillsville, but our other business partner kinda went away. We need a go-between to supply our hungry little teenie boppers with the pot they so desperately want. We want you to handle this business for us."

"I dunno," Ben said. He didn't like the sound of it.

"Well, play ball with us and we all win, Ben. Don't play ball with us, and who knows… something bad might happen," David said sternly.

"Is that a threat?" Ben asked.

"You bet your life it is," David said.

Suddenly a bolt of fear shot up inside Ben. He remembered those rough-looking bikers. "Okay," he said, "I'll help you out with the high school. What do I have to do?"

"Not much. It's real easy," Terry explained. "There's a kid in the high school who handles our sales for us. He has a whole bunch of customers. So, you meet up with him. He pays you and you give him the stuff. Then you bring us the money, and we give you your stuff."

"Okay, I guess," Ben said, "but that's all I'm gonna do for you. Deal?"

"Deal," David said.

"Deal," Terry said.

Terry placed his arm over Ben's shoulder and said, "Hey, kid, now we're business pards. This could be very good thing for all concerned. It's a win-win-win type of deal, where everyone gets what they want. What could be better than that? So tell me, what kind of stuff are you looking for? We can get most anything, but some things take a bit longer."

They chatted business for a while, and then Ben left them and returned to his residence.

David and Terry walked back together to the staff parking area where their cars were parked. "I feel good about this new development," Terry said as they walked. "We get our business going smoothly again and make some quick cash. That kid's not going to snitch on us."

"I'm surprised he agreed to do the high school," David said.

"Yeah, we'd still have to play ball with him, even if he didn't agree. Whatever is motivating him must be very powerful."

"What would you know about that?"

"Hey, I'm a bona fide professor of criminal psychology, remember," he said, laughing. "When you told me there would be a job opening at the college I read everything I could find on the psychology of criminal behavior. Anyway, it kinda comes naturally to me. That's how I learned to play bridge. I read a few books, took a few lessons online. Now I'm a pro. I'm what they call a quick study. IQ of 165. Use it or lose it, Davey boy."

"Is that why you play bridge, to keep your brain sharp?"

"Partly. I played poker in prison with the boys, but it was too easy, man. Sure, I could be a pro poker player, but there's no mental challenge with it. It's all bluff and intimidation. I'm all about the brain, man. I gotta use it or I go crazy!"

"Poker, you can win millions," David pointed out.

"Yeah, I know, poker's easy money, but by the time I'm finished here, I won't need money. My plan is to build up enough cash to go live in some cheap, sunny place, maybe Costa Rica. With my salary and the income from a few little sidelines I have going on, I'll have enough cash set aside by the time I leave here. After I get settled, I'll just play bridge for the hell of it. Maybe play tournaments and take on the world-class players, you know. Poker is easy, but bridge is where it's at, mentally," he said tapping his head and laughing. "Like the drug business, you just gotta find the right partners!"

Then they got in their separate cars and drove home for the night.

As Ben walked back to his residence, he thought about this new business venture with Terry and David. He was feeling somewhat conflicted, knowing that he was entering into a scheme that was risky and possibly even dangerous. On the other hand, he figured if the head of security and a professor were in it, it couldn't be so bad.

CHAPTER 14

 PRESENT DAY — 3:45 A.M.

"I'm going for another Red Bull," Brian said. "You want a refill?"

"Sure, thanks," I said. Brian walked over to the counter and ordered the drinks as I sat back and reflected on the rest of the story. When Brian returned, I filled him in on some of the events leading up to the fatal bridge night.

"As the end of the year approached," I said, "things were heating up at the bridge club. There were tensions in other areas too. For example, we learned that David Bartholomew and Terry Digman were having some issues, based on their mutual business interests."

"Oh yeah? What kind of issues?"

"Well, if honor among thieves is uncommon, honor among drug dealers is even less so. Remember that altercation that Barb Baker reported? David found out that Terry had been cheating him," I said, taking a sip of coffee.

"David was in a bind. He felt he had no choice but to help Terry because Terry knew the truth about his past. So David agreed to keep campus security in the dark, and in return, Terry paid David twenty percent of their business deals. And it wasn't just the drug business, either. Terry had recruited women on campus to entertain his business friends, in more ways than one!"

 WEDNESDAY, DECEMBER 3, 2008 — 3:30 P.M.

The relationship between David and Terry went back several years. They first met in Canada, when Terry was not Terry Digman. In those days, he was Stanley Karakchuck.

David had a drinking problem. He was working for an old friend who owned a trucking company in Hamilton, Ontario, when he was convicted of aggravated assault. He had a prior conviction, so this time the judge gave him a time-out in prison. He was incarcerated in the same prison as Stanley, who was doing time for investment fraud.

They became friends and Stanley taught David to play bridge. A few months after his release, David returned to the U.S., where he took courses for corporate security work. Stanley stayed in Canada after he got out of prison, and set himself up as a business consultant.

When David applied for the security job at Kensington he needed references, and Stanley helped him by setting up fake companies to provide those references.

When Jill Wilmington checked David's references, she received glowing reports from all three companies, not realizing they were coming from the same source, namely Stanley.

At the job interview, David used his charm to secure the job. David was very pleased with the way things had worked out. He had landed a legitimate job with a good income. He didn't see himself as a criminal in the classic sense. He just wanted a regular life with the usual trimmings. His time in prison was due to bad judgment and getting drunk, not because he wanted to pursue a criminal lifestyle.

Stanley, on the other hand, was a career criminal. He enjoyed finding ways to further his ambitions without making the usual commitments for legitimate enterprise. He liked to make money without much effort, from goods and services that were lucrative. With his good looks and quick thinking, Stanley was able to fool most of the people most of the time. Many gullible people willingly gave him money for ventures that never saw the light of day.

Life was good in Canada once Stanley got out of prison. Working as an independent financial consultant and stock promoter, he used his ingenuity to build a network of friends and acquaintances ranging from drug addicts to corporate executives to frustrated housewives. However, he knew that good things never last when they are procured through false means. When he noticed a plain-clothes police presence in his neighborhood, he decided it was time to move on.

Like the good bridge player he was, always thinking ahead, he had prepared for the time when he would have to disappear from view quickly. It could be when his buyers caught on to his habit of diluting the drugs to make more of a profit for himself, or perhaps when the police received a complaint from another lonely widow who had lost her life savings to a lover with a hard-luck story.

Developing fake identities was one of Stanley's specialties, and he sold them for thousands of dollars to his criminal friends. He had a new identity as Terry Digman ready to go. He kept these documents at the local bank in a safety deposit box. When Stanley realized it was time to move on, he packed two large suitcases, closed his bank accounts, picked up his fake identity documents and drove across the border into New York state.

When the police raided his apartment a day later, they found only Stanley Karakchuck's belongings and a pile of bills. There was no hint of Terry Digman to be found.

Terry rented a motel room outside Buffalo, New York, for a few days and got busy on the Internet. He opened a Hotmail account with a new handle and sent coded emails to his connections on the Native American reserve near Cornwall, Ontario. His friends there would keep him supplied with the drugs he needed to pursue his business stateside.

Now living with his new identity, Terry contacted David when he learned about a job opportunity as professor of criminal psychology at Kensington. Terry thought this would be the perfect cover to pursue his criminal activities while working in a real job that would require little effort on his part.

He borrowed psychology texts from the local library and learned just enough to fake his way through a job interview. He provided forged transcripts and university degrees to support his application, and created false references for his consulting business. One of his friends was Ken Trotter, who had been an officer in the R.C.M.P. for several years, but was fired for dereliction of duties. He was an alcoholic, and for a few bucks, he would do anything for Terry. Ken provided a reference from the R.C.M.P.

When Terry Digman showed up for the job interview, he was pleased to see two women across the table, Dr. Primrose and Jill Wilmington. Terry turned on his charm, spoke with confidence and assured them he was an expert in criminal behavior. He knew from David that both Gayle and Jill were bridge players, and when he revealed his own passion for the game, he knew it would help him get the job.

David did his part to move the process along. He offered to do a deep background check on Terry Digman, something Jill normally handled. The report David produced had nothing but good things to say about Terry.

Shortly thereafter, Jill contacted Terry and offered him a two-year contract to teach at the college. The R.C.M.P. connection had impressed Gayle, and she needed someone with international law enforcement experience to fill the position temporarily.

When Terry arrived in Mount Salem, he found an apartment in a building close to the college. It came furnished and had a secure entrance.

He obtained the exams from previous years to help him devise lectures and tests. He figured the teaching would be easy for him. He planned to talk about his own areas of expertise: white-collar crime. The students would have to learn theoretical material from textbooks and research journals.

Once ensconced in his new job, Terry developed relationships with some of his students outside the classroom, and soon learned about their recreational drug use. He made a secret deal with a young man from Oregon who was looking to score. Terry said he would give him a good mark in criminal behavior if he managed the campus drug business. This student, a senior in the Sigma Chi frat house, jumped at the chance to provide himself and other students with a steady supply of pot, and to get a good mark in the process.

That arrangement worked for a year, but then the Oregon student graduated, and Terry found himself needing to find another student to handle the business.

David agreed to make it easy for Terry to conduct his drug business on campus for a cut of the profits. David knew that Terry's contract was only two years, and in the meantime, the money Terry paid him would be the start of a nice retirement fund.

By 2008, Terry's second year of his contract, the business arrangement between Terry and David was thriving, until one day in December David learned that Terry was cheating him. David overheard Terry on the phone talking about money to Ben, and something didn't sound quite right. David caught up to Ben later and Ben confirmed that the amount of money he had given to Terry was much larger than the amount Terry had reported to David.

When David found out about the discrepancy, he was livid. He wasn't risking his job and his future for what turned out to be a mere 5% of the take. The risk-reward equation was out of whack.

David cornered Terry outside the Arts Building and accused him of cheating, leading to a scuffle behind the recycle bins.

Terry denied the accusation at first, but when David roughed him up, and revealed his conversation with Ben, Terry caved, saying, "Sorry, man. You're right. I'm a prick. Let me make it up to you."

"I want it all," David said, "going all the way back."

"Well, I just changed the formula in the summer," Terry said, "before we got Ben going."

"Whatever," David said, dusting off his coat. "I don't care. Just have the cash in my hands by tomorrow."

"Okay, partner," Terry said. "No problem." And they went their separate ways.

The drug trade was not the only action Terry had going on campus. A month after he started working at Kensington, in October of 2007, he recruited some female students to offer fun times for his trucking friends. These guys hauled freight for companies doing business across the border, and they were always looking for some kinky girl action en route, mostly threesomes. Terry put up a website and advertised it in anonymous posters placed discreetly around the campus.

The posters said: "Girls! Girls! Girls! Want to make extra money and have fun at the same time? Hiring five or six beauties for occasional entertainment and hospitality work. High hourly rate for the right girls! Go to www.girlsgirlsgirls.com for more information!"

Once the girls connected through the website, Terry contacted them by telephone and explained what was involved. As expected, some girls were interested in earning money and others were intrigued by the naughtiness of the work. He would tell the girls where to go to meet their 'date', and then deposit money in a prepaid debit card account, so he never had to meet them face to face. Some of the girls, he was surprised to discover, were in his criminal behavior class.

Then, at the bridge club Halloween party, he was surprised and intrigued with Emily's portrayal of Nurse Ratched. On a hunch, he approached Emily to see if she'd be interested in making some extra money on the side. Terry knew some clients who would get a kick out of Emily's evil nurse persona, and he also knew she was looking for ways to earn extra money. He thought it would be a win-win-win situation, and he was very pleased when she agreed to do it.

But what pleased him even more was another discovery.

In early January 2008, Terry was hanging out at his favorite bar in Beaumont, when the lights dimmed. There was a small platform at the end of the barroom. Spotlights came on and some sexy music started as a woman walked on stage.

The woman was dressed in a tight-fitting silver outfit that shimmered as she moved. Her stage name was Ice-Is, adapted from Isis, the Egyptian goddess. She had long black hair and she wore bright red lipstick. Her face was powdered to look very pale. Terry could tell she had very good bone structure underneath all the makeup.

She moved her arms up and across her body and swayed around in time with the beat. As the music swelled, she started dancing with more purpose. Suddenly she stripped away her silver outfit to reveal a sequined halter-top and skimpy satin shorts that barely covered the intended body parts.

This earned some whistles and hoots from the audience. Terry was really beginning to enjoy the show. He noted that the dancer had very good legs. She began to prance around the stage, moving her body in time with the music, and turned around to jiggle her satin-clad bottom. The audience loved it. She continued her routine for several minutes as the men moved in closer to get a better look. She seemed to sense their interest as she went down to the floor, spreading her legs apart enticingly as she arched her back.

Then she rolled over on the floor, and in the process she unsnapped her top and it slid off her body onto the floor. When she stood up, her breasts were now bare except for nipple rings with little jewels that sparkled under the lights. Her pink nipples were hard and stood straight out.

Ice-Is began a new routine as she contorted her body into poses that maximized her physical assets to the viewing pleasure of the onlookers.

For her finishing act, she let her satin shorts drop to the floor, to gasps and approving howls from the audience. Her body was magnificent, toned, tanned and perfectly proportioned. She was completely hairless between her legs. She clamped her legs closed and swayed her body to the music, moving her hands seductively over her body and fondling her nipple rings. The whistles and howls of approval continued. With her legs still closed, she slowly turned her back to the audience, swaying her buttocks in time with the music. Still with her back turned, she opened her legs and bent down with her hair cascading to the floor, exposing her butt hole for a brief moment. Something glittered between her legs. She had genital piercings! A jewel on a small gold chain dangled between her legs. As she moved her hips, the little chain moved around and the jewel twinkled, sending the male audience into a frenzy.

Terry was intrigued, and he moved in very close to get a better look. He could tell her body was very supple.

The dancer was writhing on the floor again. She raised her legs and stroked them with her hands, then swiveled around and slowly rose back onto her feet, swaying seductively to the music.

She was nearing the end of her act when she faced the audience. She gradually moved her legs apart and lowered herself to the floor, doing the splits with ease. She angled herself so the men could get a good view of her pierced privates glistening in the spotlight. After a few seconds, she swiveled around and raised herself up on her feet again, crossing her legs as the music stopped. She bowed slightly and smiled to howls of appreciation from the audience, and shouts of "Do it again, Ice-Is!"

Terry was the only man in the room who was not staring at her body. He was fixated on her feet. Unlike many men who go for a woman's breasts or backside, Terry was attracted to the lower regions of a woman's body. If her legs were long and in good shape, and her feet well kept with painted toenails, he was in erotic heaven. He would spend hours massaging her legs and feet, rubbing and kissing them, and he especially enjoyed sucking toes. Some women found this very stimulating and it certainly got his mojo working. He would slowly work his way up the woman's calves and over her knees to massage and kiss her thighs, opening her legs to get into the more delicate areas of her body, where he would spend an excessive amount of time licking and kissing until she was completely satisfied. Then he would enter her and finish off quickly. His style of lovemaking never involved kissing her breasts or her mouth. In fact, he had made love to many women without ever looking into their eyes.

Terry moved closer to the stage to check out the dancer's feet and noticed a tattoo on her right ankle. It was an angel. He had seen that ankle before. He suddenly realized the dancer on stage was the H.R. manager at the college, Jill Wilmington. She was wearing a black wig, but now he could see it was Jill. And she had magnificent legs and feet.

The audience's enthusiasm gave him an idea.

A few days later, Terry called Jill on her office extension and invited her out for a drink in the faculty dining room. She agreed to meet him after work.

"What's this about?" she asked, settling into her chair at a small table near the fireplace.

"I caught your act the other night, in the bar in Beaumont," he said.

"Oh, really?" she said, sipping her drink. She didn't seem surprised. "What did you think of it?"

"I liked it very much," he said. "You are very talented."

"Thanks," she said.

"And you have great legs. Any time you want an erotic leg massage, let me know."

She gave him a 'get lost' look.

"So, I wonder if you'd like to do some private dancing, for a fee," he said.

"What? For you?"

"Not me. For friends of mine. Businessmen. They have private parties and they like to be entertained. They would love your act."

"I'm not sure," she said, although she was intrigued. "I don't allow physical contact. I'm not a hooker. I'm just into the dancing," she said.

"I understand," Terry said. "I can pay you $350 per performance."

"That's good money," she said. The bar paid her only $50 plus whatever tips she earned from the audience. "Well, if I agree to do this, you must keep my real identity a secret."

"That's no problem," Terry said. "I totally understand, believe me."

"You can't let anyone at work know about my little hobby," she said.

"I get it," he said. "I have my own private hobbies, you know. We'll keep our business arrangement strictly between you and me. Just another way to make some extra money the government won't know about."

Jill accepted the arrangement with mixed feelings. She didn't like Terry, and she didn't trust him either, but now that he knew what she did in her spare time, she saw no harm in practicing her special hobby for his business friends, far from the judgmental eyes of her campus peers.

From then on, they agreed to maintain a cool relationship on campus.

Jill enjoyed the work that Terry arranged for her. She found it exciting to display her body for the viewing pleasure of these men. The strong desire she had to expose herself in public was contrary to her upbringing, but her family would never know. She would have danced for no money at all, just for the thrill of it, but the money made the whole experience that much sweeter.

Jill hoped that her secret hobby would not get back to Gayle. She didn't think her dancing would put her job at risk, as there was nothing in her contract that stated she could not work off campus on her own time, but she was concerned about her image and reputation on campus.

The only person other than Terry who knew about her passion for erotic dancing was Barb. But Barb was her special friend, and Barb would never tell.

Of course, secrets like this are hard to keep forever.

CHAPTER 15

📅 PRESENT DAY — 4:00 A.M.

Brian was astounded. "So, Terry Digman and David Bartholomew were partners in crime going way back," he said. "I'm surprised about Jill Wilmington being a stripper. And Emily Warren making money as Nurse Ratched... who would have guessed?"

"As I said before, there were some interesting characters in this case," I said. "Let me get back to the story. Going back to the first week in December 2008, the bridge club was buzzing with anticipation over the preparations for the big Christmas bridge dinner — and of course they were competing for the annual prize to attend Dr. Primrose's New Year's Eve dinner party."

📅 FRIDAY, DECEMBER 5, 2008 — 2:00 P.M.

Gayle hated making this phone call every week, but she wanted to get it over with. She dialed Daniel's office number.

"So, Daniel," she said when he answered, "How's the book coming along?"

"It's coming along, Gayle. I'm making great progress," he reported.

"So we'll see something soon?"

"Sure, Gayle. The draft will be ready in a couple of weeks."

"That's good news. I'm so happy to hear that. Let's talk about our special event for the bridge club next week. You know it's the Christmas theme."

"Right."

"I'm ordering sandwiches from the Delish Deli, as I'm on a budget this year. I've put up decorations for Christmas in the dining room this week, so it will be nice and festive. I've arranged for some Christmas music too."

"Excellent! Sounds like we'll have a jolly good time."

"Right. So I'm going over the list for the potluck dinner. I have you down for snacks. What are you bringing?"

"Snacks? That's not right. I'm bringing curried chicken balls."

"No, Daniel. There's nothing on here about chicken balls. You are bringing snacks. You know, chips or something."

"Fine! I'll bring chips as well as curry. Maybe some naan bread too, from the Indian shop in Beaumont."

"All right, if you insist," she said with a sigh. "I'll let you get back to your work, then. Bye, Daniel."

"Bye, Gayle."

Daniel replaced the handset, and then he rang through to Emily's extension.

"I just talked to Gayle. She's got everything organized for the Christmas bridge dinner. She's having bloody sandwiches catered by the Delish Deli," he said.

"That's right," Emily said. "And I'm bringing cupcakes. I've got all the ingredients. I'll make them Tuesday night."

"I guess we'll have enough to eat. Bah... why sandwiches? I'll be glad when Gayle gets off this austerity program she's on. At least we'll have free drinks," Daniel grumbled, and rang off.

The Christmas bridge dinner was a bright light in the bleak, winter darkness every year. Gayle would allow the players to have any drink they wanted from the bar. Daniel indulged in the single malt Scotch, his favorite. With the fire crackling and the alcohol flowing, people were always in a good mood.

The previous year, roast beef had been catered by the college chef, compliments of Gayle. The beef was tender, juicy and dark red in the middle, just how Daniel liked it. The players brought vegetables and casseroles to complement the roast beef, and they even had Yorkshire pudding. Some players brought dessert. They made delicious Christmas cookies, squares with candied fruit and other fillings, slices of golden yellow pound cake with lemon icing, chocolate fudge brownies and cupcakes with jellybeans on top.

The cupcakes were Emily's specialty. Last year, Daniel asked Emily to decorate the icing with sprinkles rather than the jellybeans she always used. "I don't care much for jellybeans," he said. "They stick to my dental work."

"Well, my mom always put jellybeans on top. It's our family tradition. If you don't like them, you can always take them off," she replied, a little miffed that he had criticized her cupcakes.

This year Daniel didn't mention her cupcakes. However, he did express concern about the sandwiches. It was obvious Gayle was not going to the same trouble or expense for the Christmas dinner this year. That was a shame, he thought. He much preferred roast beef to sandwiches.

After she ended the call with Daniel, Gayle reviewed her list. She had confirmed several of the contributions from the players, but some were still outstanding. She rang Anne-Marie Boland.

"Accounting," Anne-Marie said when she answered her office phone.

"It's Gayle, Anne-Marie. Just checking up on a few things. Are you working on my year-end report?"

"Yes, I sure am. I'm about three-quarters of the way through it now. It'll be ready before Christmas break."

"Very good. I'll review it over Christmas. We need to have a meeting before the end of the year to finalize the details and deal with any discrepancies. I have my board meeting the first week of January, and it has to be ready for the governors to rubber stamp."

"I know, and I'm well prepared for that."

"Thank you, Anne-Marie. I know I can always count on you. So, let's talk about the bridge dinner next week. I'm going over the list of food that people are bringing. I have you down for potato salad, is that right?"

"Yes. I'm preparing our favorite winter recipe. It has apples and nuts in it, with a touch of curry."

"That sounds interesting. I'm looking forward to it already. It will go well with Daniel's chicken balls," Gayle said. "I'm providing the main. It's going to be catered by the Delish Deli. Just sandwiches this year. I'm making sure some of them are vegetarian, just for you."

"Thank you."

"It's no problem at all. Okay then, I'll wait for your report next week. I'm concerned that some of the faculties have overspent their budgets this year, and I don't want to draw any more funds from the war chest to cover overruns. It was bad enough last year when we had to do the renovations on the sports complex without the governors finding out. Some of those old geezers don't have any idea how important it is to maintain these sophisticated facilities if we want to attract quality students. They are so out of date!"

This was a recurring theme in Gayle's conversations with her chief accountant. Anne-Marie knew that part of her job was to camouflage some of the spending on Gayle's pet projects so the governors would not find out or question the details. Gayle, for her part, knew she could count on Anne-Marie's creative accounting abilities and her utmost discretion in these matters.

Gayle rang off the call with Anne-Marie, and then contacted Sally Brighton. Sally was in class, so she left a voice mail message. Then she called Terry Digman.

"Professor Digman," he said upon answering the call.

"Hello, Terry. It's Gayle. I'm calling about next week's bridge dinner."

"Gayle, the light of my life! How goes the battle?"

"Fine, thanks. I'm just wrapping up some details for the dinner, and I want to confirm what you're bringing. I have you down for bread and cheese. Is that right?"

"Yes. I've ordered some special Balderson cheddar through my contacts in Canada. And French baguettes from the bakery in Beaumont. They do them right. Very light and crusty."

"Sounds good."

"So, Gayle, you know I'm leaving at the end of the spring term. This is my last kick at the can. I want to be at your New Year's Eve party. And I'm betting that you can make it happen."

"Sorry, Terry. If I make a special case for you, the others will get upset. The only way you can attend my party is to win the prize. That's it. And it's only fair."

"Okay, so I'll win the prize then. Simple. If things don't add up, you're the one who does the calculations on your little laptop there. You can get Anne-Marie to help you fudge the numbers a little. She's good at that."

"What?"

"Oh, I know about your arrangements with her, Gayle. She's your… what do you call it… creative accountant… or partner in crime?"

"Terry, you're skating on thin ice. You don't know anything. And I'm not fudging the numbers for you. The bridge prize goes to the team that earns it. Legitimately. So, if you want it, you have to win the next two bridge sessions. Just like the rest of the players."

"Aw, come on, Gayle. You can indulge me this one time."

"You're incorrigible!" she said, exasperated. "I'm not going to undermine the competition just for you, and that's final."

"Have it your way," he said smoothly. "Sally and I have a strategy to win the prize anyway. Piece of cake."

"Fine. If you win it, I'll be the first to congratulate you."

"And I will kiss you on both cheeks," he said.

After her irritating call with Terry, Gayle called David Bartholomew.

"Security. How can I help you?"

"David, it's Gayle. I'm wrapping up the details for the bridge dinner. Everyone has confirmed what they're bringing except Sally, the Blacks and

Karl Schultz. Would you mind following up with them for me? I'll email the list to you. I've got a headache, and I want to go home early and rest."

"If there's anything else I can do for you...?"

"I'll call you."

CHAPTER 16

📅 PRESENT DAY — 4:05 A.M.

Brian shifted in his chair as I took another sip of my coffee.

"It's getting late," he said. "How much longer?" His need for sleep was beginning to overcome his curiosity about the case.

"Hey, I'm just getting warmed up," I said, grinning. Coffee had that effect on me. One coffee after 10:00 p.m. will keep me up all night.

"To really understand what happened that night, we needed to catch a break," I continued. "And we did, when Skip's research and my interrogation of one of the suspects helped to get these people to spill the beans. That's when it got really interesting."

Brian opened another can of Red Bull. "I'm still listening," he said, stifling a yawn.

"Well, we got the ball rolling when I received the M.E.'s report at 6:00 p.m. on Thursday, December 11. At this point, all we really knew about the first victim, Terry Digman, was that he had a reputation as a sarcastic S.O.B. and a flirt. Barb Baker had told us about his argument with David Bartholomew, so we knew something was going on there, but we didn't know what. We also knew that Barb and Jill had a very low opinion of Terry. We couldn't find any dirt at all on Anne-Marie Boland. Her husband refused to talk to us. I had a suspicion that Ben Chong was hiding something, but at this point, he wasn't talking. Daniel Post was being a pain in the butt about his book, but he was more of an annoyance than anything else. Our investigation was stuck in first gear," I said.

"But once we got the M.E.'s report, things started to happen." I pulled another clipping from the folder. "This is another radio report by Sharon Sharpe."

> THURSDAY, DECEMBER 11
> KENSINGTON COLLEGE MYSTERY AWAITS M.E.'S REPORT
>
> ANNOUNCER: Sources close to the investigation into the sudden deaths of two people at Kensington College last

night acknowledge that the police have no idea what caused their deaths.

With no physical trauma and no obvious wounds, the investigation is stalled until the Medical Examiner produces his report, expected later today.

Sharon Sharpe, News Radio 1015's crime reporter, is following the story. Sharon, what have you got for us now?

SHARON: Beaumont Police Captain Juno explained it to me this way. (begin audio clip) "What could kill two healthy people in such a sudden and gruesome way? We don't know if it is a virus, a toxin or an allergy to something they ate, but the M.E.'s report will clarify that soon, we hope." (end audio clip)

The Captain would not comment as to whether the deaths were the result of a homicide or terrorist plot. He said it could be a case of food poisoning or bad drug interactions. (begin audio clip) "We can speculate until the cows come home, but I'd rather wait for the M.E.'s report and go from there." (end audio clip)

The radio station has already received several phone calls from concerned parents about the safety of students on campus.

One parent complained that they were not getting any information from the police, and he was worried that it might be a terrorist attack with a deadly toxin, like ricin, or some deranged person going around poisoning people for the fun of it.

David Bartholomew, Chief of Security for Kensington College, would not comment, except to say that they have a private security service that provides 24-hour patrols on the campus.

I went to the campus today and met Mr. William Horner as he waited for his 20-year-old daughter outside her residence. He told me he was taking his daughter home until he was satisfied the campus was safe for her to return.

Dr. Gayle Primrose, Kensington College President, called me after receiving some phone calls from worried parents. (audio clip) "We have never had any security problems on campus, except for some minor incidents involving recreational drugs years ago. We have completely eradicated these drugs from our campus." (end audio clip).

Our files indicate that three years ago, an illegal drug trafficking ring was operating at Kensington, and several students needed medical treatment after taking drugs. Five members of a local biker gang were arrested and found guilty of drug trafficking, and since then, the drug scene on campus has disappeared from view.

I asked Simon Leung, an executive with the SOD (Stamp Out Drugs) organization, what he thought of the situation. (audio clip) "This doesn't mean they have a perfectly drug-free campus. If college kids want to get high, they will find a way to get their hands on drugs. The only way we can stamp out drugs on our campuses is to train our children to 'Refuse to Use'. That is the theme of SOD's drug awareness campaign for college campuses." (end audio clip).

Dr. Primrose said she was unaware of SOD, but that she would look into their program at the appropriate time.

I looked at Brian and grinned. "Cap was so pissed off when he heard this report! He came charging into my office and said, 'I'm never speaking to Sharp Sharon again! She's making us look like a bunch of incompetent yahoos!'

"Sharon was just doing her job. She knew we were at a standstill. I told Cap he should ask her out on a date, and then maybe she would be nicer to us in the future. He just glared and me and stomped back into his office."

I chuckled at my recollection.

"So everything hinged on the M.E.'s report?" Brian asked, the Red Bull kicking in.

"At this point, without knowing the cause of death, we just had to wait. But once we confirmed the cause of death, we went into high gear."

After their interview with Michael Schwartz at the high school, diLongo and Skip returned to the station. At 5:45 p.m., diLongo called Sam Baldwin's extension.

"Baldwin," he growled. Sam was a man of few words.

"Hi, Sam, it's diLongo. Do you have something for me?"

"Uh-huh."

"Good. I'll be right there." She told Skip to accompany her, and they took the elevator down to the bottom floor.

"Hey, Sam," she said upon entering his stainless steel empire called the morgue.

"Here you go," Sam said, handing diLongo a folder filled with papers and medical forms.

"Give me the ten cent tour."

"Well, I was suspicious when I saw the bloody eyeballs," Sam said. "So I had the lab guys look into it. It's a toxin all right, from a plant called *Abrus precatorius*, also known as Rosary Pea. It's a decorative garden plant and grows all over North America, but mostly in the south. It gets its name from the bright red berries that are sometimes used as rosary beads. The berries contain seeds that have a poison called abrin. This poison is so toxic that, if swallowed, it will cause severe vomiting, drooling, highly elevated nervous tension, liver failure, bladder failure, bleeding from the eyes and convulsive seizures, and will result in death unless treatment is provided immediately. Not a plant to be toyed with." He looked very smug. "The poison was in something they consumed. That much I can tell you. The rest is up to you."

"Good work, Sam," diLongo said. "How long does it take for this poison to kill a person?"

"Well, that depends on several factors: how much was ingested, how large a body mass we are talking about, the health of the victims. In this case, with the high concentration of poison in the bodies, I would say…" and he paused for a moment, "…a few minutes."

"Not an hour or two?"

"No. I said minutes. Half hour tops."

"Okay, thanks Sam. I'll read this report and I'll let you know if I have any other questions for you."

"Hold on. I still need contact information for next of kin for the male. And Chris Boland wants me to release his wife's body so the funeral home can pick it up. I'm preparing the release, unless you have an objection."

"Go ahead," diLongo said. "I'll get back to you on the next of kin for Mr. Digman."

DiLongo took the M.E.'s report back to her office and read it through to see if there were any further clues to help solve the case. Skip followed her into the office.

"The M.E. says it takes only a few minutes for the toxin to kill a person. It was in the food or drink that Mr. Digman and Mrs. Boland consumed at the bridge club."

She pointed to the chart on the wall and said, "Let's take a look at what the two victims ate and drank, and maybe we can figure this out."

They examined the chart.

Under Terry Digman's name, the chart listed the following items: beer, roast beef sandwiches, chicken balls, veggies with dip, coffee, cupcake.

Under Anne-Marie's name, the chart listed the following items: water, egg salad and tomato and avocado sandwiches, bean salad, garden salad, tea, cupcake.

"There's only one thing that both victims consumed," diLongo said. "A cupcake." Then she looked at Skip. "That must be the link, then," she said. "The cupcakes killed them."

Skip shook his head. "If the poison is in the cupcakes, why didn't it affect any of the other people?" he asked. "Lots of them ate cupcakes!"

"Good point," diLongo said, mulling it over. "Why did these two die, and not the others?"

Skip looked at her, shaking his head and diLongo shrugged. They stared at their chart. Suddenly Skip perked up. "Well, it's the only link. Since no one else got sick, the toxin had to be in only two cupcakes — the two cupcakes that Boland and Digman ate — and not in the others."

DiLongo nodded. "Makes sense. So how did the toxin get in these two cupcakes?" Then she jumped up from her chair. "We have to talk to Miss Warren right away. She made the cupcakes. It's logical that she could be the one who contaminated them."

DiLongo dialed the number for Gayle Primrose, who was still in her office.

"Dr. Primrose, this is Detective diLongo. Would it be possible to meet with you and Emily Warren in one hour?"

"Let me get back to you," Gayle said.

A few minutes later, diLongo's phone rang. It was Gayle.

"I reached Emily before she left to go home," Gayle said. "She is coming here to my office. We'll wait here for you."

"Good. We are on our way," diLongo said. "Please set up an office where we can speak with Miss Warren privately."

Then she said to Skip, "We're going back to the college."

They drove in silence as diLongo formulated a plan for the chat with Emily. When they arrived at the admin building, Gayle unlocked an office for diLongo and Skip to use to question Emily.

DiLongo took a small recording device out of her pocket. "Now, we're going to talk to Miss Warren. I'm going to record the conversation. I want you to watch her every move. We can't use the recording as evidence, but it might help us with our note-taking."

When Emily came into the office a minute later, she appeared calm.

"So Emily," diLongo said, settling down into a swivel chair. "How are you doing?" Skip sat in the chair next to diLongo, and Emily sat down opposite them.

"I'm fine," she said. "A little tired. It's been a long day and I didn't sleep much last night."

"I understand," diLongo said. "Mind if I turn on this device? Saves us from taking copious notes, and ensures that we have an accurate record of what you say."

"Okay, no problem," Emily said.

"I love these gadgets," diLongo said as she fiddled with the device. "They combine phone, camera and recorder. When I get back to the station, I just plug it into my computer, and the voice recognition software listens to the words and produces the text on screen. I can also broadcast through the phone. There's a very sensitive microphone here. Picks up everything. Saves me a lot of time. Very high tech stuff."

Emily nodded. "That's nice," she said.

After identifying the speakers, location and time diLongo began the interview. "So let's start with what we know. We now have the M.E.'s report. He has confirmed the cause of death for the victims," she said, and paused. Emily sat with her hands folded in her lap and waited for diLongo to continue. "The victims were poisoned — by a toxin they consumed shortly before they died. The toxin is called abrin, and it is from a poisonous plant called Rosary Pea. Are you familiar with this plant?"

Emily nodded, "It grows in my mom's garden and I've seen it on campus too. But I didn't know it was poisonous."

"Thing is, Ms. Warren, the M.E. has confirmed that the victims died within minutes of consuming the toxin. We have determined that both victims ate one of your cupcakes a short time before they died, and the M.E.

will testify that the toxin was, in fact, in the cupcakes they ate," diLongo said, stretching the truth a little bit. "Now, how do you account for that?"

Emily's mouth opened, but no words came out. She just shook her head.

DiLongo took a long, hard look at Emily, who now appeared far less calm than before.

"Miss Warren, did you deliberately kill Digman and Boland by contaminating their cupcakes?"

Emily suddenly found her voice. "No, of course not! I wouldn't do such a thing. I have no reason to! Anyway, other people ate my cupcakes, and they didn't get sick."

"That's because only two of the cupcakes were contaminated."

"Well, I didn't poison my cupcakes."

"Okay, then if you didn't, who do you think might have done it?"

Emily frowned. "Maybe Chris did it? Maybe he wanted to kill his wife for some reason, and Terry just got the poison by accident."

"Why do you think he would want to get rid of his wife? From all accounts, they appear to be a happily married couple."

"Every couple has their problems," Emily countered.

"Meaning…?" diLongo said, encouraging Emily to continue.

Emily sighed. *It's going to come out sooner or later,* she thought. Aloud she said hesitantly, "Well, I know they were having problems in the bedroom."

"Go on."

Emily chewed on her lower lip. "Listen, before I tell you this, I want you to know that I had absolutely nothing to do with their deaths. I didn't poison them. I have ambitions to be a doctor, to help people. I plan to go to Africa or someplace where they really need doctors to help the poor people there who are suffering from starvation and disease, especially the children."

"That's very admirable, Miss Warren," diLongo said, without conviction.

"But a few years ago, my dad died, and my mom got sick. So I had to stop my medical training and I got a job here working in the English department. I thought I could save enough money to go back to medical school in a few years. But my salary minus the taxes I pay are just barely enough to pay my bills," she said, and paused.

"So?" diLongo prodded.

"So, I looked for other ways to earn some money, you know, off the books."

"You freelanced?" diLongo asked.

"Sort of. Let me explain," Emily said.

"Please do."

"Will you keep this confidential?" Emily asked anxiously.

DiLongo looked at her and said, "Listen. This is now a homicide investigation. If you have information that is material to the case, I cannot promise to keep it a secret."

"Well, I don't know if it's material or not," Emily said.

"I'll be the judge of that. If it doesn't affect our case, I'll keep a lid on it."

"Okay," Emily said reluctantly. "I expect you will find out about this anyway," and she sighed. "Last year I attended a Halloween party for the bridge club. The theme of the party was to come dressed up as a character from a movie. At the party, we had to act out our character, and the one who did the best job of acting their character would win $500. That's a lot of money! I figured if I won the prize, I could put the money aside in a special account I am building up for my education. I went as Nurse Ratched, you know, the character played by Louise Fletcher in *Cuckoo's Nest*. She was named the fifth worst movie villain, by the way. It was a brilliant performance," Emily said. "Anyway, I borrowed a nurse's uniform, did my hair up to look like Louise Fletcher, and wore lots of makeup. I really wanted that prize money to save up for my education, so I put a lot of effort into my performance." Emily paused to take a breath.

"Well, it turned out I won the $500. I had a lot of competition from Jill Wilmington, who came as Hot Lips Houlihan, because all she wore was a white towel — you know, from that scene in *M*A*S*H* where the guys let the shower stall down and she's standing there naked. Jill got a lot of attention that night because her towel kept slipping down, but she didn't seem to care. I think she did it on purpose to distract the men at the bridge table! Terry came as James Bond and Sally came as Miss Moneypenny and they won a bottle of champagne. Daniel came as Klinger, you know, the Lebanese cross-dresser in *M*A*S*H* who pretends to be nuts in order to get out of the army? He won a bottle of Scotch. Gayle came as Miss Jean Brodie. David was Captain Hook — I thought he was going to get the $500 prize because she seemed quite taken with him all night. Chris and Anne-Marie came as Brad and Janet from *Rocky Horror*. There were others, too, but I forget them all."

"Sounds like quite the party," diLongo said. "Please go on."

"Well, a few days later, I got a call from a guy who said he knew about my Nurse Ratched performance. It sounded like he was speaking with marbles in his mouth to disguise his voice. He said he was a businessman and his clients could benefit from my special acting talents. He asked me if I'd like to make some extra cash. I asked him what I would need to do, and he said, 'Just act like Nurse Ratched.' I said, 'Okay. How much could I earn?' and he said, 'At least $250 for each performance.' And he said I could earn tips on top. He said it was perfectly safe, and all I would need to do is come to the Lakeside Inn once a week, wait in one of the rooms in my Nurse Ratched costume, and take care of his clients who would come to me. I told him I was not a hooker, and he said I didn't need to fuck them, just role-play. I wanted the money, so I said I would try it and see how it went. He said he knew the men and he could vouch for them. He said the men would hand me an envelope with cash in it. So I thought it couldn't be that bad. I would be in the Lakeside Inn, which is, you know, very upscale. They have good security there for the guests. They have panic buttons in all the rooms so I could always call security if things got out of hand. So, I agreed to do it."

"Sounds risky to me," diLongo said, frowning. "You went along with it?"

"Well, when you are desperate for money, you do things you might not normally do," Emily said. "It was a calculated risk. I figured I would be safe enough at the Inn. Just to be extra cautious, I brought a syringe with me, loaded with a drug that would knock out any guy who got out of control."

"You had a drug-filled syringe?" diLongo asked incredulously.

"Yeah, for my own protection."

"And where did you get this drug?"

"Well, I have a friend who works at a psychiatric hospital."

"Okay, but you know what you are doing is a gray area, legally?" diLongo asked.

"Yes, officer. But I've stopped doing it now."

"Why did you stop?"

"That's what I'm coming to. Okay, so once a week or so, this man would call me and tell me what room to go to at the Inn. He left a room key in an envelope for me with the concierge. So I would just get the key and go up to the room."

"I see," diLongo said.

"The clients would come in to the room, one after the other, four or five a night. And all I did was play-act Nurse Ratched, which culminates in the men taking off their pants and bending over so I can insert a dildo into their rectum, which gets them off. I never actually fucked any of them. Then one night, a few weeks ago, this guy comes in. He's a first timer. And

I nearly dropped my syringe. It was Chris Boland! He gave me the cash, so I started the game. He said he couldn't get it up anymore without fantasizing about being dominated. I could tell he was nervous, and when it came time for him to drop his pants, he stopped and said he couldn't go through with it, even though he had an erection. He said it was a mistake. And then he left. So that's how I know they were having problems in the bedroom."

"Do you think he recognized you?" diLongo asked.

"I don't think so. I kept my voice very low, and I was wearing a lot of makeup. But I suppose it is possible that he recognized my costume from the Halloween party. Anyway, after that, I decided to quit. I thought it was getting too risky, and if anyone else connected to the college should turn up I would be exposed. I didn't want people from the college knowing about it. I wanted to keep my freelancing a secret."

"Did you ever meet the guy who set you up with these clients?" diLongo asked.

"No, but here's the really weird thing. I think it was Terry Digman!"

"Really? What makes you think that?" diLongo asked, looking sideways at Skip, who raised his eyebrow.

"A couple of times, he forgot to disguise his voice on the phone. Also, at the Halloween party, he kept commenting what a great Nurse Ratched I made. He was always making these snide comments to me at the bridge club, you know, alluding to some sex act or other. I didn't connect the dots until later," Emily said.

"So, you think Terry was involved in this?"

"Yes, I am convinced it was him."

"Right," diLongo said, and she glanced at Skip. "Well, what all this tells us is that Chris Boland has a kinky side, but he didn't go through with it for some reason. Guilt, maybe. He's a devout Baptist. Maybe he confessed to his wife that he almost deviated from the narrow path of Christian morality. Do you think that's possible?" diLongo asked Emily.

"Sure. It's possible," Emily said.

"Or maybe he did recognize you, and that's why he couldn't go through with it. Maybe he confessed to his wife and told her the woman in the nurse's outfit was you. And maybe his wife was upset about that. What do you think she would do?"

"I have no idea, but I think she would be pretty mad," Emily said. "Not just about the morality of it. He spent $500 for nothing, and they are not rich people."

"$500? I thought you said it was $250," diLongo said.

"No, I said I earned $250, but the men paid another $250 to the man who hooked us up — who I now realize was Terry," Emily said. "Some of these guys were regulars, you know. They dropped a lot of money every month to get off that way."

"I see," diLongo said. Skip tried to keep a straight face. "So you think his wife would be upset with him? Or with you?"

"Well, I think she would be mad at him. And she would probably be disgusted with me for doing this kind of work. She was very uptight about stuff like that."

"Right, that's what I think, too. And do you know what else I think?" diLongo asked.

Emily shook her head.

"I think she was so outraged," diLongo said, "that she told you off for trying to corrupt her husband. Maybe she threatened to tell Dr. Primrose or your boss about your extracurricular activities. And that's why you poisoned her and Digman, to keep them quiet and preserve your squeaky clean reputation!"

Emily stared at diLongo for a few seconds, as the color drained from her face. Then she said in a cool, even voice, "I came here to answer your questions and help you, but if you are going to accuse me, I'm not saying another word. I'm calling my lawyer. If you want to talk to me further, you can set it up with him. Mr. Evan Thompson. He's in the Beaumont phone book."

And with that, she got up out of her chair and marched out of the room.

Skip turned off the recorder and looked at diLongo. "Wow," he said. "That was the last thing I expected to hear!"

"I know," diLongo said. "She comes across as Little Miss Innocent. But underneath that candy-sweet exterior we find the evil Nurse Ratched just dying to come out and wreak havoc."

Skip just shook his head in amazement. "So, what's next?"

"We have to organize a search warrant for Miss Warren's apartment, office and car for hard evidence to link her to the crime," she said. "If she's the one, we need evidence to convict her. We have no time to waste."

DiLongo went back to Gayle's office to speak with her.

"We've finished interviewing Miss Warren and she has gone home. I'm going back to the station now. Will you be available this evening?"

"Yes," Gayle said. "I'll be at home. Here's my home address and phone number." She handed diLongo a business card.

DiLongo left with Skip and they drove back to the station. DiLongo instructed Skip to draw up the paperwork for the search warrant. "While you are doing that, I'm going to have a private chat with Dr. Primrose," she said.

DiLongo called Gayle and told her she was heading over to discuss the case. Then she left the station and drove back to Mount Salem.

She arrived at Gayle's house forty minutes later, and parked in the driveway behind Gayle's Jaguar. There was a narrow garden with flower beds and shrubs alongside the driveway leading up to the front of the house. As diLongo walked up to the door to ring the bell, she noticed a vine with bright red berries next to the front steps. *Very interesting,* she thought.

Gayle opened the door and let her in. "Good evening, detective," Gayle said. "Let me take your coat."

DiLongo shrugged out of her coat and Gayle placed it on a chair in the foyer. Then they went into front room and sat together on Gayle's white leather couch in front of a crackling fire.

"What can you tell me about the investigation?" Gayle asked, anxiously.

"Well," diLongo said, "we know what caused the victims to die. It's a poison, actually. From a plant called…" and here she referred to her notes, "…*Abrus precatorius*, commonly known as the Rosary Pea." DiLongo watched for Gayle's reaction.

Gayle's hand shot up to her mouth. "Oh!" She said. "Are you sure? I have one of those plants in my garden. David gave it to me two years ago."

"David?"

"David Bartholomew, the college's head of security. He came over with a plant for my garden just after we hired him. It was a thank-you gift for being hired," she explained.

"Do you realize the berries are poisonous to humans?" diLongo asked.

"I had no idea," Gayle said, shaking her head.

"Someone extracted the seeds from the red berries, and we think they somehow contaminated the food that Professor Digman and Mrs. Boland ate," diLongo said.

"Oh my God," Gayle said. "You mean they were murdered?"

"Yes," diLongo said. "That's how it looks."

"Do you have a suspect?" Gayle asked.

"Yes, eighteen of them — everyone who was playing bridge that night," diLongo responded.

"Oh!" said Gayle, with dismay. "I'm a suspect too?"

"I'm sorry, but we have not ruled anyone out at this point. and since you have the plant in your garden, and have access to the poison, I certainly can't rule you out yet. You were also responsible for getting the food organized, so that gives you ample opportunity."

"Well," Gayle said stiffly, "I can assure you I had nothing to do with these murders. I am absolutely shocked that this has happened in my college. I cannot imagine why anyone would want to kill either Terry or Anne-Marie. I want you to find the killer as soon as possible, so we can get back to some semblance of normalcy around here. I'm getting calls from frantic parents and reporters, and I'm concerned about the reputation of my college."

"I understand. The local press is already on the story. We can't stop that. But we will do our very best to find the killer, or killers, and bring them to justice," diLongo said.

"Whatever I can do to help, please let me know," Gayle said, recovering her composure.

"In the meantime, since you are still on our suspect list, I want to advise you not to go anywhere until this case is cleared up," diLongo said.

"That's not an issue," Gayle said. "I have no plans to travel before next February, when I'm scheduled to speak at a conference in Munich."

DiLongo got up to leave. "By the way, I'd like to have access to the employment files of all the bridge club players. We need to do our own background checks on everyone. Can you make that happen?"

"Yes, I can and I will," Gayle said. "I'll have them ready for you tomorrow morning."

"I also need the contact information for the parents of all the students who were playing bridge that night. In case I need to follow up with them for any reason," diLongo said.

"That's no problem. I'll get that for you."

"One more thing," diLongo said, as she pulled her coat on. "I'd like to take a sample of your Rosary Pea plant back to the lab. Just routine," she said.

"Help yourself," Gayle said. "I'll get some scissors and a baggie." And she went into the kitchen to fetch the scissors.

DiLongo snipped a small branch with red berries off the vine, and handed the scissors back to Gayle. She then placed the branch in the baggie.

"Thanks, and good night, Dr. Primrose," diLongo said.

"Good night. And good luck, detective. Please solve this quickly!"

CHAPTER 17

📅 THURSDAY, DECEMBER 11, 2008 — 8:00 P.M.

After diLongo left, Gayle pondered her options. Then she picked up the phone and called a number on her speed dial.

"Hello," David said.

"David, I'm getting concerned! I had a chat with that detective tonight," Gayle said. "She told me Terry and Anne-Marie were murdered with a toxin from the Rosary Pea plant. That's the plant you gave me when you first got hired here, remember?"

"Yes, of course I remember," he said.

"Where did you get it?" Gayle demanded.

"I dug it up from one of the gardens, you know, on campus and put it in a pot for you," he said.

"You didn't buy it from a nursery?" she asked, incredulous.

"No, I was strapped for cash back then. Before I got my signing bonus."

"Oh, my goodness. So the plant you gave me came from my campus!"

"Yeah. It grows in many of the gardens," he said.

"Well, that's a relief, in a way. I'm not the only one with access to the plant. Anyone could have got it, which means any one of us could have murdered Terry and Anne-Marie." Then she paused for a moment. "David, you didn't murder them, did you?"

"Me? No, not a chance," he said, and chuckled. The sound of his laugh reassured Gayle.

"I know, I just had to ask. I didn't either. DiLongo thinks the murderer is one of the bridge players. But I can't imagine who it could be. I'm getting worried about this investigation. They want all the personnel files of every bridge player in the club. Who knows what they will turn up?"

"Where are the files?"

"Jill Wilmington has them. Why?"

"I want to check on something about Terry."

"Okay. I'll have Jill bring the files to my office in the morning, and you can take a look then. David, I'm worried. DiLongo said we are all suspects!"

"Take it easy, babe," David said. "You have nothing to worry about. Wait a sec, I'm getting a text," and he paused for a moment. "They don't suspect you. My buddy Earl at the station just sent me a message. They're focused on Emily. They think she poisoned some of the cupcakes. Problem is, they have no hard evidence to link her to the crime, so they're getting a search warrant for her place tomorrow."

"Emily! My goodness, I would never have guessed she'd be capable of something like this," Gayle said, somewhat relieved. "Well, that explains why the police were interviewing her tonight. I hope they find the evidence they need to convict her, or else we all remain under suspicion and the police will keep poking their noses into our lives. And with Emily free, who knows when she'll strike again?" The thought dismayed her. "This is stressing me out!"

"Yeah, I see what you mean," David said.

"Emily's a bright girl. She wouldn't be stupid enough to leave evidence lying around her apartment," Gayle said. "They probably won't find anything."

"You're right. She would've got rid of it by now," David mused.

"We're not safe as long as she's free, David. What if she decides to attack someone else?" Gayle sounded a little hysterical. "What should we do? For the first time in my life, I'm really scared and I don't know what to do!"

"Well, you don't have to do anything, babe. Let me handle it," he said. "I'll make sure things work out just fine."

"Oh, dear David. Thank you! I feel better all ready." Her voice softened. "What would I do without you?"

They ended the call, and Gayle sat back on her sofa and tried to relax. She had so many things buzzing around in her head that she couldn't think straight.

I wonder what David will do, she thought. Then she smiled. For the last three years, David had been her secret lover. He was the only man who had ever called her babe and taken her forcefully in the bedroom and other places. The thought of that excited her unexpectedly. She hadn't been interested in any bedroom activities in the last week leading up to the Christmas dinner, as her work schedule had been too heavy, but now she needed something to take the edge off. She picked up the phone and called David again.

"Be at my place in half an hour, okay? I'll be wearing something comfortable," she said in her sexiest voice.

"Roger that," he said, smiling. 'Wearing something comfortable' was their code for planning sex. While Gayle waited for David to arrive, she picked up the phone and called Jill's cell number.

"Hello Jill, this is Gayle Primrose. I need to speak to you about something."

"Sure. What is it?" Jill asked.

"It's very confidential," Gayle said.

"Of course. It always is, Gayle."

"Right. Well, I heard tonight from the police detective that it was poison that killed Terry and Anne-Marie — some kind of toxin from the Rosary Pea plant that grows all over the campus. I have some in my garden, too. I'm going to have all the Rosary Pea plants removed from the campus as soon as possible." Gayle said. "Anyway, the police think Emily did it!"

"Emily? That's hard to believe!" Jill exclaimed.

"You never know about people," Gayle said. "I try to run a tight ship here. I hire only the best staff and teachers to attract the best students and get the donations to keep this college at the leading edge. You've heard this speech before. And then something like this happens," Gayle moaned. Then she composed herself. "Tomorrow they are going over to Emily's place to search for evidence to link her to the crime, and once they get that, they will be charging her with the murders."

"Okay, so what's on your mind?" Jill asked.

"What if they don't find any evidence, Jill? We'll have a killer walking freely amongst us here on campus. Who knows where or when she'll strike again."

"What can we do about that?" Jill asked. "Put her in a cage?" and she laughed at her own joke, but Gayle did not find it funny.

"No, but I want to ask your opinion about something. When it gets out that one of our staff is suspected of cold-bloodedly murdering two people, our reputation as a college of high repute will be tarnished. I've worked too long and too hard over too many years to let that happen. I want to be proactive and deal with this as quickly and as quietly as possible," Gayle said.

"I see. What do you have in mind?"

"What would it take to immediately remove Emily from our staff?"

"You mean, fire her?"

"Something like that," Gayle said hopefully.

"Well, I'm not a labor lawyer, so we'd have to consult our legal counsel to find out all the consequences if you did fire her. In my opinion, if Emily is simply under suspicion, you don't have a leg to stand on. If she is charged with the crime, you may be able to put her on indefinite suspension. If she is convicted, I believe she would be in violation of her contract with the college, and you would be able to fire her for just cause."

"I see. I wish I knew what to do," Gayle said.

"Sit tight, Gayle. You may be ringing alarm bells unnecessarily."

"But Jill, I'm so worried," she confided.

"Well, we should all be worried. I believe we're all under suspicion until the police rule us out," Jill said.

"I'm sure I'm above suspicion," Gayle murmured.

"Don't count on it. Until they actually charge Emily with the crime, we can't take anything for granted."

"Well, I didn't do it. I have no motive. And if you are suggesting that I had anything to do with this, you are sorely mistaken, Jill. I have way too much to lose to risk murdering two of my staff. If I did want to get rid of them, I'd do what I'm doing now, calling you for advice on how to fire them legally!" Gayle was getting worked up again.

"Hey, Gayle, I'm not accusing you of anything. I'm just saying we are all under suspicion until the police catch the killer."

"I told you, they think the killer is Emily. What's that you said about putting her on indefinite suspension if she is charged?"

"I'll look into it tomorrow," Jill said.

"Okay. Good. Get the papers drawn up, just in case. And Jill, the detective wants the employment files for all the bridge players, including you and me. Have them sent over to me first thing in the morning. And I also want the contact information for the parents of all five of the students who were there. And… um… thanks for your help, Jill. You're invaluable to me."

After talking to Jill, Gayle felt somewhat relieved, but her nerves were still on edge. "Good thing David is coming soon," she thought, as she went upstairs to get ready for his visit.

Gayle needed this distraction. She keenly felt the pressure of having the police talking to her staff and investigating their lives. She was very worried that her relationship with David might come to light. That would hurt her image with the Board of Governors, and she'd have to do some fancy footwork to convince them that her liaison with David had not affected her work or professional judgment in any way.

As she prepped herself for her lover, Gayle thought about her large, extended family in Georgia, and how outraged they would be to know about her relationship with David. Gayle had never felt comfortable in the South as a teenager in the 1960s. She moved north, and after her husband died, Gayle devoted herself to the college. Her romantic life took a back seat to her business and professional pursuits. She did not see the need, nor did she have the desire, to bring another man into her life.

That changed when David applied for the position as security chief. Gayle had already interviewed several candidates, but she didn't care for any of them. When David, a tall, burly African-American man, walked into the room for the interview, she was immediately charmed by his easy manner and deep voice. She felt her body responding to his presence. She wanted him.

She instructed Jill Wilmington to check his references, including the letter of recommendation from his previous employer, the owner of a trucking company in Canada.

When Jill reported back that David's references checked out, Gayle offered him a signing bonus to take the job, which he eagerly accepted.

Gayle was aware of her physical attraction to David right from the start, but she was reluctant to act on her feelings until his three-month probation period was up. She was also worried about the propriety of becoming romantically involved with someone on her staff.

But her desire for him overcame her concerns, and one day when they were walking in the quad, she asked him if he'd like to join her for supper at her place. He agreed. Since then they had been sharing more than meals, and enjoying every minute of it.

She knew that they were an odd couple. She was fair-skinned and he was very dark. He was also a few years younger, but that didn't seem to be an issue for either of them. As a rebellious youth in the 1960s, she supported the civil rights movement and spoke openly for the desegregation of public schools, much to her parents' dismay. The desegregation issue was what got her interested in pursuing a career in education. Over the years, she slowly stripped away her southern identity to develop the persona she had today: a modern, educated, open-minded, independent woman of high accomplishment. Her new life was in complete contrast to her upbringing in the closed-minded world of the 1950s and 1960s.

In her old world, the idea of dating a black man was abhorrent to her family. In her new world, taking a black man as her lover gave her a special thrill. David was her forbidden fruit, and he excelled in one very important area: copulation. Never had she experienced the thrill of sex like she did with him. He took charge and made it exciting for her. He screwed her anywhere he pleased, inside the house or outside. He used his tongue liberally to make sure she was ready for him and he entered her repeatedly.

His kisses rocked her world, and the scent of him made her long to be in his embrace.

Occasionally he didn't bother to remove all her clothes. One time they did it like that in her office. After embracing and exchanging passionate kisses, David closed and locked her office door and lifted her up on the desk. She giggled in surprise as he pushed up her skirt and pulled off her panties and stockings. Their lovemaking was particularly enthusiastic that time.

They often went away on weekends to upscale hotels in Vermont and Maine. There was something about the anonymity of a hotel that turned Gayle on. One time they were alone in a hotel elevator. David pulled her to him and felt up her skirt and discovered she was not wearing any panties.

"Hmmm, what's this?" he said, caressing her wetness. He pulled up her skirt and pushed his face between her legs, forcing her legs apart as he slipped his tongue inside her. For a few moments, they both forgot they were in an elevator, much to the amusement of a young couple on the 33rd floor when the elevator doors opened.

Gayle thoroughly enjoyed her relationship with David, but she could not afford to make it public. She was his boss, and she didn't want people making judgments about them or questioning her motivation in hiring him.

For his part, David didn't want Gayle to be found in a conflict of interest and possibly be forced to let him go. He knew she would give him a good buy-out package, but that would not be enough to keep him in the lifestyle he wanted. He needed his position at the college to do that. David figured that so long as he could satisfy Gayle's sexual needs, his job was secure. In any case, he enjoyed their bedroom activities. Sex with Gayle was one of the perks of his job.

So, for their own individual reasons, Gayle and David wanted to keep their personal relationship top secret.

At 9:00 p.m. sharp, David inserted a key into the lock of Gayle's front door and entered. Gayle was waiting for him in the front room, wearing a long, silky robe that was tied loosely together at her waist. David smiled approvingly. He suspected she was naked underneath.

Logs burned and crackled in the fireplace, and two glasses and a bottle of wine sat on the marble coffee table. Gayle's wine glass was half full. His was empty.

"Hi, babe," he said, closing and locking the door behind him. She was sipping her wine and she waved for him to come and join her. He removed his coat and shoes, and sat beside her on the white leather sofa. Before she said a word, he pressed his lips against hers and explored the inside of her mouth with his tongue. "Mmmm," he said. "I taste red wine. Give me some, babe."

She poured a glass for him, but instead of giving it to him, she took a sip herself. Then she kissed him and squirted the wine from her mouth into his.

"Now, that's the way I like it," he said, licking his lips after their kiss.

"That's the beauty of our relationship," she responded, rubbing her hand against his crotch until his penis became hard. "We know what the other likes, and we deliver." She giggled like a teenager.

They continued chatting, cuddling and kissing for a while, avoiding any mention of the murder investigation. Gayle's robe loosened, exposing her left breast. When David saw this, he undid the tie and pulled the front of her robe apart so she was fully exposed. As expected, she was naked. He cupped her left breast in his hand and fondled her nipple to make it hard. He kept working the nipple and nuzzling her neck, until she could no longer stand it. They almost tipped over the coffee table in their haste to make love. It had been over a week since their last session, and Gayle was more than ready for him.

Following their torrid encounter in her living room, they had a late dinner in the dining nook off the kitchen and then a bubble bath in her big Jacuzzi upstairs, followed by more lovemaking in her bedroom.

David stayed with her for several hours, then returned to his apartment, located only five blocks from the campus. It was an old-fashioned house with a high roof and two apartments. He used the back staircase to climb up to the second floor. His elderly landlord, Dick Henderson, who was almost totally deaf, slept in the front room on the first floor, so he would not hear David's arrival.

David took a beer out of the refrigerator and sat down at his kitchen table to think.

He had promised Gayle he would take care of things, so now he had to deliver. He had formulated a plan that was simple and could be accomplished with little fuss, he thought. He went over the details in his mind for the tenth time, to ensure he had everything worked out.

He finished his beer and headed to the bathroom for his nightly ritual before bed: empty bladder, wash face and hands, brush teeth, in that order.

As he fell into bed, he felt a little thrill of excitement, or was it anxiety? He shrugged it off and went right to sleep.

The next morning he quickly showered, dressed and drove to the campus. He stopped in to Gayle's office for a few minutes to examine Terry

Digman's personnel file. When the secretary was not looking, he removed the report that he had done on Terry's background. Then he went on to his office to take care of a few things and catch up on emails.

He had a plan, and he would execute it over his lunch hour.

CHAPTER 18

📅 FRIDAY, DECEMBER 12, 2008 — 12:00 NOON

DiLongo called Skip into her office. It was Friday just after noon, and she had briefed the shift change on the status of their case. The issue she needed to deal with now was finding enough evidence to charge Emily Warren.

Skip took a call on his cell phone, and reported to diLongo. "Chris Boland called. He wants to know if we've made any progress with the case."

"Call him back and tell him I'll give him an update later on today," diLongo said. "Make sure he's available, in case I need to ask him more questions."

Skip went back to his desk and made the call. Then he returned to diLongo's office. DiLongo indicated towards a chair for him to sit.

"Okay, let's review our case. We know the C.O.D. is the toxin, we know the murder weapon is the cupcake, we know Miss Warren has the means and opportunity," diLongo said, "but we need hard evidence that links her to the crime before we can charge her."

"Well, I prepared the paperwork for the search warrant before I left last night," Skip said, "and one of the officers took it to Judge Malloy's office this morning. We should have it any time now."

"Okay, perfect," diLongo said, continuing her thoughts. "And then there's the issue of motive. What's her motive? We can only speculate that Mrs. Boland called Miss Warren and threatened to expose her extracurricular activities. We can maybe make the case that Miss Warren fingered Digman as her pimp and decided to eliminate him before he spilled the beans, but honestly, it's not as strong a motive as I would like. Unless we find the toxin on her person or her property, we don't have much of a case against her."

"Hmmm," Skip said, thinking out loud. "If the search warrant comes up dry, we'll be up the creek without a paddle."

"Let's cross that bridge when we come to it," diLongo replied, chuckling at their clichés. "By the way, Dr. Primrose left me a voice mail this morning. You can pick up the personnel files from her office when we go to execute the warrant."

A few minutes later, an officer handed diLongo the search warrant. She arranged for a second cruiser to follow them as backup as they headed up to the college. She told Skip to drive so she could call Gayle Primrose.

Gayle answered on the first ring. After the preliminaries, diLongo said, "Please have Emily Warren come to your office, and keep her there until we arrive."

Gayle agreed, and diLongo ended the call.

Then to Skip she said, "First, we'll go to the Baxter Building. You can get those personnel files and we'll pick up Miss Warren and take her with us. I want her to be there when we search her place. I don't want any suggestion that the police planted evidence against her, in case we do find something," Then she impatiently gestured towards the road. "Drive! We have no time to waste!"

The two police cars sped along the highway to Mount Salem with their lights flashing the entire way. Upon arriving at the campus, diLongo instructed the other two officers to wait in front of the Baxter Building while she and Skip climbed the stairs to Gayle's office. When they entered the office, Emily was seated in a chair. She looked worried.

"What's this all about?" she asked.

"Miss Warren, I am here to inform you that we have obtained a search warrant for your home, your car and your office. We will be executing the warrant immediately at your home. Please come with us."

Emily looked at Gayle and said, "You knew this was happening, and you didn't warn me?"

"Sorry, Emily. I couldn't," Gayle said coolly.

Emily turned to diLongo. "What are you looking for?"

"We are looking for evidence in the murder investigation of Terry Digman and Anne-Marie Boland," diLongo said.

"And you think you're going to find something in my place? Good luck," she said.

"Please come with us now," diLongo said briskly.

They drove with lights flashing to Emily's apartment. The two officers following them turned on their siren as they sped towards Emily's apartment building. "Nothing like alarming the neighborhood in the middle of the day," diLongo muttered.

By one o'clock on Friday afternoon, Daniel Post was getting antsy. He was trying to work on his novel, but his mind kept wandering. He was waiting for a phone call from the police department to let him know whether he would be allowed to monitor the investigation into the deaths of Terry Digman and Anne-Marie Boland.

He shook his head and wiped his eyes. For some reason, he could not focus his mind on the task at hand. In the pit of his stomach he could feel the pinch of anxiety threatening to take hold.

"I need to find out where I stand," he muttered. He picked up the phone and dialed the number on diLongo's card. The call went to her cell phone.

"DiLongo here," she said.

"Detective, this is Daniel Post. I'm calling about the investigation into the deaths of my two colleagues."

"I'm very busy at the moment," she said. "Please call back later this afternoon."

"Wait just a minute," he said. He could hear a police siren in the background. "This morning, I sent you an email requesting the opportunity to shadow your team and observe your investigation into this matter. Would you mind advising me of the status of my request?"

"I will be happy to when I get back to the station, Mr. Post. I will call you back later today," she said. "I'm busy doing police work right now."

"Well, can you tell me this much: am I a suspect? Is that why there is a delay?" he persisted.

"All I can say is that our investigation continues. I'll get back to you later today regarding your request. Good day, Mr. Post," she said, and hung up.

"Him again?" Skip asked diLongo. They were nearing Emily's neighborhood. Emily was in the other police car following them.

"Yep. He's very insistent on having his name cleared so he can observe the investigation. I wonder if he knows we're looking at his assistant?"

"I don't see how he would."

"Well, you know the rumor mill. Sometimes people learn things they are not supposed to know," she said. "I like to keep a lid on things."

"Yeah, maybe Dr. Primrose figured out last night we are looking at Miss Warren as the murderer. She could have tipped off Mr. Post," Skip speculated.

"Still, he has a point," diLongo said. "If we cleared his name, we could let him observe some of our procedures. What do we have on him, anyway?"

"Well, as you requested, I've been looking into the backgrounds of all the suspects. It will be easier once I go through their personnel files," he said. "But there's a lot on the Internet about Post, because he's a celebrity of sorts. His wife died just a few years ago. I talked to one of his past colleagues and also to an editor at his publishing house. Apparently he was known as an eccentric before he ever came to Kensington College. Many creative people are super sensitive, it seems." Skip paused for a breath. "His colleague put me onto a couple, the Bentleys, who live in Washington and knew both Mr. and Mrs. Post socially. Mrs. Bentley was a childhood friend of Marion Post. She told me that after their marriage, Daniel Post settled down and the next twenty years were his most productive, work-wise. He wrote several bestselling novels. He also wrote articles for the New Yorker and he was a frequent guest on talk shows. He was seen in the company of people like Oprah and Bill Clinton. Then Gayle Primrose hired him to teach a creative writing class. It's a cushy job. He teaches one class a day, and the rest of the time he writes books. He was writing one when his wife died suddenly of ovarian cancer. That's when he went off the deep end — had some kind of breakdown. His book still isn't finished."

"I know. He thinks that observing our investigation will help him work out some details for his book," diLongo said. "No wonder he wants to shadow us."

"So far, I don't see anything suspicious in his background. He's just an eccentric old guy who makes a living from writing books and teaching," Skip said.

"I see," diLongo said. "We'll have to get back to him later after I talk to Cap. I still have some questions about the crime. How did the toxin get into the cupcakes? And what is the motive?"

"And how did Miss Warren know which cupcakes the victims would eat?" Skip added.

📅 SEVERAL MINUTES EARLIER…

David was finally ready to execute his plan. Thanks to his buddy Earl, he knew the police were about to search Emily's place.

As he left his office, David noticed the two police cars parked in front of the Baxter Building. He hurried to his Explorer and gunned it out of the parking lot.

"Geez," he thought, "they got here faster than I expected."

He didn't think Emily would leave evidence lying around her apart-ment. She was too clever for that. His plan was to ensure the police would find the evidence they needed to charge Emily with the crime. As head of security, he had the tools to pick locks, in case someone got locked in a classroom or there was some other emergency. It would be easy enough for him to sneak into Emily's apartment during the day when she was working at the college, place a twig of Rosary Pea berries that he had snipped from Gayle's garden in one of the cupboards, and sneak out again. The whole job would take no longer than two or three minutes.

"When the police find the berries in her home," he thought, "they will have the evidence they need to charge her. No matter what Emily says, they won't believe her."

He wanted Gayle to be able to relax and focus on the administration of the college so things could get back to normal. David had another reason to want the police to stay away from the campus. He didn't want them to stumble across his moonlighting activities. That would not go down well with Gayle. In fact, it would cost him his job!

It took only a few minutes to drive to Emily's neighborhood. David parked his SUV on a side street and walked the rest of the way. He knew the police would turn up soon, so he had to move quickly without attracting attention. He pulled a wooly hat on his head as he rounded the corner to Emily's building. He looked both ways, but there was nobody on the street.

"So far, so good," he thought.

He crossed the street. There were three walk-up apartment buildings in a row sharing a common parking lot at the back. He walked over to the first building and went down the driveway that led to the private parking area in the back.

Emily's building was at the far end. He walked up to the back door of her building and glanced around. Then he pulled on a pair of thin surgical gloves. He quickly picked the lock on the back door of her building and let himself in.

He found himself at the foot of a narrow staircase that led to the upper floors. Seconds later he was on the second floor, in front of Emily's back door. He knocked first, just in case someone was inside. He would say he was in the wrong building or something if a person came to the door.

Suddenly, he heard a noise. It came from the landing above him. The door opened and a male voice called out, "Someone there?"

David froze. He stopped breathing.

Hearing nothing, the man above closed his door, muttering something. David sighed, and as quietly as possible worked on the lock. He hoped there was no chain on the inside of the door. Why would there be? It was a very safe neighborhood. Click. He was in luck. No chain.

He opened the door just enough to let himself in. The kitchen was down the hallway to his right. *Emily keeps a very neat kitchen,* he thought. There were a few breakfast dishes in the sink. Everything else was cleared away, with only a toaster and a blender sitting on the small counter.

He took two steps towards the row of cupboards above the counter. A loud squeak sent shivers up his spine. He froze for a second. *It's just a weak floorboard below the tiles,* he thought.

He opened the first cupboard door. It contained dishes. He opened the next cupboard door, and smiled. This was her pantry cupboard, with all her baking supplies in clear sight.

He removed a baggie from his front pocket and placed it in behind the baking supplies, where the cops would be sure to find it.

Then he heard a police siren. "Crap!" he muttered.

He closed the cupboard door and suddenly felt something move against his leg that made him jump.

"What the hell!" he cried. Instinctively he kicked his leg out to the sudden yelp of a large calico cat. The cat ran back into the living room and hid under the couch.

By now his heart was racing and his breathing was rapid. He went to the back door of the apartment, and just as he was opening it, he heard noises coming from the front stairwell. They were already here! David carefully pulled the back door closed behind him just as the front door opened. He hurried down the stairs to the door that opened on to the parking lot. He paused and opened the door a crack to see if the way was clear. Seeing no one, he let himself out. He knew he couldn't walk out to the front of the building now, so he moved to the corner of Emily's building to see if anyone was on or near the driveway. It was clear. He launched himself across the driveway into the bushes that divided Emily's building from a house next door. This would provide some cover, but not much. He couldn't hide here if the cops came to the rear of the building. He looked around for a better place to hide. There was a garden shed in the back yard of the house next door.

If the door was unlocked, he could hide in there. He decided to check it out. He snuck alongside the bushes as well as he could, terrified that someone in the house might look out the back window and see him in their yard. That would definitely raise some alarm bells. This was his lucky day. The shed door was unlocked, and the house seemed to be vacant. *People at work,* he thought. He let himself into the shed and quietly closed the door. Then he waited.

As they entered the apartment, diLongo said to Emily, "Miss Warren, you may contact your lawyer if you wish. We are going to search your apartment, then we'll take you back to the college and search your car and your office until we find what we're looking for."

"Go ahead," Emily said. "I have nothing to hide."

"Kitchen first," diLongo said to Skip. "I want you to observe our search, Miss Warren, to ensure it is on the up and up."

"I guess I'd better, huh?" Emily did not disguise her annoyance.

The three of them went to the kitchen and Emily stood at the doorway, watching Skip and diLongo go through her things.

"Hello, what's this?" Skip said, pulling out the little plastic bag with the Rosary Pea plant inside. "We'll have to confirm this back at the lab," he said, and placed it in an evidence bag.

Emily looked shocked. "How did that get in there?" she asked.

They continued searching, and diLongo pulled out a white plastic bag. "What's in here?" she asked Emily.

"Look inside and see for yourself," Emily said, noting that her lawyer had advised her not to say anything to the police.

"It's a mortar and pestle," diLongo said, looking inside the bag. "I have one of these at home, to grind up herbs and spices. Here," she handed the bag to Skip. "Put this in an evidence bag."

They continued searching and located and bagged the cupcake pans that Emily used to bake her cupcakes, the electric mixer, the stainless steel mixing bowls and various ingredients commonly used for baking cupcakes. They also bagged her garbage.

DiLongo turned to Emily and said, "I think we have all we need. I want you to come with us to the station while we examine this evidence."

As they left the kitchen, Emily noticed her back door was unlocked. She was sure she had locked the door when she left that morning, but she was too distracted to say anything about it. Instead, she used her cell phone to call her lawyer.

"Mr. Thompson, please help me," she said in a panic. "The police are taking me to the Beaumont police station. They searched my apartment and found something!"

"Don't say another word. I'll meet you at the station in one hour," Evan Thompson said.

DiLongo and Skip escorted Emily outside to their cruiser. Emily kept silent on the drive into Beaumont as she pondered her situation.

Back at the station, diLongo brought Emily into a small room the police used for interviews.

"I'm not saying a thing until my lawyer gets here," Emily said.

"That's fine," diLongo said. "Wait here. We're going to process the evidence in the meantime."

DiLongo left to go to the lab where the techs were unloading the evidence bags. She asked the supervisor to process the twig with the berries first. She watched as the other techies swabbed the baking utensils and various items for traces of the toxin. An hour later, she returned to the interview room and found Emily, accompanied by a silver-haired man in a gray suit. The silver was premature. Evan Thompson, lawyer, was still in his thirties.

DiLongo placed two plastic bags on the table.

"You have some explaining to do," she said to Emily. "This is the baggie we found in your cupboard. It contains Rosary Pea berries. The toxin that killed Mr. Digman and Mrs. Boland is from this plant."

"I don't know how that got into my cupboard. I have never seen it before. Someone is trying to frame me," Emily said firmly.

"We also examined this item," diLongo said, removing the mortar and pestle from the bag. "We found traces of the same toxin on it."

Emily looked at her lawyer and then at diLongo.

"That's impossible," she said.

"Miss Warren, we collected this evidence from your home today, in your presence. This is hard evidence that connects you to the crime. We have you on the opportunity, the means and the evidence. I am now placing you under arrest for the murders of Terry Digman and Anne-Marie Boland. You have the right to remain silent," she said, and she continued the Miranda warning.

Emily looked stunned. "Wait a minute. I didn't do this! I'm being set up!" she protested.

Evan stood up and said to diLongo, "This evidence is all circumstantial. Without a motive, I'll drive several tractor trailers through the holes in your case."

"The motive," diLongo said, "will become clear as we continue our investigation."

Then she called in an officer to take Emily away and book her for the murders of Terry Digman and Anne-Marie Boland.

CHAPTER 19

📅 FRIDAY, DECEMBER 12, 2008 — 4:00 P.M.

After booking Emily, diLongo sent Skip out to pick up some Chinese food for their dinner. There would be no time to go out for a meal.

With Skip on his mission to find food, diLongo went to speak to Captain Juno about Daniel Post's phone call and his desire to participate in the investigation.

"Got a minute, Cap?" she asked, walking into his office.

"Sure. What's up?" He looked up from a binder of crime stats and reports.

"We have this situation with the Digman/Boland case. Daniel Post, you know, the professor who's writing a book? He wants to shadow our investigation — be embedded with us, so to speak — to see how we solve this case. He says he wants to help. I keep putting him off. Is there any reason to tell him we can't let him in on it, now that we've charged Emily Warren? He's no longer a suspect."

"DiLongo, let me ask you something," Cap said. "How is it going to help us to have him looking over our shoulders? Hmm? We already have Miss Warren in custody. I don't want that girl's lawyer making it an issue! Tell him the answer is no. And that goes for Dr. Primrose, too, if she calls again. Sheesh!"

"Okay, Cap. I'll get Skip to call him as soon as he returns." DiLongo left his office and returned to her own to clear up some paperwork until Skip turned up with the food.

By 5:30 p.m., when they had finished eating, diLongo decided to dig a little deeper into some of the other members of the bridge club.

"It's time to take the gloves off," she said to Skip. "I think Ben Chong knows more than he's letting on. Please call him and have him come in ASAP. "

"Now?" he asked. "I have all these background checks to do."

"Yes, now," diLongo said. "And please hurry."

Skip nodded. He called Ben's cell phone, then grabbed his coat and rushed out to the police cruiser.

DiLongo then called Chris Boland.

"Mr. Boland, I have some questions for you. Mind if I drop by your place for a few minutes?"

"I told you, I don't want to talk to the police," he said, "if I'm still a suspect."

"Well, we've made an arrest in the case. Emily Warren. And I need to talk to you to clear up some details."

"Emily! That's surprising," he said. "Okay, I guess I can talk to you, then." He sounded at little more cooperative.

DiLongo took her own car and drove twenty minutes to Chris Boland's address in a small subdivision between Beaumont and Mount Salem. He invited her inside and they sat in the front room. It was strewn with children's toys and he shooed two of his children out of the room so they could talk.

"Again, let me say how sorry I am for your loss," diLongo began.

"Thank you. I'm... I'm still in shock about it."

"Have you told the children anything?"

"Annie's mom came here last night. We told the kids together."

"They must be very sad," diLongo commented. She wondered how her own kids would react if anything happened to Paul or herself. It made her shudder. "Just so you know, we are doing everything we can to build the case against Emily Warren and ensure she is convicted. We found evidence in her apartment today."

"I still can't believe Emily did it," he said. "What did she have against my wife?"

"You never know about people, do you? The most innocent-looking suspects are sometimes the most deadly."

"Well, I never would have suspected her," he said. "Why did she do it?"

"That's a good question," diLongo said. "We are looking into her activities and connections to understand her better. But she is claiming innocence. So our job now is to find a motive for the crime."

"I see," he said. "How can I help you?"

"We think there may be a connection between Miss Warren, Mr. Digman and your wife. That is what I'd like to talk about," she said.

He looked surprised. "Okay. Go ahead," he said.

"We discovered that Miss Warren was freelancing as a... what shall I call it... a dominatrix of sorts. She dressed up as Nurse Ratched and played some kind of game with clients sent to her by Terry Digman. We also know that one of her clients was you, Mr. Boland."

Chris remained silent as the color drained from his face.

"No need to deny or confirm it," diLongo said. "And I don't care how you found out about her activities or why you went to see her. We just want to know if you said anything about it to your wife."

Chris shook his head. DiLongo was disappointed, but she pressed on.

"If you said nothing to her, there would be no reason for your wife to contact Miss Warren. If you did say something, we think your wife may have been outraged and disgusted enough to confront Emily and threaten her with exposure, and this might have given Emily the motive to kill her. So, I ask you again: Did you say anything to your wife about your encounter at the Lakeside Inn with Nurse Ratched, a.k.a. Emily?"

"No," he said, emphatically. "And I don't want my kids to learn about this. Please keep it out of your investigation," he pleaded.

"I will do what I can," diLongo said. "But understand this: without a motive, it will be difficult to get a conviction on circumstantial evidence alone. If that happens, Emily will go free, and she could strike again. It's very important to know, for sure, if you mentioned this to your wife. Maybe you felt guilty about it and wanted to confess to her to get it off your chest. Are you sure you did not mention it to your wife?"

"I am sure, detective," he said firmly. "I know what I said to her, and what I didn't say. And I did not say anything to her about that."

DiLongo sighed. She was sure that this had been the connection between Emily and Anne-Marie Boland, but as Chris was insisting that his wife did not know about his encounter with Emily, she would not get very far with this line of thinking.

"Well, in that case, there must be another link that we need to discover to understand why Miss Warren would take it upon herself to commit these murders," she said. "You have already stated that there was no relationship between your wife and Mr. Digman — at least, to your knowledge. Do you think it's possible your wife learned about Mr. Digman's involvement with Miss Warren, and Miss Warren found out and decided to eliminate them both?"

Chris looked skeptical. "My wife spent all her time working, looking after the house and the children and going to church," he said. "And once a week we played bridge. If she knew what Terry was up to, she would have told me. She was a very moral person."

"Okay, Mr. Boland, thank you for your time. I will be in touch if there are any further developments in the case," diLongo said.

"It's tomorrow at 2:00 p.m.," he said.

"What is?" diLongo asked, as she stood up to leave.

"Annie's funeral," he said. "The McGregor Funeral Home is handling the arrangements."

He looked so downcast that diLongo gave him a sympathetic pat on the back. "Thank you. I'll try to attend the funeral." Then she said good-bye and returned to her car and drove back to the station.

An hour later, Skip arrived at the station with Ben and took him to an interview room. Then he went to diLongo's office.

"What took you so long?" she asked.

"Had a hard time locating Mr. Chong," Skip said. "He was out with his frat buddies, doing whatever."

"Okay, let's go talk to him," she said. "Why don't you start this time?"

Skip nodded, and they both went into the interview room where Ben was sitting at a small table.

"Good evening," diLongo said.

"Hullo," Ben replied, fidgeting nervously.

"Thank you for coming in this evening. We want to talk to you about the bridge club murders," she said.

"I understand," Ben responded in a low voice.

DiLongo nodded to Skip, who consulted his notes. "What we want to know, Mr. Chong, is what you are not telling us," he said without any friendly preliminaries. "We need your information."

Ben looked down at his hands. "I don't know what you mean," he said.

"Mr. Chong, we don't have time to mess around here. If you know anything about either of the two victims, or anyone else, for that matter, you need to speak up now. Tell us what's going on." Skip was using his most serious 'don't mess with me' voice.

Ben examined his hands, but said nothing. Skip shrugged, and looked at diLongo.

"Okay, then," diLongo said. "We'll have to do this another way. Skip, please go see the Captain and ask him for the 'N' form."

"What's that?" Skip asked.

"Just do it," she said, and she closed the door after him.

"All right, Ben," she said in a softer voice, using his first name to put him at ease. "We're alone now. It's just you and me. Tell me what you're afraid of."

He remained silent, and shifted in his seat.

"You're here on a student visa, right?" diLongo said, changing tactics.

He nodded.

"Are you afraid if you talk, you might lose your status here?"

He looked up at her, and nodded.

"Okay, then. If you know something that will help our case, and you tell me now, I promise you will receive full immunity from any prosecution, deportation or other punishment."

"You can do that?" he asked.

"Yes. I will talk to the District Attorney right away, and get an immunity agreement done up for you. If, on the other hand, you continue to remain silent and we find out you are hiding something — and trust me, we will find out — then you will not be protected at all, and you will go to jail. Your choice," she said.

"I can't let my parents know," he said. "They would be very upset."

"You want jail?" she asked pointedly. "What's worse?"

He shook his head. "I don't want jail."

DiLongo waited as Ben shifted in the chair. She noticed beads of sweat on his upper lip.

"Okay," he said reluctantly. "I'll talk, but only when I have the immunity document in my hand."

He must be into some deep shit here, diLongo thought. She looked at Ben and nodded. "Okay, I'm taking you to a room where you can sit tight for a couple of hours. When I have the immunity document signed, I'll come and get you. Okay?"

"Okay," he said.

"Look Ben, don't worry. You're doing the right thing," she said, but his eyes revealed his anxiety.

She took Ben into a small waiting room where he could watch TV and read some magazines that were stacked on the table.

To the officer on duty, she said, "Make sure he doesn't leave."

When she returned to her office, Skip was waiting for her. "There's no such thing as an 'N' form," he said, petulantly. "Cap just laughed."

"Oh, dear boy, you have so much to learn," diLongo sighed. "The 'N' Form is just a ploy to get Ben to talk. He's going to fill us in now, but I have to get the D.A. to sign off on his immunity first. I am sure Ben knows something that will help us solve this case."

DiLongo then prepared a short document and faxed it over to the D.A.'s office for sign-off.

DiLongo called Skip into her office. "Skip, let's go see Ben Chong," she said. "We have the immunity document."

They walked over to the room where Ben was waiting, and entered.

"Here you go," diLongo said, handing him a document. "I signed it here. D.A. signed it there. You keep this for your records," she said. She placed her own copy in a folder on her desk.

Ben read the document, folded it and put it in his jacket pocket. DiLongo then turned on a recording device and said to Ben, "I'm going to record our conversation, okay? It's just to make sure we keep accurate notes, etc."

He nodded. "Okay, I understand."

After setting up the recording, she said, "So, Ben, what is your involvement in this situation? Do you know either of the two victims, Professor Digman or Mrs. Boland, personally?"

"Just Terry, that is, Professor Digman. Not Anne-Marie."

"And what is the nature of your relationship with Digman?"

"Drugs."

Skip blinked in surprise, and diLongo raised her eyebrows.

"Okay. What kind of drugs."

"Recreational party enhancers. Pot, mostly. A little coke, too."

"You got the pot from Digman?"

"Yeah."

"Do you know where he got it?"

"Yeah, from some bikers."

"Are these drugs for your own personal use?"

"No, I supply them to someone else."

DiLongo looked at Skip and shook her head. Skip turned away as he rolled his eyes.

"You sell the pot to... whom?" diLongo asked Ben.

"I don't want to say," he said. "It can't get out that I told you."

"If it is not material to this case, we'll keep it confidential," she assured him.

"I promised I wouldn't tell. He said if I supplied the drugs, he could get me into the Sigma Chi frat house. He said it's the only way they'd let me in."

"Go on," she said.

"He said their previous supplier graduated last spring. So we made a deal. I would get the pot and he would help me get into the frat."

"How did you get involved with Digman in the first place?"

"My contact told me to go to a bar in Beaumont where I could get fixed up. The bartender pointed out some guys sitting in a booth. That's when I saw Terry and David talking to the bikers."

DiLongo looked at Skip, who was sitting behind Ben. Skip's eyes were wide with surprise.

"You saw Terry Digman *and* David Bartholomew — the security chief at the college?" diLongo asked, incredulous.

"Yeah."

"So what did you do?" diLongo asked.

"Nothing. I went home. I was freaked out."

"No wonder," diLongo said.

"But I figured that I had something on them now. I knew they were dealing in drugs. So the next night, I saw them at bridge. I talked to Terry, and later I met him and David on the quad where we made a deal."

"And what was the deal?"

"They would give me the drugs and I would sell them to the frat boys. And they also wanted me to sell drugs to a high school kid in Hillsville. So I agreed to do it."

"You can tell us who your frat buddy is later, if it becomes important. Right now I want to know the name of the high school kid."

"Do I have to say? He has nothing to do with any of this!" Ben said.

"Yes, you have to say, Ben. Who is he?" diLongo demanded.

Ben looked down and sighed.

"Mike… his name is Mike. I don't know his last name."

DiLongo looked at Skip who raised an eyebrow.

"Okay, what does he look like?" diLongo asked.

"He's about 16 or 17. Black hair. Kinda stocky." Ben took his iPhone out of his pocket and dialed up a photo. "This is him."

DiLongo and Skip exchanged glances.

"Where do you meet him?" diLongo asked.

"At Poppa John's. I give him the stuff, he gives me the money," Ben said.

"What is Mr. Bartholomew's involvement in all this?" diLongo asked.

"I think he just makes sure things are cool on campus. The other security officers don't seem to have a clue what's going on, or they just ignore it," he said.

"Do you have any idea who would want Digman dead?" diLongo asked.

"No, unless he double-crossed someone. Maybe the bikers?"

"Ben, it has to be someone in the bridge club," diLongo said.

"Oh, I see. Well, I dunno."

"What about Mrs. Boland. How does she figure into this?" diLongo prodded.

"I dunno," Ben said. "I never had anything to do with her, except to play bridge."

"I warn you, Ben. Tell the truth, or you will lose your immunity," she said sternly.

"I am telling the truth. I honestly don't know anything about her!"

"Okay, Ben. What else is going on that I should know about?"

"This may not mean anything," he said, "But I saw Terry and Jill Wilmington driving together in his car late one night. But she's always saying how much she doesn't like him, so I thought that was odd."

"Hm-m-m. The H.R. lady. Well, we'll check it out," she said. "Now that we know Digman is involved with drug trafficking, we'll have to look into all of his connections. So, Ben, is there anything else you can tell me about Digman and what he's doing on campus?"

"Nope, only that I've heard some of his students find his course very easy. Like, he just talks and talks about crime and stuff. And get this: one girl I know in his class keeps getting A's on her assignments, but she doesn't do any work. Now that's what I call a bird course!"

"What's that girl's name?" diLongo asked.

"Cynthia, I think."

"Cynthia who?"

"I don't know. I overheard one of the students talking about her," he said.

"Okay, Ben. Anything else unusual going on at the college?"

"No, not that I can think of. I like it there. I want to stay," he said.

"You must realize that your illegal drug trafficking gig is over, right?"

"Yes, ma'am."

"I'm curious, Ben," she said. "Why do something so risky? You must have known that selling drugs to kids on campus, let alone high school kids, is illegal and you could be jailed or deported for doing it."

"Yeah, I know. But since Terry and David and the frat boys were involved, I figured it would be okay. Terry's a prof and David's the security chief. And it was the only way I could get into the fraternity."

"Why is that so important to you?" diLongo asked.

Ben looked down. Reluctantly he said, "I'm half Chinese, half English." He hesitated.

"Go on."

"I've been an outsider all my life. I just want to be accepted and make some American friends. I want to build a life here in America and blend in. It's a big melting pot society. A lot of American students are into pot and other stuff, so I thought it was cool to do that, to get accepted."

"I hope you realize you made a wrong choice," diLongo said. "There are better ways to blend into American society. Keep your nose clean, work hard, pay your bills and your taxes and give back to your community," she lectured. "That's how you blend in here."

"Yes ma'am. Please don't tell my parents. They would be so disappointed." He looked genuinely remorseful.

"Ben, did you have anything to do with Digman's death?" she asked pointedly.

"No ma'am. I had nothing to do with that," he said. "Honest."

DiLongo switched off the recording device. "Okay," she said. "Skip, you can take him back to the college, and then meet me back here."

Then to Ben she said, "I want you to stay out of trouble for the rest of the time you are in this country," she said. "Or else. I'll be watching you."

He nodded, and walked out the door with Skip.

When Skip returned an hour and a half later, diLongo was busy working on some details for the wall chart.

"You know, I think Dr. Primrose has some explaining to do," diLongo said. "Look what's going on right under her nose! These two, Digman and Bartholomew, are running a drug ring to students on campus and the high school. What other illegal activities are they involved in? And who are these bikers supplying them? And Miss Warren — doing the kinky in hotel rooms with dates that Digman sets up for her? And what is Miss Wilmington up to, being out with Digman when she says she doesn't like the guy? Then these two murders happen."

"It's supposed to be a good college," Skip said, "but it's looking more like a cesspool of crime."

"What have you been able to get on Digman and Bartholomew?"

Skip shook his head. "I haven't finished yet," he said, "but so far, I don't have much on either one of them. I'm checking their references from the employment files, but I haven't been able to reach anyone yet."

"Okay, let's run Digman's prints through the system. Sam will have them on file by now. And we need to run Bartholomew's prints, too. And check with the R.C.M.P. in Ottawa. Both Digman and Bartholomew were working in Canada for a while, so the Mounties may have some information on them. I've got a sneaky feeling they are a couple of really bad apples."

Then she said thoughtfully, "You know, all this stuff that's going on with kinky sex and illegal drugs… it's all very interesting. But we can't lose sight of the fact that we're investigating a murder case. Two people died, and we still don't know why. We need the motive for Emily Warren. Remember that."

While Skip continued with his background checks, diLongo decided to have another chat with David Bartholomew. She called him on his cell phone.

"Mr. Bartholomew," she said when he answered. "Detective diLongo here. I was wondering if I could meet with you for a few minutes."

"Something up?"

"Yep. I need your help."

"Sure thing," he said. "Anything I can do, just ask."

"Okay, meet me at the Donut Heaven in twenty minutes."

DiLongo told Skip where she was going to meet up with David. Then she poked her head into Juno's office. "Hey, Cap, I'm going to meet Bartholomew — you know, the guy responsible for security on campus. I'll be back in an hour."

"Something going on, Dee-Dee?" he asked.

"I need to check something out, is all," she said. Then she left in a police cruiser.

At Donut Heaven, she waited until David turned up, and then offered to buy him a coffee. He accepted. "One milk, two sugars," he said.

She returned with the coffees in disposable cups and sat down opposite him.

"So, I hear you have Emily Warren in custody," he said. "Your case solid?"

"Well, we know the two victims were murdered, and we have physical evidence that links her to the murders," diLongo said. "So we have charged her and now we're just doing some clean-up, you know."

"I see. How can I help you?"

"You're responsible for security at the campus. Does that also involve background checks on your staff?" diLongo asked.

"Yeah, sometimes, if Jill needs a hand. I do the senior people, not janitors or parking lot attendants," he said.

"Okay," she nodded. "So that explains why you did the check on Terry Digman?"

"Yep. Checked him out," David said, sipping his coffee.

"Good. Anyone else in the bridge club that you've checked out?"

"Hmm," he said. "No, just him. The others were already on staff when I arrived, so I guess someone else must have done the background checks on them."

They chatted for another twenty minutes as diLongo probed him on different bridge players, but she learned nothing new.

When they finished their coffees, diLongo said, "Thanks, Mr. Bartholomew. You've been very helpful."

They walked out together and David got into his SUV and drove back to the college. DiLongo went back into the donut shop. She removed an evidence bag from her pocket and used it to pick up David's coffee cup from their table.

Back at the station, she found Skip working at his computer. She placed the bag containing the coffee cup on his desk.

"Get the prints off this cup," she said. "And run them through the system. Do it now."

EARLIER THAT DAY

By 2:30 on Friday afternoon, there was a chill wind on the mountain, and dark clouds were swirling overhead. *Snow is coming soon,* Daniel thought.

He drummed his fingers on his desk as his right leg vibrated. He was losing patience waiting for the response from diLongo. He was tired of waiting for them to make a decision. He was worried about the time he was losing when he could already be involved in the investigation. He was also worried they might turn down his request, but he didn't want to think about that.

He got up and paced the room. "Marion," he whispered. "What am I going to do if they say no? I need this for the book."

He kept pacing, deep in thought. "Marion, Marion, help me. I need to be part of the investigation, just for a little while. It will give me the reality component that I need for my book. I'll integrate the real investigation into my story, and it will be a unique literary form. They might name it after me: The Post DocuNovel! I'll be famous again. Not only famous in my lifetime, but famous forever, like Shakespeare," he muttered.

You have to take matters into your own hands, dear. Push harder. If I were you, I would just march right down to the station and demand access to the case!

"I've already been there, and it got me nowhere. It's maddening that they're investigating this crime without me. What have they got to lose?"

Why don't you threaten them instead... tell them how you'll make them look like total idiots if they don't let you in. Tell them your editor is ready to go with that scenario!

Daniel flopped down on the couch and closed his eyes as he contemplated Marion's last suggestion. Then he fell into a deep sleep.

Daniel was still napping when his office phone rang.

"This is Daniel Post," he said, groggily.

"Hello, Mr. Post. I'm Officer Crane from the Beaumont Police Department. I'm working with Detective diLongo on the investigation into the murders at the college."

"Yes, I know who you are."

"Okay, great. Well, I'm just calling to let you know that unfortunately we cannot grant permission for you to participate in any way in the investigation."

Daniel slammed down the phone with a scream of rage. His hopes of getting involved in the investigation were over.

"Christ almighty!" He picked up a heavy book and threw it across the room.

On the other side of the quad, David and Gayle were having a meeting in her office. David got a text message and said to Gayle, "Okay, they've charged Emily with the two murders."

She put a hand to her mouth. "What a relief! Now we can relax. I can advise the parents who are calling that they have nothing to worry about, and we can get back to normal around here." Gayle smiled at David. "So, what do we do about the bridge club? Are we going to play this Wednesday? There's the issue of replacing the two members who died, and Emily. We need to look at the waiting list and see who our best candidates are."

"Gayle, do you honestly think anyone wants to play bridge now, considering what happened?" David asked. "Just because the cops have charged Emily, they still have to convict her, or get a confession, before we can really breathe easy about this."

"Hmmm, I see your point. So, you think I should cancel bridge for the rest of the month?"

"That's what I would do," he said. Gayle went to her computer and quickly typed out an email message and copied it to all the members of the Faculty Bridge Club. She wrote:

Dear Faculty Bridge Club Members,

I am writing to inform you that, with regret, I'm canceling the bridge club for the remainder of the year due to the murders of Terry Digman and Anne-Marie Boland. In case you have not heard, Emily Warren has been charged with these crimes.

In consideration of all this, I am also canceling the annual prize, since it will not be fair to award the prize this year. Once we get though this unfortunate state of affairs, I will re-open the bridge club and get things back on track in the new year.

Sincerely,

Gayle Primrose

Daniel was still seething over the bad news that he would not be allowed to shadow the investigation when he heard the ding on his computer informing him of an incoming message. He was tempted to ignore the email, but then he thought it might be Captain Juno getting back to him with a change of heart.

He went over to his computer and looked at the email, and then let out a loud howl. It was a message from Gayle, canceling the bridge club and the annual prize, and mentioning Emily's arrest.

In a sudden rage, Daniel picked up the computer monitor and heaved it across the room, where it crashed into a bookcase. Then he yanked the cables out of the wall and pitched the computer at the shelves as books tumbled down. He picked up his leather chair and heaved it against the window, breaking the glass. He emptied the metal trashcan onto the floor and flung it against the wall. He picked up an ornamental planter and threw it against the wall, shattering the planter in a thousand pieces.

When he could find nothing else to pick up and throw, he sat down on the sofa, his head in his hands.

Well, don't you have a fine mess on your hands?

"Marion, it's over. I can't get the reality component for my book now. The police finally have a murder investigation but they won't let me in! I can't believe they would sabotage me like this!"

There's no accounting for stupidity.

"Gayle has canceled the annual prize *and* the party!" he moaned. "I wanted to win that this year! It's the only thing that matters, after the book."

Gayle doesn't deserve to have you on her staff, the way she is treating you! You are a famous author. She needs to be more patient!

"She doesn't care anymore!"

The whole situation is unfair. You can't be expected to work under these conditions. It's her fault for putting you under so much pressure. What's your next move?

Daniel held his head in his hands. A few minutes later he stood up. He strode over to his desk and rang Gayle's number.

"What's this about Emily?" he demanded, when Gayle came on the line.

"Daniel, I was just about to call you. The police have charged her with the murders. They searched her place and found some damning evidence. I can hardly believe it, but apparently she poisoned them!"

"No!" he cried. "Not Emily! I need her to help me with my book. How will I ever finish it on time? Oh, this is more than I can bear! I can't take any more!"

He hung up the phone, then called the office of Dr. Dunlop, his personal physician.

"Put him on now," he said in his most imperious voice. "It's an emergency!"

When the doctor came on the line, Daniel spoke rapidly. "Doctor, I need help. I need help now! I'm going to kill myself if I don't get some help!"

"Daniel, just calm down and tell me what's going on."

"Doctor," he wailed, and started sobbing. "Everyone's against me. I'm going to be fired. I hear voices. I can't control it anymore. I can't sleep. I can't eat. I want to throw myself out the window!"

"Okay, Daniel. Where are you?"

"At my office."

"Okay, good. You did the right thing to call me. You remember we've talked about this before? You have to admit yourself into the duBarry Center for a few days of observation. They will take good care of you. I'm going to make the arrangements now. I'm sending an ambulance to take you there, and I'll meet you at duBarry."

Daniel mumbled something in agreement.

When the ambulance attendants arrived to take Daniel, Belinda greeted them and brought them to his office. She knocked on his office door. When she heard no response, she opened the door to find Daniel sitting in a corner, stark naked, hugging his knees, rocking back and forth, moaning and muttering.

"That's him," she said to the attendants. When Daniel saw the ambulance officers, he became limp and docile. They brought in a stretcher and strapped him down under a sheet and blanket, gathered up his clothes and wheeled him out to the waiting ambulance.

Belinda watched from the window as they put Daniel into the ambulance, and then she walked over to the other side of the office to speak to the other secretaries.

"What's going on?" Mary asked.

"He's really lost it this time," Belinda said. "Delusional, if you ask me. He took off all his clothes, would you believe! I don't expect he'll be back soon. It's weird, because he seemed to be in a good mood lately, for a change. You should see his office. He's made a real mess of it."

Belinda went back to her desk and sat quietly for a few minutes. With Emily in jail and Professor Post taken away for who knows how long, she wondered who would be in charge of the office. She picked up the phone and called Gayle.

"Dr. Primrose, please," she said to the secretary who answered. "It's an emergency!"

When Gayle came on the line, Belinda gave her a hasty report.

"They took Professor Post away in an ambulance," she said in a rush. "He trashed his office again. Emily's not here, either. What should I do?"

Gayle calmed her down and said, "Do you know where they're taking him?"

"Yeah, duBarry," Belinda said. "It's the psychiatric hospital — you know, the funny farm."

"Yes, I know it," Gayle said. "So he's had another episode, I guess."

"Seems like it," Belinda said.

"I wonder what triggered it this time?" Gayle mused.

"I have no idea. He seemed to be in a good mood lately."

"Okay, thanks, Belinda. You can take the rest of the day off," Gayle said. It was already close to quitting time. "We'll meet on Monday to reorganize the department." After hanging up the phone, Gayle sat back in her chair and shook her head. "What more can go wrong around here?" She decided to go home early and pour herself a stiff drink.

CHAPTER 20

After being formally booked, Emily had a brief meeting with her lawyer, Evan Thompson.

"You'll have to stay in custody over the weekend," Evan said. "There will be a bail hearing Monday morning, and then I hope to get you out of here."

"Thanks," she said, "I really appreciate your help." Then, in a lower voice, she said, "I think I know what really happened to the victims. I need you to do something for me."

"What's that?" he asked.

"Call Belinda. She works in the cubicle next to mine. Where's your pen?" He gave her his pen. "Here's her home number." Emily wrote the number on the palm of his hand. "Ask her to meet you at my office. She has an access card to get in. Tell her to find my flash drive. It's in the top right-hand drawer of my desk. Get that flash drive and print out all the documents in the folder marked *Private*."

"You think there's something on the flash drive that will help your case?" he asked.

"Yes, if I'm not mistaken. I'm starting to get a clear picture of what happened, but I need to review those documents," she said.

"I'll get on it right away," he promised.

"Thanks, Mr. Thompson. I really appreciate your help," she said, as the police officer came to escort her to her cell.

"That's what I'm here for," he said. "So don't worry. Sit tight. We'll have you out of here soon, the good Lord willing and the creek don't rise," he said affably.

The officer cuffed Emily's hands behind her back and led her down a long corridor towards the detention area.

Evan went to his car, but before he started driving, he took out his cell phone. He called Belinda and told her about Emily's arrest, and made arrangements to meet her at the Arts Building later that evening.

Satisfied that there was nothing else he needed to do immediately, Evan went for dinner at an Italian restaurant in Beaumont. An hour and a half later, he drove to the campus to meet Belinda. She was already standing out front of the building waiting for him.

He went up to her and introduced himself. She seemed nervous. "I hope I don't get in trouble for this," she said, her head bobbing up and down.

"Don't worry. You are not doing anything wrong," Evan said, "and it might help Emily beat the charges against her."

She opened the front door with her access card and disarmed the alarm.

"You think she's innocent?" Belinda asked, as they entered the building.

"You bet," he said. "Now we just have to prove it."

She walked up the stairs with Evan following close behind her and they made their way to the second floor where the English department was located.

"It's in here," she said, unlocking the door to the suite of inner offices. "That's Emily's desk."

"Okay. She told me to look in the right-hand drawer," he said, pulling it open. Underneath some papers he found a flash drive. "This must be it."

"Great. Let's go, then," Belinda said. "This place gives me the creeps at night."

CHAPTER 21

Evan returned to the police station with the flash drive in his pocket. He spotted diLongo walking down the corridor towards her office.

"A word, officer?" he called, and trotted after her.

"What is it?" she asked.

"The evidence you collected at Emily Warren's place. You know, I believe it's a setup. If the D.A. goes ahead with this case, I guarantee your department will look foolish and your career will suffer!"

"I'm listening," she said.

"If you want to catch the real killer, I'll need your cooperation. Otherwise, see you in court, as they say."

"Mr. Thompson, if you have any information that is material to this case, you need to tell me now. If it's just a theory, you can present it in court. As they say."

"Okay, do you have half an hour for me?"

DiLongo nodded.

"Let's meet at the Blue Bird Café on Main Street, where I know we can talk in private. Then you can decide what you want to do."

She said, "Okay, we'll meet you there in ten."

DiLongo walked back to her office to collect Skip. "Where we going?" he asked. "I have to work on this report."

"We're going to hear a story," she said. "Come on."

They grabbed their coats and drove a few blocks down Main Street to the Blue Bird Café. Evan was sitting in a booth at the far end, well away from the windows and the other diners.

"Here's the deal," Evan said, after they ordered coffee. "My client is currently in jail. She is innocent. I want her out. She has information about the real murderer and I need her to be out on bail so we can confirm our information."

"What is this information?"

Evan just smiled and shook his head.

"Look, the evidence against her is overwhelming," diLongo said as she counted each item on her fingers. "She actually made the murder weapon, for God's sake. She was present at the scene. We found the poison plant in her kitchen cupboard. We found the poison on the mortar and pestle she used to grind up the seeds. We know she had an unsavory relationship with Mr. Digman and she may have had a problem with Mrs. Boland too, although we're still looking into that. We have more than enough evidence to convict her."

"But she didn't do it," Evan said.

"So you say," diLongo said, "but where's the evidence that will exonerate her?"

"There's some information I want to share with you, but bear with me for a minute. Let's assume that she didn't do it. In that case, there must be some other explanation for the evidence you have found. Correct?" said Evan.

"Mr. Thompson," diLongo said with a sigh, "If you have some specific information we can work with that changes our case, let me have it and I'll investigate. Otherwise, the only thing that will change our case is if someone confesses to the crime."

diLongo's cell phone rang. She listened, nodding several times. "Well, that's interesting," she said after hanging up. "Daniel Post is in Cloud 9 on a voluntary admission."

"Emily's boss?" Evan said.

"Yes. It appears he had some kind of mental breakdown. Stress."

"Oh, I see. How strange," Evan said. "So, you think the only thing that will clear Emily is someone else's confession?"

"Yep, she's good for the crime otherwise. Of course, if there is a confession, there has to be some evidence to support it, or the D.A. will throw it out. In a high-profile case like this, some idiot is bound to come forward and confess just for the attention."

"I need to see Emily. It's important."

"I thought you wanted to share something?" diLongo asked.

"Yeah, well, I've changed my mind," he said.

"You dragged us out of the station to tell us something, and now you won't?"

"I'm sorry, but I think it's better if I talk to my client first."

"Tonight?"

"Yes, right away."

"Okay," diLongo said, "I'll play ball with you, for now. But don't push it. I have to get this wrapped up pronto. Captain's orders."

They paid for their coffee and went back to the station. DiLongo sent Skip to bring Emily into a small conference room where Evan Thompson was waiting.

A few minutes later Skip returned with Emily and diLongo joined them in the room. Evan told Emily about Daniel's breakdown and admission to the hospital.

"What does that mean, 'Cloud 9'?" she asked.

"It's what some people call the DuBarry Center for Mental Health. It's a private treatment center for people with psychiatric and emotional problems," diLongo said.

"Oh, yes," Emily said. "I know about it. My friend Rachel works there as a nurse."

"With a voluntary admission," diLongo said, "he can leave whenever he feels like it, as long as he is not a risk to others. By the way," she added, "DuBarry is very strict about allowing visitors or any other communication with patients."

"Yes," Evan said. "They keep the center as a safe haven for mentally disturbed patients. They call it a healing place, away from the stresses of everyday life. They don't allow patients to have cell phones, laptops or pagers, and they have only limited access to computers and the Internet. Outsiders are not allowed. You practically have to have a court order to get inside. They have a wall surrounding the grounds and a locked gate that opens electronically. If you don't have the right pass to enter, you can't get in there. Or out."

"A cuckoo's nest," Emily commented.

"Well, not that bad," Evan said. "They don't take psychopaths or violent types. People pay a lot of money to dry out there, if, for example, they have a substance abuse issue. And parents can send problem children there for evaluation. The accommodation is similar to a first-class hotel. They offer a private room for sleeping or watching TV, upscale recreation facilities, nice lobbies and reception areas, beautiful dining rooms and libraries. There are secure floors for patients who may be a danger to themselves — you know, suicide threats, slashers and so on. They have a state-of-the-art security system in place," Evan said.

"How do you know so much about it, Mr. Thompson?" Emily asked.

"When I was a law student a few years ago, I had a summer job working there as a security guard. Now they call me when they need legal advice."

DiLongo drummed her fingers impatiently on the table and added, "The kids there load up on uppers or downers. They call it Cloud 9 'cuz it's like heaven compared to their home or school life."

"And it's not cheap," Evan said. "It costs thousands of dollars a month for patient care, so the patients are mostly short-term. However, if you're rich and crazy, you can stay as long as you want."

DiLongo stood up. "Emily, your bail hearing is set for Monday morning, so you have to remain in custody over the weekend. If you get out on bail, you have to let us know before you leave the local area. If you try to escape to Canada, we'll pick you up. We have your passport flagged, so you won't be able to board any international flights."

Emily shrugged. "I have no intention of leaving the area. What do I need to do to clear my name?"

"If you truly believe there is another explanation for the murders, I strongly advise you to give us your evidence so we can investigate the situation. As I told your lawyer earlier, unless you have hard evidence that implicates another person at the bridge club, the only thing that will change our case is a confession," diLongo said. "And it had better be a good one."

"Wait a minute," Evan said. "There's a huge hole in your case against Emily. What's the motive? You'll have a hard time convicting her on circumstantial evidence alone."

"We'll find the motive, don't you worry about that," diLongo said. But she knew Evan was right. With no plausible motive, the D.A. would not be happy to go to trial with just a twig and a mortar and pestle that anyone could have planted in the apartment. She would have to keep looking for the motive, and at this point, she didn't know where to look. She was half hoping that Evan would come back to her with evidence that implicated someone else as the killer — someone with a real motive.

"Now, I want to speak to my client privately," Evan said. "Give us five minutes."

CHAPTER 22

📅 PRESENT DAY — 4:30 A.M.

My coffee was cold, so I decided to get a refill. Brian ordered a ham sandwich with a bottle of water. We settled back down at our table.

"Sharon Sharpe was all over this case," I said. "It was the most exciting case she'd worked on for quite a while. She was driving Cap nuts, as usual, with her pointed questions. Here's another story she wrote for *The Record*."

I laid another newspaper clipping on the table and started reading.

SATURDAY, DECEMBER 13, 2008
BEAUMONT POLICE CHARGE SUSPECT IN KENSINGTON MURDERS

Late Friday afternoon, police arrested a suspect in the deaths of two people at the Kensington College bridge club Wednesday night.

Emily Warren, 27, a secretary in the English department at the college, was charged with two counts of first-degree murder. She is currently in jail awaiting a bail hearing on Monday morning.

Police Captain Juno said in a statement, "We are pleased to announce that Emily Warren has been taken into custody and charged with the murders of Terry Digman and Anne-Marie Boland. We executed a search warrant at her home on Friday and found incriminating evidence that links her to the crime.

"The two victims were killed by a toxin from the Rosary Pea plant. This toxin was administered to the victims in a dessert prepared by Emily Warren for a Christmas celebration at Kensington College. The toxin causes almost instant death to humans.

"Further details will be provided as they become available."

When asked about the motive, Juno said, "We will provide information about that at the appropriate time."

Evan Thompson is a local lawyer representing Warren. He claims that his client is innocent of the crime and that the evidence against her is circumstantial.

"The police will have a hard time proving their case in court," he said.

When Dr. Gayle Primrose, the president of Kensington College and Warren's employer, heard about the arrest, she said she was relieved.

"I'm glad the police solved this case so quickly," she said. "Many parents have expressed their concerns about the safety of their children on campus. Now we can get back on track and put this unfortunate incident behind us."

Not everyone is relieved, however. Some students are worried that Warren may not be the killer.

"What if they charged the wrong person?" asked one student, who did not want her name to be published. "I know this Miss Warren, and she's not the type to go around murdering people. The police have not offered a motive for the crime. If it's not her, who is it? And is the killer still on campus? Should we be taking precautions?"

The police have not detailed how the toxin was introduced to the dessert in question without the victims' knowledge. And the biggest question remains: Why?

In a separate incident, the head of the English department at Kensington College, Daniel Post, a celebrated author of crime fiction, was admitted to duBarry Mental Health Center Friday night, shortly after Warren's arrest. Warren has been working as Post's secretary in the English department.

Dr. Primrose said, "Mr. Post has a nervous condition that was exacerbated by the events this week, causing him to become temporarily incapacitated. He is going to be under observation for a few days. His doctor is looking after him. I fully expect him to be back at work very soon."

> The funeral for one of the victims, Anne–Marie Boland, will be held today at a local Baptist church. The McGregor Funeral Home is handling the arrangements. The police are still trying to contact next of kin for the other victim, Terry Digman. His body remains in the county morgue.

📅 SATURDAY, DECEMBER 13, 2008 — 1:00 P.M.

On Saturday afternoon, the sky was clear and sunny, but the temperature was near freezing. DiLongo drove her personal car, an aging silver Taurus, to the Mount Salem Chapel of Redemption, where Anne-Marie Boland's funeral service was being held. The small Baptist church was located on the main street heading into the village of Mount Salem. She found a parking spot on a side street half a block away. She noticed several other people walking towards the church, their heads bowed against a strong breeze that had suddenly started swirling around them.

DiLongo was used to the imposing Catholic Church that she attended in Beaumont, with its high bell tower and statues of Mary and Jesus smiling down on the people. This little white chapel seemed very unpretentious in contrast.

Inside the church, the hard wooden pews were already filled, and some people were standing at the back and along the side.

DiLongo recognized a few people from the college. Gayle Primrose and David Bartholomew were sitting near the front. Jill Wilmington and Barb Baker were seated near the back. Karl Schultz was also sitting near the back with a gray-haired woman diLongo took to be his wife. She noticed Melissa Fielding standing at the back of the room. DiLongo looked around, but she did not see Ben Chong, Sally Brighton or the Blacks.

The service began with a prayer and then the pastor opened his Bible and read some passages of comfort and spiritual salvation. The organist played a few hymns and the congregation sang along. Chris Boland stood up and said a few words about what a wonderful person Anne-Marie was and how much her family and friends would miss her.

The service was over in less than half an hour. The pallbearers carried Anne-Marie's coffin out to a hearse for the short drive to the Mount Salem Community Cemetery.

As friends of Ann-Marie gathered to give their condolences to the grieving family members, diLongo waited her turn. When she reached the family, she spoke briefly to Chris Boland and Anne-Marie's mother, who was dabbing her eyes and nodding, barely able to speak. Another family member ushered the children out of the church into one of the black limos from the funeral home.

As diLongo left the church to return to her car, she spotted Mason Schwartz, owner of the Delish Deli, chatting with someone. She went over to speak with him.

"Hello again, Mr. Schwartz," she said.

"Detective," he said. "I'm surprised to see you here."

"Well," she said, "I was invited by Chris Boland."

"Nice service," he commented. "Short."

"Yes," diLongo said. "Not like our Catholic services."

"Nor like our Jewish ones," he added.

"I'd like to have a word with you about the murder investigation," diLongo said.

"What's up? I hear you have someone in custody," Mason said.

"Yes," she said. "We're still investigating, however. Just wrapping up a few things. Anyway, I thought I should mention to you that we discovered that your son, Michael, is involved in supplying illegal drugs to the students at his high school."

"What!" Mason said, shocked. "Are you sure you're not mistaken?"

"We're sure," diLongo said in her semi-official voice, "It came out in our investigation. I'm telling you this for your own good. If Michael continues to supply drugs to his friends or other people, we'll catch him. Then he'll be charged with drug trafficking, and not only will he go to jail, but he'll get logged into the system and have a criminal record for the rest of his life. That will not be a good outcome. So, this is your heads-up. Let your son know that we're on to him," she said sternly. "If he doesn't stop, he'll wind up in jail."

Mason's attitude changed. "He's working in the deli today. I will go see him right now and get to the bottom of this. I promise you he will not be dealing drugs anymore when I'm finished with him!"

"Thank you," diLongo said.

"No, thank *you*," Mason replied, and shook diLongo's hand. He hurried over to his car and headed back into the village.

DiLongo looked around and noticed that many of the people who attended the service were departing in their cars. Some were following the hearse procession to the cemetery, and some were heading home.

DiLongo decided not to go to the cemetery. She drove back to Beaumont and dropped into the station to speak with Skip. She found him working at his desk, going through a stack of folders and logging information into his computer.

"Hey, Skip," diLongo said. "How's it going?"

"Man, oh man," he said. "I've been going through these personnel files to fill in the backgrounds on all these folks. Trouble is, it's the weekend, so it's hard to reach people. I'm waiting for some call-backs now."

"Well, keep at it," diLongo said. "We have to uncover a motive. There's got to be a connection between Warren, Digman and Boland that we're missing. There's a triangle here, but the sides are not coming together. It bothers me that she's maintaining her innocence in spite of the evidence in her apartment. Something smells, and I don't like it," she said.

"Okay," Skip said. "I'll do what I can over the weekend and give you a report on Monday morning."

"Sounds good," she said. "Now I'm going to spend some time with my family. It's Morgan's birthday tomorrow. He's turning nine and I have a cake to bake."

CHAPTER 23

📅 MONDAY, DECEMBER 15, 2008 — 11:00 A.M.

At Emily's bail hearing on Monday morning, Evan Thompson argued effectively to let Emily out on $50,000 bail. He pointed out to the judge that Emily had a clean record, the police had no motive, the evidence was circumstantial and she was maintaining her innocence.

The judge reviewed the file and agreed with Evan. "I can see your point about the evidence," Judge Malloy said. "Just make sure your client is available for her court appearance."

As they left the judge's chambers, Evan and Emily walked over to his car.

"Let's go to my office. It's not far from here," Evan said. "We'll take a look at the documents I printed off from your flash drive."

Evan had a small two-room office on the second floor of a commercial strip. They parked behind the building and walked up a narrow set of stairs. At the top of the stairs they turned right and went halfway down the corridor. Then Evan opened a door and walked into the outer office that served as a reception area and waiting room. There were two clerks working behind a moveable partition. The office looked disorganized, with books and papers piled up on every surface.

Evan ushered Emily through another door and seated her in a comfortable armchair. His private office was clean and tidy, with glass-fronted bookcases full of legal texts and binders, and filing cabinets along one wall. He handed her a folder with some papers inside.

"This is what I printed off," he said. "I took a quick look but I couldn't make much sense of it all."

"Okay, let me see," she said.

"Where did you get these documents?" he asked her, handing over the folder.

"From Daniel's computer. He has a habit of trashing his office. A few weeks ago, he threw his computer at the wall and it didn't work after that. I gave the hard drive to our IT guy, who copied the information onto a flash drive for me. We got Daniel a new computer, and I copied the files from the flash drive onto his new computer." She tapped the flash drive. "I kept the flash drive to update it every few days, just in case he decided to trash his computer again, so I'd have his files backed up here."

"Aren't these files already backed up onto the university's central server?" Evan asked.

"Not these. He keeps them separate, for confidentiality. He's paranoid someone will see his stuff before it's finished," she said. "'A writer's work process is sacred,' he says."

"So what do you make of the pages I printed off?" Evan asked.

"Not sure yet. Some of the information relates to the book he's been working on. I think he's on version twenty-five now. He's been trying to write this book for six years, but he keeps starting over. He'll write about hundred pages and then scrap them. Sometimes he'll go for months without writing anything. Then he'll get on a roll and write furiously for days on end, sometimes writing all night long. A lot depends on his mood. When he's feeling good, he writes. When he's feeling down, he can't seem to write at all."

"I see," Evan said. "Go on."

"Well, lately he's been writing again. He's writing in fits and starts, so the material is disjointed and doesn't make much sense. But I noticed a few things when I copied his files, and I want to take another look to see if my memory is correct."

Emily leafed through the pages in the folder, reading quietly while Evan worked on his laptop.

Then she looked up. "Right," she said. "Here it is. He was doing some research on several common garden plants. Look at this, Evan," she said, handing him a sheet. "See, he researched the Rosary Pea plant. He knew it was deadly. Do you see? He planned the whole thing! He's the murderer."

Evan reviewed the notes and whistled. Emily said, "We could give these to diLongo and then she'll believe me. Daniel did it!"

He looked at Emily with concern. "But I'm afraid this isn't enough to clear you, Emily. Even though it looks suspicious, the police will argue that you were in possession of the flash drive, and you could have written these notes and placed them on Daniel's computer."

"Oh, I see," she said, looking disappointed.

"The good news is," he said, "we now know that Daniel could be the killer. But you still need solid evidence or his confession. That's not going to be easy to get, with him locked away in duBarry."

"Yeah, that's the problem," she agreed. "And we don't know why he did it."

Evan looked at his watch. It was nearly 1:00 p.m. Emily was staring out the window, deep in thought. Her face was pale and her shoulders were slumped. It pained him to see her looking so distressed.

"Listen, Emily, let's take a break," Evan said. "I bet you could use a nice meal. Come on, I'll take you to the best lunch place in town."

Emily was very quiet as Evan drove five blocks down the street to the Blue Bird Café, where they found a table by the window.

"We're lucky it's not so busy today," Evan said, helping Emily off with her coat. They got settled into their seats, and Emily studied the menu, but her mind was elsewhere. When the waitress came to take their order, she still had not decided.

"You order for me," she said. "I can't focus on the menu."

"Fine," Evan said, and he ordered two Caesar salads with chicken and two club sodas with lime.

While they waited for their lunch to arrive, Emily took stock of her situation. "So, Daniel's notes aren't enough to clear me."

"The big thing against you is the evidence they found in your cupboard — the berries and the mortar and pestle with traces of the poison. DiLongo told me the only prints they found on it were yours," Evan said.

"Well, Daniel borrowed my mortar and pestle last week to grind some spices for an Indian food recipe," she said. "He must have used surgical gloves when he handled it. He gave it back to me in a white plastic bag the day before the murders. I brought the bag home and put it in the cupboard with my other kitchen tools. That's where the police found it. No one else touched it."

"I see. That explains it. Thing is," he said carefully, "from the police's perspective, we only have your word for it that Daniel borrowed your mortar and pestle. He could easily deny it. And what about the Rosary Pea plant?" he said.

"I have no idea how that got there," she said, shaking her head. "You've got to believe me."

"Well, if someone planted the Rosary Pea twig to implicate you, it means they also had access to the mortar and pestle before the police arrived," Evan mused. "They could have contaminated it, I suppose. So maybe they're the killer, and not Daniel."

"No, Evan. Remember, Daniel's notes clearly indicate that he was researching poisonous plants, including the Rosary Pea plant. And one day his office door was open a little bit, and I heard him talking — I don't know who he was talking to — but he was talking about creating a murder for his book. I didn't think he meant a real murder. And he was the only one who had access to my mortar and pestle. He deliberately held on to it until the day before the murders. He knew the evidence would still be on it. So he deliberately framed me for the murders."

"That's premeditation," Evan said. "Murder one."

Emily nodded. "I don't want to think about that. He's a mixed-up man, for sure. Why he would do such a thing is beyond me. That's the real mystery." Then she paused for a moment. "I don't understand how he poisoned the cupcakes, though. I baked them the night before, and decorated them in the morning. Then I covered them with tin foil and I brought them over to Gayle's office. Monica, her secretary, put them into the refrigerator to stay fresh. Gayle has a private kitchen connected to her office, you know, to offer refreshments when people come to see her. I don't see how Daniel could have tampered with the cupcakes."

"Well, that's something we need to find out."

"Yes, I need him to confess!"

"That won't be easy while he's in duBarry," Evan said. "It was clever of him to get admitted and lock himself away like that."

"You think he's capable of being so devious?"

"We're talking about a twisted, egocentric psychopath. If you are right that he planned the murders, he certainly could have feigned this breakdown to avoid being questioned."

"Well, I don't have much choice. He did it, all right. If he doesn't confess, I might be convicted of his crime and he'll go free. He might even kill again." Emily looked concerned. "I can't let that happen."

"You're right. Even if we offered the police your theory of the crime, Daniel can just deny everything and it would be his word against yours. With the evidence they have, the D.A. will concoct some kind of motive for you and the jury will have to decide. It's a huge risk, for sure."

Emily nodded slowly. "You know, I noticed after my apartment was searched that my back door was unlocked, and I always lock the door when I leave. What if someone broke in and planted the Rosary Pea evidence in my cupboard? I'm positive it wasn't there when I left Friday morning!"

"That implies someone is working with Daniel, unless you think Daniel could have planted the twig evidence himself."

"This whole situation is so twisted, I honestly don't know what to think. Anyway, how could he get in? He doesn't have a key to my place."

"It's easy to pick the lock, if you know how and have the right tools," Evan said. "What kind of building do you live in?"

"It's a walk-up triplex. I'm in the middle apartment."

"Okay, who lives above you and below you?"

"My neighbors? A lady lives below with her twelve-year-old son. She works at the bank in Mount Salem and her son is in school. The man above me lives alone. He's on a disability pension."

"So your upstairs neighbor would have been at home on Friday morning?"

"Probably. He doesn't go out much."

"We need to find out if he saw anything or heard anything unusual on Friday morning," Evan said.

"I'll ask him —" she began.

"No, Emily. Let me talk to him. I don't want you speaking to anyone about the case, you understand?"

"Okay," she said.

"Just get me his name and telephone number, and I will call him," Evan said.

After lunch, Evan drove Emily back to the college. Emily was quiet for a while. Then she said, "Well, if I can't use the files on the flash drive as evidence, I'll have to plan an alternative strategy."

"Do you have any ideas?" Evan asked.

"I'm a bridge player, Mr. Thompson. When you play the hand at bridge, before you play to the first trick, you look at the dummy and decide on a plan to make your contract. You often have choices on how to proceed. Some choices are obvious, some less so. You should play the hand in a way that will make the contract with the least amount of risk, and have a back-up plan. For example, if you are missing the king of trumps, you can try a finesse. But, if the finesse fails, you have to look for a way to make an extra trick in the other suits. So you might try for a squeeze or an endplay. Right now, I'm faced with a finesse that didn't work, since the files on the flash drive are not enough to exonerate me. So I will just have to come up with another plan that will get the result I want."

"Intriguing. Maybe I should look into… uh… learning how to play bridge. Seems like an interesting game!"

"You bet it is," she said, laughing. Evan was pleased to see her smile. "If you're serious about it, I'll give you some bridge lessons — after I get out from under these ridiculous charges, that is."

He smiled and nodded in agreement. "I'd like that," he said. "So what is the back-up plan you're considering?"

"Well, it's a long shot, but if I play my cards right, it might work," she said. "First, I have to go talk to my friend Rachel. She's a nurse at duBarry. Then we'll need to get diLongo to cooperate."

"Before you do anything, let me know so I can advise you of any legal issues."

Emily agreed. Arriving back at the campus, she picked up her car from the staff parking lot, then drove home.

As Emily was unlocking her back door, she called to her cat, Patches. She knew the cat would be hungry and displeased for being left alone all weekend without food. Sure enough, Patches jumped down from the sofa and walked stiff-legged into the kitchen, twitching her tail the whole way. She sat by her feeding bowl with her back to Emily, who got the hint. Before she took her coat off, Emily put out some fresh food and water for Patches. The hungry cat did not acknowledge this offering until Emily left the kitchen to hang up her coat. Only then did Patches sniff her food and start eating.

Emily sat down on her sofa and phoned her friend, Rachel Mayberry, who lived a few miles away in Fairview.

"Rachel, I need your help," Emily began.

"Hey, Emily, I'm glad to hear from you. I read something about you in *The Record*. Is it true you've been charged with murder?"

"Yes," she said. "But, Rach, I didn't do it. You've got believe me. I swear I didn't do it!"

"Of course I believe you, Emily," Rachel assured her. "Why did the police arrest you?"

"It's a mess, Rach. They found evidence at my apartment. Listen, I know who did it, but I need your help to clear my name!"

"What can I do?"

"The killer is a patient at duBarry."

"Oh my God, Emily, are you serious?"

"Yes, I am. The killer is my boss, Daniel Post. He poisoned those two people and planted the evidence against me, so now I've been charged with the murders!"

"You know this for sure?"

"Uh-huh. I have the proof, but it's not something the police can use until I get Daniel's confession. So that's why I need your help."

"Okay, tell me what you want me to do," she said.

"Daniel was admitted to duBarry on Friday afternoon, apparently after having a breakdown. Belinda, one of the secretaries in our department, told my lawyer that he went nuts in the office, took off all his clothes, and threatened to kill himself. So his doctor arranged for him to be admitted," she said. "But I don't know if it's a true mental breakdown or if he's faking it to get into the psych ward."

"Well, he's probably on the third floor, where they have patients who are potentially a threat to themselves. It's a very secure floor. No one can get in or out of there without the proper authority. You have to know the security codes to gain access to the floor."

"Well, that's unfortunate," Emily said.

"Not so much. Guess what? I'm working that floor this week, so I have the security codes. What do you want me to do?"

"Can you go and talk to him? Ask him about the murders. See if he'll divulge anything to you. I mean, he won't suspect you of anything, right? He might talk to you, if he thinks you're sympathetic."

"I'll give it a shot," she said. "I work from four to midnight this afternoon, so I'll let you know how it goes."

"If he confesses to you, then you could testify in court and the jury might actually believe me then," Emily said. "I know it's a long shot, but it's worth a try, don't you think?"

"Leave it with me, Em," Rachel said. "If anyone can get him to talk, it's me."

"Thanks, Rach," Emily said, "You're a life saver!"

For the next few hours, Emily busied herself with some household chores and then made dinner. When she was finished eating, she turned on the TV and curled up on the sofa with Patches, who had finally forgiven her and was purring contentedly on her lap. Emily's phone rang just after eight o'clock.

"Em, it's Rachel. I'm sorry, but I have no good news for you. I tried to talk to Mr. Post tonight, but he told me to bugger off. Those were his exact words. He said if I didn't leave him alone he'd push his call button, and then the orderlies would come to investigate and that would not be a good thing. So I had to leave. I am so sorry!"

Emily sighed. "Thanks for trying, anyway. Tell me something. Do you know if they're giving him any drugs?"

"According to his chart, he's just on a mild tranquilizer that acts as a sleeping pill at night, and they're keeping him under observation for a week or so. Then I guess the doctors will assess his case and see what kind of treatment he needs."

"Does he seem normal to you?"

"If being bad-tempered is normal, then yes," she said.

"Well, I guess I'll have go to Plan C," Emily said. "I really need him to confess."

"What's Plan C?" Rachel asked.

"Let me map it out for you," Emily said. "It's time for some bold action."

After filling Rachel in on her plan, she called Evan Thompson and gave him the name and telephone number for Barry Coin, her neighbor upstairs. Then she told him about Plan C.

"I need you to talk to Detective diLongo and get her to go along with this," Emily said. Evan agreed to meet diLongo the next morning.

When Emily went to bed on Monday night, she fell into a deep, satisfying sleep with the hope that her situation was soon going to be resolved one way or the other.

After eating dinner at home and speaking with Emily on the telephone, Evan called Barry Coin, Emily's upstairs neighbor.

The phone rang five times before Mr. Coin answered.

"Good evening, Mr. Coin. I'm Evan Thompson. I'm a lawyer representing your neighbor downstairs, Miss Emily Warren."

"Okay," he said.

"How are you doing, Mr. Coin?"

"I'm just hunky-dorey. What do you want?"

"We're looking into the circumstances of a case involving two deaths at Kensington College…" Evan began.

"Oh, that," he said. "Yeah, I heard somethin' about that on the radio. They already caught the killer!" he said. "That was fast work."

"Well, the police have charged my client, but she's innocent until proven guilty. And we have ample reason to believe she is innocent."

"You mean, they charged Emily? I didn't catch that on the news," Mr. Coin said. "She's such a nice girl."

"Yes, she is," Evan said. "If you don't mind, I have a question for you."

"Go on," he said.

"Think back to Friday. Were you at home during the day?"

"Yeah, all day," he said. "I don't go out much, on account of my back."

"I'm sorry to hear that. So, on Friday, did you see anything or hear anything unusual?"

"Hmm… there was a big commotion in the afternoon when the police arrived. They made a lot of noise going up and down the stairs," he said.

"Right," Evan said. "Before the police arrived, did you notice anything unusual?"

"Yeah, come to think of it. I heard someone knocking on my back door, but when I opened the door, no one was there," he said. "I don't move so fast since my accident ten years ago. I was a logger," he explained. "I thought maybe whoever it was went back downstairs. I look out my kitchen window and I see this guy walkin' around suspicious-like, and he goes into the neighbor's backyard."

"Do you know when this happened?"

"Yeah, it happened when the police cars arrived," he said.

"Can you describe the man you saw out back?" Evan asked.

"Well, I didn't see his face. He was wearing a dark jacket and a cap," Mr. Coin said. "A big fella."

"Okay, thanks Mr. Coin. You have been very helpful," Evan said.

"Anything else I can do, let me know," Mr. Coin said. "I like Emily."

"Okay, I will. Good night, Mr. Coin," Evan said.

"Bye," he said.

Evan was pleased with his chat with Mr. Coin. If this case went to trial, he could use Mr. Coin's testimony to build his theory that someone else entered the apartment that day and planted the incriminating evidence against Emily.

CHAPTER 24

PRESENT DAY — 4:45 A.M.

"So," Brian said, "it's starting to look good for Emily to get off."

"At the time, we still thought Emily was guilty, but what bothered me was the lack of a suitable motive. I didn't see how eliminating these two people would benefit her in any way, except to win the bridge prize, and that's a pretty thin motive for murder."

"Well, I'm curious about the Christmas dinner. How did the poison get into the cupcakes? I can't see anyone sneaking into Dr. Primrose's office, accessing her private kitchen and doctoring the cupcakes. And if they did, there would be no motive, other than the desire to kill randomly. So what happened?"

"We were able to piece together most of the player interactions that took place that night," I said. "As I suspected, the players were very focused on the competition for the annual prize. Terry, in particular, was being quite obnoxious about it."

WEDNESDAY, DECEMBER 10, 2008 — 7:00 P.M. CHRISTMAS BRIDGE DINNER

One of the highlights of the year for the Faculty Bridge Club was the annual Christmas potluck dinner. Gayle always decorated the faculty dining room and had a big fire burning in the stone fireplace, with scented candles on the bar and a tall Christmas tree adorned with red bows, silver balls and twinkling lights.

"Cheers!" Gayle called out, raising her glass of wine as each new person entered the dining room. "Help yourselves to a drink!" she chirped, directing them to the bar where wine, beer and liquor of all sorts stood ready.

When everyone was assembled with their drinks in hand, Gayle made a short speech.

"Welcome, friends, to our annual Christmas bridge night. We'll have some great food, great spirits and, hopefully, great bridge too! I have the scores from last Wednesday right here." She raised her hand with several sheets of paper. "The winners from last week are Terry Digman and Sally

Brighton for East-West — good job, Terry and Sally! — and Daniel Post and Emily Warren for North-South. Well done! You can pick up your prize money at the end of the session tonight." She set the papers down on the bar. "We're down to the wire for the annual bridge prize to attend my New Year's Eve dinner party, folks. There's only one more session to go after tonight, before we break for Christmas. And three pairs are tied for first place. So next week we'll have the winners!" she said. "This year, I have a spectacular guest list, including a Nobel prize winner, a leading New York publisher, a Hollywood icon, an Olympic gold medalist, a late-night talk show host, a famous Italian wine-maker and some other celebrities," she said enticingly. "Of course, I will keep their identities secret until the party, as a surprise for you," she said with a big grin. Then she checked her watch.

"It's time to eat, folks, and the food is ready. Help yourself to sandwiches and salad. We'll have dessert at the break, at around 9:30. Coffee and tea will be available by then. So, without further ado, let's eat, shall we?"

Some of the players hurried to the food table, while others drifted over to the bar to pick up the results from the previous session and learn if they were still in the running for the prize. The prize was awarded to the pair that was 'in the money' the most throughout the year. As Gayle said, it was a tight race this year. Tied in first place were Terry and Sally, Daniel and Emily, and Anne-Marie and Chris, each pair having been in the money nine times. Barb and Jill and Gayle and David were very close behind.

Barb and Jill went to see the results. "Look at that," Barb said, pointing to the East-West results for the previous session. "We came in third, just below Karl and Ben, by less than one percent! Let's see where we lost ground."

Jill reviewed her copy of the results and said, "I think I see where we lost it. Look at board nine. They bid three clubs and made four. We bid three clubs, and made three. I wonder how Karl got the extra trick."

"Well, they must have got a gift," Barb pointed out, "'cuz you can't make more than nine tricks with proper defense," Barb said.

"Pity," Jill said. "But look, we're only one behind the leaders, so we can still win, but we have to come first in the next two sessions."

Barb grinned. "Piece of cake!"

"Speaking of that, let's grab some food."

Daniel too reviewed the results from the previous week. He was very happy. He and Emily were first for North-South. They were in the running for the prize, but they would have to be at the top of their game in the last two bridge sessions to win it.

"We can't afford to make any mistakes tonight," he warned Emily.

"Yes, Daniel. I see," she said, reviewing the results. "We will win, with a little luck!"

"Luck has nothing to do with it," he said. "You have to concentrate, Emily. Watch my discards. I give you very clear signals, but you don't always see them."

"I'll remember tonight," she said. "We're so close to the finish line."

Terry also picked up a copy of the results from the last session, and smiled. He and Sally had scored over 65%! He showed the results to Sally.

"The prize is in the bag, baby. Just stay cool and I'll carry you over the finish line."

Sally pursed her lips. "Why do you always have to be so fucking obnoxious?" she snapped, and walked away.

"Hey," he said, following her to the food table where players were lining up. "Don't get all hormonal on me… I'm just saying, we have a good shot at the prize. And I don't like to lose, so get with the program, honey."

Sally turned to him. "I want to win as much as you, or anyone else. And I am with the program, *honey!*"

"Oooo, I love it when you sweet-talk me!" He patted her backside as she turned away. She glared at him over her shoulder.

I can't wait to be rid of him, she thought, turning her attention to the food.

A line had formed at the food table, and slowly the players moved along, choosing the items they wanted and loading up their plates. The sandwiches came from the Delish Deli. Players contributed the rest of the meal: a bean salad, a potato salad, a garden salad, some fresh veggies with dip, chicken balls, bread rolls, snacks and desserts.

When the dinner was over and dishes cleared away, the players helped set up the tables for bridge. They laid table covers on each table, placed a card with a number identifying the table, placed bidding boxes on each corner, distributed pencils, scoresheets and table slips, and waited for Gayle to distribute the boards.

Gayle stood by the roaring fire and held up her hand to get their attention.

"I hope everyone enjoyed their dinner and had enough to eat?" she said, to murmurs of appreciation. "I know it was simple fare this time. Maybe next year, if budgets permit, we'll have our amazing chef prepare a magnificent meal like he did last year." The players applauded this idea.

"Great! So tonight, we have five full tables and no skip. We have four boards per table and twenty-five minutes per round. I'll give you a two-minute warning for each round. So, enjoy!"

Two staff members arrived to clear away the food and dirty dishes left over from dinner as the players began the first round of bridge. Gayle told the staff to go home once the tables were cleared.

In spite of the festive atmosphere, the players became very serious once the game started. At this time of year, heading towards the finish line for the annual prize, there was more tension than usual at the bridge table. Some players took extra time to make their bids or play the hand, and other players insisted on following the rules to the letter, calling Gayle, the director, over to settle any disputes.

Gayle called the end of the first round, and all the East-West players moved to the next table in ascending order, while the North-South players remained at their table and scored the last hand. They passed all the boards with the hands they had just played over to the next table in descending order, in the opposite direction of the East-West players.

At the end of the third round, Gayle announced it was time for the coffee break. She went over to the dessert table, removed the plastic wrap and tin foil that covered the desserts, and made sure the coffee and hot water were ready.

As players started lining up for dessert, Daniel said to Emily, "You stay here, I'll get your dessert. It's already crowded up there."

Emily smiled. "I'd like a brownie and date square, please."

It wasn't often that Daniel offered to do anything for her, but he had been in a better mood lately, so she just hoped it would continue. There was quite a crowd at the table, and she was pleased to see people choosing her cupcakes. Emily decided to visit the ladies room while Daniel was getting her dessert.

Barb and Jill walked over to the end of the bar where they could talk privately.

"I think you should have just asked for aces on that last hand," Barb said to Jill. "Then we'd get to the heart slam."

"I couldn't," Jill countered. "I had a void,"

"Well, cuebid your void, then!"

"But what if you think it's a second suit? I knew we had a fit in hearts. Four hearts was a safe bet."

"Safe, yes, but we missed the slam," Barb pointed out.

"We won't be the only ones. Slam is not a slam-dunk here," Jill said, and laughed. "The two that played it so far went down one in six hearts.

Anyway, we can check the travelers at the end of the night and see how we did on that board."

Barb and Jill joined the line-up for the dessert table, behind Terry and David, who were deep in conversation. When Terry heard Jill's voice, he turned to speak to her.

"Hello, gorgeous," he said with a wink. "How goes the battle?"

"We're doing just fine," she replied, "and we're gonna beat your ass after the break tonight."

"Ooh, I love to have my ass beaten," he said. "Any time! My place or yours?"

"Get out of here," Jill replied coolly.

Barb said to Terry, "Don't flatter yourself."

He looked down at Barb and replied, "You could stand to be flattered," indicating her rotund figure.

"Go to hell," Barb replied.

Terry turned back to Jill. He leaned in towards her to speak softly into her ear. "I think you are the hottest girl on campus. And you know what I mean!" he said, running his hand down her back and over her hip.

"Hands off!" she said sternly. "Please move, so I can get a cupcake."

He moved aside, but as she leaned over the table for a cupcake, he reached over her, pressing his groin into her backside in the process. "Let me help you," he said, choosing a cupcake for her with his long reach. "See, I'm a nice guy," he said, placing the cupcake on a small plate and handing it to her.

Jill took it and moved away from the table. Then she turned around and said to him, "I've changed my mind."

He smiled expectantly and raised his eyebrows.

"I don't want this after all. Here." She handed the plate with the cupcake back to him.

"What did that jerk have to say to you?" Barb asked Jill, as they walked back to their table.

"Oh, the usual crapola," Jill said.

"He was flirting with you again, wasn't he?" Barb asked.

"He was trying," Jill replied. "Very trying!" She giggled. "Don't worry about him. We'll beat the pants off him tonight."

"What are you having with your tea?" Barb asked, noticing that Jill did not have any dessert.

"Oh, I don't know. I'll go back up in a minute," she said, "when it's not so crowded up there."

"These cupcakes are delish," Barb said, taking a big bite. "I might go back for another one."

"Well, get one for me too, then," Jill replied, taking a sip of her tea. "I wanted a cupcake, but not the one Terry got for me." She made a face. "I don't want to eat anything he's touched!"

"I don't blame you. There's Karl talking to Daniel," Barb said. "He's a funny old duck, don't you think?"

"What do you mean?" Jill asked.

"Well, he looks like an old fuddy-duddy, but he's a pretty sneaky player. You have to be careful, 'cuz he'll make some incredible leads."

"Yeah, he uses upside-down carding, too," Jill said, "like a real expert."

"I'm concerned about Karl and Ben. They're like the dark horses that come from behind. I think we should watch out for them."

"I agree," Jill said.

"I'm also concerned about Daniel and Emily. Em's a much better player than she lets on, and Daniel is not overbidding so much lately. If they keep playing like that, they could actually beat all of us," Barb said.

Jill sipped her tea and placed her cup on the saucer. She looked fondly at her friend.

"Barb, you worry too much, and over-analyze too much. Just relax. We have as good a chance as any to win this year," she said.

"*You* can say that — relax!" Barb said, "Everybody loves you, but they look down on me. But if we come first this year, they'll have to give me more respect at the bridge table, at least!"

"Barb, what makes you think people don't respect you?"

"Oh, I don't know," she said, frowning. "It's this college crowd. When they look at me all they see is an ugly, fat girl in boots. They think I'm a low-life or something. They don't really see me as an equal."

"I think that's all in your mind, Barb," Jill said. "They just don't know you. I love you, and anyone who gets to know you will love you too. So chill, already."

Barb smiled, and settled down to finish her cupcake. Then she went back to the dessert table to get another one for herself and one for Jill.

Karl returned to his table, and Ben asked him if he wanted something for dessert. Karl patted his rotund middle and said, "I think I'll pass, but perhaps you could bring me some tea, Ben."

Ben nodded, and walked to the other side of the dessert table where the tea and coffee were located. The table was still crowded with bridge players reaching for the sweet treats and drinks. Ben poured tea into a cup, and took a bottle of water back to the table.

"Here you go," he said to Karl, "I'll go back and get some cookies for myself. Just be a minute."

He made his way back to the dessert table, squeezing past Terry and David, who were standing at one end of the table next to Chris Boland and Melissa Fielding.

"Well, excuse me," Terry said sarcastically, as Ben maneuvered around him. "If it isn't our little Chinaman going for some cookies! These aren't fortune cookies, you know."

Ben glared at him, but said nothing.

"He's trying to do a squeeze play at the dessert table," Terry continued, directing his comments to David. "He needs to learn some manners!" Then he turned to Ben and said, "Where are your manners, boy? Did you leave them in China? Maybe you should go back home and get them." Terry moved to block Ben so he couldn't escape.

"What's your problem?" Ben said, trying not to be rattled by Terry's goading.

"Oh, nothing much. You executed a squeeze on me once, but you and I know it was pure luck, not skill. Better keep taking lessons from old Karl over there. Maybe one of these years you'll actually learn this game."

"Piss off," Ben said. "You don't want me talking to Gayle, do you?"

"As if!" Terry said derisively. "You're not going to shoot yourself in the foot. Anyway," he said more jovially, "it's just bridge talk. Just trying to make you think twice when you play at my table. Right, Davey boy?" he said to David. Ben and Karl were sitting East-West, and they would be moving to Terry's table when Gayle called the next round.

"Yeah," David said. "All's fair in love and bridge, as they say. Even Terry and I get on each other's case at the bridge table. But we're friends. Very close friends," he said, nodding. "Remember that."

Terry stepped aside and Ben returned to his table.

Karl was watching and he could tell that Ben was rattled. "Don't let that guy bother you," Karl said to Ben, as he returned with his cookies. "He's just trying to push your buttons."

"I know," Ben said. "He better not push too hard, or he'll regret it. I know how to get him."

"Just concentrate on your bridge, Ben, and you'll be fine," Karl said. "Remember to count all the suits."

At the dessert table, David lowered his voice and said to Terry, "That kid, he's not gonna rat us out, is he?"

"Ben? All I have to do is mention 'Hong Kong' and he'll behave," Terry said.

"How do you know that for sure?" David asked.

"I figured he had his reasons for coming here," Terry said. "So I warned him a while back if he was dumb enough to talk about our business deal, I'd report him to my friends in the immigration department and he'd be on the next plane back to China. You should have seen the look on his face!"

"You bluffed him," David commented. "Sweet."

Melissa Fielding was also at the dessert table, and she moved closer to Terry to reach for some dessert.

"Well, hello!" Terry said as Melissa leaned over the table for the cookies. "Impressive bazookas," he said, indicating her partially exposed bosom. He moved in closer to her and lowered his voice so only she could hear. "But, you know, I'm a leg man, and you have some very nice pins, baby. You and I should get together sometime. What do you say?"

"I say, out of my way," she said, but her smile showed her amusement. She took a big bite of her cookie, and moved around the table to speak to Chris.

"Look at that," Terry said to David. "Chris Boland is chatting up Melissa again. What do you think is going on there?"

"Oh, come on," David said. "Chris is happily married with kids. He wouldn't mess around. He goes to church every Sunday!"

"Don't be so sure about that," Terry replied. "I know things. For example, I know about you and Gayle."

"Only because I told you… and you promised to keep it a secret!"

"Yeah, yeah," Terry said. "I'm good at keeping secrets. But what's the good of having knowledge if you don't use it?"

"What do you mean?"

"I may have mentioned something to Gayle last week. I told her I knew something that she wouldn't want the Board to find out about."

"Oh shit," David said under his breath. "Why did you do that?"

"Well, it gives me more leverage to do what I want. Anyway, I told her I'd keep a lid on it. She knows I'm planning to leave in a few months. And by the way, she's giving me a nice 'going away' package," Terry said, and grinned.

"You devil," David said. "She's paying you to keep quiet!"

Just then, Terry spun around as someone bumped into him. It was Daniel.

"Hey, watch it," Daniel said.

"No, you watch it, old man," Terry said. "You bumped into me."

"My apologies," Daniel said. "It's crowded up here."

Daniel moved out of the way as Anne-Marie Boland came up to the table and reached for two cupcakes. Then she motioned to her husband, Chris, who was standing beside Melissa. "I have some dessert for you, dear. Can you bring us some tea?"

"I'll be right there," he said, and turned back to Melissa. "Duty calls," he said, as he nodded towards his wife.

"Wait," she said. "Grab me a cupcake, will ya?"

"With pleasure," he replied. He turned around, placed a cupcake on a plate and handed it to Melissa. Then he poured two cups of tea and left to join Anne-Marie at their table.

"Where's John tonight?" Anne-Marie asked Chris. John was Melissa's husband.

"Dunno," Chris said. "Out late somewhere."

"Is he still off work?"

"I really don't know," Chris said. "I don't grill Melissa about what her husband is doing. She has a hard enough time with a full-time job and caring for her baby."

"Really. You seem to know a lot about her life. What has she been telling you?"

Chris looked annoyed. "What does it matter? She's a nice girl, and she's having a tough time right now. I lend an ear sometimes. It's the Christian thing to do."

Anne-Marie bit into her cupcake and sipped her tea. "You are right, dear. We should show our love and support to those in need. I'd like to include her family in our prayers tonight."

"Fine," he said. "Now let's focus on the bridge game. There are two more rounds, and I think we have some top boards, but we also have a couple of bad ones. Stick to the strategy, dear. Aggressive when we are not vulnerable. Careful when we are vulnerable. If I double anything up to three spades, it's for takeout. And don't forget about the Unusual Notrump bid. It can happen even at the four-level."

"Yes, dear," she said, through a mouthful of cupcake.

Back at the food table, Daniel was fussing with some dessert plates. Then he noticed Terry talking to David.

"Looks like we're tied in first for the annual prize," Daniel said to Terry, interrupting them.

"For now, but don't get too cocky, old boy. We're gonna leave you in our dust by the end of the evening," Terry replied.

Terry was still holding the small plate with Jill's cupcake on it. He picked up the cupcake and sniffed it. "This smells awfully good," he said.

"Yes, Emily does a fine job on them," Daniel said, indicating the cupcake on his own plate. "She bakes them from scratch, you know."

"Hey, where'd you get the black jellybeans?" Terry said. "I didn't see them earlier. I thought they were all green and red for Christmas."

"She ran out and had to use some black ones," Daniel said. "Actually, I'm not fond of jellybeans. I like sprinkles, but Emily insists on jellybeans."

"In that case, I'll trade you." Terry said. "I like the black ones. I hate red ones."

"Well, okay," Daniel said, exchanging cupcakes with Terry, "but don't expect any more gifts tonight. Emily and I are playing near-perfect bridge."

"I know, I see your scores," Terry said. "Not bad. But the night is not over yet."

"Now get out of my way," Daniel said, "I want to take this dessert back to Emily." He was holding a plate with a brownie and date square.

Terry turned back to David and they continued their discussion.

Daniel returned to his table with the desserts and then he went back to get a coffee for Emily and a tea for himself. As he settled into his seat, he removed the red jellybeans from his cupcake and peeled off the paper case. Then he took a big bite, getting some white icing on his nose in the process.

"Mmmm, delicious," he said. "I could eat one of these every day!"

"Well, I could make them more often and bring some into the office," Emily said, enjoying her date square. Daniel offered her his jellybeans. She popped them into her mouth and smiled. "Thanks," she said. "I love jellybeans! Especially the red ones!"

When she was finished eating, she said, "I'm going for some tea. The coffee is too strong for me. You want some more tea, Daniel?"

"Thanks, Emily," he said, smiling. "One milk, two sugars. You know, the usual."

Emily walked over to the dessert table and selected two cups. She poured in the milk, and then the tea, and added two cubes of sugar to Daniel's cup. Several players were still milling around the dessert table, and as she moved away, she bumped into Terry, and the teacups spilled. He moved his arm to avoid the tea, and his cupcake nearly bounced off the plate, but he caught it just in time. "Hey, watch it!" he said.

"Oh, sorry, Terry!" Emily said. "My fault. I didn't see you there."

"No problem, Emily," he said. "You know," he said in a lower voice, "I love your cupcakes but not as much as those sweet cheeks of yours," and he winked and patted her backside.

She frowned at him and said. "Mind your manners," and hurried over to join Daniel at their table.

"What was Terry saying to you?" Daniel asked.

"It was nothing," she said.

"Well," Daniel said, "he was at the dessert table when I was there. He told me that he and Sally are going to leave us in their dust for the prize this year. What cheek!"

"We'll prevail if we concentrate and play up to our potential," Emily said. "I'm not concerned about our play of the hand — it's the bidding that gets us into trouble sometimes. If we bid properly, we'll always come first."

Then Gayle's deep voice cut through the break-time chatter.

"Okay, folks, next round begins now," she boomed.

The players settled down to start the next hand. The chatter gave way to the sound of bidding boxes clacking as the players selected their bidding cards.

The bidding boxes were a recent addition to the club. In the past, players had to say their bids out loud, but that made it noisy and other players might overhear the bidding. Several minutes after the play began, Anne-Marie suddenly stood up at Table 1, holding her stomach.

"Ohhhh," she groaned. "My stomach hurts!" Her faced drained of all color, and her eyes rolled back in her head as blood seeped out from under the lids. Then she collapsed on her hands and knees. Her body convulsed and she vomited several times.

"What's wrong?" her husband shouted as he knelt beside her on the floor. "Annie? Annie, what's wrong?" he kept asking as she thrashed from side to side, making horrible retching sounds. The blood and vomit covered her face and clothes.

Chris shouted, "Call a doctor!" He started giving his wife mouth-to-mouth to revive her. Players at the next table jumped up to see what was happening.

Gayle took out her cell phone and called the college clinic. "Send a doctor over to the faculty dining room immediately. We have an emergency. Someone has collapsed."

Players crowded around, offering advice: "Give her some water!" "Get some ice!" "Move her over to the sofa!" As the players were attending to Anne-Marie, Terry Digman suddenly let out a loud groan and fell out of his chair, writhing on the floor. "Oh God, oh God," he gasped, and then his eyes rolled up as he convulsed. Blood oozed from his eyes as vomit erupted from his mouth. He curled up in a fetal position, screaming in agony.

"Bloody hell!" Daniel shouted, "Terry's down, too!"

"Oh, my God," Sally cried. "Terry!" Everyone started shouting at the same time.

The four students huddled together. "They're dying!" one student shouted. "Who's next?" someone else cried out. Emily elbowed her way to Terry and started trying to revive him. "Someone call for help!" she shouted as she continued CPR. Then pandemonium broke out as the players huddled together in panic at the sight of their stricken friends on the floor. "Christ Almighty!" "What's going on?" "Are you okay?" "What's happening?" "Is it contagious?" "It's something they ate!" "Look at all the blood!"

Dr. Morrison, the college doctor on call that night, arrived on the scene a few minutes later. He was horrified to see two people lying on the floor, already dead. There were flecks of foam and dark vomit around their mouths and blood around their eyes. He told Emily to stop doing CPR while he knelt down to see if there was a pulse. Nothing. He was too late.

Panicking, unsure of what to do, he turned to Gayle and said, "They're gone. Better call the police. This looks suspicious to me. There's nothing I can do for them."

And then he headed over to the bar and poured himself a Scotch, which he drank in one gulp and then poured another.

Gayle picked up her cell phone and called 911. "We have an emergency!"

CHAPTER 25

"Things really heated up after the weekend," I said, "when Skip came into my office with some updates about the background checks he was doing on the players. I did some more interviews and discovered another angle and possible motive for the crime, but in the end, it was Miss Warren who took charge of the situation and helped us solve the case. Her lawyer came to see me to make the necessary preparations. I was skeptical at first. I mean, I don't like involving civilians, especially murder suspects out on bail, in police work. But Evan Thompson was very persuasive, and I considered the possibility that we might have made a big mistake charging Emily Warren."

MONDAY, DECEMBER 15, 2008 — 11:45 A.M.

While Evan and Emily were having lunch at the Blue Bird Café, Skip and diLongo had a brief meeting about the case. Skip had worked through the weekend.

"Anything new?" diLongo asked him.

"Nothing out of the ordinary so far," Skip reported. "Emily Warren's background is squeaky clean. Not so much as a parking ticket.

"Sally Brighton has an impeccable academic record, no criminal activity, a few speeding tickets, no other issues.

"Chris Boland is clean, except for his escapade with Nurse Ratched. He attended church every Sunday with his wife and kids, coaches Little League baseball, supports several charities and has a steady job. No convictions. He does have some debts, and the life insurance money will help him out there, but not if he is convicted of murdering his wife. The insurance would not pay in that case.

"Daniel Post is a celebrity, having written several bestselling novels. He was educated at Cambridge, came to the U.S. thirty years ago, married his wife Marion, no kids, no criminal record, etc. He is known to be rather eccentric and sometimes difficult to work with, but nothing extreme.

His wife died four years ago. He hasn't published anything since, but he's working on a new book.

"Barb Baker, the printing and post office manager, has family in the area. Her father is a factory worker and her mother is a nurse. The family is solid, working class. No trouble with the law. There's some speculation that she is a lesbian, but no proof about that. She doesn't like Professor Digman very much, but she has no motive to kill him or Mrs. Boland.

"Jill Wilmington, the H.R. manager, checks out. She has a good employment record and no debts or convictions."

"And the others?"

"Melissa Fielding is married with a baby at home. She was a wild child as a teenager and ran away from home a few times. Then she settled down, went to business school and got a job at the college doing administration work. She got married and pregnant, not necessarily in that order. Her husband, John, is a computer technician, out of work right now. Melissa is the main breadwinner. Seems they're not the happiest of couples."

"Well, we could look into that… see if she has any private connections with Professor Digman or Mrs. Boland," diLongo mused.

"I'm checking out the students now. Maybe they were buying drugs from Ben Chong, and found out Digman was the source, but that doesn't give them a reason to murder him. And they have no known connection at all with Mr. or Mrs. Boland," Skip reported.

"Okay," diLongo said, "We already ruled out Mrs. Kingston, the nurse, who was just filling in that night," diLongo said.

"Right. Karl Schultz has been teaching at the college for about thirty years or so. He's married, with two children and four grandchildren. The kids all live in different cities, so he lives alone with his wife. He has no convictions, not even a speeding ticket.

"Ben Chong also checks out. He's here on a student visa. Parents live in Hong Kong. He's an A student. No convictions for anything. He arrived two years ago and has been studying at the college this whole time.

"There's nothing on the Blacks, either. They seem like solid people. They've been working in the IT department for about ten years. They do some programming and trouble-shooting on the college's computer system.

"And then there's Dr. Primrose. She's been working at the college for over twenty-five years. She has no criminal record, no traffic violations, a few parking tickets. No debts. Her academic credentials check out. She earned her Ph.D. at Syracuse University before moving here to teach at

Kensington. Her husband died in a boating accident. She didn't remarry. She's got a lot of connections to rich and powerful people.

"I'm still checking out David Bartholomew. I'm waiting for someone at the training college where he acquired his papers for security work to get back to me. No one was there on the weekend. I did made contact with the owner of the trucking company in Canada. He said Mr. Bartholomew was an excellent employee."

"What was Bartholomew doing before he lived in Canada?" diLongo asked.

"He had a series of odd jobs with small companies that are no longer in business, so it's hard to confirm anything. He was in the army, too, so I'm trying to find out more about that," he said. "And I'm also waiting for information on Digman. I sent his prints and photo to the Mounties in Ottawa. Since he worked as a consultant for the R.C.M.P. before coming to Kensington, they should have some information about him. According to his resume, he's been an independent consultant for many years. The security report was not in his file for some reason. Anyway, it's hard to connect with people on the weekend. I can't locate his next of kin, either. He left that part blank on his employment form."

"So we're no further ahead. Everyone has the opportunity and the means, but no one has a motive," diLongo said. "If Miss Warren is innocent, that means someone set her up, so there must be something we're missing," she said. "People don't commit homicides like this without a motive, not unless..." she paused for a moment, "not unless they're a psychopath, which means we may have a predatory killer on our hands. We've already determined the killer is one of the bridge players. There has to be something in their backgrounds that will illuminate the truth."

"Okay, I'll keep digging," he said, and hurried back to his desk.

"Thanks, Skip," diLongo said. "Now I have to do a report for the shift change."

CHAPTER 26

📅 MONDAY, DECEMBER 15, 2008 — 4:30 P.M.

Late Monday afternoon, Skip charged into diLongo's office.

"I finally got some intel on Terry Digman," he said. "You won't believe this. He did some consulting work for the R.C.M.P. all right. But he died ten years ago! His prints don't match our Terry Digman, because our Terry Digman is not Terry Digman at all. He's Stanley Karakchuck, from Hamilton, Ontario, who spent four years in a Canadian prison for investment fraud and some other white-collar crimes. He's a con man, Dee-Dee!"

"Really? So, what — he stole Terry Digman's identity?" she asked.

"Exactly. I also have some information on David Bartholomew that you'll find very interesting," he said.

He handed the file over to diLongo, who took a minute to look through it. Her eyes widened in surprise as she read. "Thanks, Skip. Good work. Would you call Dr. Primrose and have her come in for a chat? And I also want to speak with David Bartholomew and Jill Wilmington. And come back here when you're done."

Skip went to his desk and rang Gayle's office number.

"Dr. Primrose, this is Officer Crane. We have some news about the investigation into the murders of Mr. Digman and Mrs. Boland."

"Please, tell me," she said.

"We would like you to come down to the station immediately to discuss a few things with you."

"Of course," she said. "I'll leave right away."

"Thank you," Skip said. Then he rang David Bartholomew and Jill Wilmington and gave them the same message.

Gayle rang David's cell. "I got a call from Officer Crane," she said. "They want me to come to the station. They have some news about the investigation."

"He called me too," he said. "We might as well go together."

"I wonder what's up," she said. "Anyway, I can be ready in ten."

"I'll drive over and pick you up," he said.

Gayle went into the private washroom attached to her office to straighten her hair and fix her make-up. She peered at herself in the mirror, noting the pallid color of her skin and the dark circles under her eyes. The strain of the last few days was showing in her face. She opened a drawer in the cabinet where she kept her personal supplies and took out some blush. *A little dab'll do ya,* she thought, as the old commercial for Brylcreem popped into her head. She noted that the additional color made her look prettier and younger in the daylight. She always wanted to look her best when she was in David's company.

As she exited the building, she noticed that the afternoon sun was sinking behind the mountains and dark clouds were gathering overhead. Gayle looked up. *This is the darkest time of day in the darkest month of the year,* she thought. She smiled as the festive lights on the trees in the quad suddenly came on. *Thank God for Christmas!*

She stood inside the front door to keep warm while she waited for David's SUV to appear outside. She was curious about the new development in the case. She wasn't sure why they wanted to talk to her, as she had already told them everything she knew, and given them all the personnel files they asked for.

Then she saw the SUV as David drove up to the curb. He got out and opened the door for her. She resisted the urge to kiss him, and instead she just smiled and cooed, "Oh, David, you are such a gentleman."

"Why, thank you, ma'am. I always aim to please," he said, smiling broadly.

He helped her into her seat, giving her arm a little squeeze. Then he went around to his side and drove onto the highway that took them through the village of Mount Salem towards the town of Beaumont.

"I can't imagine what the news might be," she said, "considering that they've already charged Emily Warren with the murder. She's out on bail right now. I sent her a message to take a few weeks off with pay, until her trial. I don't want her hanging around the campus, being a murderer and all," she said. "I changed the programming on her access card so she can't get into any of the buildings after hours now. And if she shows up during the day, I want you and your staff to escort her off the campus."

"As you wish," David said, and patted her left hand with his right.

"Maybe after the interview at the police station we can go somewhere nice for dinner," she said. "There's a cute Italian place just outside Beaumont where no one will recognize us. And the food is very good, too."

"Sounds like a plan," he concurred.

"Good food, good wine, good company — that would be a nice way to spend the evening," she said. She looked sideways to see his profile as he drove. "Maybe, if we get in the mood, we can relax at my place this evening…"

"For some good nookie," he suggested with a grin.

She laughed, "You are a mind reader!"

They chatted amiably all the way into Beaumont. For a few minutes, Gayle forgot about her troubles at the college and just enjoyed the moment.

It was the last moment she would enjoy for quite a while.

CHAPTER 27

📅 MONDAY, DECEMBER 15, 2008 — 5:30 P.M.

When Jill arrived at the station, Skip escorted her into an interview room and asked her to wait for diLongo. He gave her some magazines to browse through.

A few minutes later, diLongo came in to the room with Skip, and they sat facing Jill across a small table.

"How are you today?" diLongo asked Jill.

"I'm fine," she said coolly. "How can I help you?"

DiLongo opened a file she had brought in with her.

"As you know, Dr. Primrose was kind enough to provide us with the personnel files of all concerned," diLongo said. "Including yours, I might add," and she leafed through some pages in the file. "We checked you out."

"Okay," Jill said, unfazed.

"You graduated with honors from a recognized university. You worked for a hospital, a car manufacturer and a food distribution company before landing your job at the college. Quite the diverse job history," diLongo said.

"I'm versatile and flexible," Jill answered.

"We know. We talked to all your past employers, and they had nothing but good things to say about you: very professional, competent and reliable. And Dr. Primrose speaks very highly of you. So, no issues there."

"Thank you," she said.

"Where I do have an issue," diLongo continued, "is with your professional activities at the college."

"What do you mean?" she asked.

"Well, it seems that you hired someone who is not who he said he was, and I'd like to know how he slipped through your fingers, so to speak," diLongo said.

"Really? Tell me more," Jill said, intrigued.

"No, you tell me, Miss Wilmington. Tell me how you let Terry Digman get hired as a psychology professor?"

"I didn't *let him* get hired, Detective. I reviewed his resume and credentials, and I checked his references. Everything checked out. Gayle and

I interviewed him personally. Gayle wanted to hire him, and I concurred, after doing our due diligence. I don't see the problem," she replied.

"If you checked him out, why didn't you discover that he was using a false identity, that he had a criminal record in Canada and that his real name was Stanley Karakchuck?"

"What?" Jill looked shocked. Then she recovered and said calmly, "Well, that explains a lot!"

DiLongo gave her a moment before prompting her to continue. "What do you mean?"

"Terry always seemed a bit slimy to me," Jill said. "I never liked him. He made off-color comments to the staff, especially the women. No one complained officially, so I couldn't do anything, but he was skating on thin ice for a sexual harassment complaint. I also heard comments from the staff in the psych department that his teaching style was unorthodox. But apparently the students loved him. It's no wonder, with the high marks he handed out to everyone, especially the girls."

DiLongo flinched. She had received an A+ when she took the criminal behavior course with Terry Digman. With this new information about him, she wondered whether the whole course was bogus and if she had wasted her time and money.

"Is there anything else you can tell me about his background or activities?"

Jill took a breath. *This is where things could get a bit dicey,* she thought.

"You said he has a criminal record. What was it for?" she asked.

"Investment fraud," diLongo said.

"Not drugs and prostitution?" Jill asked.

"No, but we're looking into that angle. Do you know something about that?" diLongo asked.

"Just that… he might have had a few female students working for him to, you know, provide sexual services for his buddies from out of town," Jill said. "He said he had some girls working for him, and he said it in a slimy way, but I didn't take him seriously at the time. I thought he was just blowing smoke."

DiLongo made a note of that. "Did he mention any names?"

"No, he didn't mention anyone by name, except—" and then Jill stopped herself.

"Go on, Miss Wilmington," diLongo said.

"I don't like to speak about people behind their back," she said, "but I guess you'll find out about this anyway, and you have already charged Emily with the crimes," she said, and paused. "Terry told me he hired Emily to do some role-playing games with guys who are into that kind of thing. She dressed up as a nurse and pretended to abuse these guys. You know, a little kinky action, but nothing serious."

"Okay," diLongo said, "we already know all about that. Anything else?"

Jill paused again. She wondered if she should confess that she also worked for Terry as an exotic dancer. If she didn't disclose it, and they found out about it anyway, it would make her look untrustworthy. She decided to be forthcoming. As far as she was concerned, she had done nothing wrong, but it wasn't something she wanted to broadcast, either.

"Well, I have to admit something, but I want you to keep it confidential," she said to Skip and diLongo.

DiLongo said, "Depending on what it is, if we can keep it confidential, we will."

"It's not material to your case," Jill said, "but it might come out in your investigation into Terry's activities."

"Okay. Go on."

"I have a hobby. I perform for people in bars and at private parties," Jill said. "I'm an exotic dancer. Terry saw my act and hired me for some of his parties."

Skip sat up straighter, opened his notebook and clicked his pen.

"That's it?"

"Yes."

"How many times did you perform at his parties?"

"Oh, maybe ten or fifteen times. I lost track."

"These parties, was it just men who attended?"

"Yes, of course, no wives." she said.

"And did you offer sexual services as well?" diLongo asked pointedly.

"Absolutely not. I just danced. No touching. That was part of the deal with Terry," Jill said emphatically.

"Do you know any of the men who attended?" diLongo asked.

"I don't think so. But I don't look closely at them when I dance. I'm in my own little world up there. So I would not be able to recognize any of them," she said, anticipating the next question.

"I see," diLongo said. Skip was writing furiously in his notebook, trying to keep a straight face.

"Well, I don't know if this will get into the final report on this case, but we'll try to keep the information confidential," diLongo said. "It all depends on how the investigation goes."

"I understand," Jill said, relieved that she had told the truth. Then she added, "I am not ashamed of my hobby. It's only because of my job on campus that I keep it a secret. Since Terry was also involved, I didn't think he would talk. He had too much to lose."

"This Terry Digman was quite a character," diLongo said. "He was also into procuring drugs for students. Did you know about that?"

"No, he never mentioned anything like that to me," Jill said. "But I think he was using, sometimes. I don't use drugs of any type, not even the legal kind. I'm strictly into medicinal herbs."

"Some people consider marijuana to be a medicinal herb," Skip said.

"You're right, and it will likely be legalized for medicinal purposes, if not for personal recreational use," Jill said, "but probably not in my lifetime."

"So, do you use it?" diLongo asked.

"No, Detective. My herbal remedies are strictly on the up and up," Jill said. "I get them from a naturopath or make them up myself."

"Do you know anything about plants that are toxic to humans?" diLongo asked.

"You mean, like wild mushrooms and poison ivy?" she asked.

"No, really toxic plants like the Rosary Pea plant?" diLongo said.

"Oh, yeah, I heard about that," Jill replied.

"Indeed," diLongo said. "Word travels fast on campus."

"Gayle told me she's going to have all the Rosary Pea plants removed from the campus," Jill said. "As a precaution. It's going to be a 'Rosary Pea-free campus', she said."

"Okay," diLongo said. "Let's get back to Terry Digman, or shall we call him by his real name, Stanley Karakchuck? Who did you call to check out his references?"

"I contacted the references he gave on his resume."

"You personally called these people?" diLongo asked.

"Yes. Or I emailed them. I don't honestly remember. It was over two years ago. It should be in the file," Jill said.

DiLongo took out another file and opened it up. "It says here you talked to someone in Ottawa for the R.C.M.P. reference."

"Oh, yeah! That's right. I got him on the phone. I forget his name, though."

"And you have copied some emails here from two other references," diLongo said.

"Right. I guess I couldn't get them on the phone, so I emailed them," Jill explained.

"And they gave you glowing reports for Terry Digman?" diLongo prodded.

"Correct."

"Would it surprise you to know that all these references were faked?" diLongo asked.

"Not anymore," Jill said, "but at the time, they seemed very legitimate."

"You didn't do a background check on him? Credit rating, marital status, criminal record, that kind of thing?" diLongo asked.

"Oh, sure we did. David Bartholomew did that part. He's our security chief," Jill said.

"I know who he is," diLongo said. "Did he give you a report?"

"Yes, and I filed it," Jill said.

"But it's not here," diLongo said.

"Well, it should be there," Jill insisted.

"Who else has access to these files?" diLongo asked.

"Just Gayle," Jill replied. "Gayle and I are the only ones who can access the files for the senior administrators and teaching staff."

"Miss Wilmington, you've been very helpful. Would you mind sticking around a while longer, while we verify a few things? We may have some further questions for you."

"All right. But do you have any better magazines to read? These suck," she said.

DiLongo shook her head, and motioned for Skip to leave the room with her.

David and Gayle had arrived at the station while Jill was being interviewed. "I think Dr. Primrose has some explaining to do," diLongo said to Skip. "But first I want to talk to David Bartholomew. Please show them into separate interview rooms."

Once Gayle and David were settled in different rooms, diLongo and Skip went into the room where David sat at a small table. She and Skip sat down across from him.

"How you doin'?" diLongo asked as she sat.

"Could be better, could be worse, I guess," he said calmly.

"Right. Well, I hope you can clear some things up for me," she said. "Mind if I turn on this recording device? Saves me from taking notes."

He nodded to go ahead.

After setting up the recording, diLongo started her questioning.

"I want to talk to you about your friend, Terry Digman. In particular," she said, "I want to know about the background check you did on him before he was hired at Kensington College. The report is missing from the file. What happened to it?"

David just shrugged. "Why are you asking me? Anyway, what do you want to know about Terry?" he asked.

"I want to know how you managed to miss the fact that Terry Digman has a criminal record in Canada, and he isn't Terry Digman at all, but a guy by the name of Stanley Karakchuck?" she asked pointedly.

David was stunned, but he kept his composure enough to say, "I have no idea what you're talking about."

DiLongo smiled at him, and then said to Skip, "Please pass me the file on Mr. Bartholomew."

Skip handed her a file marked *David Bartholomew, Background*.

David shifted in his seat and stared at the file. Before diLongo opened it, she said, "Would you like to tell me anything about your own background, Mr. Bartholomew?"

"Not really," he said warily.

"Well, I will tell you, then," she said, opening the file. "Officer Crane was busy the last few days doing his own background checks. He did a very thorough job, I might add. We obtained your fingerprints and ran them through the system, and we also sent them to Canada. And guess what? We found out that you were incarcerated in a Canadian prison for aggravated assault causing bodily harm, and it wasn't your first conviction. Now this is what I am wondering, Mr. Bartholomew: Why doesn't this show up in your employment file at the college?"

"I have no idea," he said. "How did you get my prints?" And then it dawned on him. "The coffee shop."

DiLongo smiled.

"Hand me that other file, will you?" she asked Skip. This file was marked *Terry Digman, Background*.

"My colleague here discovered that Terry Digman, when he was Stanley Karakchuck, was also incarcerated in the same prison at the same time as you. Now, isn't that an interesting coincidence?"

"So?" David said, smiling to cover his unease.

"So, the two of you were released the same month. After your release you worked for a trucking company, and then you returned to the United States and settled down in Beaumont. When Stanley Karakchuck got out, he continued his criminal activities in Canada, before changing his identity to Terry Digman and fleeing to the United States just ahead of the R.C.M.P., who were about to arrest him. Lo and behold, he gets hired at Kensington College as a phony psychology professor, facilitated in large part by the so-called security check you did on him. The two of you are quite a team, aren't you?"

David realized he was in deep trouble. He said, "I want my lawyer."

"Okay. Call your lawyer. I'm going to come back in a few minutes," diLongo said. She motioned Skip to come with her, and they left the room.

"Now," she said, "we go talk to Dr. Primrose. This should be a very interesting conversation!"

CHAPTER 28

DiLongo and Skip went to the kitchen to get some coffee and donuts and take a little break before questioning Gayle Primrose.

"Funny thing about these types of investigations," diLongo said. "When you scratch the surface, you never know what you'll find brewing underneath. In any case, there's more going on here than meets the eye, and the more we dig, the more we find out. So let's keep digging," she said.

"Will do," he replied.

"Now let's discover what Dr. Primrose has to say for herself," diLongo said, and they left the kitchen with coffees in hand and a bottle of water for Gayle.

"So, Dr. Primrose," diLongo began, turning on the recording device, "you might be interested to know we have uncovered some surprising things regarding your employees, starting with Terry Digman."

"I see. What have you found out?" she asked as she unscrewed the cap on her water bottle.

"First, you might be surprised to learn that Terry Digman is dead," diLongo said.

Gayle stared at her blankly and said, "Yes, I know that," she said.

"Yeah, but what you don't know is that he died ten years ago!" diLongo watched for Gayle's reaction to this news.

"What?" Gayle looked puzzled. "What do you mean?"

"The real Terry Digman died ten years ago of a heart attack. He lived in New York City. He did some work with the R.C.M.P. as a consultant in Ottawa for a few years, but he never studied at the University of Toronto. His degrees were from Columbia."

"Oh. That's where I took my undergraduate degree," she said.

"Right," diLongo said, and then she paused for a moment. "Did you hear what I just told you, Dr. Primrose? The man you knew as Terry Digman was an imposter! He stole Mr. Digman's identity, and then passed himself off as a psychology professor to get a job at your college."

"Well, that's impossible. You must have made a mistake," Gayle said confidently. "We thoroughly check out our new hires before they come on board."

"Is that a fact? How thoroughly did you check out David Bartholomew?" diLongo challenged her.

"David? We checked him like we always do. Checked his references and credentials. We also did a background check," Gayle took another sip from her water bottle.

"And Mr. Bartholomew checked out okay?"

"Yes, he did. His references were stellar." Gayle frowned, unsure of where this was going.

"Well, Dr. Primrose, we also checked the references from his file ourselves. And guess what we found out?"

"You found out the same as we did, I assume," she said blandly.

"We found telephone numbers that were no longer in service. Further investigation showed that they had been pre-paid cell phones. The companies he claimed to have worked at do not exist, and never have existed, except for the trucking company in Canada. It turns out the owner is an old friend of Mr. Bartholomew's, so he provided a good report for his buddy. So, you see, the references for Mr. Bartholomew were basically false."

"But… but…" Gayle could only sputter at this point. She didn't know what to say.

"And here's something else that should have shown up on his background check. He has a criminal record in Canada for aggravated assault causing bodily harm," diLongo said.

Gayle looked stunned. "Oh, my," she finally said as her hand covered her mouth in shock.

"There's more. He was incarcerated in the same prison as Terry Digman, a.k.a. Stanley Karakchuck, who was serving time for investment fraud."

"I don't understand," Gayle said, in disbelief.

"The bottom line is, David Bartholomew and Terry Digman were in cahoots. They worked together as a tag-team to con people. Both Terry and David were selling illegal drugs on campus, and organizing a ring of student prostitutes. There's more, but I just want you to think about this for a minute," diLongo said.

Gayle swallowed, breathing heavily.

DiLongo was just getting warmed up. "What sort of college are you running, Dr. Primrose? You have two criminals working for you, one posing as a teacher and the other providing security, for Christ's sake! You have prostitution and drug trafficking going on right under your nose! You have a professor with a criminal past teaching kids about criminal behavior, giving them A's for doing nothing, and recruiting them to be prostitutes! And two murders have taken place in front of your eyes, and the poison is growing in your garden. Now, what do you think I should make of all this?"

Gayle looked from diLongo to Skip, and back again. Then a strange sensation came over her as the implications finally began to sink in. Gayle got up and paced the room to release some of the nervous tension that suddenly welled up inside her.

She finally turned to diLongo and said, "I am sorry. I am so sorry. I've let everyone down, including myself. But most importantly, I've let down all the people who look to me for guidance, safety and progressive thinking. I've let my personal needs cloud my judgment. I'm a very bad administrator," she said mournfully. "How could I have let this happen?"

"How indeed," diLongo said, sarcastically. "Do you realize that this Digman imposter has also conned all his students? Their marks are meaningless! What they've learned has no merit! What will these students think when they find out, I wonder? Do I hear the bells of doom ringing in the form of a class action suit?"

"Oh my God," Gayle said. "Could that really happen? I honestly had no idea all this was going on!"

"What you do now is up to you," diLongo said. "I'm just giving you the facts."

"I don't know what to say…" Gayle suddenly felt drained. She sat down again. "I need to think."

"You think," diLongo said. "I'll be back."

She turned off the recording device and left the room. Skip followed her back to her office and closed the door. DiLongo wanted to take a break from the interviews and to get her own feelings under control.

"God damn. I worked my ass off for that course!"

"Is that why you're upset?" Skip asked.

DiLongo sat down at her desk. "Have a seat," she said. "Look, Skip, I've worked hard to get where I am. It's not easy being a woman in this business. Law enforcement is still a man's world, in many ways, but I believe I can make a valuable contribution to the community. I also have a family to support. I want my kids to grow up normally and have a chance at a good life. You know, go to college and all. We're smart people, but being smart is not good enough these days. You have to have a plan and work hard. That's why I take all these courses. I want to set a good example for my kids, and further my career." She paused for a moment. "I thought Digman's course sounded really interesting. So I read everything on the course guide. I gave up precious family time to work on the assignments and I studied like mad for the exam. Now I find out the course was bogus because the prof was a fraud? All that time and effort for nothing!"

"Well, look at it this way," Skip said, "You learned about criminal behavior from a professional crook. That's got to mean something." He laughed.

She threw her notebook at him, and sighed.

"Yeah, I guess I'm just disappointed. But I'll get over it. You know, there's something bothering me about this case," she said, changing the subject.

"Yeah? What's that?"

"How does Emily Warren fit into all these new developments? She murdered two people but she just doesn't seem the type. When you consider the Nurse Ratched thing she looks more culpable. But I just don't see a motive. She doesn't seem like a mentally unbalanced individual, so unless she has multiple personalities and one of them is pure evil, what kind of motive would drive her to murder two people?"

"The motive," Skip said reflectively.

"The motive," diLongo repeated. "What is the motive? The other thing that bothers me is her lawyer, Evan Thompson. I know him and he's a straight-up guy. If Emily were guilty, with the evidence we have against her, he'd talk her into making a deal with the D.A. But he's arguing that she's been set up. He's not the kind of guy to waste taxpayers' money by defending a murderer for the heck of it. So he must believe her story. We have all this evidence — her cupcakes were the murder weapon, she had the opportunity, and the evidence linking her to the crime was in her home. The only thing to clear her now is for another person to confess. And it has to be plausible. Then we can all relax." DiLongo paused for a moment. "You know what? I'm not feeling very relaxed at all."

"I could do some more research into Miss Warren's background," Skip suggested. "If she is the perp, maybe something will pop up."

"Before you do that, let's go have another talk with our friend Miss Wilmington. She's the head of H.R. She must know something more about these people that she's not telling us."

CHAPTER 29

📅 MONDAY, DECEMBER 15, 2008 — 6:50 P.M.

DiLongo returned to the room where Jill was waiting and playing a game on her phone.

"Can I go now?" Jill asked. "I'm hungry. I need dinner."

"In a couple of minutes," diLongo said. "I have a few more questions for you." Then she opened her notebook. "As the head of H.R., you have some knowledge of everyone at the college. What more can you tell me about any of the players in the bridge club — their habits, their connections with each other, their private interactions, their professional interactions, any info at all?"

Jill looked at diLongo for a few seconds, and then she stood up. "Detective, I am now officially ticked off with you and your sidekick with these ridiculous questions. I'm not going to compromise my professional or personal ethics to betray my friends. If you have something specific to ask me, something that is related to the murders, ask away. But if you are on a fishing trip to see what kind of dirt you can dig up on my friends, I'm not going to be party to it!"

DiLongo sighed. "Okay, I see your point, Miss Wilmington. So, let's just say for a moment that we're looking for a motive that explains why Miss Warren murdered these two people. Can you think of anything, from your experience, knowledge and interaction with Miss Warren, that might explain why she would do something like that?"

"Emily is a sweet girl. Very clever and dedicated. She's also a very good bridge player," Jill said. "Having said that, I don't hang out with her. I don't know much about her motivations, other than her desire to become a doctor. I cannot think of any reason why she would want to kill anyone, let alone Terry and Anne-Marie. Unless she just snapped, for some reason. Maybe Terry was putting too much pressure on her to perform as Nurse Ratched, or maybe he threatened to expose her activities, or something. In any case, she seems perfectly normal to me, always in a good mood, and always trying to please her boss and her co-workers. I've never had a discipline problem or any complaints about her. So there you have it. I can't help you with a motive, and I can't think of anyone else who would want to murder Terry and Anne-Marie. That's your job, I believe. Now, can I go?" she asked again.

DiLongo nodded. Jill picked up her purse and her coat and walked out of the room. "Enjoy your dinner," diLongo called after her. Jill just waved her hand and quickly left the station.

DiLongo called Skip to follow her, and they returned to the room where Gayle was waiting.

"Dr. Primrose," diLongo said, "I'm waiting for Mr. Bartholomew's lawyer to show up, and then I will have some more questions for him. In the meantime, I thought we could talk a bit more, to try and figure this whole thing out. Will you help me?"

"Of course," Gayle said. "It's the least I can do."

"All right, then. I'd like to hear your take on Miss Warren's motive for killing Mr. Digman and Mrs. Boland. Do you have any ideas?" diLongo asked.

"Emily came to us several years ago with solid credentials and she has been a valuable member of my staff ever since. I cannot fathom why she would ever do something like this." Gayle looked down. "But my track record on character assessment seems to leave a lot to be desired. I'm still in shock about Terry and David. I had absolutely no idea about any of this. How sad is that?"

"Why sad?" diLongo asked.

"If I tell you something, will you keep it under wraps?"

"I can try," diLongo said.

Gayle sighed. "You must understand. I have never had problems like this at the college before. I run a tight ship — at least, I thought I did. Now that I know David's true nature, I can see I should have been more diligent about reviewing his past.

"The truth is that I wanted to hire him for personal reasons, which are hard to explain. Let's just say that the reason I moved here from my hometown in Georgia was to get away from the backward thinking and immoral social conditions where I grew up." She blinked back tears.

"But now, I don't know what effect this trouble will have on my college's reputation, and my own reputation. It may destroy the legacy I wanted to leave." Gayle sighed again. "It makes me sad to know that my life's work is in jeopardy, all because I turned a blind eye and allowed my carnal desires to overcome my good judgment." She sniffed.

"Please explain," diLongo said, as Skip opened a new page in his notebook, pen in hand.

"You see, when I was holding interviews for the security position, several men applied, all ex-military, and none of them were suitable for the college. Then David walked in, and he impressed me right away. He was so easy-going, so warm and mature. I thought he would be perfect for the role. But that's not the only reason," she said, and she paused before continuing.

"I try to encourage people of different races and backgrounds to join our staff, and since he is black…" She paused again. "There's also another reason, I'm ashamed to say. Personally, I found myself very attracted to him." She dabbed at her eyes as they brimmed with tears.

DiLongo looked at Skip, who rolled his eyes as if to say, "Here we go again."

"I couldn't help myself," Gayle sobbed. "I just felt so safe and secure in his presence. I thought all the people on campus would feel that kind of safety and security with him in charge." She paused to gain her composure. "But now I realize that I just wanted him. It's one of those strange attractions that comes over you when you least expect it."

"So you two are lovers?" diLongo asked, surprised.

"Yes! After his probation period ended, once I was sure he was really suitable for the job, we became lovers, and have been ever since. But I needed to keep it a secret. I didn't want the Board of Governors to find out, because they would consider it a conflict of interest and force me to fire him," she explained. "What's going to happen now when they find out the truth? I even gave him a signing bonus to ensure he'd accept the job! They will roast me over hot coals for this. I might even lose *my* job." Gayle's face crumpled. "And that's why I'm upset. I've let everyone down, including myself." Tears rolled down her cheeks.

"Dr. Primrose," diLongo said, "In spite of everything, I really don't think it's your fault. You were the victim of a fraud, cleverly thought out and executed by a team of hardened criminals. The real problem you have, as I see it, is dealing with the aftermath of your lack of good judgment. You hired a criminal to teach criminal behavior. That's not going to go down well with anyone, including the students."

Gayle looked at diLongo with a long face. "I know, and I feel horrible about that."

"And you hired another criminal, one convicted of assault causing bodily harm, to provide security on your campus. That will not go down well with parents."

"I know," Gayle said, her chin trembling. "I know."

"Then you have two murders committed right under your nose. This will not reflect well on you either. So, I ask you now, is there anything you can tell me that might help us understand what is going on here?" diLongo demanded, with no sympathy for Gayle in her tone.

"Okay, let me think… let me think… Yes, there is one thing," Gayle said, "and I don't know if I'm reading this correctly or not. But the night after the murders, I told David I was really upset. I was worried about how these suspicious deaths might affect the reputation of the college. David said he would see what he could do to help the police. I didn't know what he meant at the time, but now that I know he's a criminal and a fraud, I think he's capable of anything."

"If he was going to help the police, so to speak, maybe he wanted to deflect the investigation away from himself," diLongo suggested. "He had an argument with Mr. Digman the week before. Do you think he could be the real murderer here, knowing him as intimately as you do?"

Gayle shot diLongo a sharp look. "Must you?" she said. Then she thought for a minute. "All I know is that he said it would all be over in a few days. He also said he had someone on the inside here at the station who was feeding him information about the case. That's how he knew about the search warrant."

"Really?" diLongo asked, surprised. "So he knew we were going to search Miss Warren's home before we went there?"

"Yes. He knew the night before. He got a text message from his contact at the station here. And he has a police scanner, too."

"All right then. Do you think he could have planted the evidence in Miss Warren's home to implicate her?" diLongo said. "And why would he do that?"

"He could have. This might sound silly now," she said, "but I think he would do something like that for me. He knew I was worried about how this situation was going to affect the reputation of the college. I know you think he's a despicable criminal, but he and I were lovers and I know he cares about me. He would do anything for me. Except tell me the truth, it seems." Gayle suddenly got a pained look on her face. "And now it turns out he's betrayed me in the worst way!" Her demeanor changed suddenly and she jumped up. "My God, he's lied to me and used me for his own purposes! Just wait till I get my hands on him! He's ruined me!" she exclaimed.

Then Gayle sat down and started to sob again. "No," she said through her tears. "It's not all his fault. I'm really the one to blame. I ruined my own life by letting my feelings get in the way of my judgment. If I hadn't done that, none of this would have happened."

"Oh, it would have happened," diLongo said, "just not here, just not now."

And with that, diLongo and Skip exited the room and left Gayle to wallow in her angst.

CHAPTER 30

📅 MONDAY, DECEMBER 15, 2008 — 7:00 P.M.

Following the revealing interview with Gayle Primrose, diLongo went into the next room, where an officer was waiting with David. They were playing cards.

"No lawyer yet?" diLongo asked.

"He's on his way," David said, not looking up.

"Okay. When he gets here, you can ask him about making a deal with us. You tell us everything you know, and we'll go easy on you. You clam up, and I'll throw the book at you. Got it?" she said.

David looked at diLongo, and smiled. "Thank you, my sweet," he said sarcastically. "I'll take my coffee with milk and two lumps of sugar."

DiLongo shook her head at him and left the room. She went over to the vending machine and got a soda and brought it to Gayle, who was sitting alone in the room, looking very dejected.

"Here you go," diLongo said. "I thought you could use a cold drink. I'm going to talk to Mr. Bartholomew in a little while. I'd like you to stay here, in case I have any further questions for you."

"Thank you," Gayle said, accepting the soda. "You are most kind."

Keith Towers, David Bartholomew's lawyer, arrived at 8:00 p.m. He was a short, pudgy man in his thirties with a receding hairline. DiLongo knew him as the 'biker lawyer' because he often represented bikers who got into trouble. Keith had a private session with David for a few minutes, and then he emerged from the room.

"We'll talk to you now," Keith said curtly.

DiLongo and Skip entered the room and sat down facing David and Keith. DiLongo waited. Keith said to diLongo, "Okay, you start."

DiLongo said, "No. I want to hear what Mr. Bartholomew has to say for himself first."

Keith nodded, and David began speaking slowly. "A few years ago, I was working up in Canada for my old friend Barney at his trucking company. I got into some trouble. Nothing big, I just got drunk and got into a fight. I hurt the guy pretty bad. It was the second time for me. I guess I had a bit of a drinking problem back then. Anyway, I was convicted and spent time in prison, where I met Stan. You know him as Terry Digman." He paused. "Well, after I got out of prison, I went back to my job to make some money and figure things out." He paused again. "Then I decided to come back to the States. I wanted to turn my life around. Prison sucks. I just want a straight life with a real job and a nice home. I don't want the criminal life and all the bullshit. That's why I covered up my past when I applied for the job at the college. I thought I'd be able to work there for a few years until I was ready to retire. I'm not getting any younger, you know."

"So what happened?" asked diLongo.

"I tried to go straight. I got my papers for corporate security work, but the only jobs available don't pay for shit. So when I applied to the college, I kinda re-wrote my resume and Stan — I mean Terry — helped me with that. He's good at that kind of thing… or he was."

"We know you two were partners in crime," diLongo said. "Go on."

"When he came stateside and changed his identity to Terry Digman, Stan said he wanted a legit job as a cover. He's a real smart guy. There was an opening coming up for a psych prof, so he applied. I offered to check his background, and Gayle agreed. I faked some things for the report and gave it to Jill, and she put it into his file."

"But the report is not in the file now," diLongo pointed out.

"That's because I took it out after Terry died. I knew the cops would be asking for it and I wanted to make it disappear. I did that Friday morning."

Keith intervened. "If we tell you any more, we want a deal."

"If he cooperates, if he tells us everything he knows, I'll work out a deal with the D.A. to go easy on him," diLongo said. "But we already know he's been procuring drugs for the college kids, so that's not going to go over very well. Tell you the truth, I'm not so fussed about the drugs. College kids will find a way to get drugs if that's what they want. I'm just trying to tie up loose ends for my murder case."

Keith looked at David and shrugged as if to say, "It's up to you."

David sighed. "What do you want to know?"

"You and Gayle Primrose. Tell me about your relationship."

"What do you mean?"

"Your personal relationship."

"We're friends, I guess."

"Are you in love with her?"

"No. Why do you ask?"

"Because she's been telling us about you being her secret lover, that's why."

"Oh," he said. "Well, yeah, we get it on. Once or twice a week or so."

"That's it? You 'get it on'?" diLongo asked skeptically.

"Well, yeah. It's convenient for me, and it's very nice for her, or so she says," he added with a smirk.

"Did anyone know about your private liaison?" diLongo asked.

"No. Well, I guess Terry did. I told him one night over beers," David said, chuckling.

"Really?"

"Yeah, he noticed some chemistry between us and asked me about it," David said. "Some things are hard to hide. You know what I mean."

"Right," diLongo said, sighing. "What else can you tell me?"

"Well, Terry's the kind of guy who always works the angles, you know."

"Yeah, go on."

"I guess he said something to Gayle about it."

"So, it wasn't a big secret after all," diLongo commented.

"Oh yeah, it's still a secret. Gayle doesn't want the Board of Governors to find out about us; she thinks it could reflect badly on her. Anyway, she agreed to pay him off to keep quiet."

"What kind of pay-off?"

"A 'good-bye' package of some sort, for when he leaves in a few months. Guess he won't be getting it now," David said.

"No," diLongo agreed, "he won't." She shook her head as she made some notes.

"I want to know more about your relationship with Dr. Primrose. Did you know her before you came to work at the college?"

"No. I applied when I saw the ad on the Internet," he said.

"So your relationship began after you got hired?"

"Yeah. I just wanted a job, you know, but she was real nice to me. Gave me a signing bonus too. She wanted me bad, you know how it is," he said smugly. Skip nodded. DiLongo shot him a look.

"When did you find out we were going to execute a search warrant on Emily Warren?" diLongo asked.

"Oh, I guess, Thursday night. I was at Gayle's and we had a late dinner. I got a text message from my buddy in the station here, Earl."

"Earl!" diLongo said. She did not like Earl Doggan much. He was lazy and sloppy in his work, and his careless attitude rubbed her the wrong way. She would deal with Earl later.

"Is that when you decided to plant the evidence in Emily's house?" diLongo asked sternly.

"How do you know about that?" David blurted out.

"Lucky guess," diLongo said. "You knew about the search warrant. Someone had access to her apartment that day. Why did you do it?"

David looked at Keith, and Keith just shrugged his shoulders. David said, "I just wanted the police to have the evidence they needed to charge Emily, you know, and take the heat off Gayle. We both thought Emily did the murders, and Gayle was paranoid that Emily might strike again. Emily's too smart to leave stuff lying around, you know, so I figured I would just help the process along and let the cops find what they were looking for," he said, hoping this would mitigate his guilt.

"The cops would be me," diLongo said sarcastically. "And here's some news — I don't need your help. How did you manage to plant this evidence?"

"Easy. I just snapped a branch off the Rosary Pea plant in Gayle's garden when I left Thursday night, and put it in a plastic baggie. I picked the locks and snuck into Emily's apartment. I got there just in time, you know. I could hear you guys coming up the front stairs as I was leaving out the back," he said, chuckling. "Then I hid in the neighbor's shed for a while, until you guys left. And I went back to the office after that."

"Where did you put the baggie?" diLongo asked.

"In her cupboard, behind some baking stuff."

"What about the mortar and pestle?" she asked. "Did you plant that, too?"

"No, ma'am. I just put the baggie in the cupboard, and then I left. I don't know anything about a mortar and pistle."

"Pestle. You left through the back door?"

"Yeah, and down the back stairs lickety-split. I didn't want to get caught at her place. No way," he said.

"Okay, so now you've planted evidence to implicate someone in a double homicide. How many years do you think you should get for that?" diLongo asked.

"Hey, I'm cooperating, aren't I?" he protested.

"I'm just so disgusted," diLongo said, not able to hold it back any longer. "You have no regard for anyone but yourself. What if she's innocent? We've charged her with murder based on the evidence we found at her apartment — the evidence *you* planted!"

"Hey, I'm trying to reform. I'm fifty-two years old. I can't go back to prison," he whined. "I just want a straight job with a decent income, you know. Is that too much to ask?"

"Well, despite your age, you haven't learned how to live a straight life with a straight job, have you?" she asked him pointedly.

"No, I guess you're right. I haven't," he said. "Damn, if Terry hadn't shown up, none of this would've happened. I had a good thing going here, you know," he said.

"Them's the breaks," diLongo said. "You live by the sword, you die by the sword. Okay, listen. Let's say for a moment that Miss Warren did not murder Mr. Digman or Mrs. Boland. Who among the bridge players do you think is capable of such an act?"

"I dunno. Look at the husband. Isn't it usually the husband who kills the wife?"

"That would explain Mrs. Boland, but what about Mr. Digman?" she prodded.

"Terry can be an ass, so he could have made an enemy of any of the bridge players. Maybe there's a jealous woman, or maybe an envious man. Who knows? My money is still on Emily. She's likes to act like Nurse Ratched, you know."

"Yeah, we know all about that," diLongo said. "So you think there could be two perps? One who killed Anne-Marie, and the other Terry? Like in that movie where two people make a pact to kill each other's spouses, so there would be no motive linking them to the crime?"

"Sure. That's possible," David said.

"Yeah, and it's possible that you killed Mr. Digman and Mrs. Boland was just collateral damage!" diLongo said.

"Wait a minute," Keith said. "You have no evidence linking my client to the crime."

"Hold on," she said, raising her hand. "He planted evidence to implicate someone else. And we know that your client and Mr. Digman had an argument a week before the murders. What was that all about, Mr. Bartholomew?"

"How did you find out about that?" he asked anxiously. He looked at his lawyer, who nodded his head.

"Go ahead," Keith said. "Tell them."

"I had a little disagreement with Terry on how he was dividing the proceeds from our drug business," David explained. "But we settled that, and he reimbursed me, so there was no problem. We were making some money on that business, and I was saving it up for my retirement. I don't have a pension, you know. And Social Security isn't enough to live on when you retire. You need a nest egg."

"Yeah, well maybe you wanted the whole drug business for yourself, and with Digman out of the way, you could have it all," diLongo suggested.

"If you think I murdered them, you're wrong!" David said emphatically. "And if I did, I wouldn't have done it this way. I'd think of something a lot more... masculine. Murder by cupcake? Give me a break!" He laughed out loud.

"We've got you on drug trafficking, prostitution, planting evidence and hindering a police investigation, Mr. Bartholomew. I would not be laughing too hard, if I were you."

"Sorry," he said, still chuckling. "It was the image of the cupcake."

"Do you think Dr. Primrose had anything to do with the murders?" diLongo asked. "Maybe she wanted Terry out of the way, once he revealed to her that he knew about her secret love life on campus. He was blackmailing her, after all."

"No way. I'm sure she's innocent!" he proclaimed. "She's not that good of an actress!"

"Alright then. Is there anything else you can tell me about your activities the night of the murders or thereafter?"

"No. I can't think of anything. I was as surprised as anyone about the murders. Doesn't make sense to me why Emily would do it, you know. But people do surprising things," he said ruefully.

"Yeah, like your involvement with drugs and prostitution. You were making money off the girls too, weren't you?" diLongo said, barely hiding her disgust.

"If you don't mind," Keith interjected, "we'll have that discussion later, if and when my client is charged with anything."

DiLongo sighed.

"Okay, then you can go. About the charges for these other crimes, I'll see what I can do to make it easier on you. But if you leave town I'll have you arrested and I'll throw the book at you, understand? So don't go anywhere."

David nodded, and he left the building with Keith.

DiLongo returned to the room where Gayle was waiting. "Dr. Primrose, I have learned something very interesting about you from Mr. Bartholomew."

"What do you mean?"

"Why didn't you tell us that Terry Digman was extorting money from you to keep quiet about your affair with Mr. Bartholomew?" diLongo asked aggressively.

"Oh, that," she said, waving her hand. "Well, I didn't think it was important."

"Oh, really? It's not important? How about this idea: it gives you a motive to murder him!"

"For goodness sake, Detective," Gayle said. "You have charged Emily for the murders! Anyway, I didn't kill him. He planned to finish his contract and then he was leaving the country. He just wanted a few thousand dollars to help him on his way, and I agreed to pay him. It was no big deal."

"What happened to the money?"

"He didn't get it yet. The deal was that he would keep quiet, and when he left, I would provide him with a bonus for a job well done."

"So, you don't have to make the payment now. How much was it, anyway?"

"Twenty thousand."

"People have been killed for less," diLongo said.

"That's quite enough, Detective!" Gayle said, visibly irritated. "I didn't murder him. If you persist in this line of questioning, I shall call my lawyer and you won't get another word out of me!"

"All right, Dr. Primrose. Is there anything else you are hiding? You might as well come clean. We'll find out anyway."

"Honestly, Detective, there is nothing else," Gayle said, in a more conciliatory tone of voice. "But if I think of anything, I will let you know. Now I want to go home and figure out how I am going to clean up this big mess. When the Board of Governors finds out that both Terry and David have a criminal past, they'll have my head on a platter!"

"You are free to go, Dr. Primrose. We'll be in touch," diLongo said.

"Just make sure you convict Emily Warren! I don't want her back on campus, under any circumstances," Gayle said.

Then Gayle got her coat and called a taxi to take her back to Kensington College where her car was parked. Upon getting into her car she leaned back in her seat, closed her eyes and seethed. *How could David do this to me?* she thought. *He's been lying to me since day one!*

She felt violated and humiliated, as if someone had stripped her bare and paraded her in front of the whole town. *I was stupid, I guess,* she thought. *Stupid and in love, or was it just lust? I guess it was lust. But I don't deserve to be treated this way, by anyone. He's going to pay for this!*

David went to dinner at a local steak house with his lawyer. They talked about their strategy to get a deal with the D.A.

"We'll ask for three years, and settle for five," Keith said. "Agreed?"

"I guess. But I really don't want to go back to prison," David said.

"If you don't go for the deal, you could get ten years or more," Keith said.

"I know," David said, groaning. "That's the problem."

After their dinner, David got back into his SUV. The drive home was a lot lonelier than the drive into Beaumont earlier in the day, and he was not looking forward to the next conversation he would have with Gayle.

He pounded his fist on the steering wheel several times, saying, "Stupid. Stupid. Stupid."

CHAPTER 31

Back in her office, diLongo and Skip took a look at the chart on their wall.

"Okay," she said to Skip, "We're going to start connecting the dots," she said. "Let's clear the board."

Skip used a cloth to clean off the whiteboard.

"Okay," diLongo said. "Let's start by putting the victims in the center of the board."

Skip wrote *Terry Digman* and *Anne-Marie Boland* in the middle of the board.

"Now we'll write the names of all the bridge players on the board, starting with Gayle Primrose and David Bartholomew," she said.

Skip wrote the names of all the bridge players in a circle around the two victims.

"Now we'll draw some lines to show the connections between the players," diLongo said. "We want to look at their connections outside of normal work and bridge relationships.

"We know that Gayle Primrose and David Bartholomew are lovers, so you can connect them. Dr. Primrose is now connected to Digman — the extortion angle. Digman is also connected to Ben Chong, who is connected to David Bartholomew through the drug business.

"Digman was a busy boy. He had Miss Warren play-acting as Nurse Ratched. Mr. Bartholomew was his partner in crime. Miss Wilmington worked for him as a stripper and Mr. Chong was the go-between to sell drugs on campus and at the high school. Sally Brighton was his bridge partner. Is that all she did with him? We might want to look into her a bit further. And then Mr. Boland is one of Digman's kinky clients with Nurse Ratched, a.k.a. Emily Warren. So all the lines lead to Terry Digman, and no lines lead to Mrs. Boland, yet she was one of the victims. It's puzzling," diLongo said.

"Yes, it is puzzling" Skip said. "The rest of the players don't have any known connections with either Terry Digman or Anne-Marie Boland outside of their work and bridge relationships. It sure looks like Emily is the murderer, doesn't it? She's the only one who links up with both Mr. Digman and Mr. Boland, who, by extension, links her to Mrs. Boland. But he claims he never spoke to his wife about his kinky sex night with Nurse Ratched, and he has no reason to lie about it, does he?"

"So, if these victims were targeted for murder, we still need to find the link between Miss Warren and Mrs. Boland," she said.

Skip made a note in his book just as Captain Juno stuck his head into diLongo's office and asked her to come see him for a minute.

"What's happening?" he said. "I noticed you had some people from the college in here for questioning."

"Yeah. We've been looking into the backgrounds of the victims, Digman in particular. Turns out he's a con artist with a fake identity, and he's been involved with drugs and prostitution on and off campus."

"Well, that's all very interesting, but he's dead, and we have already charged Miss Warren with the crimes. Why are you pursuing this further?"

"I have this nagging suspicion that there's more to this story than meets the eye... and I am not totally convinced that Miss Warren is the perp. Her lawyer says she is innocent..."

"He's her lawyer — of course he'll say that!" he interrupted.

"But I know him and he's a good guy. He would try to make a deal if his client is guilty, but he fights like hell if his client is innocent. So he's convinced Emily is innocent. And there's the issue of the motive. I can't find a good enough motive for Miss Warren to kill these two. So, that makes me wonder if someone else has a motive to kill."

Juno sighed in frustration. "You have Miss Warren on opportunity," he said, counting off the items on his fingers, "she was at the scene. You have her on means — she made the murder weapon, the cupcakes. You have her on evidence — we found the poison in her home. Surely to God you can find a motive! What's the problem?"

"Well, we learned tonight that Mr. Bartholomew and Mr. Digman go way back, and Mr. Bartholomew planted the evidence in Miss Warren's apartment. He broke into her apartment and put the bag that contained the Rosary Pea twig in her cupboard. He said he wanted us to find hard evidence to link her to the crime, to take the heat off Dr. Primrose, with whom it turns out he's having an affair. So we know that at least half the evidence we found was bogus," diLongo explained.

"I see," Juno said, frowning. "But what about the traces the lab found in the mortar and pestle?"

"Mr. Bartholomew said he didn't touch that," diLongo said. "So that hasn't been explained away yet."

"Right on," Juno said.

"Yeah, it certainly makes her look guilty," diLongo said, sighing. "Still, I'm having a hard time finding a motive. Chris Boland says he didn't tell his wife about his kinky encounter, so there's nothing to suggest that Mrs. Boland knew about the Nurse Ratched episode. Digman was not likely to expose Emily — she was working for him and making money for him and he wouldn't want that to come out. He would want to keep his activities under the radar. So who could benefit from their deaths? David Bartholomew has no link with Mrs. Boland that we know of, and he had no reason to kill Digman. He needed Digman to keep the drugs and girls going and keep the money coming in. So he had every reason to keep Digman alive," diLongo said.

"There is another possible scenario," she continued. "We found out tonight that Digman knew about the affair Dr. Primrose was having with David Bartholomew. He was blackmailing her. Maybe she concocted this murder to shut him up. She's very eager to have us convict Emily for the crime. But if she's the perp, how does Mrs. Boland fit into the picture?"

"I'm concerned about the amount of overtime you and Skip are racking up over this case," Juno said, irritably. "We have enough to convict Miss Warren. So why can't you just wrap it up?"

"It's going to be tough without her confession. And if she isn't the perp, and some new evidence comes up at her trial to exonerate her, won't we look stupid if we don't do a thorough investigation?" she asked. "When I'm satisfied we have charged the right person, I'll let you know."

"I'm sorry, diLongo. I'm running out of patience and budget," Juno said. "I'm up to my eyeballs here, getting phone calls from worried parents wanting to know if it's safe for their kids at the college. And Sharp Sharon keeps calling me for updates. And I've already heard from someone at CNN. They're calling it the Cupcake Murders! Reporters know we've charged Miss Warren and we'll have a lot of explaining to do if you suddenly switch gears. I want this thing wrapped up, pronto."

"Yes, Cap," she replied. "We're working as fast as we can."

CHAPTER 32

 MONDAY, DECEMBER 15, 2008 — 8:45 P.M.

On his way back to his apartment in Mount Salem, David contemplated his options.

On the one hand, he could just pack up and leave in the night, disappear from view, change his identity and start a new life somewhere else. He knew it was possible from watching Terry do it. *But on the other hand,* he thought, *what if I get caught? I'll wind up doing the maximum amount of prison time. But if I stay in town, I'll have to face Gayle!* He groaned at the thought: *She'll be furious! I'm stuck between a rock and a hard place, and there's no easy way out.*

He was still trying to figure out his best options when he drove the SUV into his driveway. When he got out of his vehicle, he saw Gayle pacing on the front porch, waiting for him. In her hand was a can of pepper spray.

He walked slowly towards her. She glared at him.

"Hey, babe," he said, in a conciliatory tone as he approached her. "Don't be mad. I'm gonna make this up to you."

"Really?" she said sarcastically. "How do you plan to do that? You are nothing but a common criminal! You've ruined my life, my job and my reputation! And you had to tell the police about our affair and how Terry was blackmailing me!" She hurled these words at him from pursed lips.

"Babe, it's just one of those things, you know. I didn't expect anything to develop between us. It just happened. And then it was too late for me to tell you the truth. I just had to go along with it, you know. I wanted to tell you, babe. Honest, I did. Many times."

"Bullshit."

"What can I do to make it up to you?" he asked, moving closer to her.

She held up the can of pepper spray. "Stay back," she warned. "You think you can make it up to me? With what? Your big, black dick? Oh, excuse me, that's right. It's not so big, is it?" she said. Then she stopped, shocked at herself for using such a nasty racial slur. She took a deep breath as David looked down at his feet.

"Can you get any more despicable?" she continued, pacing all the while. "I can't believe I fell for your lies. I've been a complete ass — a foolish, misguided, middle-aged ass! I, of all people, should have known better! Whatever did I see in you to begin with? It boggles my mind that I have spent the last three years lusting after you, letting you know my most intimate secrets — letting you into my home, into my bed, into my body, without any restraint! How ridiculous am I? Huh?" she goaded him. "How ridiculous have you made me?"

"Gayle, babe," he pleaded. "I did my best to please you! Isn't that what you wanted?"

"Oh, yeah, that's what I wanted," she said, "but without the baggage you so conveniently forgot to tell me about! You betrayed me in the worst way! You lied to me every day. The only reason I know the truth is because a detective told me all about you. How do you think that makes me feel?"

He hung his head and said nothing.

"Right. You have nothing to say for yourself, because you are nothing. You are nothing but a low-life, lying, despicable criminal. You're not even very smart, but I guess you outsmarted me, didn't you? You must be really proud of yourself, taking advantage of a vulnerable, lonely woman. My

God, you make me sick!" she said, and she pushed past him to go down the front steps to the walkway that led out to the street.

"Wait!" he cried. "Don't go! Let's talk about this. I can explain everything!"

"Don't waste your time! And just for the record," she said, as she turned to face him, "you are fired! You can pick up your last paycheck from Jill in the morning. And I never want to see your face on my campus again after that."

And with that, she strode purposefully to her car, and drove off.

David stood there for a few moments to calm his nerves. Then he opened the front door and walked up the stairs to his apartment. He felt completely deflated.

I'll never get another job around here, he thought morosely. *I'm going back to prison and when I get out, I'll be a white-haired old man with nothing to show for my years on this earth.*

He went to the kitchen and took a bottle of Jack Daniels from the cupboard. He poured some into a glass, and sat down in his living room with the lights out.

My life is over, he thought, and poured the drink down his throat. Then he went back to the kitchen, returned with the bottle and poured more whiskey into his glass. *What am I gonna do now?* he thought, taking a big gulp. *Get drunk, I guess…*

As Gayle drove home, she experienced mixed emotions. On one hand, she felt a strange kind of elation for having given David a piece of her mind. On the other hand, she was sad that the relationship had ended so badly. The pain of betrayal was hard to experience, but the confrontation with David had allowed her to vent and expel most of it from her system.

I need a stiff drink to calm my nerves, she thought.

When she got home, she lit a fire in the front room fireplace and went to her desk, where she had a laptop computer. She sat down and composed her letter of resignation. She also sent an email to Jill explaining that David was no longer an employee, and to make the necessary arrangements.

With that task done, she poured herself a dry martini and went upstairs to run a hot bubble bath in the Jacuzzi. She settled into the bubbles with her drink and finally started to relax.

The martini reminded her of the early days with her husband, when they were young and in love. *What would Garry think of me now, if he could see me? I bet he'd be so disappointed in me,* she thought. *I'm so disappointed with myself!* She shed a few tears over what she had lost when he died, knowing he could never be replaced in her heart or her mind.

As she finished her drink, Gayle refocused her mind on the task at hand.

Tomorrow is another day, she thought. *Maybe it's time for me to retire and become a bridge director on cruise ships, like I've been planning to do for so many years.*

With that happy thought, she emerged from the bubble bath, wrapped herself in a thick terrycloth housecoat and went downstairs to fix some dinner.

CHAPTER 33

📅 TUESDAY, DECEMBER 16, 2008 — 3:30 P.M.

The winter skies were filled with dense black clouds that threatened to blanket the region in snow as the temperature dropped below freezing. A large black sedan sped along the two-lane highway that meandered alongside the dark waters of the Salem River. The car slowed down as it approached the gated entrance leading to the duBarry Mental Health Center. Rachel Mayberry powered down the driver's side window and waved to the guard.

"Good afternoon, Mrs. Mayberry," the guard greeted her.

"Good afternoon," she replied. Rachel drove up to the gate and used her access card to open it. Then she drove down a long, straight driveway lit on either side by electric lamp posts.

The duBarry Mental Health Center was a modern building with wings that sprawled in different directions from a main core. The core was designed like a hub, with a reception area on each floor where the elevators were located. There was a central staircase inside the hub, and additional staircases at the end of each corridor for emergency use.

Rachel headed for the underground parking garage where staff parked their cars. She used her access card to open the garage door, and then she parked her car in spot number 125.

She looked around, and seeing no one, she unlocked the trunk of her car; Emily stepped out. Emily was wearing a trench coat with a scarf over her head. Rachel locked her car and straightened her coat before walking over to the security door that led to the elevators and central stairwell. Rachel pointed out the security camera that was trained on the door leading into the facility from the garage.

"Just keep your head down," she said. "The security guards will think you're one of the nurses coming in for the evening shift."

Rachel punched a code into the panel beside the security door, and then opened the door. They went in and walked to the stairwell. Rachel punched in her code again and opened the door to the stairwell. Then they walked up the stairs to the third floor, encountering no one.

"If we take the elevator, someone is sure to see us," Rachel explained.

The door of the stairwell opened into a dimly lit reception area. Two burly orderlies sat at the security desk, playing cards. Rachel motioned Emily to stay in the stairwell. Then Rachel walked onto the floor and waved to the orderlies, as she walked down the hall to the nurses' station.

"You're early, Mayberry," Nurse Simmons, the nurse on duty, said.

"I know," she squeaked through a sudden coughing fit. "Gotta get some water. Feel crappy tonight. Might have the flu."

"Well don't spread it around," the nurse said, disapprovingly. "If you don't feel well, you should take off sick."

"We'll see how it goes," she said in a gravelly voice, feigning a cough. She tapped the computer keyboard to log in her name and time of arrival. Then she removed her coat and hung it on the coat rack.

"I've got some cough drops for you," Nurse Simmons called out, and then she returned to her paperwork.

"Thanks," Rachel said. "I'll maybe get some later."

"I'll have a briefing for you in a minute," Nurse Simmons said.

Rachel went back to where Emily was standing in the stairwell. Emily removed her coat and scarf, and placed them in the corner of the stairwell. She was wearing her Nurse Ratched uniform, minus the nametag. She had on a blond wig that matched her friend Rachel's hair, and a pair of black-rimmed glasses just like Rachel's. In the dim light, she hoped she looked exactly like Rachel.

Rachel told her that Daniel was in Room 304, down the corridor on the east side of the reception area.

"There's a security desk in the middle of the reception area where two orderlies guard access to the corridors," she whispered. "They offer assistance to the nurses when the patients misbehave or need to be moved to another room."

Emily nodded.

"The nurses' station is in the west wing. There are always two nurses on the night shift," she said. "Tonight it's me and Diane Lessik. She's an older woman... been here forever. When Diane gets here, Simmons will go home. "

Emily nodded again, and Rachel continued. "I'll go to the nurses' station and stay out of sight. To get to Daniel's room, you'll have to walk past the orderlies. They play cards, so they probably won't notice what's going on. They'll think you're me. If they say anything, just hold a Kleenex to your face and cough as if you have a cold, and they'll leave you alone."

"Geez," Emily said nervously. "I hope this is gonna work!"

Rachel gave her the access card to open the door to Daniel's room. "Knock first," she whispered, "so you don't startle the patient. Then open the door and go in."

Emily took out a tissue and tucked the access card into her front pocket. Then she squeezed Rachel's hand and said softly, "Wish me luck!"

"Good luck," Rachel said.

Emily opened the door of the stairwell and entered the reception area. She walked quickly past the orderlies, who glanced up briefly from their cards. As she reached the door to the east wing corridor, an orderly spoke to her.

"Hey, Mayberry. What's doin'?" Emily froze, and then she remembered to cough with her tissue up to her mouth, keeping her face turned away from them. She waved to the orderlies and then pulled the door open and entered the corridor leading to Daniel's room. A few seconds later, with her heart racing, she was standing in front of Room 304.

"Here goes," Emily thought. She pulled a mobile device out of the pocket of her nurse's uniform and dialed a number. Then she slid it into the front pocket of her uniform, and knocked on the door.

"What?" Daniel said in his loud, irritable voice.

Emily swiped her card and entered the room. "Room check," she said, keeping her voice low. "Good evening, Mr. Post."

Daniel didn't bother to look up. He was seated on a narrow hospital bed, propped up against some pillows, doing a crossword puzzle.

"Well, you can see everything is perfectly fine," he said.

Emily moved closer to his bed. She wanted to make sure he could not reach the call button that was on his bedside table, should he panic at her being there.

"I just want to check the electrical outlet," she said, moving towards the head of the bed. Something in her voice made Daniel stop working on his crossword and look up at her. She rolled the bedside table out of his reach, carefully keeping her body sideways to him so he could not get a good look at her.

"You're not Nurse Mayberry!" he said irritably. "Who are you?"

"You're right," Emily said in her normal voice, and she suddenly turned towards him and pulled off her blond wig and glasses. "I'm Emily Warren, your office assistant. Remember me?"

"Emily," he said, not quite comprehending the situation. "What are you doing here?"

"I came to pay you a visit, Daniel. I need to talk to you," she said, trying to keep her voice from trembling.

"Well I'm not supposed to have any visitors," he said. "I'm a sick old man."

"You're sick, all right," she said. "Sick and evil, too! You murdered Terry and Anne-Marie and then you implicated me. Why did you do it, Daniel?"

"I don't have to talk to you," he said, lunging for the panic button on the bedside table. "I want you to leave."

"Not so fast," Emily said, moving the table further out of his reach. "I know you are very clever, Daniel. Brilliant, in fact. I read all your notes. I know how you were planning to write your new novel by integrating a real live police investigation into the story. All you needed was the crime itself. I understand how it must have infuriated you when the police turned you down."

"What do you know about anything? You're just a secretary, and not a very good one either!"

"Your insults don't affect me anymore, Daniel. I know you planned the murders to create the case you wanted for your novel. How demented are you, really? Do you think the police would really let you get involved in their case?"

"Ha! Once they cleared me as a suspect, they said they would, so there!"

"But they cleared you when they charged me with the crime, and they still didn't let you in on the case then, did they?" she countered.

Daniel pursed his lips and remained silent. Then he suddenly sat up straight.

"How did you get my notes?" he demanded. "They're confidential!"

"Oh, that was the easy part. Remember, I signed an NDA so I could have access to everything. I just copied them from your computer onto a flash drive... in case you trashed your computer again. I didn't know what they were all about, at first. But now I understand."

"You crazy little bitch," he shouted. "Get out of here!"

"Look, Daniel," she said, thinking fast, "I have the computer files so I know it was you who planned the murders. Maybe you can fool the police, but you can't fool me, so stop trying to pretend you're innocent."

"Why did you come here?" Daniel asked, settling back onto his pillow.

"I want you to tell me why you did it!" she said.

"Why should I tell you anything? The cops charged you for the murders. You're the one they're after."

"Oh, you mean, because you implicated me with the poison from the Rosary Pea plant," she said accusingly. "I know it was you who put the poison in the mortar and pestle."

Daniel eyed her suspiciously.

"Thing is, Daniel," Emily said, softening her voice, "I just want to understand your motive."

"As if I'm going to talk to you!" he said derisively.

"Look, Daniel, it's just you and me here. You're safe inside this hospital for as long as you want. You're right, the police think I did the murders and I'll likely be convicted. This is the only opportunity you'll have to explain to me why I'm doing the time for your crime!" She paused for a moment. "It was a brilliant plan," she continued, trying to appeal to his ego. "No one else could have pulled it off the way you did."

Daniel smiled. He *was* rather pleased with himself. "You are going to spend a long time in jail now," he said. "Have fun!"

"So tell me," Emily prodded. She was starting to get anxious that he would clam up and refuse to speak any further. "What are you afraid of? Even if I told the police how you did it, they wouldn't believe me. It would be your word against mine, and the evidence is already piled up against me!"

"Yes, I'm the celebrated author, and you're a nobody," he said, gloatingly.

"You don't want to go to your grave with no one knowing your brilliant plan, do you? How you pulled off the perfect murder?"

Daniel smiled. *She's right,* he thought. *It is the perfect murder.*

"It's ironic, isn't it?" he said. "You, little Miss Perfect, got caught with your pants down, didn't you? Ha-ha, you had no idea," he said laughing. "You think I can cook Indian food? Give me a break. I just opened a jar of Patak's!"

"Yes," she said, her confidence that he would talk now building, "it was a stroke of genius when you asked to borrow my mortar and pestle for spices. Instead, you used it to grind up Rosary Pea berries and make the poison. That's how I figured out it was you who poisoned the cupcakes. I knew you were the only person who could have contaminated the mortar and pestle. But Daniel, I still don't understand how you got the poison into the cupcakes. How did you do it?"

He scrutinized her, contemplating his options. He could stop this charade right now by screaming for help. A nurse, or the orderlies, would hear him and come to the room. Or, he could explain to Emily how he did the murder, and savor the moment of illumination on Emily's face.

Hubris won out. "My dear Miss Emily," he said in his most condescending voice, "the poison wasn't in the cupcakes. It was in the jellybeans!"

Emily looked at him with a puzzled expression on her face. "In the jellybeans?" she repeated. And then she realized how he did it. "Of course. You poisoned the jellybeans and then you put them onto the cupcakes during the break at bridge!"

"Bingo!" he said, laughing hysterically now. "It was so easy, too. I just had to decide who would get my special treat. I figured that with Terry out of the way, I'd win the prize this year and earn a seat at Gayle's New Year's Eve party. So, I just traded him my cupcake with the black jellybean one that I poisoned. And he asked for it, as I knew he would. Stupid idiot that he is. Was."

"But I didn't use black jellybeans this time," she protested. "I used green and red ones."

"Well, I brought my own special ones from home," he said.

"You knew Terry liked the black ones?"

"Sure! He told me so at the Halloween party. We were talking, and I said I didn't like jellybeans, so he asked me for mine and said he only likes the black ones. So I gave them to him. At the bridge dinner I knew he would want the black ones, so I poisoned two and put them on my cupcake. Once they were on the cupcake, you couldn't tell the difference," he said. "All I had to do was show him my cupcake, and he wanted it."

"But what about Anne-Marie? Why did you poison her?" Emily said, egging him on.

"Well, she was just random. I needed one more victim to make it interesting for the police, so I put my special jellybeans on another cupcake. Who's going to get it? Who knows? Who cares?"

Emily stood with her mouth open in disbelief. "How appalling!" she finally said. "Anne-Marie never did anything to you. She was the mother of five children!"

"Five little brats, no doubt," he said, making a face.

"Okay, so let me get this straight," she said, remembering her instructions from her lawyer. "You poisoned two people so you could win the bridge prize. But why implicate me? I'm your bridge partner. If I'm in jail, you can't win the prize!"

"Sure I can! That's the most brilliant part of my plan! I'll be Sally's partner with Terry out of the way," he said, smugly.

"You are truly a sick, sick man, Daniel. Sick and twisted! You killed two people and implicated me in your crime for the bloody bridge prize!"

Emily paced back and forth, and then stopped. "You know what is really ironic, Daniel? Gayle has canceled the prize because of these murders. So who's the idiot now?"

"There's always next year," he said, and shrugged. "Anyway, it wasn't just for the prize, Emily. Sure, it was convenient to eliminate Terry from the competition. But more than that, what I really wanted was to be part of the investigation, for my book. And since the local cops didn't have a major crime to investigate, I created one for them."

"You are unbelievable!" Emily said with disgust.

"It's actually a thing of beauty, Emily. It's the perfect set-up, and you're the perfect patsy. You played right into my hands. I finally found my inspiration, and now I will finish my book. It will be a bestseller, and I'll be a star again," and he settled back into his pillows. "When I get out of here, I'm going right down to the police station to get the material I need for my book. And you'll be cooling your heels in jail. It's a brilliant endplay. Too bad for you!" He grinned at Emily.

"Well, Daniel, I have my own brilliant endplay for you," Emily said, and she pulled the mobile device out of the pocket of her nurse's uniform and showed it to Daniel. "Detective diLongo, did you get all that?" Emily asked. She heard diLongo's acknowledgement.

"Bloody hell!" Daniel said. "You're not allowed cell phones in here!"

"Tell it to the cops." Emily held up the cell phone as Daniel looked stunned. "I now have what I wanted — your confession! The police heard everything," she said. "See, this device has a very sensitive microphone. DiLongo gave it to my lawyer, who passed it to me to use for your confession."

Emily put her blond wig and glasses back on and backed up towards the door, keeping her eye on him.

"No!" he yelled, and jumped off the bed.

Then he came after her. Emily opened the door and ran down the hall towards the reception area. Daniel ran after her screaming. "Stop! Stop!"

The two orderlies were engrossed in their card game and oblivious to the drama taking place in the east wing. As Emily opened the door to the reception area, she called to the orderlies, "We need help here!"

Nurse Simmons heard Emily and she came rushing out of the nurse's station just as Emily entered the reception area to escape Daniel's wrath. "Daniel Post — stop him! He's a murderer!" Emily cried.

"Orderlies, are you deaf? Get over here!" Nurse Simmons shouted, as she hurried past Emily to intercept Daniel. "Back in your room, Mr. Post!" she said, in a very authoritative voice.

"Move out of my way!" Daniel screamed, trying to get around Nurse Simmons, who kept stepping in front of him. The two orderlies arrived and added their bodies to the confusion.

"Mayberry, get over here and help me!" Nurse Simmons ordered, as she blocked Daniel's attempt to go past her. "Mayberry! Where are you?"

"You idiots!" Daniel screamed. "Stop hurting me! That's not Mayberry! Get her! She's trying to kill me! Get her! Get her!" Daniel kept screaming about Emily, but the orderlies didn't pay any attention.

Rachel heard the commotion and came running down the hall, passing Emily who was hovering in a dark corner of the reception area. "Go to the stairwell!" Rachel hissed to Emily as she went to assist Nurse Simmons. The orderlies were already tussling with Daniel as Rachel arrived on the scene. Emily disappeared into the stairwell and flattened herself against the wall.

The orderlies finally got a good grip on Daniel and carried him back to his room and threw him on the bed. They held him down while the two nurses worked on the straps that were attached to his bed frame.

"Mr. Post," Simmons said. "You are safe. No one is trying to kill you. Be calm." She continued to try to soothe him, but he was thrashing and spluttering with fury and frustration. She looked at Rachel and said, "Who was that other nurse in here? I thought she was you."

Rachel shrugged and said, "What nurse?"

When Daniel was securely strapped down, Rachel left the room and ran to the nurses' station to get her coat. Then she raced back to the stairwell and opened the door, just as Nurse Simmons returned from Daniel's room.

"Where are you going, Mayberry?" Nurse Simmons called out to her.

"I told you. I'm sick," she said. "I'm going home."

"What? We have an emergency here. You can't leave now!" Simmons protested.

"You have it under control, Simmons," Rachel said. And with that, she disappeared into the stairwell.

"Let's go," she said to Emily, who had donned her coat and hat. They scampered down the stairs to the parking garage.

"Oh no," Rachel said, as she opened the door to the garage. "There's the guard. Wait here."

She opened the door and entered the garage. "Hi, George," she said.

"Mrs. Mayberry. Everything okay?"

"Yeah, just feeling sick. The flu. Better not get too close to me. Going home."

"Okay, sorry to hear that," he said, and he continued walking through the garage on his rounds. Rachel opened the door for Emily and said, "We'd better be quick. He'll be back here in a minute, and Simmons may suspect something by now."

They quickly walked to her car. Rachel popped open the trunk and Emily got inside. Rachel closed the trunk, took a quick look around, and then got in the car and started the engine.

"Here we go," she thought, pulling out of the parking spot and driving out of the garage. It was now dark outside, and she flipped on her headlights to navigate down the long driveway towards the gates. She slowed down at the gate. The guard held up his hand to make her stop the car.

"Nurse Mayberry," he said.

"Hey," she answered.

"You leaving?"

"Yes, I'm sick. Going home."

"You're sick and going home," he drawled. Then he took out a notebook. "It's so unusual for you to be leaving at this time. I thought something might be wrong." He wrote something down in his book.

"Nope. Just sick," she said.

"So, why didn't you log out?" he asked her. "I can't let you leave if you don't log out."

"What? Oh, I guess I forgot," she said. "Must be the flu medication I'm taking."

"Oh, I see," he said. "Well, I'll log out for you, this time. But, don't let it happen again, or I'll have to write up a big report. I hate writing reports," he said, grinning.

"Thanks," she said, as the gate lifted. She gunned the engine and sped out to the highway. A mile up the road, Rachel stopped the car and let Emily out of the trunk. They hugged each other and laughed with relief.

"Did you get what you needed?" Rachel asked.

"Oh yes!" Emily said. "I've just been talking to Detective diLongo on this special phone she lent me, and she said she heard everything. It's a really fancy phone that recorded the conversation while she was listening on her speaker at the other end. She told me she will look into dropping the charges against me now. My lawyer was there too. I think Daniel is toast!"

"Yahoo!" Rachel cried, and hugged Emily again. "You did it, girl!"

"Thanks to you, Rach. I owe you my life!" Then they got back in the car and carried on towards Rachel's house in Fairview, where Emily picked up her car and drove back to Mount Salem. On the way, Evan called her on her cell with some good news.

"DiLongo is doing the paperwork to drop the charges against you," he said. "I'm so proud of you."

"Thank you for all your help and support, Mr. Thompson," Emily said.

"Please just call me Evan."

"You believed in me, and that means the world to me right now!"

"That was awesome, what you pulled on Daniel," he said.

"Let's hope he gets what he deserves."

"That will depend on how the judge handles his confession. At least it was enough to get you off the hook! But the police still need to come up with hard evidence to implicate Daniel, in case the confession is thrown out."

"Why is that?"

"Daniel isn't stupid, and he has financial resources. He will hire a good lawyer, who will argue that the confession was coerced, or obtained by illegal means — in other words, not admissible in court."

"Is that a problem for me?"

"DiLongo believes you. I also told her about the files on your flash drive, but she agrees that they will not be enough. What she needs to convict Daniel is evidence of his plan, something he wrote in his own handwriting, or a witness who knew what he did. It would help if they find traces of the poison in his house or office. DiLongo is getting a search warrant as we speak."

CHAPTER 34

FRIDAY, DECEMBER 19, 2008 — 7:30 P.M.

A few days after the charges against Emily were dropped, Evan asked her out for dinner to celebrate the victory over Daniel.

"Let's meet at the Lakeside Inn Friday evening," he said. "My treat. I know the food is really good there, and this time of year the Inn will be beautifully decorated for Christmas."

Emily agreed, with pleasure. She liked Evan, and he had earned her respect during the investigation. Over dinner, they chatted about the case and her plans for the future.

During the investigation, Emily had revealed to Evan her short-lived career as evil Nurse Ratched for guests at the Lakeside Inn. "It's nice to be here as a guest myself this time," she said, reflecting on her past activities, "sharing a gorgeous meal with the best lawyer a girl could ever want." She raised her glass. "Here's to you, Evan. Thank you so much for helping me and believing in me!"

"Well, I think diLongo should be thanking you," he said, taking a sip of his wine. "After all, you solved the case for her!"

"She had doubts about my guilt," Emily said, "but the evidence was stacked against me and she couldn't do anything about it. The captain was pressuring her about the budget and the D.A. was pressuring him to wrap up the case!"

"Yes, sadly, Emily, you're right. Sometimes politics and budgets can get in the way of real justice. The system is far from perfect. Maybe we should call it the conviction system rather than the justice system. Sometimes you have to manipulate the situation to get justice, like you did this time. You took things into your own hands and you made it happen."

"I knew I was innocent. That's a big motivator!"

"You know, the public just wants to be safe," he said, fiddling with his napkin. "People get upset when criminals get off with a light sentence or get acquitted for lack of evidence, and I understand that. You hear their concerns on radio talk shows all the time. But what's the alternative? Some countries have no legitimate legal system in place. The authorities are not subject to any rule of law. They simply pick people up and throw them in

Chapter 34 | 281 |

jail with no trial or evidence, or they'll cut off a person's arm for no reason. And if they think someone is opposed to their dictatorial rule, they will send private armies to kill the person and their family and even their entire village. These thugs use their power to terrorize the entire population and many innocent people fall victim to their evil ways." His napkin was now folded into a small square. "At least in America the authorities must prove their case against a citizen, based on rules of evidence. Sure, it means some criminals are allowed to get away with their crimes, and I guess that's the price we pay. Our system of law and order is not perfect, and that's why I fight like hell to defend the clients who are innocent and hope that the guilty ones..." He stopped midsentence, suddenly realizing that his sermon was not the most charming dinner conversation.

"Yes, it scares me to think how close I came to being convicted of a crime I didn't commit," Emily said.

"So what will you do now? Any plans?" he asked, changing the subject.

"Not yet. I'm just happy to be out of jail! In the New Year, I'm going to look for a new job, I guess. With Daniel gone, so is my position. And I don't think Daniel will ever finish his book. Even if he does, he won't be giving me the acknowledgement he promised — not after what I did to him! At least Gayle has given me two months off with pay to help me with the transition. There are hardly any jobs around here, so I may have to move away, but I'm not making any immediate decisions," she said.

Then she lowered her voice. "You know, I always wanted to be a doctor, but I had to give up that dream when my dad died and my mom got sick. I was saving up to go back into med school when this debacle happened. Now I need to take some time and come up with a new plan."

"That's very sensible," he said. "And it's almost Christmas. Will you go to D.C. to be with your mom?"

"Oh, yes," Emily said. "I spend Christmas with her every year."

"I bet she appreciates that," he said.

"What will you do for Christmas?" Emily asked. She realized she had never talked to Evan about his personal life. She didn't even know if he had a wife and children.

"I'll go to Chicago for a few days," he said, "to visit my folks. We have a big family gathering every year at Christmas. Lots of nieces and nephews to spoil!"

"That's nice," she said. "What do you think will happen to Daniel now? He's still in duBarry, right?"

"Yeah, on Cloud Nine, taking his happy pills," Evan said laughing. "He'll be there for quite a while, and then he will be transferred to a more secure facility where they will do a thorough psych evaluation to see if he's fit to stand trial."

"It's hard to know what's real and what's fake with him," Emily said. "When I was talking to him in the hospital, he seemed very lucid and alert. But then, when he realized that I had tricked him into confessing, he changed into a madman. How can someone flip like that?"

"I'm not a shrink, so I can't answer that question, but he's obviously unstable. The bigger issue, to my mind, is whether he's legally insane. Where's the line between pure culpable evil and legitimate insanity? That's a question the courts have to deal with all the time."

"Yes, I see what you mean. To deliberately poison a person for no other reason than to further your own personal ambitions, and to randomly poison a second person as part of the plot, and set up a third person to take the fall… it seems so diabolical and premeditated… and evil," she said.

"There are many cases just as diabolical," Evan said. "Mothers drowning their children so they can go to parties with their boyfriends, fathers killing daughters who dare to challenge their religious ideology, children killing their parents to get access to their trust funds. It goes on and on." He stopped again. "I'm sorry… this is not a very nice topic to discuss over dinner, is it?"

"I just hope they keep Daniel under lock and key for the rest of his life. I don't care if he's in prison or a mental institution, so long as he's securely locked up. It gives me nightmares to think how close I came to being one of his victims," she said.

"Well," Evan said, "let's change the subject to something more pleasant. I seem to recall that you offered to teach me how to play bridge when the murder investigation was over. So, is that offer still on the table?"

"Oh, yes. Sorry, I forgot all about that. Sure, I'll teach you the fundamentals, but if you really want to learn this game, you have to read bridge books and practice, practice, practice."

"Well, I'll drink to that," he said, smiling as he clinked his glass with hers.

Emily studied Evan's face for a moment, and for the first time she noticed his clear, blue eyes and engaging smile. She smiled back at him.

"By the way," she said, thinking out loud. "Gayle has announced that because of the murders and everything that's happened, she's invited all the bridge players to attend her New Year's Eve party, as a way to compensate. It's so ironic: Daniel wanted the prize so much he killed for it, and now he is the only one who won't be there! I think there's some kind of justice in that, don't you?"

Evan laughed in agreement.

"So, I was wondering," she said shyly, "What are your plans for New Year's Eve?"

EPILOGUE

📅 PRESENT DAY — 5:30 A.M.

As I finished the story, Brian drank the last few drops of his fifth Red Bull. He looked wired.

"That's some story. Wish I'd been there!"

"Yes, it was quite a case," I said.

"So, what happened to the killer? Did he get convicted?"

"Well, we got the search warrant and found incriminating evidence in his house. He had diaries beside his bed, not even hidden in a wall or anything. Apparently he spent hours at night scribbling in these diaries, mapping out his plan to win the annual prize and also to get his crime story by creating the crime himself. Eventually the D.A. put Daniel Post on trial. His lawyer argued that he was not responsible for his actions because the medication the doctor prescribed for him caused him to have delusions and act out of character, but the D.A. provided evidence that Mr. Post acted with callous disregard for the rights of others and that his actions were premeditated and deliberate. The evidence against him was very strong. Halfway through the trial, the D.A. made a deal with the defense, and Mr. Post changed his plea to 'guilty but mentally ill' to stay out of prison. Now he's locked up in an institution for the criminally insane, where he will remain until he dies, I expect. His doctor, by the way, was also disciplined for medical malpractice. Apparently he prescribed the wrong medication for Mr. Post, and that contributed to his delusions."

"Oh, my God," Brian said. "Are you saying they think the pills made him do it?"

I shrugged. "Not sure, but some anti-psychotic drugs can make you crazy, if they are not prescribed properly. Personally, I think he's damaged goods, unbalanced in a seriously evil way with no hope of rehabilitation. He needs to be locked up forever, meds or no meds."

Brian shook his head. "So, what happened to the others?"

"We finally tracked down Terry Digman's family — I mean, Stanley Karakchuck's family. They lived in Niagara Falls, New York. Both his parents were alive, but quite elderly. Stanley was adopted and his biological family background is unknown. His adoptive parents were in their forties when Stanley came to them at about four or five years old. He was already acting out, even at that young age. He was known to be very bright, but he misbehaved badly in school and was constantly in the principal's office. He quit school and left home when he was seventeen and made his own way in life after that. He didn't bother to stay in touch with his family. Both his parents were getting on in years by the time we located them. They couldn't quite comprehend what Stanley had been up to for the last twenty years. Anyway, they took possession of his body and buried him in their local cemetery."

"Did Gayle Primrose leave her job?" he asked.

"She tried to resign, but the college bigwigs wouldn't let her go. They took the position that hardened criminals duped her, and it could have happened to anyone. However, she had to reimburse the college for the signing bonus she gave to Mr. Bartholomew. I think she got off easy, don't you?"

"Yeah," Brian said. "And Emily Warren, what happened to her?"

"She landed on her feet, actually. After she helped us unmask the real killer, she took time off from work and in the process she got engaged to Evan Thompson, her former lawyer. Now they are married and she's at home with two small children. I hear she's waiting for them to be in school, and then she's going to finish her medical degree."

"Good for her," Brian said. "She sounds like a nice person."

"Uh-huh," I said. "I'm really glad we didn't convict her of murder."

"And what about David Bartholomew?"

"We charged him with a few of his crimes, but he earned some leniency by cooperating with us during the investigation. Instead of twelve years, he got five. I have no idea what he's doing now. He'll probably wind up working as a bouncer in some bar, or maybe pumping gas. With his record, he won't be able to get any kind of decent job. It's too bad, because he's nice enough guy. He just wasn't able to get his life together in any meaningful way, and he was always looking for an easy solution to his problems."

"And the others?"

"Oh yeah… the big surprise! We learned that Chris Boland was not exactly the devoted husband that he portrayed himself to be. In fact, he was having a wild romance with Melissa Fielding in the weeks before his wife died. I guess Mrs. Fielding got his mojo working. Anyway, a few weeks after the funeral, she moved in with him, along with her baby. Left her husband high and dry!"

"Wow, I didn't see that coming!" Brian exclaimed.

"Nobody did," I said. "Just one of those things!"

"And Miss Wilmington, is she still at the college?" Brian asked.

"Yep, she's still there, doing her H.R. thing. We managed to keep her exotic dancing out of the news reports. I heard she joined a nudist resort near Lake Champlain, so maybe that will keep her exhibitionist tendencies under control," I said, chuckling.

"And Ben Chong, what happened to him?"

"Ben graduated with honors. He was a good kid — just wanted to fit into American society. Unfortunately, he met the wrong people and got a warped idea of what it means to be American. I heard from Gayle Primrose that he is now in Boston working for a big technology company. Welcome to America!"

"And Karl Schultz, is he still teaching?"

"Oh, sure he is. He's one of those old-time academics who lives to teach. I expect he'll be teaching until the day he dies."

"Who else is there? Oh yeah, Barb Baker. What became of her?"

"Miss Baker is still doing her mail delivery and printing job on campus. She'll probably be there until she retires. I don't expect to hear much about her in the future," I said. "She's just a hard-working cog in the wheel. Keeps her nose clean and does her job. As far as I know, she and Jill Wilmington are still friends and they play bridge together."

"And Sally Brighton?"

"That's a bit of a mystery. She took off. She just quit her job at the end of the school year and left the area. Gayle thinks she may have gone to Washington to work for some political outfit, but that has never been confirmed. I think she was very ambitious, and Kensington was just too small a pond for her. Maybe she would have been interested in the college president's job if Dr. Primrose had resigned, but that didn't happen, and won't happen for many years to come, I think. "

"And the Blacks?"

"They are still in the I.T. department of the college," I said. "They are solid tech professionals — no issues with them at all."

"And I guess the students just carried on?" Brian asked.

"Uh-huh. The students in the bridge club finished their studies and graduated. Gayle tells me they still play bridge online, and two of them have gone on to compete in local tournaments. The bridge club has many new players now."

"Do you keep in touch with anyone at the college?"

"As a matter of fact, I do. Gayle Primrose calls me about four or five times a year and we get together for lunch or dinner on my days off. We've become friends, sort of. She refunded the money I paid for the bogus course I took and gave me a free pass into another course on criminal behavior from a bona fide professor. I got an 'A' and this time it was legit. By the way, Gayle has a new boyfriend. He's some big shot businessman, a former football player who started a chain of restaurants after his playing career. She has a thing for black guys! Can't wait to meet this one," I said, chuckling.

"So, the case didn't ruin the college's reputation after all?" Brian asked.

"The way I hear it," I said, "the college is doing better than ever. The publicity around the case made more people aware of the college and Dr. Primrose took full advantage of the situation. She turned a P.R. nightmare into a bonanza. I gather she's raking in more donations than ever. More power to her!"

Brian looked at his watch. "Holy shit, it's 5:30 already!"

"Time to hit the road," I said. "My kids will be up in an hour, and I have to get them ready for school!"

Driving home, I reflected on the events and people involved in the Kensington College bridge club. There must be a reason why so many highly intelligent people are so passionate about bridge. One day, when the kids are grown and I have more leisure time, I'm going to take some lessons and learn how to play this game!